I0647617

Chariot Canyon

Also by Larry M. Edwards

- *Dare I Call It Murder?: A Memoir of Violent Loss*
  Winner, Best Published Memoir, San Diego Book Awards, and
  Pulitzer Prize nominee
- *Food & Provisions of the Mountain Men: A Guide to Authentic
  Provisions of Fur Trappers, Traders & Explorers in the Early American
  West*
- *The Pandemic Sessions: New Tunes in the Old-time Style (mostly)*
- *Official Netscape Internet Business Starter Kit*

Chariot Canyon

~ *A Rent Beacham Mystery* ~

Larry M. Edwards

Wigeon
Publishing
San Diego

Copyright © 2024 by Larry M. Edwards. All rights reserved. No part of this book may be used or reproduced in any manner whatsoever without written permission of the author, except in the case of brief quotations used in critical articles or reviews.

The scanning, uploading and distribution of this book via the Internet or via any other means without the permission of the publisher is illegal and punishable by law. Please purchase only authorized electronic editions, and do not participate in or encourage piracy of copyrighted materials. Your support of the author's rights is appreciated.

With one exception, this novel's story and characters are fictitious. Certain long-standing institutions, agencies, and public offices are mentioned, but the characters involved are wholly imaginary, aside from the one exception.

Published by Wigeon Publishing
ISBN: 978-1-7323650-7-0
Library of Congress Control Number: 2024916422
FIC022090: FICTION / Mystery & Detective / Private Investigators
FIC031010: FICTION / Thrillers / Crime

Cover design by Timothy W. Brittain
Cover images: Larry M. Edwards, iStock
"The Fiddler" sketch: Vicky Johnson

Printed in the United States of America

For Connie Saindon, who saved my life.
I only wish I could have done the same for her.

I believe that the best definition of man is the ungrateful biped. But that is not all, that is not his worst defect; his worst defect is his perpetual moral obliquity, perpetual—from the days of the Flood to the Schleswig-Holstein period. Moral obliquity and consequently lack of good sense.

—Fyodor Dostoyevsky

Author's Note

Although this is a work of fiction, the underlying story about welfare fraud is real, and I have presented that aspect of the story as I would have written it for a newspaper or magazine as a nonfiction news feature.

All but one of the characters in this story are fictional; I have included a real person, Connie Saindon (1941-2023), who founded Survivors of Violent Loss. She dedicated her life to helping survivors develop strategies for learning to live with the aftermath of a homicide, including safety issues, dealing with the criminal justice system, addressing the news media, and coping with traumatic grief, while preserving the memory of a loved one.

Chariot Canyon Companion Contests

Virtual Fiddle Contest — Win a Prize!

Identify the names of fiddle tunes and other references to music and song in the novel Chariot Canyon by Larry M. Edwards. There are more than 40 such references. Some will be obvious, others a bit more subtle or obscure.

Prizes awarded to the top five entrants—those who correctly name the most references. (And, if you wish, your name will be memorialized as a character in the next book from Mr. Edwards.)

The contest begins on October 11, 2024, upon the official release of the book. The contest closes at midnight on December 31, 2024. The winners will be announced in early January 2025.

Send your contest entry to fiddlecontest@larryedwards.com. In the Subject line, write: Virtual Fiddle Contest. *No* attachments; your answers must be listed as text within the body of the message.

The entry must cite each reference and the number of the page on which the reference appears.* Entries will receive bonus points for providing additional details regarding a reference, such as composer, songwriter, or performing artist, or trivia about the item. These bonus points will be used as a tiebreaker in the event of a tie.

For more information and prize options, go to <u>LarryEdwards.com</u>.

Participants are encouraged to enter the Virtual Literary Contest as well.

A Grand Prize winner—the entrant who has the most correct responses in both the Fiddle and Literary contests combined—will receive a special prize.

———

* This does not include any references in front matter or back matter, only within the story itself.

Virtual Literary Contest — Win a Prize!

Identify the names of books and other references to literature, movies, and TV shows in the novel Chariot Canyon by Larry M. Edwards. There are more than 50 such references. Some are obvious, others a bit more subtle or obscure.

Prizes awarded to the top five entrants—those who correctly name the most references. (And, if you wish, your name will be memorialized as a character in the next book from Mr. Edwards.)

The contest begins on October 11, 2024, upon the official release of the book. The contest closes at midnight on December 31, 2024. The winners will be announced in early January 2025.

Send your contest entry to litcontest@larryedwards.com. In the Subject line, write: Virtual Literary Contest. *No* attachments; your answers must be listed as text within the body of the message.

The entry must cite each reference and the number of the page on which the reference appears.* Entries will receive bonus points for providing additional details regarding a reference, such as an author, other works from an author, featured characters or actors. These bonus points will be used as a tiebreaker in the event of a tie.

For more information and prize options, go to LarryEdwards.com.

Participants are encouraged to enter the Virtual Fiddle Contest as well.

A Grand Prize winner—the entrant who has the most correct responses in both the Fiddle and Literary contests combined—will receive a special prize.

———

* This does not include any references in front matter or back matter, only within the story itself.

Chariot Canyon

~ A Rent Beacham Mystery ~

1

Rent Beacham cursed himself as he struggled to block all thoughts of immediate danger and recall the irony of how a seemingly innocent decision to take a soothing drive to the mountains led him to his lightless prison.

He leaned against the hard wall of igneous rock, holed up in what would likely be his grave: A gold mine near what in its heyday had been the boom town of Banner City, down valley from Julian, California. A single stick of dynamite—or a black-powder charge— could collapse its walls, precariously shored up by rotting timbers. Or the approaching atmospheric river, as the meteorologists called it, could flood the mine and drown him.

I think I'd prefer the explosion to slowly drowning. Then again, I'd rather be alive. At thirty-two, I've got a lot more years ahead of me.

He snorted in disgust at his own angst. Why could he never be satisfied with just doing his job and enjoying his leisure time like all those perfect people in the TV commercials? Perpetually plagued by dissatisfaction with the status quo, his restlessness had led him to a small mountain town, then to the desert, then to the discovery that opened his Pandora's box. A box whose lid had come precariously close to banging shut—and literally burying him alive.

Then he chuckled. No, it wasn't funny, but he had been cursed with a propensity to laugh at the ironic. It had gotten him in trouble in the past when he couldn't keep such thoughts to himself.

Being an investigative journalist did that to him. Or was it the other way around? His knack of seeing a laughable lament even in the darkest of circumstances.

Maybe that's what led me into journalism? he wondered.

At that moment, however, he could laugh his lungs out and no one would be subjected to his macabre brand of gallows humor. No one could hear him. Not while he sat trapped in the shaft of an abandoned gold mine miles beyond Bumfuck.

What else can I do? I may as well laugh, even if it is at my own expense. Crying and whining will get me nowhere.

If nothing else, his predicament spared him from his editor's chastisement over a looming deadline. But the only person who might be able to figure out where he had gone also wished him dead—at least in the figurative sense. His lady friend had become his foe.

As he waited in the dark for his would-be killer's next move in a game in which he had become the wuss to his foe's puss, he retraced in his mind the steps, in a relentless, inevitable progression, that had led him to this potentially fatal fix—and maybe come up with a way to get out . . . alive.

2

Day 1, morning

Rent Beacham draped an arm across his eyes. "Crap," he muttered. A shaft of intense morning sunlight had found the lone chink in his bedroom's armor—a slat in the mini-blinds had been bent at a painful angle, giving entry to a rogue ray of light whose laser-like beam had pierced his still-shut eyelids.

He lay there in what he thought of as a cocoon, not wanting to glance at the clock, though it had become a reflex he could no longer control—6:48 a.m.

It's Sunday. I have a right to sleep late, damn it.

It also happened to be the dead of winter. At least according to the San Diego Zoological Society calendar—whose playmate of the month featured a Frobisher's Marble-winged Warbler, or some such winged creature—hanging on the fridge. February should be cool, blustery, rainy. He wanted nothing more than to sleep late, nurse a carafe of coffee while reading the morning newspaper, then settle in with a G.M. Ford novel by a chuckling fire and dispel all thoughts of the pedestrian world.

Still, he felt guilty for not being outside and enjoying the fine weather—weather the majority of the country would kill for. *San Diego, cursed with the perfect climate,* he thought. *Maybe it's time to move back to the Pacific Northwest whence I came, where the term "winter" at least held some meaning. . . . Nah. Months of overcast skies leads to drearipression.*

That's why Rent had landed in the self-anointed America's Finest City in the first place—for real sun, not that "liquid sunshine" as folks in the Pacific Northwest had euphemistically dubbed the persistent drizzle. But after nearly a decade, Rent had begun to miss the seasons. The postcard-blue sky that made San Diego a tourist mecca had become boring. He recalled the Hawaiians he knew while a student at the University of Washington. What possessed them to leave paradise to attend school in the Emerald City?

"The seasons. We like the seasons," they had confessed. He told them they were nuts.

Now, here I am saying the same thing.

Of course, they could always scurry back to Hawaii when the doldrums descended.

Maybe I should move to San Diego's mountains. At least it snows there once in a while.

But the 60-mile commute would be a killer, could be a killer, literally. State Route 67 had achieved notoriety for its fatal traffic accidents. Impatient drivers of SUVs and big pickups, fueled by alcohol and the arrogance to think it couldn't happen to them, that they could defy the laws of physics: take corner too fast, pass on curve, obit.

Except the scofflaws often were not the ones with the obits. "It's always the innocent mother with two toddlers who gets the funeral," Rent muttered aloud.

Cynicism went part and parcel with working in a newsroom.

He tossed back the bed covers and, in a fluid motion that bore years of repetition, got his feet to the floor and his torso upright. *Ugh.* He sat motionless, staring blindly at an erupting volcano of dirty clothes begging for attention.

At least the sun is out of my eyes.

He wrapped his bare frame in a terrycloth robe and stumbled toward the kitchen to start the coffee, then padded outside to retrieve the newspaper. He had been assured his story about scandalous travel expenses at the San Diego Port District would be on the front page, above the fold—every journalist's wish. But it had been superseded by yet another wearisome story about the homeless encampments and dire predictions of high winds and torrential rainfall of biblical proportions, threating life and limb, especially of the "unhoused."

The kettle shrieked as he returned to the kitchen. His daily infusion of caffeine—his one true vice (well, that and gin)—almost ready. He poured the scalding water over the unsuspecting coffee grounds in the stained Melita filter cone, then turned to the newspaper as the acrid brown liquid trickled into the waiting carafe.

As he leafed through the thick-but-thinning Sunday edition, the real estate section caught his eye. He rarely gave it a second glance. Not since he bought his condo on the north rim of Mission Valley. But the siren song of seasons still fluttered through the backroads of his mind.

I could drive to Julian and check out some acreage.

If not to live year-round, at least a mountain retreat where he could get a measured dose of winter when the fancy struck him. He envisioned a log cabin, a roaring fire, a big dog and . . . a sexy female companion.

Cut!

Rewind.

Stop at the big dog.

Leave the vision of the sexy female companion on the cutting-room floor. Dogs are loyal. Feed them and they will follow you anywhere. Women turn on you when you least suspect it.

His current mantra.

He knew his tune would change with time as loneliness, wishful thinking, and hormones began to creep out from the shadow of embittered memories, but for the time being he would enjoy the uncomplicated existence of sailing single-handed and the freedom it gave him.

He grabbed the real estate section and headed for the bathroom. A bathroom he didn't have to share. No sarcastic soliloquies from the "petticoat"—as Charlotte Brontë might phrase it—beyond the door suggesting he think of someone besides himself for a change. Never mind that Charlotte Brontë never wrote a single word about anything so mortifying as personal hygiene.

"YES!" RENT SHOUTED FROM the cab of his Toyota pick-em-up. Once shed of the freeway free-for-all and forced to drive at a sane pace, he got into the rhythm of the curves as the narrow, two-lane state road slowly climbed into the mountains in east San Diego County. He dipped through Santa Ysabel Valley and stopped at Dudley's for a blueberry scone and more coffee, and a loaf of the bakery's renowned date-nut bread.

Life is good.

The final climb up the grade to Julian brought into view patches of snow on the pine-clad hills. That is, the pine-clad yet to be burned in a Santa Ana-blasted wildfire. He cranked up the heat in his aging truck, then down-shifted. The shuttered fruit stands told him he was almost there.

The small town of Julian, huddled below the towering peak of Volcan Mountain, came into being in 1870, after escaped-slave-turned-cattle-herder A.H. "Fred" Coleman spotted the glitter of gold in a small creek while watering his horse in Spencer Valley in late 1869. His news quickly spread the highly contagious gold fever, and thousands of miners laid siege to the tranquil mountain meadows claimed by the Kumeyaay Nation of Native Americans.

Ironically, Julian City, as it was known at the time, had been founded by a family of Confederate veterans of the Civil War, among them Drury Bailey and his cousin Mike Julian, the namesake of the ram-shackle new town. The gold rush lasted only a few years, but because of Julian's temperate climate and good soil, the town survived when the mining boom went bust and apple and pear orchards flourished.

These days, Julian's citizens mined gold from the pockets of tourists—*flatlanders* to the locals—escaping their stress-filled lives in the city by the sea. The big event each year had been Apple Days, the centerpiece of the annual rite being the all-American apple pie. Although, Rent recalled, 90 percent of the apples were imported from his home state of Washington. The town fathers and mothers realized they could strike the mother lode if they promoted the town year-round instead of just a few big weekends a year.

As he approached the town proper, Rent began humming Bob Wills' famous ditty: ". . . he can eat an apple pie, and never even bat an eye. Roly Poly, daddy's little fatty. Bet he's gonna be a man some day."

Rent pulled up to Main Street and turned right, inching southward through the three-block-long business district. Most of the buildings were constructed in Western motif. He found a parking space in front of a store offering wood-burning stoves, locked up, and began strolling—still humming

Roly Poly as he passed the portly owner of a fresh pie emerging from the Julian Pie Co.

He had arrived early enough that he easily found a parking space on the main drag. By noon, parking would be at a premium, and the narrow sidewalks would be as crowded as a shopping center on Black Friday. The apples were out of season, but the unseasonable amount of snow attracted crowds as well. It made for great TV news when idiot drivers skidded on the ice, crashed their cars, and cracked their skulls.

"As the saying goes, 'If it bleeds, it ledes,' " he muttered, reciting the local-television news mantra.

In Julian, the real estate offices outnumbered the pie shops, but luckily for Rent most of them had photos in their windows, along with lengthy lists of available properties. He wouldn't have to actually endure listening to the litany of a fast-talking salesman, or saleswoman.

Or is it salesperson in this woke world? . . . Oh, right, the proper term is agent, or even Realtor, if licensed.

He stopped at the window of the Coleman Creek Real Estate office where he scanned the photos and read the property descriptions. He shook his head and scoffed as he noted the prices. He had figured he could pick up a nice five-acre plot for a few thousand bucks. But the asking price even for property that only a bighorn sheep could love was going for $25,000 an acre and up.

Imagine what a piece with a flat patch on it would command.

Of course, these were the show pieces. Surely, there were lower-priced parcels available, but not pushed as hard because the commissions were also lower.

And there are always the cheapskates who think they can do better selling it themselves.

"Good morning!" an unreasonably cheerful voice greeted him from behind. Rent turned to discover a young woman wearing an Eddie Bauer trapper cap, knee-length quilted parka, and Ugg boots, and cradling a pastry box and two cups of coffee.

She smiled radiantly. And he froze, a deer in the headlights. Before him stood the sexy woman from his *sitting-by-fire-in-a-log-cabin* fantasy. Her chestnut hair fell to her shoulders, framing a well-formed countenance set off by exuberant hazel eyes. The parka subdued the contours of her body, but Rent's imagination filled in the blanks.

"Come on in and warm up," she invited.

Rent stared to the point of making the woman uncomfortable. He felt torn between melting into a panting puppy dog who would follow her anywhere and steeling himself into the hard-bitten rejected lover he wanted to be. Hard-bitten prevailed—but only just.

"Thanks, but I'm widow shopping . . . er . . . window shopping," he stuttered. Besides, he rationalized, he was enjoying the cool morning outdoors. It left him feeling alive and an excuse to dust off a flannel shirt, wool sweater, and stocking cap.

"Looking for anything in particular? I'm sure we've got something you'd be interested in," the woman persisted, her perfect white teeth straight out of a toothpaste commercial.

Rent felt his spine soften, threatening to turn into putty. His inner Cynic immediately began shouting words of warning: *She's a Siren, you pitiful moron! She doesn't care about You! She's only interested in your wallet! She is the witch they named that creek after . . . and that wildfire. It's the hormones generated by your genetic code that make you attracted to her, not because there's anything intrinsically good about her.*

Rent, recovered and back on form, replied, "Yes, I'm interested in this 345-acre ranch." He pointed to a picture in the window. Then added, gesturing as he glanced around the still sleepy town, "I'm with a medical practice that wants to establish a leper colony in this bucolic environment you have here."

The woman's smile collapsed, then returned but tight-edged. "I need to get this coffee to my associate before it gets cold," she said as she struggled to open the door. Rent leaned forward and opened it for her.

"Thank you," she said, stepping through the doorway, then turning to speak again. "I can schedule an appointment for this afternoon, if you'd like, Dr. . . .?" and her voice trailed off.

"Watson," he said quickly. "Dr. Watson."

"Abby Wilburforce. Nice to meet you, Dr. Watson," she said, bobbing her elbow in a mock handshake, her hands still cradling the coffee and pastry box. "Let me give you my card. I have several properties I could show you."

She crossed to her desk, deposited the donuts and coffee, and returned with a business card. Rent felt chagrined that his little charade had backfired. "Yes, thank you," he said in forced politeness. He pocketed her card without looking at it and backed out of the doorway, moving out of view. There he took a deep breath while mentally kicking himself for his smart-ass demeanor.

There actually were a couple of properties that interested him. Rent pulled a reporter's notebook, something he never left home without, from a back pants pocket and began jotting down a few place names—the actual addresses being closely guarded secrets only the Siren Realtor could disclose—and decided to cruise the local roads on his own to get the lie of the land, and maybe spot a promising for-sale sign.

Before he could finish writing, the door to the real estate office opened again. The dreamy smile, this time accompanied by a devilish crinkle around her beckoning eyes, poked out.

"My, my. I didn't know medical professionals made it a habit of carrying around a reporter's notebook, Dr. Watson. Or is it Mr. Holmes?"

Busted.

Rent blushed as his log-cabin fantasy flashed through his mind. The Siren would lure him onto Broken Heart Rocks. "Holmes is my first name," he replied. "My parents had a bizarre sense of humor."

"Uh-huh," she replied, nodding but obviously not believing a word of it. "Well, Dr. Holmes Watson, if you need some *clues* . . ." Heavily emphasizing clues and making no effort to hide the sarcasm. ". . . regarding the location of those properties you have written down, you know where to find me." She chuckled at her own joke.

"Or," she continued, smiling wickedly. "You could always homestead like those social misfits in Chariot Canyon."

"Chariot Canyon? Never heard of it."

"Down by Banner, at the foot of Banner Grade. They say they're working the old mining claims, but some folks believe they're hiding from the law. Maybe cooking meth. They also carry guns," she added, then pulled her head back and closed the door.

Rent turned and marched double-time back to his truck, mentally kicking himself for having been taken to the mat by, of all things, a real estate agent—and a female at that. Yet, a feisty female. One with a quick and clever mind. Still, the memory of her snide smile and razor-witted retort rankled. He shook his head to clear the image as he started the engine.

3

Rent drove southward to where the road split at the edge of town. Banner: straight ahead, Cuyamaca: turn right. He instinctively went straight ahead, although not sure why, except that in his mind he still carried the image of the gun-toting social misfits in Chariot Canyon she had mentioned. The thought intrigued him. "Might be a story that," he said aloud.

His route took him past the high school and the library, and wound past a few small businesses. After less than a mile it began its descent toward Banner and the Anza-Borrego Desert.

Banner Grade, which dropped 1,500 feet to what was left of the old Banner City townsite, had more bends than a sidewinder. Rent drove slowly, keeping an eye out for any for-sale signs, as the flora transformed from a forest of pine and oak to desert scrub and chaparral. The west side of the mountains trapped the rain, with Julian averaging nearly 40 inches per year, and leaving the east side a haven for cholla and ocotillo cacti, mesquite, brittlebush, and other drought-tolerant plants.

Near the foot of the grade, he came to a store, one of the few remaining structures from the once bustling mining town. Rent pulled into the store parking lot to get his bearings. His auto club map fell short on details and didn't even identify Chariot Canyon. He dug out his Thomas Bros. Guide and found the page with Banner. Not much help there, either. Yes, he owned a "smart phone," but he didn't care for GPS. He had never progressed from his days as a Boy Scout—paper map and compass.

A gunshot startled him. He peered through the windshield and saw a man holding a pistol in one hand and fist-pumping the air with the other.

Rent got out of his truck but kept his distance.

"Damn thing's got no business here," the man said. "A body could get bit if he's not careful."

Rent stared at the man, a frown creasing his brow. He judged the man to be in his mid-thirties.

"Coyote. Didn't you see it?" the man asked.

Rent shook his head. "Uh, no. Must've been blocked by the building. Did you kill it?"

"Nah," the man said, then grinned. "But I scared the livin' shit out of 'im, that's for sure."

"You could add me to that list."

"Ah, just havin' a little fun, that's all. Gotta keep these varmints in line. Elsewise they think they have the run of the place. Take our cats, dogs, chickens."

"They help control the rodent population," Rent said.

"If they stuck to rats, mice, gophers, and squirrels, that'd be fine," the man replied. "But they don't. Them do-gooder city folks think they're all cute and cuddly, like their domesticated cousins, their dogs, but they're not. Coyotes . . ."—he pronounced it as *ky-otes*—"are vicious opportunists and see any small critter as fair game for a meal."

"You mean like humans do?"

The man blinked rapidly as if trying to comprehend what Rent had just said as he shoved the pistol in a holster on his belt. Rent didn't know much about guns, but that pistol, and the man, reminded him of Clint Eastwood as gun-totin' Dirty Harry. The man turned toward the store. Rent held open the door for him, then followed him in.

"Hey, Gabe," a man behind the cash register called out. "That you doin' the shootin' out there? No snakes this time of year."

"Just giving a coyote a scare, that's all. No harm done."

"As long as you don't hit one of my donkeys."

"Not even close."

"How's the diggin' comin' along?"

The face of the man called Gabe flashed a toothy if insincere smile at the storekeeper. "Haven't struck the mother lode yet, but making progress. Following a quartz vein that looks promising," he said as he made his way to the back of the store.

Rent thought the greeting and reply sounded rehearsed, as if they were acting out a familiar script. The storekeeper greeted Rent with a nod.

"Getting a few trail rations," Rent said.

"Help yourself," the storekeeper replied as the man called Gabe approached with a half-case of beer and a gallon of milk, and set them on the counter.

"I'm gonna grab a few more things," Gabe said as he strode toward an aisle with shelves of canned goods.

Rent grabbed a Dr. Pepper from the cooler and a packet of beef jerky, then returned to the front of the store.

"If that's it, I'll ring you up first," the storekeeper said. "He'll be another minute or two."

Rent set the items on the counter, extracted his wallet from a pants pocket, and handed over a ten-dollar bill.

As the storekeeper gave Rent his change, Gabe returned and set his items on the counter, then extracted what appeared to be a debit card from his shirt pocket.

"Okay to use this? The milk and bread are for the kids," Gabe said. The storekeeper nodded and Gabe swiped the card through the card reader next to the cash register. "Beer, too," Gabe added. "I gotta get somethin' fer babysittin' them two brats."

The storekeeper narrowed his eyes and glanced at Rent.

"He's nobody," Gabe said.

The storekeeper shook his head. Gabe rolled his eyes in disgust, pulled a wad of cash from a pants pocket, peeled off a twenty-dollar bill, and tossed it on the counter. The storekeeper gave Gabe his change, then shook open a paper bag and placed the items in it.

Rent had stood aside as the two men completed the transaction.

The storekeeper gave Rent a questioning glance. "Somethin' else I can help you with?"

"I'm just wondering. What can you tell me about Chariot Canyon?" he asked.

"You be careful going out there, especially in that old pickup of yours," the man replied.

"It's a four-wheeler," Rent said of his Toyota Tacoma TRD.

Gabe interjected. "Yeah, but it's gotta be twenty years old or more."

Rent shrugged. "More or less."

"You ought to have something with newer technology in case you break down, especially with the roads as muddy as they are. Once it dries out, you might be all right on the main road, but you could get stuck easy on them side roads. Why do you want to go there? Do some shootin' or some such?"

Rent shrugged. "Just curious. A friend had mentioned it."

Gabe stared at Rent a long moment before again offering his facsimile smile. "Curiosity killed the cat," he said, then picked up his purchases and left the store, the door closing with a bang behind him. He walked over to a late-model Toyota Land Cruiser the color of trail dust and sporting a snorkel accessory, opened the rear hatch, and placed his groceries inside.

Rent's eyes followed the man, who wore what appeared to be a new outfit of Levi's jeans, denim shirt, sheepskin vest, burnt-orange beanie, and unscuffed work boots.

Doesn't look like much of a miner to me. Just wants to dress the part. Or maybe it's his Sunday-go-to-meetin' outfit.

The storekeeper looked at Rent and cleared his throat, his brow furrowed in a questioning manner. Rent turned his gaze back to the storekeeper and forced a smile of his own.

I may be out of my element here.

"Don't mind him. He just gets suspicious of strangers poking around. Had a few run-ins with snoopy interlopers, or so he claims. But he's right about your truck."

"Good point," Rent replied. "I thought you were going to warn me about the characters inhabiting the nether regions of the canyon."

The storekeeper chuckled. "Characters is right. They are that. But they's good folk. Don't harm nobody. They just like to keep to themselves."

"Do they come in here often?"

"Oh, I see 'em off and on. They'll drop by for a few things. Beer and chips, mostly."

"No ammo? They have to be on the lookout for coyotes and rattlesnakes, don't they?"

"Can't sell ammo no more. Have to jump through too many hoops to get a license, this being California, run by a bunch of damn libtards."

Rent gave a slight nod of acknowledgement.

"But you can't be too careful when it comes to rattlers. Not a problem right now, but come spring, they crawl out of their holes. Course, those folks get a bit suspicious of the two-legged variety, too. You ain't the law are you?"

Rent smiled, shaking his head. "Nope. Not the law. I was just up in Julian looking at some property and a woman said there were a bunch of gun-toting social misfits working some of the old mines in Chariot Canyon, or brewing meth."

"Me, I try not to judge people," the storekeeper said. "Their money's good here. Even if I do have to give 'em credit once in a while. Some take longer than others to pay up. Some of 'em are on the dole. But I never been stiffed yet."

"She said something about homesteading. Is there land available back in there? I came up here looking at maybe buying some property, but the prices are as high as that Volcan Mountain out there. Although I can't imagine there'd be much water."

"You get some water in the creek, especially this time of year, but most of the time dry as bone," he replied. "As for homesteading, that's BLM land."

"B-L-M?"

"Yep, Bureau of Land Management. Under the jurisdiction of the federal government. Can't really homestead it, at least not any longer, but you can stake a mining claim and stay on the land as long as you pay the annual fee."

"Is there any gold left? As I recall, the mines played out pretty quickly."

"The easy gold is gone, but there's still paydirt in there if you're willing to dig for it. Back-breaking work though. That's hard rock. Not like panning in a stream. And the mine shafts flood during heavy rain. I'll pass, thank you very much."

Rent nodded. "I hear ya."

"Say, do you like peanut brittle?"

"Yeah, sure," Rent answered with a shrug.

The storekeeper glanced out the window, then reached under the counter, pulling out a small dish containing pieces of peanut brittle. "Have a sample."

Rent tasted it. "Mmmm. Nice," he said, although he thought it had an unusual taste to it.

"The best in the world. Her secret ingredient is the honey."

"The honey?"

"Mmm. We keep bees out back. The bees get into the cactus and mesquite. Gives the honey a very unique flavor."

"Hmm . . . interesting," Rent responded.

"Only three dollars for a small bag, five dollars for the bigger one," the storekeeper said, producing one of each. "Homemade. Granny's peanut brittle. The best in the world."

Rent looked at the unmarked zip-lock bags. He wasn't big on sweets, and he knew he was being hustled. But he felt sorry for the aging shopkeeper who probably didn't get many customers in this isolated part of the county. And, he rationalized, he could always set it out in the newsroom. If nothing else, Greg would eat it. Greg ate anything, everything. He was known in the newsroom somewhat derogatorily as the "Meal Machine." Donuts left in the break room never stood a chance.

Rent still had change from his purchase in hand, which just happened to be three dollars and twenty-three cents. He handed it back to the storekeeper.

The man returned the coins. "No tax," he said. Then he leaned over the counter and spoke in a low, conspiratorial tone. "The reason we keep it behind the counter is because it's bootleg peanut brittle. Granny got busted a few years back for not having a health permit. So now we just sell it on the side. To the regulars. The folks in the tiny houses and campers."

"How do you know I'm not from the health department?" Rent asked with a wink.

"'Cause those lazy bastards don't work Sundays," the shopkeeper replied. "Only been back here once since the big bust. He learned not to fool with us. His two rear tires mysteriously went flat about half-way up the grade. No one hereabouts would help him. He had to leave the car and come back the next day with someone from the county motor pool."

"Hmm, did he, now," Rent acknowledged.

"Oh, he had one spare tire—but not two," the storekeeper continued with a chuckle. "It's amazing what a little ol' piece of buckshot will do when it's seated on top of an air valve."

Rent knew the old prank. Remove the safety cap from the valve stem, drop in a bee-bee or piece of buckshot, then replace the cap. It creates a slow leak—and a very flat tire given enough time. He laughed at the stunt. The "guv'ment" man had been made a fool by the back-country bumpkins. He picked up the peanut brittle and turned toward the door.

"You take care, and have a blessed day," the storekeeper said.

4

Back in his truck, Rent popped open the soda and took a long swallow. The air didn't feel hot, but it was much warmer, and dryer, than it had been in Julian.

He backed out, then crossed the state road to where the Chariot Canyon road split off. He pulled into the shade of a live oak, opened the package of jerky, and examined the canyon road as he chewed the tough, dried meat. No pavement, only dirt, with diagonal ruts cut by rain runoff. It led up a steep grade, then doubled back on itself, a cut that wound its way around the side of the ridge and into the canyon proper. Nearby stood two trucks with horse trailers attached.

He wanted to explore the canyon and get a glimpse of its storied inhabitants but thought better of it. He didn't want to get stuck out there.

As Rent chewed on another piece of jerky, he tried to recall the name of the real estate agent. *Abby . . . Abby Wil . . .*

He withdrew from his shirt pocket the card she had given to him and examined it. *Abby Wilburforce.* Then a smile crept to his lips. *She got me even better than I thought.*

He started the engine and retraced his route up Banner Grade. On a particularly tight corner, he had to jam on the brakes and swerve to avoid hitting a flock of wild turkeys.

Why did the turkey cross the road?

Rent spent the afternoon driving the backroads of the Julian area, eventually stopping at the Menghini Winery. He did a tasting and bought a bottle of Syrah. From there, he drove westerly on Wynola Road, dodging Miatas and Hondas hot-rodding on a road that had more twists and turns than a Hickory Farms pretzel.

From Wynola, which featured antique stores and two or three restaurants, he headed back toward Julian, then on a whim turned south into Pine Hills. He saw a few for-sale signs and jotted down the addresses, but figured they'd be out of his range. Paying the mortgage on his condo took a big chunk of his paycheck as it was.

Journalism is a career for ideological watchdogs, but not a path toward independent wealth, he mused.

He stopped at Heise Park and walked through the campground, thinking a camping trip might be in order, once the weather warmed up a bit. At least it would be affordable.

As the sun streaked the distant marine layer with crimson ribbons on its downward trek to kiss the Pacific Ocean, he returned to Julian to find a place to eat dinner. But his first challenge became finding a place to park. He got lucky when a car pulled out, leaving him an open slot in front of a bookstore.

Might as well check it out while I'm here.

He stepped inside and browsed, not looking for anything in particular, although a book about Julian might be useful. "Historical or maybe travel?" he muttered.

A young girl stopped beside him. "May I help you?" she asked.

Rent looked down and smiled. "Why yes, you may. I'm looking for a book about this town, about Julian. Do you have anything like that?"

The girl crinkled her face, then answered, "We have a kid's book, but you're probably too old for that. Unless—"

"Rachel," a woman's voice scolded. "That's not polite, calling the man 'old.'"

She pouted. "I only meant that . . ."

"No problem," Rent said to the girl. "I know what you meant. I appreciate your help." He turned around to face the voice . . . and froze.

"Rent?" the woman said.

"Hannah?" he replied.

"Mom, do you know this nice man?"

Hannah looked past Rent to her daughter. "From a long time ago. Now go finish shelving those books like I asked you to."

Rachel rolled her eyes and sighed, then walked toward the back of the store as Hannah turned her eyes back to Rent.

"Umm, it's been a while," he said.

"You could say that," Hannah replied, stone-faced.

"I'm surprised to see you here."

"What, you think because I dropped out of college I don't read?"

"Come on, you know that's not what I meant. Here, in California, in Julian."

"Life is a meandering stream that takes us where it takes us."

"I live in San Diego."

"I know. The famous Rent Beacham. Read all about it. I thought this might happen eventually."

Rent cocked his head. "Yeah?"

"Our paths crossing."

"Yet you made no effort to get in touch."

"Why would I?"

He shrugged.

"How can I help you?" she asked. "Looking for anything in particular? Maybe *50 Ways to Leave Your Lover*, you dirty bastard."

"Whoa, Hannah, I don't know what . . ."

Rachel returned to stand beside Hannah but stared into Rent's eyes before shifting her gaze to her mother. "I'm all done. What's next?"

"Just give us a minute, hon, will you? I need to finish up with Mr. Beacham."

Rachel looked questioningly at her mother, then returned her focus to Rent.

"Go on, mind the register for a minute. I'll be right there."

Rachel sighed again and dramatically crossed her arms over her chest. "Oh-kay." She walked away, but not without a backward glance at Rent.

Rent smiled at the adolescent, then turned back to Hannah. "My, what a precocious child you have. What is she, eleven, twelve?"

"Twelve, going on twenty."

"I'll bet she's a handful . . . or will be in few more years."

"Yes . . . until she meets someone like you and has her heart broken."

"Hannah, look, it's been long time. Can't we let bygones be bygones and at least be civil to one another?"

"Easy for you to say."

"What about it? Meet me for coffee and we have a chat. Catch up."

"Why? You have a guilt complex or something?"

He blushed. "Uh . . . no. I'm just curious, wondering how you ended up here."

Hannah scoffed, then Rachel's voice interrupted her.

"Mom, customer."

"I gotta go," Hannah said and turned away.

Rent watched her, taking a deep breath and releasing it slowly. *Wow. This is a surprise.*

Only then did he realize his forehead had broken out in a sweat, which had begun to seep into his eyes. He wiped away the stinging moisture with a sweater sleeve, then strode to the front of the store and stepped out onto the boardwalk. The cool air felt good on his face. He turned left and headed uptown to find a place to eat.

He hadn't taken ten steps before he heard the girl's voice again.

"Hey, mister, Mr. Beacham, wait a minute," Rachel called as she ran toward him.

Rent turned and waited for her.

When she caught up, she blurted out, "How do you know my mom?"

Rent noted the intensity of her cornflower-blue eyes. He started to reply, but Hannah came out of the store and ordered Rachel back inside.

"It's time to close up," Hannah said.

Rachel did an encore of her disappointed adolescent routine and stomped back to the store. He sighed and returned to his quest to find a place to eat.

At this point, anything will do.

The Nugget intrigued him, and the menu in the window looked inviting enough. He entered what appeared at first glance to be a museum of mining equipment and artifacts. The walls had black-and-white photographs from the nineteenth-century boom days.

A man wearing a red-checkered shirt and sporting a bushy white mustache greeted him and said a table would be available in ten to fifteen minutes, if he wouldn't mind waiting. Rent nodded his acquiescence and tried to identify the various implements hanging on the walls. Then he heard a woman's voice calling, "Dr. Watson. Dr. Watson."

He caught sight of a hand waving and the woman from the real estate office gesturing for him to join her. He crossed the room to her table, where she sat alone, although he noted two place settings and wine glasses.

"I think I've been stood up," she said. "I couldn't decide whether to have another glass of wine or just go home and eat leftovers and feel sorry for myself. Do you want to join me? The wine's already open."

"Sure. I would've been eating by myself anyway."

"I hope you like red."

He pulled out a chair and seated himself. "Anything but merlot."

She laughed. "No problem. I'm more of pinot noir kind of gal."

"*Sideways.*"

"You've seen the movie too," she said as she poured wine into the empty glass and topped off her own. "I haven't ordered yet, but I'm leaning toward the meatloaf and mashed potatoes. It's been that kind of a day."

Rent glanced at the menu, which featured basic family fare and the Miner's Special, pork and beans with crusty sourdough bread. "Yeah, why not. I'll have the same."

A matronly server stopped at their table. "New beau, Abby?" the woman asked with a wink and a teasing quality to her voice.

Abby's face flushed as she responded. "Ha, ha, Alice. No. This is . . ." She looked at Rent, puzzlement crossing her face. "Dr. Watson, I presume?"

Rent chuckled. "Okay, full disclosure. I am Rent, Rent Beacham."

Alice frowned. "That name almost sounds familiar. You been in here b'fore?"

"Nope. First time."

"Well, Mr. Rent Beacham, what'll it be?"

"The meatloaf, please."

"Fries or mashed?"

"Mashed."

"Same for me, Alice," Abby injected.

"That's an odd name . . . Rent," Alice said.

"Yeah, it's because I'm always behind."

"Behind? . . . Ah, funny boy. Behind on your rent," Alice replied. "You sure know how to pick 'em, Abby. Two meatloafs comin' right up."

Abby leaned forward and asked in a low voice, "Rent? Is that really your name? Or are you still being evasive?"

Rent grinned and lifted a shoulder in a half shrug. "That's my name. Short for Regent, my grandmother's maiden name."

Abby didn't look convinced, so Rent pulled his wallet from a pants pocket and withdrew a business card.

"Here, see for yourself," he said as he handed her the card, adding, "Miss Sales Associate."

"Miss . . .?" She sighed. "Yeah, I can explain. I'm studying for my Realtor license and will take the exam . . ."

Rent waved her off. "No need. I already sorted it." He lifted his glass as if to offer a toast. "Here's to transparency," he said, and they clinked their glasses.

Alice returned with a basket of bread and butter pats. Rent helped himself, washing it down with wine.

He and Abby chatted while waiting for their meals to arrive. Rent confirmed the information on the card he had handed her, that he worked for the *San Diego Herald* as an investigative journalist.

"So, what are you investigating?"

"Today, I'm investigating real estate. Personal matter, not for the paper. I am interested in looking at some properties."

"But not three hundred and forty-five acres."

"You got me there," he acknowledged. "But how about you? What brought you to the back country? Or did you grow up here?"

She explained that she had moved to the mountains with a former boyfriend who had gotten a job at a winery . . .

"Menghini? I stopped there this afternoon . . . sorry to interrupt."

Abby nodded and continued, saying that she discovered he had been cheating on her with a co-worker. Meanwhile, she had gotten a job at the real estate office and began studying for her broker's license.

"That's when I'll make the big bucks," she said. "More wine?"

"Just a splash. Long drive home."

Abby added some to his glass and refilled her own. "I don't have a long drive home, and I'm not letting this go to waste." Then she muttered, "Selfish bastard," and immediately caught herself. "Oh, sorry. I don't mean you."

"No worries. That's an unusual bracelet you have on," he said.

Abby held up her forearm. "Survival bracelet."

"I've never seen one before. Macramé?"

"Kind of. The band is made of woven paracord, and it has a compass, whistle, fire starter, SOS light. You never know when it might come in handy around here, wandering in the wilderness."

"Nice," he said.

They were silent for a moment before Abby spoke again.

"I stayed here because I missed the seasons," she said, "and as long as I don't have that long commute, rent's a lot cheaper here than down below. It's gotten ridiculous. Did you know the average rent in San Diego is now three thousand dollars a month?"

Rent nodded. "Missed the seasons?" he questioned.

"Yeah, I grew up in Fruitland, Idaho. We have real winters there, snow and ice, not the namby-pamby weather that passes for winter in San Diego."

"I've been to Fruitland, although never in winter."

"Why on earth would you go to Fruitland?"

"Just passing through, actually. On my way to Weiser."

"Let me guess. You don't look like a cowboy, so not for the rodeo . . . maybe you play the fiddle or guitar?"

"Nailed it."

Rent had attended the National Oldtime Fiddlers' Contest in Weiser, Idaho, for a number of years, but he hadn't been back recently because of the two-day drive from San Diego.

"I worked as a page at the fiddle contest one year, fulfilling a community service requirement," she said.

"Did you enjoy the music?"

Abby looked around conspiratorially, then leaned forward. "Truthfully? I got a bit bored with it. Those tunes pretty much all sound alike to me."

Rent grinned.

Abby leaned back in her chair, a hand covering her mouth as her face flushed. "Oops. Sorry. I didn't mean—"

He waved dismissively. "I've heard that before. No offense taken. As the saying goes, 'Old-time music, it's better than it sounds.' Besides, I'm more of a dance fiddler than a contest fiddler. I got a late start and can't compete with those who started fiddling as little kids."

"There's a fiddle and banjo contest in Julian every year. You should enter."

"I've won a prize there a time or two."

"I'd like to hear you play sometime."

"I'll let you know. I played at the winery last year. Maybe I'll be invited back."

"Then I have heard you. I was there. I enjoyed that, and that singer who was there."

"I know what you mean about missing the seasons," Rent said, shifting back to the initial topic. "I'm originally from the Seattle area. That's when I started going to the fiddle contest. Not that the winters there are so bad. Just dreary. You can go months without seeing the sun. I never realized there was an alternative until I spent a winter down here as an exchange student. I enjoy a day or two of clouds and rain. Just not weeks or months on end."

Abby smiled and held his gaze for a long moment, staring over the lip of her wine glass before taking another sip.

Hmmm. I may get lucky after all, he thought, although his resident internal Cynic resurfaced in his consciousness. *No! Don't be an idiot. This woman just got stood up by her boyfriend. She probably lives over on Witch Creek.*

Rent lifted his wine glass and took a large gulp, nearly emptying the glass, as Abby's face turned grim, then to one of fear.

Crap, she can read my mind.

He felt his chair tip forward and a male-sounding voice said, "I believe you're sittin' in my seat."

That voice sounds familiar.

Rent looked over his shoulder but made no move to stand. The man pulled the chair out, dumping Rent on the floor. He glared at Rent, who stared into the man's menacing face—the man called Gabe, from the store on Banner Grade, the guy who shot at the coyote.

Rent checked the man's belt for his sidearm, then breathed a sigh of relief.

"You!" The man uttered from the back of his throat.

He stepped around the table, picked up Rent's business card, glanced at it, and tossed it back on the table. He then grabbed Abby's arm and jerked her to her feet and dragged her toward the door as other diners stared, mouths agape.

At the door, the man looked back toward Rent. "You can pay her bill." He then opened the door and shoved Abby through the open doorway. Rent got to his feet and started to follow, but the mustachioed man in the red-checkered shirt grabbed his arm. "No dine-and-dash, mister."

"I'm just trying to help her."

The man relaxed his grip as his face softened into an expression of sadness. "I wish you could. But I'm afraid—"

"She has to wise up and help herself," said Alice as she joined them at the door. "I realize he has George Clooney's movie-star good looks, but other than that I don't know what she sees in that ass."

"Alice!" the man said.

"Sorry, Bart," she replied and turned to face Rent. "Pardon my French, but that jerk is a bad man, and no matter what she does, she's never going to change that. But she has to figure it out her own self. No point tryin' to tell a woman that her man's no good when she refuses to hear it."

"So, what do I owe you?" Rent asked.

"I'll get your bill," Alice said. "Do you want me to box up your meal? I was just about to serve you."

Rent nodded and handed her a credit card.

"Might as well take hers as well."

Rent shrugged, feeling lost and out of control.

"Listen," Bart said. "How about an apple pie á la mode for your trouble? On the house. I'd hate for you to think this is a common occurrence here and that we're not hospitable."

"Thanks, but no thanks. I should be going. But could I ask you a question, if you've got a moment?"

Bart nodded and Rent wondered about the man called Gabe, explaining that he had encountered him that morning at the store on

Banner Grade, when the man had shot at the coyote. Bart told Rent that Gabe could be a real charmer, which is why Abby started dating him. But if he sees her even look cross-eyed at another man, he goes ballistic.

"He gets *ugh-lee*," he continued. "Abby's the nicest gal in the world. Like Alice said, I don't understand what she sees in him. Although, I have to admit that, for a woman, Julian is probably a bit like Alaska when it comes to eligible men."

"Oh?" Rent replied.

"The odds are good, but the goods are odd."

Rent chuckled at the old joke as Alice returned with a brown paper bag.

"You're set for tonight and tomorrow," she said. "I put what was left of the wine in there as well."

"Thanks."

She handed him the bag and his credit card. "You might as well take this back, too." She handed him his business card. "Abby left it on the table. Too bad. It might have come in handy."

"Oh?"

"She doesn't know who she's dealing with. Maybe you ought to look into it, Mr. Investigative Journalist."

Rent shrugged. "I'd need a few more details."

"Like the stuff you uncovered at city hall and got the mayor fired."

"He resigned."

"Everwhat. You laid out all that bankruptcy stuff and he had no choice. And him bein' a former judge. You'd think he should've known better."

"You follow San Diego politics do you, Alice?"

"My son works for the city, in the building department. Afraid he might lose his pension." She laughed. "I told him he could come back home and sleep on the couch like so many young'uns these days."

"He's not going to lose his pen—"

She feigned a punch to his shoulder. "Oh, I know that, son. I was just joshing him a bit. The guy's name is Gabriel Turner. Everyone calls him Gabe."

"Your son?"

"No, that ass . . . oops." She caught herself and covered her mouth, then whispered conspiratorially, "That jerk who just dragged Abby out of here. Say, why don't you leave your card with me. I'll see that she gets it."

"That's kind of you."

"She can do better. See you around, lover boy."

An hour and half later, thanks to the slow parade of vehicles leaving Julian, Rent sat at his dining table, ate the reheated meal, and finished the wine, concerned about Abby.

I don't really even know her, but surely she didn't deserve to be dragged out of the restaurant like that. Why do some men have to be such assholes when it comes to women? Not that I'm above reproach.

5

Monday, Day 2

The following morning, Rent called Abby's office, only to learn that it was her day off. He left a message and called a second number on her card, assuming it was her cell phone. The call went to voice mail, so he left a message, asking her to give him a call.

Rent wondered what Alice had implied about Gabe Turner. Could the rumor about meth labs be accurate? Or mere speculation? Or maybe something else entirely?

And why did Abby disparage the people in Chariot Canyon if the guy she's going out with is one of them?

He shook his head. As Grandma Beacham would say, "There's no accountin' for the ways o' some folk."

Still, a story about the folks working claims in Chariot Canyon could be interesting as a human-interest feature. *And if I could tie in the meth angle, all the better. If it doesn't get me killed first.*

He went to see his editor, Janis O'Connor, but she frowned and shook her head.

"Oh, yeah, I can see the headline already: There's Still Gold in Them Thar Hills." She scoffed. "No, I want you to continue digging on the EBT fraud story. We get letters from many of the stories about corruption and people gaming the system, stealing taxpayer dollars. Take a look at the trend line. Seems like the COVID pandemic, now officially over, spawned a new epidemic of crime. They may be unrelated, but you, nor I, believe in coincidences."

Rent sighed. "Yeah, all right. You're the boss."

"It may be just the tip of the iceberg," O'Connor added. "Why isn't anything being done about it? Good piece to follow your city hall bankruptcy series and the downtown real estate fiasco. Could be something big. Might win you that Pulitzer yet."

"Yeah, whatever," he responded. "Thing is, I'm stalled and keep going in circles. The folks at the county welfare office refer me to the U.S. attorney's office, who says I need to talk to the welfare office. Then there are multiple law enforcement agencies involved—city police and county mounties, not to mention crossing county and state lines. The usual bureaucratic runaround."

"What about your Deep Throat? What's he saying, other than 'follow the money'?"

"Word on the street is a whistle-blower may be fired and, if so, there could be a legal brouhaha. But he hasn't returned any of my calls going on two weeks."

"He's not the guy about to get shit-canned, is he?"

"I hope not. I'm trying to come up with a new angle, something beyond the clichéd district attorney nails another welfare fraudster."

"Keep digging. I'll give you till the end of the week to come up with a solid angle," she continued. "If that doesn't pan out, then start poking around city hall again. Just because we've got a bunch of do-gooder liberals running the show doesn't mean none of them have their hands in somebody's pocket. Like that self-righteous prig of a senator from New Jersey with gold bars stashed in his suit coat, and now the mayor of New York City. What's that old joke? 'How cold was it?' "

They delivered the punchline in unison: "It was so cold the politicians had their hands in their own pockets."

He waved a weak goodbye, thinking he would look into the Chariot Canyon story on his own time. As he returned to his desk, his phone chimed. He recognized the number—his mole at the San Diego County Health and Human Services Agency.

Must be psychic vibes floating around the ether.

He touched the Answer icon and put the phone to his ear. "Beacham here."

"Rent, it's DT at HHSA," the voice said.

"Yeah, Rod, you okay? I thought I was gonna hear from you last week."

"Sorry, I had to lie low. I've been getting suspicious looks from some of my co-workers, which tells me I'm on the right track, but I also have to cover my ass. Anyway, I have a hot tip for you."

"I see the city is instituting greater protection for whistle-blowers."

"Yeah, but lot of good that does me. I work for the county."

"Maybe the county will follow suit. What's the hot tip?" Rent replied and pulled a pen from his shirt pocket.

Rod Davis explained that an employee within the county was being investigated, but "everyone's pretty tight lipped about it, and they refuse to divulge many details about it."

"You got a name for me?"

"No. I don't know who's pulling the strings."

"Sorry. I mean the name of the guy suspected of fraud."

"Ah . . . I have to tread lightly on that as well. The authorities don't want him to get suspicious, but he's got an accomplice and I can give you some fairly broad hints that ought to point you in the right direction."

Rent sighed. "Okay, go ahead."

Davis told him that a woman, and her allegedly estranged husband, lived in the Julian area, possibly Pine Hills, but—"

"Julian? I was just up there yesterday."

"Looks like you're going back. I hope you got a big slice of apple pie."

"Actually, I passed on that, but I interrupted you. Please continue."

"The man operates a carpet-cleaning business and advertises in the local fish-wraps. He has a bunch of reviews on Yelp, including a few not-so-happy customers, although his overall ranking isn't too bad."

Rent jotted this down in shorthand as Davis continued, adding that the man also had a Facebook presence.

"He's big into Second Amendment issues and conspiracy theories, and has nothing nice to say about any politicians to the left of Attila the Hun," Rod Davis said.

"I should be able to ID him based on that. Anything else?"

"Oh, here's something. Just checking my notes. I got a message from one of my colleagues but the handwriting's not so great. Something about 'chard rot' maybe?"

"Chard rot?" Rent repeated. "Charred wood that has rotted? Or maybe it's some vegan thing."

Davis laughed. "Yeah, that must be it. Any chard around my house usually rots, that's for sure. Never understood the attraction myself. As bad as collard greens."

Rent grew impatient. "Is that it then?"

"Sorry," Davis said. "I didn't mean to get sidetracked. Actually, yeah, one more thing. This dude might have ties to a guy in Fallbrook who is involved with white supremacists. Leftovers from the Beltz days."

"Tim Beltz? The neo-Nazi dude?"

"I guess so."

"What does that have to do with defrauding welfare?"

"Maybe nothing. We have some active investigations in the Fallbrook area as well, but no direct tie to this guy in Julian that I'm aware of. I just thought if you start poking around, be careful. He could be dangerous and not take too kindly to a nosy newspaper reporter asking questions."

"So noted."

"Oh, one more thing. We've got a private investigator doing some of the legwork."

"Can I talk to him?"

"Actually, it's a woman, and, yes, you can speak with her. You might even want to go on a ride-along."

"You mean like with cops?"

"Yes, but you might find it a little boring, if not downright disgusting. She does surveillance, which can be long hours of sitting on your ass, or some Dumpster diving."

"Dumpster diving?"

"You know, going through people's trash, looking for anything incriminating."

"Yuck."

"I'll let you know what she says. It would be next Tuesday."

Okay, Rod, thanks for the heads-up," he said, then wondered, "Is it possible there's some racketeering going on? These guys recruit people, promising them easy money, do all the phony paperwork, and take a hefty cut for themselves?"

"It's possible. The problem is, we're short staffed and PIs don't come cheap, so there's probably of bunch of these cases that slip through the cracks. We used to have automatic fraud investigations of every application, but that went by the wayside a few years back due to the COVID lockdown."

"I'll see what I can find out and let you know if anything turns up."

"And do *not* forget, you heard none of this from me."

"You got it, Deep Throat. Mum's the word," Rent said. "Do you know anyone I can talk to on the record?"

"Did you get the county's press release?"

"Yeah, I have that, but I need to get beyond the hyperbole."

"Um, let me think . . . yeah, Ed Maxwell. He's a security analyst that we consult with. He can fill you in on the basics of how these scammers work. He'll give you an earful, I'm sure."

Rent jotted down the man's contact information and disconnected. He then called the PI and left a message. The ride-along meant returning to Julian. Not surveillance per se, but to interview a woman who might be able to provide information, if not be a suspect herself.

Rent reviewed his research, thinking he could at least get the background and backstory organized, set up the big picture, then add the specifics and local angle later.

He made a bulleted list of key items and highlighted the most egregious elements:

- Statistics from various sources say benefits fraud has cost U.S. taxpayers billions of dollars and continues to be an ongoing problem.
- Losses to fraud rise into the hundreds of millions of dollars due to EBT (electronic benefits transfer) card skimming, card cloning, phishing, retailer fraud known as "trafficking" (allowing benefits to be exchanged for cash or non-food items), and false applications for benefits.
- Surge in fraud since COVID pandemic.
- California now uses EBT cards to deliver financial assistance for several programs, including CalFresh, which gives food aid to 2.8 million families a year, and CalWORKs, which gives cash to more than 300,000 families a year.

- California Department of Social Services: in 2021, the state paid around $92,000 in fraud claims by July. A year later, same time frame, it paid out nearly $3.8 million to victims of EBT fraud alone.
- Low-income Californians reported $29.7 million in welfare cash stolen and $4.7 million in food aid stolen in the 14 months from July of the previous year through last September.
- In all, California lost almost $24 million as a result of such scams in just a 12-month time period.
- San Diego: thousands of people in San Diego County have seen their electronic benefit cards hacked since September.
- EBT cards do not have CVV microchip embedded, unlike credit cards and debit cards issued by banks; CVV would greatly improve security and reduce fraud.
- Elected officials claim implementing such a program is cost prohibitive.

Feeling more confident about the overall story and able to ask informed questions, Rent called security expert Ed Maxwell. The man named several types of fraud being committed, including card skimming, phishing, counterfeit EBT cards, and filing false claims for assistance.

"The false claims can come from individuals filing falsified applications regarding their marital status, household income, for children that don't exist, and so on," Maxwell said. "They also come from individuals within the government agency, working with accomplices on the outside."

"Like the guy at the county currently under suspicion," Rent said.

"Exactly."

Maxwell then described in excruciating detail how the skimming devices worked. "Skimmers are small card readers placed on top of or hidden within legitimate card readers in retail stores and ATM machines and collect data from every person who swipes a card," he began, and went on to explain that the scammers install the skimmers using subterfuge, distracting store employees, or by posing as legitimate technicians. These devices may be so well designed that card readers or ATMs function properly and, therefore, are difficult to detect. The thieves might also place a hidden camera near the phony card reader to record personal identification numbers, or PINs, used to access the accounts.

"Later, the thieves will retrieve the files containing the stolen data," Maxwell added. "With that information, they can create cloned EBT cards and extract money from the legitimate card holders' accounts."

"Where does 'phishing' come into play?" Rent asked.

"So, if they get the name and account number but not the PIN, they can contact the person and pretend to be a government official, saying there's a problem with the account and they need the PIN to access the account and correct the problem. The unsuspecting individual cooperates, not realizing they've just been scammed until they discover their account has been drained."

"What's the solution to that?" Rent asked.

"In my not-so-humble opinion, the politicians," he said. "They have to get off their asses and do something. I told them that to their faces at a recent security conference. They need to add CVV security chips to the EBT cards, like the banks and credit card companies do. But they whine about how it costs too much, so there's no political will."

"So, it's time to afflict the comfortable and comfort the afflicted, as the saying goes."

"Something like that, yeah."

"CVV, what does it mean?" Rent asked, getting back on topic.

"It stands for Card Verification Value," Maxwell said. "Typical bureaucratic gobblygook. It's another layer of security the financial industry uses to prevent fraud when people make purchases online or over the phone. It was initially used in Europe and Canada before U.S. companies finally adopted it."

"If it reduces fraud, wouldn't it pay for itself eventually?"

"In the long term, yeah, it would. And now the credit card companies are starting to use AI to help identify fraud, but implementing that cannot be inexpensive."

"AI?" Rent asked.

"Artificial intelligence. What hole have you been hiding in?" Maxwell said, then continued. "But politicians can't see past the next election. Meanwhile, it costs taxpayers millions, if not billions, every year in losses. Maybe if the reimbursements came out of these politicians own paychecks they'd do something about it."

""Can I quote you on that?" Rent asked.

"Be my guest. I'm not running for office any time soon," he said. "The sad part is that it's the most vulnerable that get hurt by this."

"The kids."

"Yeah, the kids, and seniors, and people with disabilities."

"These scumbags quite literally steal food out of the mouths of babes," Rent said.

"Don't put those words in my mouth, but, yeah, that pretty much sums it up," Maxwell replied. "Welcome to humanity."

Rent thanked the man and ended the call, muttering, "Yeah, welcome to humanity—self-serving chimpanzees with large brains. But I demean chimpanzees."

Rent called the local FBI office to ask about Eastern Europeans possibly being involved in the EBT fraud. The spokesperson agreed to speak, but on background only. She acknowledged the bureau's interest in the involvement of neo-Nazis and Eastern Europeans working at the bidding of Russian operatives trying to disrupt American governmental operations and political activities, but she provided no specific details.

Thanks for nothing.

6

Rent called Davis to let him know he would do the ride-along and asked how much information he could disclose at this time.

"If the subject's willing to go on the record, go for it, but I doubt she'll say much of benefit to you. Otherwise, you'll have to wait until the investigation is concluded and charges are filed by the prosecution."

"That could take months."

"No shit, Sherlock. The wheels of justice turn . . . oooh . . . sooo . . . sloooowly."

Another call lit up Rent's phone. Abby, finally. He touched DECLINE and sent it to voice mail, then resumed his conversation with Davis.

"What if she's not home?"

"Then you wait."

"All day?"

"And all night, if that's what it takes."

"What exactly are we looking for?"

"We have to determine if what she said on her application is in fact true. That she's a single mother, has three kids, no full-time employment, and the father has scarpered and doesn't pay child support. An anonymous caller suggested a man may be living there more on than off, and the caller only mentioned two kids, not three. I will review the application and see who gave it the green light. Oh, one more thing."

"Yeah?"

She has an instance of claiming that someone emptied her EBT account and she applied for and received a reimbursement," Davis said.

"So, she's a fraud victim as well?"

"Maybe. Or she had help and got some bonus money. Her account has been flagged in case it happens again."

"Okay, got it. Thanks again."

"No problem . . . and good luck. I'll call the PI and set it up."

Rent ended the call and listened to Abby's message.

"Hi, it's me. I'm sorry I took so long to call you back. It's just that . . . just call me. Please?"

Rent saved the message, then tapped the Call icon. She picked up after the second ring.

"Thanks for calling back," she said. "I'm sorry . . ."

"Not a problem. I just wanted to make sure you're okay. That was a bit scary."

"Yeah, he's . . . a bit possessive . . . and controlling."

"What's the deal with this guy, Mr. Chariot Can—? That's it. Ha! Chard rot, chariot."

"What on earth are you talking about?"

"I'll explain later. I was about to ask what's going on with the coyote dude."

"We're through. I told him to get lost . . . and to take his glib charm and stuff it you know where."

"Smart."

"When do you think you might come this way again? I do have some listings you might be interested in." She laughed. "I did leave the restaurant kind of sudden like."

"Truth is, I may be priced out of the market," he said, "but we could still get together. Next week I need to be in Julian to follow up on a lead. Probably on Tuesday."

"That's one of my days off. I have to run errands and do my laundry, but I could meet you in the afternoon."

"Perfect. Then we can finish the delightful meal that got so rudely interrupted."

"Yeah, about that . . ."

"Is there a problem? If you'd rather not, I'd be disappointed, but . . ."

"No, I do, I just . . . I think he's stalking me. And he's left a bunch of horrible messages, threatening me."

"Oh, shit. Can't take no for an answer."

"Exactly."

"You can get a restraining order, if that's what it takes. Save those messages."

"I am. But I don't want you to get caught up in this mess. Why do I always pick the crazies?"

Rent ignored her rhetorical question. "What if we met somewhere else? In Ramona, maybe."

"Yeah, that could work. I have to do some grocery shopping and that's where I do my laundry. Do you know how to fold sheets and towels?"

"Sheets and towels, yes. But that's where I draw the line," Rent said.

"What, you don't want to fondle my unmentionables?" Abby teased.

"Not unless you're wearing them."

"Why you naughty boy . . . I guess I asked for that."

"Uh-huh."

"So, it's a date then—at the romantic laundromat. Folding towels by candlelight. I can't wait."

"Works for me. Let's touch base sometime around noon and go from there."

"Okay. See you later, alligator," she said and disconnected.

Rent frowned at his phone. *Alligator?* Then smiled.

A female co-worker got up from her desk and smirked as she passed by. "Folding down the sheets, are we? Isn't that one of those fiddle tunes you play?"

Rent looked up. "What the—"

The woman stopped. "Haven't you figured out yet that conversations on cell phones can be quite public, even when not on speaker? You might want to have those intimate chats in a more private setting than a newsroom filled with professional eavesdroppers."

He rolled his eyes as she grabbed a piece of peanut brittle.

"Mmm, yummy," she said. "But it tastes a little different."

"She uses honey from her own hives rather than sugar."

"Excellent. I think I'll have another."

"Help yourself. If you don't eat it, Greg will."

She chuckled, then leaned down and said in a low voice, "Don't let her down too hard, Beacham. I'm sure she's had enough disappointment in her life already. Being a woman and all."

Rent glared at her. "Look, Naomi, we've been down this road before. Things just didn't work out."

"Uh-huh, and in hindsight, lucky me. But don't forget to tell her you're already married."

Rent narrowed his eyes. "Married?"

"To your job."

He sighed and shook his head.

"And don't forget your mistress."

"What the—"

"Your fiddle," she added and sauntered away, her hips swaying suggestively.

"Fuck," he muttered and turned to his computer, accessed story archives, and typed "Tim Beltz" into the search bar. A number of stories popped up, the more recent ones about his death at age 91.

Beltz, who had owned an appliance repair business, was a former Klansman and founder of a white-power group. But he and his organization had been hit with a multimillion-dollar judgment in a civil suit. The jury found them responsible for inciting a group of skinheads to violence that resulted in the beating death of a young Black man.

Rent clicked a few more links, including one dedicated to a memorial created in Beltz's honor. A number of people had written glowing testimonials about this man of "core principles."

Hmm . . . maybe the remnants of the group are still operating under the radar? Possibly funding their efforts through EBT fraud? I suppose anything's possible.

Rent opened a blank file and typed in a few notes for future reference. He then reviewed his notes from his chat with Rod Davis, again musing over "chard rot" being a mangled reference to chariot, as in Chariot Canyon. *Could it be? Did I already meet this dude?*

7

—————

Ｔhe PI's name is Alicia Velasquez," Rod Davis said, "and she's okay with you going along, but she's in charge; you're along for the ride."

"Understood, but will I be able to ask questions of the interview subject?"

Christ, did I just say that? Interview subject? I'm becoming one of them.

"Yes," Davis replied, "but the client has to be apprised of who you are and what you're doing, and she has the right to refuse to be identified in your article or even speak to you."

"That's cool. Mainly, I want to get an idea of how this process works so I can make it clear for the readers. My preliminary piece will be in Sunday's edition, so even if she agrees to speak to me and be quoted—even if she's not identified—I won't use it until I do a follow-up."

Rent got the PI's contact information, thanked Davis for setting up the ride-along, then called the PI. She told him her client interview had been set for the following week, on Tuesday.

"Meet me at my office at four a.m.," she said.

"What?" Rent replied.

"You know what they say, early bird get's the worm, and I do mean worm."

"The client agreed to talk to you at what, five a.m.?"

"No, the interview will be at nine."

"It doesn't take five hours to drive to Julian."

Velasquez sighed. "First we do the stakeout. See what's cookin', or who's cookin'."

"We're going to spy on her?"

"Pretty much. That's what I do, spy on people, only I prefer to call it 'investigating.' Then I write reports. That's the dull side of the job."

"We're going to sit there for four hours?"

"Mr. Beacham, do you want to do this or not?"

"Yeah, yeah, I do, I just—"

"Private investigators do not work bankers' hours."

"Or even journalists' hours."

"And it will take an hour or so to get there," she continued. "Look, here's how it's going to play out, assuming it all goes according to plan," the PI said, adding under her breath, "although it rarely goes according to plan."

She went on to explain that they would arrive before dawn to monitor the comings and goings in the event anything suspicious might be going on, vehicles arriving or leaving, and the drivers of said vehicles, and general activities in and around the residence. They could also check on the whereabouts of the carpet cleaning guy.

"This is to determine if there are any statutory violations occurring?" Rent asked.

"More or less," she replied. "Sleepovers, that sort of thing."

"Sleepovers?"

"Her ex or her boyfriend. She stated in her application that she is the only adult living at the residence, along with her adolescent daughter and young son. If another adult is, in effect, living there and contributing to the household expenses, then that could be in violation of the regs governing her participation in the Supplemental Nutrition Assistance Program—a.k.a. SNAP—or it could reduce the amount of her benefit."

"In other words, committing fraud," Rent replied.

"You're catching on, Mr. Investigative Journalist."

"So, we just sit there, watching for four hours."

"No. I figure a couple of hours at most ought to give us what we need at that point, then we go find some coffee and a donut, use the restroom, then return for the interview at nine, which should take no more than an hour or so, and we're done. You should be back to the office before lunch."

"And a nap."

"Barring any late-hour change, I'll see you at four a.m. sharp next Tuesday. And dress warmly. We may have to skulk in the bushes."

Rent held his phone away and stared at it, as if to conjure the woman's face and stare into her eyes. *Seriously?*

"Rent? Still there?"

"Yeah, sure. . . . uh . . . thank you for agreeing to this, Alicia."

"My pleasure. See you then," she said and ended the call.

Rent sighed as he set the phone on his desk. "Four fucking a.m. Christ on a crutch."

"Whining again? Is your glass never half full?"

Rent swiveled his chair, having recognized the voice of his editor. "That's rich, coming from one of the biggest cynics in the newsroom."

She feigned a smile and Rent continued.

"I'm working on it, but it's a challenge."

He showed her his bulleted list of key items to be included in his story.

"Excellent start. Any progress on the local angle . . . a way to personalize it?"

Rent told her about the ride-along.

"Ah, I can see how that early start might give you some leeway in the whining department. If it's any consolation, knock off early on Monday and get to bed early."

"Thanks," he replied and turned back to face his desk.

He logged on to his computer and reviewed his notes, trying to get a sense of how the fraud schemes worked well enough to be worth it economically, keeping in mind that desperate people, living close to the edge financially, sometimes take desperate measures.

After an hour, he needed a break for lunch to let the information overload settle and start making sense. Afterward, he began writing in earnest, providing an overview of the fraud schemes and the millions of dollars involved, and would wrap it up with the usual spin from authorities saying arrests are imminent on the biggest fraud racket in county history, potentially involving an employee or employees of the county government bureaucracy.

Over the next two days, Rent continued finetuning the story, making calls as needed to county, state, and federal officials for clarifications and comments. He wrapped it up Thursday afternoon and filed it with his editor. On Friday, they met to clarify a few things in his story.

While in the meeting, he'd received a call from a fellow musician, Simon Fraser, who wanted to know if Rent could sit in with his band on Saturday. Rent called him back, saying he'd love to, and got the details on time and place.

He ended the call, then thought, *Why not?*

He called Abby to see if she would be interested in getting together on Saturday. "I've been invited to sit in with the Coleman Creek String Band. They're performing at Volcan Wood-fired Pizza in Wynola."

She hesitated before answering. "Um, yeah, that'd be great."

"It's okay if you'd rather not. I'll still be in Julian next Tuesday for the stakeout."

"No, it's nothing to do with you. Saturday should be fine."

They agreed to meet there at six o'clock.

As he ended the call, a fellow journo, Dan Rowland, stopped at his desk and sat on a corner. "Some of us are going to the Newport Bar & Grill for a beer, you in?"

"By some of us—"

"Jesus, you gonna be picky?"

"If Clark—"

"Yeah, she's coming, but you don't have to sit next to her."

"You mean she won't be sitting next to me."

"Whatever. It's just for a coupla beers and mini-burgers. Or fish and chips. Maureen's hubby says they're better than what he got back home in Merry Olde. It's Campbell's farewell. At least come and offer him congrats."

"All right, I'll stop by, but I'm playing for a contradance tonight so I can't stay long, and if it starts to get ugly . . ."

"You two gotta grow up and act like adults."

"Yeah, yeah, heard it all before."

"You want to go sailing tomorrow? Gonna be on the cool side, but should be a good breeze. It'll give you a break from the tomahawk tongues of the petticoat brigade."

"I'd like to, but I have another gig tomorrow night, and I need to run through some of the tunes . . . including *Sailor's Hornpipe*. Next weekend maybe?"

"Sure. See you at the pub."

8

Saturday, Day 7

Rent slept late Saturday morning, not getting home from the contradance until nearly midnight. He puttered around the house, catching a Six Nations rugby game and an indoor track meet, and ran through some tunes for the gig that night with the Coleman Creek String Band.

He arrived at the pizza restaurant ten minutes early and waited in his truck, listening to fiddle tunes. "*Rats in the Rafters* ought to set their toes a tappin'," he said aloud.

Abby arrived 15 minutes late. And immediately apologized.

"Sorry, sorry. Wouldn't you know it, a looky-loo came in a little after five-thirty and I could *not* get rid of him. All he wanted to do was rant about how high the price of real estate has gone, along with property taxes. Like I've never heard that before."

"It's okay. Let's go inside."

They inspected the menu and ordered individual pizzas, she pepperoni and mushrooms with a glass of Chablis, he tomato and mozzarella. Then he spent more time selecting a beer.

The kid behind the counter tried to be helpful. "We have Coors Light, Bud Lite—"

"That's not beer," Rent said.

Looking offended, the kid tried again. "We have a curated selection of craft IPAs . . ."

Rent shook his head and interrupted him again.

"What's the big deal about *hoppy* IPAs? They're bitter. Do you have a curated selection of dark ales or a stout or a porter?"

The kid stared at Rent as if he had spoken a foreign language, then said, "Pacifico?"

"How about Modelo Negra?"

"No, but we have Modelo Especial."

"Fine, I'll take that."

"Bottle or draft?"

Rent sighed. "Draft."

"Fourteen ounce or twenty-two ounce."

Rent looked at Abby and rolled his eyes, then turned back to the kid. "All of this banter has left me as parched as a sidewinder in the Mojave Desert. Better make it the twenty-two."

"Will that be all? Maybe a salad on the side?"

Rent frowned and glared at the kid through narrowed eyes. A voice in the back of his mind whispered, *Give the kid a break. He's just doing his job.* Rent's face softened and he smiled. "Thank you for asking . . ." Rent paused as he read the kid's name badge. ". . . Duane . . . but no thanks. Just the pizza and beverages for now."

"Excellent choice," the young man responded. "Your order will be right up. Sit anywhere you like."

Rent and Abby turned away from the counter.

"Where do you want to sit?" she asked.

Rent looked at her. "Please, no more questions. Anywhere is fine." He then glanced around the room, spotting a family with three young children. "On second thought, that table over by the window."

"Excellent choice."

Rent shook his head again and chuckled. "Don't you start."

They took their seats and a server brought them their drinks. Abby lifted her glass as a toast to the occasion. "To a fresh start."

Rent tapped her glass with his and said, "And a happy ending."

At which Abby eyed him suspiciously, then raised her eyebrows and grinned. She took a sip of wine, while Rent downed a long pull of beer.

A commotion at the door drew their attention. Three men and a woman carrying musical instrument cases entered and wove their way through the tables to the back of the room and set their cases on a raised platform. The man who had carried in a guitar and mandolin looked around and spotted Rent, waved, and joined him and Abby.

Rent stood up and shook the man's hand. "Strummer, good to see you," he said.

"Glad you could make it," the man replied, grinning through a full beard, then glancing at Abby. A sign of recognition crossed his face, but he said nothing.

Rent introduced them, saying the man's name was Simon, but known more often by his nickname.

"I've heard you before," Abby said. "Fun music. It makes me want to dance."

"Then we must be doing something right," he replied and said to Rent, "You remember Flyrod, Hatman, and Rhoda?"

Rent nodded and greeted them.

"Where's your fiddle?" Strummer asked.

"Under the table."

"Great, join us for the second set. Now, if you'll excuse me, I have to get set up."

Rent returned to his seat and sipped his beer.

"So, Mr. Award-winning Instigative Journalist, how's the investigation going? Collared any criminals yet?" Abby said.

"Not exactly, but I've made some progress."

"Details, details. Come on. What's this ride-along you mentioned? You're going out with cops?"

"No, a private investigator."

"Really? What's that about?"

"You mean other than starting even before the crack of freaking dawn?"

"Well, yeah. I mean, is this like a stakeout? Does it involve Mr. Gabe Turner by any chance?"

"Why would it?"

She shrugged. "It wouldn't surprise me if he was doing some things on the sly."

"I can't go into specifics due to confidentiality issues."

"I can tell you where he lives."

"I'd just as soon keep you out of it. These people can be a bit unsavory, if provoked."

"Yeah, don't I know it."

She looked pensive for a moment, then said, "I've probably read some of your articles. How long have you been working for *Herald*?"

"The past few years," he replied. "Before that I worked for the *San Diego Journal of Commerce*, a weekly. I covered the waterfront, the port district, the shipping news."

"That sounds interesting."

"Yeah, other than the port commission meetings. Talk about snoresville. Although occasionally we got some fireworks when the NIMBies opposed a new hotel or convention center expansion. One time I got to tour a ship. That was pretty cool."

Rent could see Abby's eyes glazing over. "Okay, T-M-I. Pizza to the rescue."

Their food arrived and they dug in with gusto. They each ordered a second round of beverages, although Rent reduced his to the 14-ounce glass. They enjoyed the music, a mix of old-time fiddle, folk, bluegrass, and classic country.

"This is fun," Abby said. "I don't know why I don't come here more often."

Rent thanked her for seeing him, what with that disastrous scene at The Nugget.

"My pleasure," Abby replied, "and hopefully that asshole is long gone."

She devoured another slice, then pushed the remainder away, saying, "This will be lunch tomorrow. Rent ate the remainder of his slice and agreed.

The band took a break and Strummer stopped at their table. "Grab your fiddle. I'll be right back."

Rent joined the band, tuned up his fiddle, and took a seat behind one of the microphones. He played a number of solos, as well as accompanying the singing, to the delight of the diners, every table in the restaurant being occupied. Abby clapped loudly and hooted and hollered.

When the set ended, he rejoined Abby, who looked up at him, a smile of admiration creasing her face.

"I'm impressed," she said. "You're really talented."

"I can fake it with the best of 'em," he replied as he set down his fiddle case and retook his seat.

"Don't be so modest. I really liked that jazzy tune, where you were all over the place . . ."

"*Lonesome Fiddle Blues.* That requires a bit of *vascular clemensy.*"

". . . and that squirrel tune."

"*Squirrel Heads and Gravy.*"

"Ew."

"Don't knock it till you've tried it."

"What about that *Strummer's Breakdown*, did he compose that?"

"I did. It's sort of an inside joke."

The server interrupted them, congratulating Rent on his playing and asking if either of them needed anything else. Abby said they would like boxes to take the remaining pizza home, and Rent handed the young woman a credit card.

"Would you like another beer? On the house?" she said.

Rent looked at Abby, who shrugged, and he said, "Why not? But make it a small one."

Abby then leaned forward and gave Rent a mischievous look as she spoke in a low voice, "Do you believe in lust at first sight?"

"You get right to the point."

"Why beat around the bush, so to speak. We both know we have an end game in this merry-go-round we call *dating*," she said.

Rent, blushing. "Okay . . . well . . ." He stalled by gulping the remainder of his beer. "I never really thought about it in those terms, lust at first sight, but, yeah, I'm a male, aren't I? No free will in that department. Purely hormonal response to a good-looking young woman such as yourself."

Abby, teasing. "Soooo . . . do you? Do you lust after me?"

Rent, still hesitant. "If I'm being honest . . ."

Abby, still teasing. "Yeeessss?"

"I lusted after you the moment I saw you."

"Even in a wool cap, down parka, and Ugg boots?"

"I can imagine you naked regardless of how much clothing you have on."

"Wasn't that Billy Crystal's line to Meg Ryan in *Harry Met Sally*?

"As I recall, that had more to do with tits. And then her fake orgasm."

"Whatever. Do you want to stop imagining and see the real thing? Tits, and no fake orgasm?"

"Are you suggesting . . ."

"That we fiddle around? Do I have to start removing my clothes right here?" she said and began to unbutton her blouse.

Rent raised a hand to signal a stop. "Probably not a good idea. There are kids here, you know. But, hey, if you want to put on a show . . ."

The server returned with the credit card and beer, a smirk on her face; Rent signed and pocketed the receipt.

Abby stood up. "Let's go."

Rent drained half the beer in one gulp, set the glass on the table, and waved goodbye to Strummer and the band.

Exit Abby and Rent.

In the parking lot, Abby said, "Follow me, I live just up the road, in Pine Hills."

He did as instructed and parked in front of a double-wide mobile home nestled within a mixed grove of pines and oaks. Rent got out of his truck and glanced around, the tops of the trees barely silhouetted against the night sky.

"Man, this place is dark," he said.

"That's one of the things I like about it here. You can actually see the stars—when they're not blocked by the trees, that is.

" 'The darker the night, the brighter the stars.' "

"Dostoyevsky?" she inquired.

Rent shrugged.

"It's true. That's why Julian is an accredited Dark Sky Community."

"Never heard of that."

"Outdoor lighting is limited to make more stars visible at night," she explained.

"So that's why Julian rolls up the sidewalks at eight p.m."

"Exactly."

"I'm getting cold. Let's go inside," she said as she took his hand in hers and gave him a wink, "and warm each other up."

As they started up the stairs to the front door, a vehicle moved slowly past. They stopped and squinted as the vehicle continued on.

"That your old boyfriend keeping tabs on you?"

"He wasn't my boyfriend, although he liked to think so. And I doubt it," Abby said as she mounted the remaining steps. "He's probably charming the knickers off some desperate cougar at the

Lonely Hearts Club. I'm sure it's just one of the guys from the sheriff's Senior Volunteers; it's like a Neighborhood Watch. We can't be too careful these days, what with this dark-sky policy."

Rent continued to stare as the red taillights winked out of sight.

RENT AND ABBY LAY snuggled together in bed, their lustful passion expended.

"So . . ." Rent began.

"What?" Abby demanded.

"How do I put this politely . . ."

"Do I always hop into the sack on the first date?"

"Something like that."

"No," she answered, "but as I said, I fell in lust with you, and I think I want to see you again, figuring we'd end up at this place eventually, so why go through all that rigamarole only to find out you're not a good lay, and we wasted all that time on formalities."

"Hmm," Rent responded. "So, did you?"

"Did I what?"

"Find out if I'm a good lay."

"You're still here aren't you?"

Rent, in a mock gesture, pinched himself. "Yeah, I guess so."

"Well, there you go then. What about me? Did I pass?"

"I'm still here, aren't I? Besides . . ."

"What?"

"I suspect guys are . . ."

"Don't be an asshole or you will be on your way out the door, buster."

"Sorry, I didn't mean . . ."

"Drop it, or I will go all chimpanzee on you. And you would not like that." She moved her hand across his abdomen, toward his crotch.

"Okay, okay, I get it. But I still gotta ask."

Abby crept her fingers spider-like closer to the intersection of his legs and torso. "This better be good."

"What constitutes a bad lay?"

She withdrew her hand and rose up on one elbow. "A selfish man who only thinks of his own needs and doesn't care about my needs."

"I get that."

"Yeah, well, some guys don't. They think they're god's gift to women when in truth they are totally clueless. Slam, bam, thank you, ma'am, and off to dreamland, or to the fridge for another beer and slouch on the couch with TV remote in hand."

"Oh?"

"There was this one guy. We went out a couple of times, then I told him I didn't want to go out with him anymore. He acted surprised and asked why. I told him, because you're a bad lay. I mean, he was a nice enough guy, but I had to be honest with him."

"I'll bet he took that well."

"Ha, did he. Oh, well, say-la-vee, as the French put it."

"What about Turner?"

"What about him? I told you, he's history. He was a mistake. Shit happens. Besides, I never actually slept with him. He gets drunk and passes out on the couch. He's superficially charming but underneath he's controlling and the jealous type. So . . ." She shrugged.

"No lust at first sight?"

"The luster wore off pretty quick with him."

"But seriously, is this smart? Does it make sense, what we're doing?"

She looked at him in earnest. "Reason only satisfies a woman's rational requirements. But we also have needs and wants and desires and impulses. Loosely paraphrasing that famous philosopher you quoted earlier, desire is the manifestation of life. Two plus two equals five. So, rational thinking be damned."

"I believe that famous philosopher also cautioned that when we're guided by our desires, our wants, it may lead to self-destruction, because man is stupid. Man's worse defect is his lack of good sense, or words to that effect."

"So you're a fan of Fyodor?"

"Not just Fyodor," he replied. "I'll see your Dostoyevsky and raise you by one Mark Twain."

"Twain? Not even in the same league."

"Literary snob, are we?"

"Okay, give it your best shot."

" 'Life is short, break the rules. Forgive quickly, kiss slowly.' "

Abby, snuggling closer. "Mmmm, not bad, especially the last bit." And she kissed him, slowly.

A crashing sound from outside caused them to freeze, lips locked. They listened in silence. Heard the noise again.

Abby fell back on the bed. "Oh, damn."

"Is that a bear?"

"No. It's deer. They're pissed off. They're trashing my yard . . . again."

Rent shot her a puzzled look.

"Come on, I'll show you."

They dressed hurriedly and Abby, flashlight in hand, led the way out the back door. She panned the light across the darkness and several pairs of eyes lit up like green light bulbs at Christmas time, staring intently back at them, heads sprouting antlers silhouetted against the faint starlight.

"I forgot to feed them, and when I do, they turn over the feeding trough I made for them, along with the lawn furniture, the ungrateful quadrupeds."

She walked across the yard to an aluminum storage shed, opened the door, and flipped on a light as the deer retreated.

"Grab some hay while I take care of the trough."

Rent picked up a large chunk of hay from an open bale and took it out to Abby.

"Spread it out in the trough. I'll get some more." She returned a moment later with an armful of hay and added it to the trough. "That'll keep them happy . . . for now."

They returned to the house-on-wheels and she apologized for the deer interrupting their romantic interlude.

"Not a problem. I should get going anyway."

"No, don't go."

"You have to work in the morning, and I need a good night's sleep. I'll be back up here on Tuesday."

"Promise?"

"Promise."

Sunday, Day 8

Rent slept late and lounged even longer, recalling the events of the previous night. A smiled creased his countenance. He sighed and threw off the covers. *Chores to do. Gonna be a busy week.*

After putting the kettle on, he retrieved the newspaper from his front porch. As promised, his EBT fraud story appeared on the front page, above the fold, and continued inside.

As the water dripped through the grounds into the carafe, he scanned the story, looking for any further edits. Nothing to complain about. He poured himself of cup of coffee and continued to peruse the paper. A related story on the inside page below the continuation of his own caught his attention. It told of arrests made in Riverside County for EBT fraud.

"Hmm," he said aloud. "Could these guys be related to my investigation? And, if so, why didn't O'Connor tell me she was running this as a companion piece?"

His phoned dinged and he glanced at the text message:
back of or ur deed!!!!!
Obviously well educated. Either that or he lacks opposable thumbs.

Rent pinned it for quick reference later and spent the rest of the morning doing laundry and cleaning up his condo. He then relaxed as he continued reading another of G.M. Ford's thrillers featuring the discredited investigative journalist Frank Corso.

If, like Frank, I'm receiving death threats, I guess that means I'm being given some degree of credence.

Monday, Day 9

Rent entered the *San Diego Herald's* newsroom and went straight to his editor's office, where he knocked on the open door. She motioned him in, giving him a quizzical look as he tossed a page of newsprint onto her desk.

"Why wasn't I told about this? It could be directly related to my story."

Janis O'Connor's brow furrowed as she responded, "Get up on the wrong side of the bed this morning, did we?" She picked up the page and glanced at it, then lifted her eyes to meet his. "This was a late addition. The story came in after you had left. I didn't want to bother you at the pub."

Rent nodded. "Okay . . . sorry. I guess I overreacted."

"Is something eating you? I know it's Monday morning, but jeez, no need to get hot under the collar over something like this."

"No. It's just that I feel as if I'm spinning my wheels on this thing."

"Rent, you laid out the basics brilliantly and cut through the bureaucratic BS, raising important questions. You know all the TV news producers are salivating over it, trying to figure out how they can give it a different spin. Your next piece will go deeper into the weeds, once you've gone on the ride-along and followed up on the carpet cleaning guy."

Rent sighed. "Yeah, you're right as usual. I'll make a few calls."

He went to his desk, logged on to his computer, and followed up on the arrests with law enforcement in Riverside County. He found no obvious connection, but the Eastern Europeans suspected of being involved might give his investigation a new angle. The spokesperson said the investigation was ongoing, and they were hoping at least one of those arrested would talk in return for leniency.

"If we find any ties to what's going on in San Diego County, it will be noted, and we will liaise with our counterparts in San Diego. Give us a call back later in the week."

Rent thanked her and opened a new file to record his notes, thinking, *Liaise? Where do they come up with this euphemistic crap?*

"There's got to be a connection," Rent muttered. "Fallbrook is practically in Riverside County, and Beltz ended up in Hemet. But where do the Eastern Europeans come into it? Curiouser and curiouser."

O'Connor had approached his desk and waited until he had finished his call. She handed him several sheets of paper, and he gave her a questioning look.

"These are phone calls and emails from others claiming to be victims of EBT fraud, responses to the piece you wrote. Might be more fuel for your fire."

He glanced down at the top sheet of paper. "Thanks," he replied. He scanned them quickly and circled two. He then set the papers aside. "I'll deal with this after the ride-along."

He created a list of questions he had for the woman to be interviewed the next day. The PI hadn't given him her name. Why not? Maybe to keep him from jumping the gun?

Rent then called Abby. She answered without even a hello.

"You better not be bailing out on me," she said.

"No, no, it's not that. But can we move it to Wednesday? Tomorrow's going to be a really long day. We're starting before dawn, and I would probably end up doing a face plant in my food, I'll be so tired. I doubt I would be much fun."

"Okay, but you better not be stringing me along."

"Not at all. I'm in lust, remember? On Wednesday I'll be a fresh daisy and you can pluck my petals and play he lusts me, he lusts me not."

"Well," she replied, drawing out the word. "Since you put it that way, how could a girl refuse? Besides, something else came up, so this works out perfectly."

Rent disconnected and called the PI to say he would meet her in Julian, rather than ride up with her. That would save him a return trip. He then researched accommodations in the area and found a B&B that touted itself as a "Hubbell house"—designed by the renowned artist James Hubbell. He made reservations for Tuesday and Wednesday nights.

Rent grabbed his jacket and headed for the exit. As he walked out the main entrance, he caught sight of a dented Toyota Camry idling in the passenger loading zone and a moment of terror swept through him as he recalled the death threat.

Sunlight reflected off the windshield, making it impossible for him to see anything beyond a silhouette behind the steering wheel. He stepped back to the doorway to catch his breath without taking his eyes off the car. He recited the series of letters and numbers on the license plate, committing them to memory.

A moment later, the entrance door slid open; a woman came out and got into the car on the passenger side. The car then drove off. Rent exhaled heavily, his body still trembling.

Dan Rowland stepped out and stopped beside him. "Man, you look like you've just seen a ghost."

"Yeah, my own," Rent replied.

"Got time for a beer?"

"Maybe two. The usual?"

Rowland nodded. "I need to make a stop on the way. See you there."

Rent went to his truck and headed for the Newport Bar & Grill in San Diego's Ocean Beach neighborhood.

I could use a pint of Guinness and a plate of those decadent onion rings. Forget the fish and chips.

As he sipped his stout, he reviewed the case in his mind, then pulled a legal pad out of his leather briefcase. He drew a series of circles and inside the circles he wrote the names of the key players, creating a crude flow chart.

Rowland joined him at the table after getting a pint of brew from the bar, taking in Rent's notes. "Do you ever stop working?"

Rent scoffed. "Sure, but right now I can't make sense of this mess." He gestured at his scribblings on the legal pad. "I have a lot of dots but I can't connect them."

He got another pint, then laid out the issue as well as he could and Rowland agreed it was a puzzle in need of more clues. "All you can do is keep on digging. O'Connor pressuring you?"

"As always."

"That's her job. Let's take a walk on the pier while we still can. One more big storm and it may be closed forever."

They left the pub, Rent put his briefcase in his truck, and they strolled down Newport Avenue to the beach, where they walked out on the aging Ocean Beach Pier. At the end of the iconic landmark, they leaned on the rail and stared out over the Pacific Ocean. A sailboat ran before the onshore breeze, heading into the Mission Bay Channel, its red and green running lights aglow in the fading light.

"I wonder . . ." Rent mused. "I just got an idea. See you later." He did an about face and strode off the pier.

9

Tuesday, Day 10, early morning

Rent arrived in Julian early and parked just short of the four-way stop at Main Street. A few minutes later, a car pulled up behind him, and its lights flashed off and back on. Rent grabbed a duffle bag containing his laptop, digital recorder, and binoculars, exited his truck, and joined Alicia Velasquez in her older Honda CR-V.

"Good morning, sunshine," she greeted, giving him a 100-watt smile.

"Yeah, whatever," Rent said. She reminded him of his father, always cheerful first thing in the morning, turning on the lights and radio, when Rent just wanted quiet and to eat his Wheaties alone and in the dark.

"Nice to meet you in person," she said and offered her hand. As they shook, she added, "You're gonna enjoy this. I promise."

"I'm looking for answers, not amusement," Rent replied, noting the woman appeared to be not much older than he.

"I'm glad to see you're living up to your thorny reputation," she snapped back as she whipped her car into a 180 and sped back down the hill.

"Look, I apologize. I'm running about a quart low this morning."

"We'll take care of that in a bit, but first surveillance."

"So, where're we headed?"

She explained that they would stake out the client's residence and see what, if anything, transpires. "You can learn a lot from this."

"Does this client have a name?"

"I'll introduce you at the time of the interview."

"Why all the secrecy?"

"I know you journo types, always looking for a scoop without having all the facts."

"Whatever," Rent muttered, then closed his eyes and leaned his head back against the head restraint, seeking more sleep, if only for a moment or two. When the car slowed, he opened his eyes and watched as Velasquez made a left-hand turn onto a side road. The headlights, on bright, illuminated a road sign that indicated they were on Pine Hills Road, which he had taken to Abby's.

Moments later, she turned onto Eagle Peak Road, which took them down slope, twisting around the many ravines descending from Pine Hills toward Boulder Creek. When they reached a fork in the road, she bore right onto Boulder Creek Road and continued for another mile, then dimmed the vehicle's lights and slowed to a crawl.

She nodded to the right and said, "The house is over there, behind the oaks."

Rent peered into the darkness but could only make out the vague silhouettes of the trees. Maybe he caught a brief glimpse of a porch light.

Velasquez continued on, passing the driveway as the road veered left, then right, at which point she did a U-turn and pulled off the road into a wide spot and parked. She left the engine running to keep the heater on. The temperature displayed on the dash read 38 degrees as the clock flicked over to 5:23 a.m.

Rent shook his head. *This had better be worth it.*

Even using his binoculars, Rent could barely make out the driveway to the client's house. "Man, this place defines dark," he said.

"Yeah, we have to get closer."

"Where you gonna park, in the driveway?"

"No, we walk and hide in the bushes."

"I didn't know I'd being playing Daniel Boone."

"Oh, quit your whining. As I said, this is the exciting part. Get's the ol' adrenals running full blast. I have a spare blanket you can wrap up in if you get cold . . . wimp."

"Gee, thanks."

She turned to him and grinned. "You're quite welcome. Ready?"

"As I'll ever be."

"Be very quiet. Don't slam the door. Tread lightly and try not to fall down. Did you bring a small flashlight?"

Rent retrieved an LED flashlight from his coat pocket and snapped it on.

"Turn it off. Off. *Now!*" she ordered, her voice almost a hiss.

Rent flicked if off. "Jeez, don't have a cow over it."

"I don't want to blow our cover, you greenhorn. By the way, you do know that Daniel Boone was captured by the Indians more than once, right? Probably from doing something stupid like that."

"Yeah, yeah, spare the history lesson. Are we going?"

"Yes, let's do it," Velasquez said. She turned off the engine, then switched the overhead light to full Off so it would not come on automatically when a door opened.

They both eased out of the vehicle, closing the doors with nearly silent clicks. Velasquez led the way, crossing the road and staying on the pavement until they reached the driveway. She stopped and Rent bumped into her.

"Oops. Sorry," he said.

"I'm beginning to regret this," she responded.

"I thought you said this is the exciting part."

"I'm referring to having you along. Keep still while we get the lay of the land. We need to get closer."

The driveway curved to the right, around the line of oaks, before leading directly to the house. A faint light began to appear above the treetops lining the pine-covered hills. Somewhere a quail called.

Velasquez stepped to her left and moved behind a manzanita bush. Rent joined her.

"We've got two vehicles here, a Jeep and that van," she whispered. "I'm guessing the Jeep is hers. So, who's driving the van?"

"There's some writing on the back of the van, but it's too dark to make it out."

She handed him a monocular telescope. "Try this."

Rent accepted it and held it up to his left eye.

"Whoa, this is incredible."

"Not so loud."

He scoped the area with the night-vision device, impressed by how it lit up the vehicles, the house, and other objects in the yard.

"It's like fifty shades of gray," he whispered. "I think I'm seeing a dog. It's behind a fence or in a kennel. It seems to be sniffing the air."

"It might be picking up our scent. I just hope it doesn't start barking."

"I'm beginning to make out the lettering on the back of the van. I feel as if I'm taking the vision test at the DMV. M-A-G-I-C . . . C-A-R . . . It's the carpet cleaner. The guy my source at HHSA told me—"

"Ssh!"

The dog emitted a whine but did not bark. Velasquez laid a hand on Rent's arm.

"Gimme," she whispered.

He handed her the scope and tried to locate the dog with his binoculars, afraid to even breathe.

The dog seemed satisfied and began to lap up water from a dish sitting on the ground. It then sniffed the perimeter of its enclosure but appeared to be more curious than alarmed.

Rent put his gloved hands in his coat pockets to keep them warm as he and the PI stood motionless, waiting, while the eastern sky grew lighter.

After about 15 minutes, a light came on in the house.

"Someone's up," Velasquez whispered. "Early riser."

A few minutes later, they heard a toilet flush. Another moment passed. The light went out, the front door opened, and a person stepped out. The dog whined a greeting and raised itself on two feet, placing its front paws on the chain-link fence and wagging its tail.

The figure ignored the dog, went to the van, and opened the driver's-side door. A light came on, illuminating for a second the face of the person.

"Gabe Turner," Rent muttered, then felt a jab in his ribs from the PI.

The van's engine roared to life. The driver snapped on the headlights, shifted into reverse, turned the vehicle around, and headed down the driveway. The headlights illuminated the bush providing cover to Rent and the PI.

Velasquez immediately squatted and pulled Rent down beside her. As the van came around the bend in the driveway, its passenger side came into full view, with the signage decipherable even in the dim light: Magic Carpet Cleaning. The driver barely slowed down as he drove onto Boulder Creek Road and headed toward Pine Hills.

"Phew," Velasquez said as she stood up. "For a second there, I thought we'd been made. He didn't give any indication of seeing my vehicle, or at least having any interest in it even if he did."

Rent extended his legs fully as well. "I know that guy. Well, I don't know him, but I've met him. Seen him in action. Carries a snake gun, although this time of year he just scares off coyotes."

"Snake gun?"

"A story for another time."

"Well, he's a snake all right. A very charming snake, so I've heard."

"Are we going to follow him? Find out where he lives?"

"No need. I've already got a file on him."

"In a big hurry to get out of here. He must know about your interview."

"Oh, yeah. I'm sure they spent half the night cooking up the story . . . the lies . . . she will feed me later on."

"So, what now? I'm freezing my ass off here."

She handed him the car keys. "Here, go warm up."

"You're not coming?"

No, I'll stay here for a while longer. See if anything else transpires."

"Then I'll stay too."

"Big macho man, eh?" she teased.

"What? No. I just . . ."

The dog barked.

"Shit! Now see what you've done?" she said as she crouched behind the thickest part of the manzanita.

Rent crouched beside her, staring toward the house. The dog barked again, but more tentatively, then sniffed the air as it paced back and forth along the fence.

A light came on inside the house. A moment after that, the front door opened and the face of a short person peered out, glancing around the yard. The dog whined again and rose up, placing its front paws on the fence.

The face disappeared and the door closed. Another light came on inside the house. A few minutes later, the door opened and the short person stepped out, carrying an object in one hand.

"I think it's the eight-year-old boy," Velasquez whispered.

The youngster walked to the dog's enclosure and reached for the latch to open the gate. The dog glanced in the direction of Rent and the PI, then lifted its head and eyes to the dish-like object in the boy's hand, whining and wagging its tail in anticipation.

"Please, please don't let that dog out," Velasquez begged.

The boy cracked open the gate, pushed the dog backward, and stepped inside, then closed the gate behind him. He set the dish on the ground and the dog shoved its muzzle into it, snapping up the contents. The boy then picked up a hose and refilled the dog's water dish. He patted the dog, and said, "Good boy," then left the enclosure and returned to the house.

The daylight had increased to the point that physical objects began to assume recognizable shapes and exhibit some color.

"I think we've seen enough for now," Velasquez said. "Let's go find some coffee and muffins."

She led the way, keeping the manzanita between them and the house until more chaparral and oak trees offered cover. "Watch out for that prickly pear," she said.

Rent followed, eyes to the ground. Once out of sight of the house, Velasquez turned toward the road and went to the car. She started the engine and cranked the heat to its highest setting.

"I gotta pee," Rent said.

The PI nodded toward the exterior of the vehicle.

"Right here?"

"You're a man. You have it easy. I have toilet paper, if you need it."

Rent sighed and exited the vehicle.

A few minutes later, he opened the door and took his seat.

"My turn," she said.

Rent sat in the passenger seat and stared straight ahead, his eyes on the driveway until she returned. She fell into her seat and closed the door, then lowered the heat setting. "The joys of being a female PI," she said with a sigh.

"What now?" Rent said. "I doubt anything will be open yet."

"We sit here a little longer, see if anything else transpires."

"You expecting something?"

"Not really, but who knows? We can't assume anything. The biggest mistake we could make."

They sat in silence as the day grew brighter. Rent told her about the coyote incident at the store on Banner Grade.

"Gun totin' cowboy," she said. "Hungry? I've got sunflower seeds, a PI's favorite stakeout snack. Only thing is, have to remember not to leave the shells behind. Dead giveaway that someone's watching."

Rent declined. "I need caffeine."

She checked her phone. "It's past six. Let's do a little more poking around."

She put the car in gear but did not turn on the headlights. She proceeded at a crawl past the client's house.

"That place looks barely livable," Rent said. "Definitely needs a new roof."

At the intersection with Pine Hills Road, she veered right and up the hill into Pine Hills proper. After about 200 yards, she again slowed to a crawl as they passed a barn-like structure on the right.

"Take a look," she said with a nod.

Rent swiveled his head and peered out. Parked next to the structure, he could see the Magic Carpet Cleaner van and an old Ford Bronco, and a Toyota Land Cruiser that also looked familiar.

"So, they're neighbors as well. That's handy."

"Yeah, we've been keeping an eye on him for awhile," she explained as she picked up speed and turned on the headlights. They wound through Pine Hills and back to the main highway.

"Nothing's open in Julian, so let's go down to Ramona," she said. "I know a place that should be open by now."

SEATED IN THE KITCHEN Kountry restaurant, Rent and Velasquez ordered coffee and perused the menu. She ordered a cinnamon roll, the house specialty, and he opted for two eggs scrambled and hash browns.

"Toast or biscuit?" the server asked.

"Do you make the biscuits here?" he inquired.

"Yes, sir. Baked fresh this morning."

"I'll have that."

"No protein?"

Rent lifted his eyes from the menu to the server's face. "Protein?" he wondered aloud, frosted with a note of sarcasm. "Aren't eggs protein?"

The server, who appeared to be a teenage girl not more than fifteen, blinked rapidly. "Sorry . . . I meant to say . . . you know, meat . . . bacon, sausage, ham . . . but my boss is going all PC on me."

"I know what protein is," he groused in a vague imitation of Sam Loudermilk. "I don't understand why you didn't just give me the options without the judgmental pretentiousness."

"Do you want meat or not?"

"Not."

"Thank you." She feigned a smile and strode away.

"Are you always this cranky in the morning or is this your natural demeanor?" Velasquez asked. "The poor girl is just doing her job. A job she probably hates, but it'll give her enough money to buy a prom dress. Now, I'm wondering if maybe I should drop you back at your truck *before* the client interview."

Rent looked down at his coffee. "No."

"No, what? I can't drop you—"

"No, I'm not normally this cranky in the morning," he answered. "I'm sorry. I try to be a nice person, and kind and compassionate to others. It's just . . ."

"Something in your professional or personal life bothering you?"

Rent sighed. "Probably, if I'm honest, a little of both."

Velasquez touched his arm. "I get it, but we have to present ourselves as professionals, doing our respective jobs, and not piss off someone who might spit on your scrambled eggs."

Rent chuckled. "You've got a point there."

The server returned with the cinnamon roll and pot of coffee. She placed the roll in front of Velasquez and said, "Coffee?"

Velasquez nodded and the server refilled the cup, then shot Rent a questioning glance. He nodded. She refilled his cup and turned to go, saying, "Your eggs will be right up."

"Hey, wait," Rent said.

The server stopped and faced him. "Is there something else? Ketchup for the hash browns?"

"That, too, but I owe you an apology. I know you're just doing your job and you have to be nice to the customers and not call them 'asshole' even though you're thinking it."

The girl stifled a laugh.

Rent looked her in the eye. "I am truly sorry for belittling you."

"Apology accepted," she said, then turned and began to walk toward the kitchen.

"And please don't spit on my eggs,´ he called after her.

The teenager glanced over her shoulder and said, "Too late."

Velasquez choked on her coffee, and patrons at a nearby table gasped as Rent tried not to look as horrified as he felt.

The PI looked at Rent, a broad smile creasing her face and tears of mirth watering her eyes. "Now that's what I call a genuine ass kicking. That little gal has gumption. She'd make a great PI one day."

Rent shook his head as he raised his cup to his tremoring lips.

The server returned a few minutes later with a platter of steaming eggs and hash browns, a smaller plate containing the biscuit and butter pats, and a bottle of ketchup. She set the items on the table and said, "Bon appétit."

Rent examined the eggs carefully before initiating a tentative application of his fork. While he ate, Velasquez filled him in on the background of the client to be interviewed. Getting divorced, two kids, maybe three, depending on who's asking. Had been in rehab for alcohol abuse following a car wreck while the kids stayed with her parents. Now home, but had lost her job and trying to find full-time work while employed part-time.

"So, why is she willing to talk?"

"I suspect she's on defense and wants to shift to offense. Head the investigators off at the pass, so to speak."

Rent nodded. "It could buy her some leniency from the DA, if it comes to that."

"That's what I figure. So, we need to get as much from her as possible before she lawyers up."

The server returned with a coffee pot. Rent placed a hand over his cup.

"No, thanks," he said. "I don't want to spend the day looking for a bathroom."

Velasquez shook her head. "I'm fine, thanks."

As the server set the bill on the table and began stacking the plates, Rent said, "I'll bet you're a straight-A student and president of your class."

"Something like that," the girl replied.

"Tell me more," he offered.

She looked toward the kitchen, then back at Rent. "Senior class president, rodeo queen, and I've been accepted at UC Berkeley on academic and athletic scholarships," she answered, then added, "I'm older than I look."

"What's your sport?"

"Mainly cross country and track."

"No shit . . . oops. Seriously?"

"I have one of the top times for sixteen hundred meters in the state and I finished in the top ten at the state cross country championships last fall. But I'm not bragging. I say this only because you asked."

"Small world. I ran distance in high school and college," Rent said. "What's your name? I want to follow your career."

"Lindsey Helstrom, no relation to Ana. You can follow me on Instagram, but if you try any funny business, I will report you."

"I fear I have left you with the wrong impression."

"Oh?" she replied, crossing her arms and shifting her weight to one hip.

He pulled his wallet from a pants pocket and withdrew a business card. "No secrets about me. I write for the *Herald*."

She took his card and examined it. "I've read your stuff," she said and grinned. "I might have to cut you a little slack after all."

Velasquez again chortled and checked her phone. "We need to get going."

"What's your major at Berkeley?" Rent asked.

"I'm thinking about communications, journalism."

"Stay in touch. I may be able to get you an internship at the paper. If the paper still exists."

"I'd like that. Thanks."

A commanding voice carried across the dining room from the kitchen. "Lindsey, order up!"

"Nice meeting you and good luck to you," Lindsey said, then glanced at Alicia Velasquez with raised eyebrows and a conspiratorial nod toward Rent. "And good luck to you."

She then grabbed their plates, did a tight pirouette, and returned to the kitchen, her hips swaying.

Rent watched Lindsey move away, shaking his head, then turned to Velasquez, lips tight and eyes narrowed. "That girl is too smart for her own good. I'll bet she creates a helluva storm."

Velasquez laughed and said, "I don't know about that, but I do know that young *woman* sure as hell outsmarted you."

Rent wrinkled his nose in defiance. "Let's settle up and get out of here." He examined the bill. "I'll get this. Thirty bucks ought to cover it," he said and laid a twenty and a ten on the table and secured it with his empty cup.

He pushed back his chair and straightened up, then paused. He opened his wallet again, withdrew another ten-dollar bill, and added it to those already on the table.

10

Alicia Velasquez guided her Honda CR-V down the grade to Boulder Creek Road and retraced the route she and Rent Beacham had taken a few hours earlier.

"We're a bit early, aren't we?" Rent queried.

"We're going to do a little more James Bond," she replied as she drove slowly past the driveway and returned to the turnout where she had parked previously. She positioned the CR-V so they could watch the driveway without being visible from the house.

They waited another 15 minutes, then she started the engine. "Let's get this over with."

She pulled onto the road and approached the driveway, turned in, and pulled up beside a Jeep Cherokee that had seen better days.

As soon as they opened their doors, the dog began barking.

"Oh, shit," Rent muttered.

The dog, no longer confined to its kennel, raced toward them, barking furiously.

"A fuckin' pit bull," he added as he ducked back into the car and slammed the door. The dog came to a sudden halt as the chain that had snaked out behind it jerked the creature backward. It continued to lunge forward, hurling itself against the restraint.

Rent looked at the PI and shook his head, then shifted his gaze to the front door of the house. The door opened and a woman wearing a cardigan sweater over an ankle-length dress stepped out.

"You've got to be kidding me," Rent said.

The woman went to the dog, grabbed its collar, and led it to the kennel. She undid the chain and dragged the reluctant animal into the enclosure, then latched the gate. She turned and with the wave of an arm beckoned Velasquez and Beacham to join her.

The pair opened their respective doors and got out of the car.

"Sorry about the—" the woman began, then cut herself short as her eyes settled on Rent. "What the hell are you doing here?"

"Fuck me," Rent muttered.

Velasquez glanced at Rent, then at the woman and back to Rent.

"What's going on? Do you know this woman?" she asked.

"You might say that."

Velasquez stepped past Rent with a hand extended. "Hi, Ms. Stapleford. I'm Alicia Velasquez. Nice to meet you. Shall we get started?"

Hannah did not take the proffered hand, her eyes still glued on Rent. "Why is he here?"

"He's Rent Beacham, the newspaper reporter I told you about. He's writing articles about the EBT fraud. You agreed—"

"I wouldn't have agreed if I'd known it would be him."

"Would someone please tell me what's going on?" Velasquez pleaded.

Rent sighed. "We've met before."

Hannah huffed a sarcastic laugh. "We've fucked before, too."

"That was a long time ago, when we were young and foolish," Rent said. "Look, I'm just doing my job. I'm here to help you, if I can."

She scoffed. "Yeah, right. As if I haven't heard that before."

Velasquez glanced at Rent, her head askew.

"Look," he said. "You never told me her name, and even if you had—"

Velasquez cut him off. "Let's cut to the chase here. I'm on the clock, and the county is not drowning in dollars. Are we going to proceed with the interview or not? If not, I'll take him to his vehicle and be back alone in a few minutes.

Hannah glared at Rent and heaved a heavy sigh. "Okay, let's get this over with."

She led the way into a house that had seen better days. Exterior paint had peeled back to reveal weather-grayed wooden siding, while broken cedar shingles on the roof gave it an ominous appearance.

Inside, it looked neat, but the third-hand furniture perched upon worn shag carpet begged for new upholstery; blankets and bed sheets served as curtains. The boy they had seen earlier cowered at the entrance to a hallway that led to the back of the house.

Hannah directed them toward the kitchen. "Have a seat. Either of you want coffee?"

"No," the pair replied in unison as they took seats at the table.

"I like your dress, Velasquez said. "Laura Ashley?"

Hannah blushed as she looked down before answering. "It's a knockoff. I found it at a thrift store in Ramona."

"Still, it looks good on you."

"It's nice of you to—"

The boy appeared at the doorway between the living room and kitchen.

"What is it, hon?" Hannah asked as she went to him and kneeled, placing a hand on his shoulder. "I told you not to bother us."

The boy glanced at the PI and journalist, a taut fear spreading over his face.

He spoke haltingly, "Can I p-play my v-v-video game?"

"May I play my video game," she said, correcting his grammar.

The boy huffed in response and replied: "*Ma-a-ay* I play my video game?"

"After you finish your homework. It's due today, remember?"

The boy made fists and thumped his thighs in protest as he turned and stomped off.

"That's Samuel, my eight-year-old," she explained. "He and his sister are in a homeschool program."

Rent looked at the PI and rolled his eyes.

"I saw that," Hannah said and defended herself as she joined them at the table. "It's a good program, certified by the state. Living out here, getting the kids to and from school every day is problematic and . . ." She paused and looked at Rent. ". . . me being a single parent."

"Is your daughter here?" Velasquez asked.

Hannah hesitated before answering. "She's at my mother's for a few days." She paused, then added, "She took her schoolwork with her."

"We're not here to question your parenting, Ms. Stapleford," said the PI, who went on to explain that if the daughter was in fact living with her grandmother, then she, the mother, needs to report that to the authorities and her benefit would be adjusted accordingly.

"It's just temporary, for a few days," Hannah said. "We needed a break from each other. Her hormones have kicked in and she gets belligerent. I wanted her to cool off. And please call me Hannah."

"Where does your mother live, Hannah?" the PI asked.

"She . . . my parents . . . are in Arizona. They came and got her. She adores my dad."

"Uh-huh. I will need their names and contact information."

"You don't believe me?"

"As President Reagan famously said, "Trust, but verify."

Hannah sighed and gave the information to the PI. "But if you try to call them, you may not be able to get through," she said.

"Oh? Why's that?"

"They have an RV. They're snowbirds. They like to camp in the desert. They hang out at Quartzsite a lot, but they move around, and sometimes they can't get a signal."

"I've been known to be persistent," Velasquez said. "And don't you have a third child? I thought I read that somewhere."

Hannah seemed taken aback by the question. "No," she insisted. "Just the two, Rachel and Samuel."

Velasquez seemed puzzled but let it go. "Let's get started, shall we?"

She began by setting out a digital recording device, then pressed the Record button and a red light came on. Rent started his recorder as well.

"With your permission, I am recording this interview. It protects both of us in the event any questions arise from the statements being made. Please state your full name and age."

"Hannah Stapleford, age thirty-two."

"And you are voluntarily agreeing to your participation in this interview?"

Hannah nodded her approval.

"I need to hear it," Velasquez said.

"Yes, I agree."

Velasquez began by identifying herself and Rent, and the purpose of the interview, and stated the date and time. With prompts from the PI, Hannah explained that she was a single parent, had two children, worked part-time at the bookstore in Julian—weekends only—and homeschooled the children, who did additional educational activities with other homeschooled children in the area, such as field trips.

"They also participate in the 4-H youth development program," Hannah told them.

"So you enrolled in the CalFresh and CalWORKS programs to obtain financial aid," Velasquez said.

Hannah nodded.

"You need to respond with a statement," the PI added.

"Yes, I enrolled in the programs so I could feed my children properly, to make sure they have a healthy, enriching diet, as well as to help with the rent, utilities, et cetera, while I get job training. I'm enrolled in an online course."

Rent began to speak. "Then—"

The PI lifted a hand, signaling him to stop. "Not yet. I'll let you know when, and if, you can ask questions."

Rent rolled his eyes again and slumped back in his chair. A slight smile crept onto Hannah's lips as her facial expression softened.

The PI resumed. "Then something bad happened, is that correct?"

"Yes, my EBT card got hacked. Most of my monthly benefit was stolen. I was literally at Stater Bros. in Ramona buying groceries."

Rent sat up, pulled out a notebook, and began jotting notes. Hannah glanced at him for a moment.

"Please continue," the PI said.

"I swiped my card, entered the PIN and, *whammo*, the clerk told me there were insufficient funds in my account. I felt dizzy and almost fainted. I've never felt so humiliated in my life, standing there with my two kids and unable to pay for the groceries they'd helped me pick out."

Hannah paused to catch her breath, then continued.

"I told the clerk that was impossible, my card had just been refilled the day before, and I had only bought some milk and a few snacks at Don's Market in Santa Ysabel. But he said there was nothing he could do. So, I had no choice. I had to leave. I didn't even have enough cash to take my kids to McDonald's."

"Had this ever happened before?"

"No, never. It was a total pain in the ass," Hannah said, then covered her mouth. "Oops, sorry. I mean it really messed things up. I had my cart filled with groceries at the checkout and I had to leave it there. And that sure set the tongues a wagging. I felt so ashamed. One ass— One guy even shouted at me, 'Get a job, you deadbeat!' Can you believe it?"

"So then what happened?"

"I had to go to the field office in El Cajon and file for reimbursement. That took over two weeks, and I had two mouths to feed. Some friends loaned me money, and my parents helped out. But it was a royal pain."

"When was this?"

"About eight months ago."

"Can you be more specific?"

"It's a bit of a blur. Doesn't the county have it on record?"

"I'm sure they do, but it would be helpful to hear it from you."

"Can I get back to you on that?"

"Sure," Velasquez said, and handed her a business card. "Call or text or email me."

"And it's not just me," Hannah said. "I know others that have had their benefits hacked."

"Do you think they'd talk to me?" the PI asked.

"And me?" Rent injected.

Velasquez shot him dirty look.

"Just asking. Jeez," he responded.

Hannah replied, "I'll ask. Even Alice, who works at The Nugget . . ."

"She's on welfare?" Rent blurted.

Hannah shook her head. "No, it was her COVID benefit. You know, those cards we got during the pandemic? Hers got hacked. She had used most of it already, but it still cost her about a hundred bucks. Ask her. I'm sure she'd be happy to talk. Being Alice, the whole town knows about it."

Rent scribbled more details on the page of his notebook. *I will ask Abby about this tomorrow.*

Velasquez continued with her questions. "Have you been hacked more than just that once?"

Hannah didn't offer an immediate answer. She glanced from the PI to Rent and back to the PI, then drew a deep breath and exhaled. "Yes, a couple of months ago it happened again. Not on the first of the month, but the second week. I had already spent about half of the money. At least I knew the drill and got reimbursed right away. But if it happens again? I'm afraid I could get kicked out of the program. They're already suspicious."

"What makes you say that?"

"Just something I overheard at the field office. Some guy behind the counter said something, implying that somehow people who got hacked more than once may know the hacker and they're just trying to rip off the system."

"And?"

"What?"

"Is it true?"

Hannah looked at the PI in disbelief. "No, it's not true. Why would I?"

"To get more money, obviously," the PI replied.

"May I?" Rent asked Velasquez.

She nodded. "Go ahead."

Rent turned to face Hannah. "Theoretically speaking, as I understand it, a person could be involved in the hacking in order to get, in effect, a double payment. I've even heard about cases where a card was hacked twice in the same month. Go figure. But the program is for the kids. Ultimately, they are the ones who suffer when a parent doesn't have the money to feed them. So that leads to what some might call lax oversight. Plus, the security on these cards suck. It's way behind that used by banks and financial institutions for credit cards and debit cards, which have a special chip built into the card. That adds an additional layer of security and makes it much harder for a cardholder's account information to be hacked."

"I didn't know that," Hannah said. "But I can assure you I am not involved in this. Why would I jeopardize my own children?"

"Exactly," Rent offered. "But that's what makes these EBT cards so vulnerable, and it's innocent children who suffer."

Velasquez directed another question to Hannah. "So, to summarize, you've been victimized not only once, but twice."

Hannah nodded.

"And you have no idea how this happened or who the perps are?"

Hannah shifted her gaze from the PI to Rent, then back to the PI. "No, I told you I don't have a clue."

The PI glanced at Rent, then said, "All right, let's move on."

"Move on?" Hannah questioned with fearful glances at the PI and journalist. "I thought we were done."

Velasquez shook her head.

"I really need to use the bathroom—all that coffee," Hannah said.

"Go," the PI replied and paused the recorder, as did Rent.

As soon as they heard the bathroom door close, Velasquez faced him. "She's lying."

"Yeah," he agreed.

"How is it you know this person?"

"I haven't seen her since we were freshmen in college. In truth, I know almost nothing about her. We had a short fling, that's all, and went our separate ways. Then I ran into her at the bookstore in Julian."

"When was this?"

"Last week."

"So, I'm to believe this is all one big coincidence that the two of you are reunited just as you, Mr. Inquisition Journalist, dive into an investigation in which your former girlfriend—lover, apparently—may be up to her tits in shit."

"I know it sounds incredible, but it's true."

"What's true?" Hannah said as she re-entered the room. "Talking behind my back, no doubt."

"She's wondering how we just happened to know each other," Rent replied.

"A long, long time ago. Another lifetime," Hannah said, then leaned toward Velasquez. "As one woman to another, I had hoped to never see this lothario again. But after seeing his byline in the newspaper, I thought our paths might cross one day, but not if I could help it."

"Gee, thanks for the endorsement."

Velasquez smirked in response. "Lothario, eh?"

"Don't you start," he retorted.

She then assumed a more serious demeanor and spoke to Hannah. "As long as this doesn't compromise my investigation. If he has to recuse himself, that's his problem. . . . Now, where were we? Oh, yes."

Hannah had returned to her seat and sat at attention, arms crossed in a defiant, defensive posture. Rent and Velasquez restarted their recorders. The PI extracted a piece of paper from a file folder she had placed on the table.

"Please look at the item highlighted in yellow."

Hannah took the sheet of paper and glanced down at it, then up, a puzzled expression on her face. "I don't get it."

"Don't get what?" the PI responded.

"I don't have three children. As I already told you, I have just the two, Rachel and Samuel."

"So how did a third child . . . Ruth, age six . . . get on your application for benefits?"

"I have no idea."

"Is that your signature?"

Hannah examined the document again. "Looks like it, yeah. But I swear I know nothing about this third child."

"Did you receive an increase in your benefit amount recently?"

"At the beginning of the year, yeah, but I just figured that was part of that inflation legislation Congress passed."

"And you didn't question it?"

"Why would I? I was glad to get it."

Velasquez reached a hand across the table and Hannah returned the document.

"Now, about the living arrangements."

Hannah furrowed her brow, again casting a nervous glance from the PI to Rent and back. "As if that's any of your business."

"It's absolutely my business, the county's business. Your benefit is based on you being a single parent with minor children."

"Which is what I am."

"Then who's the dude that crawled out of your house before the crack of dawn this morning?"

Hannah gasped and glared at the PI, then Rent. "I don't believe this. You're spying on me?"

"That's what PIs do. I have been retained by the county to investigate potentially fraudulent activities within SNAP or CalFresh, whatever you want to call it . . . the EBT program."

"And here I thought you were interested in the people being victimized by these hackers stealing money from those of us who can least afford it. What a couple of slimeballs."

"We do care about the victims and want to prevent it from happening again and again. Millions of dollars of taxpayer dollars are at stake here."

"So you treat me like a criminal in the process."

"We are not accusing you of anything, nor are you being charged with a crime. You may be a witness who can help us identify and arrest some of the people committing these crimes."

"Then why the third degree about who I may occasionally sleep with? It gets lonely, living out here in the middle of nowhere, but it's all I can afford."

"We have to look into every angle to gather evidence, get the facts. That's why I'm here." She gestured toward Rent. "Why we're here. And we do appreciate your cooperation. But you have to be truthful. Otherwise, we can't help you."

"How are you 'helping' me?" she asked, making air quotes. "I'm the one doing the helping here. But now you're accusing me of committing fraud. I have done nothing wrong!"

"I apologize if that's what you think we're doing," Velasquez said. "We just want to get the facts straight. Your cooperation will help create greater awareness and, with any luck, get the politicians to do something to improve the security of the cards. It will also increase your credibility as a witness."

The son stepped into the doorway. "Mom, I'm hungry."

Hannah glared at the PI and Rent. "See? This is what I have to deal with." She then motioned to her son. "Come here, honey. Give your mother a hug."

The boy went to Hannah and nestled close to her. She straightened his hair and said in low voice. "Get yourself a granola bar and some juice. Can you do that?"

The boy nodded and helped himself, then left the room.

"How much longer do we have? I need to help my son with his schoolwork."

"I . . . we . . . just want to be clear on how many adults are living here and contributing to the household expenditures."

"Oh, I get it. You think Gabe is living here and helping me out financially, therefore I don't need to be on the dole."

Velasquez sighed. "I wouldn't phrase it like that, but in essence, yeah, I need to check that out. Can you give me his full name and address and contact information?"

"I'm no snitch."

"I could report you to the authorities for obstructing a formal investigation."

"Oh, Christ," Hannah said. "His name is Gabe Turner and he owns a carpet cleaning business. He lives not far from here, in Pine Hills. I have a business card around here somewhere."

She paused for a deep breath, then continued. "That's how I met him. He came to the door one day, handing out a flyer. Memorial Day Special or some such BS. Gave me a good deal, or so he said. He could sell igloos to Eskimos. When I first moved in here, this place was a dump, but it was cheap. I think the previous tenants kept goats in here. So I hired him."

"And you're confident that's his actual name, his legal name?" the PI queried.

"What? Not his . . ."

Rent examined her face. *She seems genuinely surprised. As am I.*

"His legal name is Joshua Gabriel Turnbull. Gabe Turner is an alias. And he's known to law enforcement," Velasquez stated.

"Why am I not surprised," Hannah said, a tone of defeat underlying her voice.

The PI continued. "And just to be clear, you are stating for the record that although he may be an occasional overnight guest, he does not live here, nor does he contribute to your household finances."

Hannah scoffed. "As if. That guy can charm your knickers off, but when it comes to money, he's tighter than a . . . well, you know what I mean. That's not even my dog out there. It's his, but he keeps him here. Claims it's for my protection. But does he provide the dog food? Rarely. And he expects me to keep the fridge stocked with beer for him."

"So why do you keep seeing him?" Rent asked.

Hannah stared at him for a long moment. "I'm human. Maybe Sigmund could answer that question for you. Or Chekhov. I don't know what else to tell you. But he doesn't live here. He just sleeps over occasionally, when he's not with one of his floozies, and to think he contributes financially, that's a joke."

"What about your husband and child support? You're still legally married are you not?"

Hannah glared at the PI and shook her head in disbelief. "I suppose you know what brand of underwear I prefer or what feminine hygiene products I use. Google and Amazon sure as hell do."

Rent had to suppress a laugh.

Velasquez breathed in deeply, then exhaled. "I understand your concern about your private life, but I have to ask these things."

Hannah bit her lower lip and looked away, shaking her head and slumping in her chair.

The PI prompted her. "Hannah? I need an answer for the record if I'm to help you."

Hannah daggered the woman with her eyes. "Will you please stop saying you're trying to help me. It's bullshit!"

"All right, but I still need an answer."

"Yes, I'm in the middle of a divorce. If you must know, the cock—" She caught herself and scoffed. "He ran off with the boy next door. He and his new partner moved to Boise. The divorce has been held up because he wants custody of Samuel, claiming I'm an alcoholic and an unfit mother. I'm fighting to retain custody and get child support. He says he will only pay child support for our son, but not Rachel, because he's not the father."

"Alcoholic?" Rent inquired.

"Yes. I'm an alcoholic but I don't drink," she retorted and straightened up, sitting erect. "I went into rehab for two months and I joined AA. I was in a car wreck. I shouldn't have been driving, but I didn't cause the accident. Ironically, I got hit by a drunk driver on the 78 one night on my way home from work in Ramona, where I waited tables at Di Carlos. Broke my leg and it gave me neck and back problems. I learned my lesson. I'm sober now and don't drink anything stronger than orange juice."

"I'm sorry you have to go through all this," Velasquez said. "I really am."

"Not as sorry as I am."

"But for the record, you are not receiving any financial assistance from your husband."

"How many times do I have to say this? No! Not one fucking dime."

"What about Rachel's father?"

"What about him?"

"Have you asked him for child support?"

"I can't."

"Why not?"

Hannah glared at the PI, her face reddening. "Because I don't know who he is."

"Hmm, I see."

"No, you don't."

Hannah sighed and jerked a thumb toward Rent. "After he dumped me, I had a couple of flings on the rebound. Just got drunk and slept with two or three guys. It could be any one of them."

"You could have gotten DNA tests."

"I know, but I was too embarrassed to admit what I'd done."

"It's not too late. Think about it."

Hannah did not respond, her eyes downcast, focused on her chipped nail polish.

"Okay, I think that's enough for now," the PI said as she stopped the recording. "But I may need to follow up with you."

"And what now?" Hannah said, turning her gaze toward Rent as he clicked off his device. "Am I going to see my name plastered all over your stupid newspaper, the butt of some great cosmic joke?"

"Short answer, no," he replied. "I would like to use some of your comments about your EBT card being hacked and how it affected you and your children. At this point, I'm only interested in the challenges you have faced as a victim of fraud. It personalizes the story, makes it real, and evokes sympathy rather than scorn for those who find themselves in unfortunate situations beyond their control or through no fault of their own, especially since children are involved. That, in turn, can increase public awareness and, with any luck, more pressure on our elected officials to do something about it."

"Oh, how magnanimous of you," she replied.

"Hannah, this doesn't have to be adversarial," he said. "My job is to uncover corruption and fraud, and expose the perpetrators, and, hopefully, further the pursuit of justice. I will not use your name or say anything that may identify you, unless you give me permission to do so."

Her features softened. "Okay, I'll think about it."

Velasquez raised a hand to get Hannah's attention. "May I use your bathroom?"

"Of course. Down the hall, on the right."

Rent and Hannah sat silent for a moment, then Rent spoke.

"I'm not trying to pry, but you seem rather upset about her contacting your parents. Is there something you're not telling us? That your daughter is living with them?"

Hannah sighed and grew misty-eyed. "I might as well tell you, but this is between you and me, okay?"

Rent nodded.

Hannah's eyes misted over and her voice broke as she replied. "I sent Rachel away due to Gabe's unsavory advances toward her. You've seen her. She's very pretty and not a kid anymore. I don't like the way he looks at her, especially after he's had a few beers. He likes to hug her, tight, and longer than needed, and he teases her about her 'little titties.' "

"How long has she been gone?"

"Just since the weekend, and it's only for a few days. I'm through with him. I'm seeing him for what he really is. He's cheated on me. I think he has a girlfriend in town, and one of my friends told me she saw him cozying up to some woman at the Rongbranch. And now I find out he's using an alias."

"Yet we saw him leaving before dawn this morning."

"He passed out on the couch. I didn't let him anywhere near my bed."

Rent seemed skeptical.

"Look, I made a mistake, all right?" She shook her head. "After he finished my carpet and was about to leave, he said, 'You are beautiful. What can you do for me?'

"I actually fell for that because I thought this must be a brilliant man to actually use a pickup line as ridiculous as that." She scoffed. "The real brilliance is that it was the most honest thing that any man . . . including you . . . ever said to me: 'What can you do for me?' . . . And now here I am. Apparently, he meant exactly what he said."

"We're looking more into his background and activities," Rent replied.

"Be careful. He hangs out with some seedy characters. Scary men."

"How so?"

"They're like skinheads, militia types. They came around here a couple times. I told him I never wanted to see them here again."

"Okay, thanks for letting me know. But I'm a bit puzzled. How long has this been going on?"

"You mean those other men?"

"No, Gabe the carpet genie."

"Don't you dare judge me."

"I'm not judging you. I'm just thinking it may not be as simple as you telling him to get lost. He sounds like someone who doesn't take no for an answer."

"Yeah. As the saying goes, 'it's complicated.' "

"You may have to get a restraining order."

For a brief moment, a look of terror rippled across Hannah's face and she swallowed hard.

Velasquez returned and Rent rose from the chair. They walked toward the front door, Hannah following. The PI stopped and looked at a framed photograph sitting atop the television.

"Cute kid," she said.

"Thanks," Hannah replied.

The PI then glanced at Rent, nodded downward at the photo, and raised her eyebrows.

BACK IN THE CAR, as they drove away, Velasquez said, "I still don't believe she's telling the whole story, even if what she has told us is true. Did you see her hands, twisting her hair, and the way she wouldn't look at us when answering? I'm going to dig a little deeper. If she is lying, she's gonna be toast."

"Yeah, and her leg jackhammering a hundred forty beats per minute. If that's not high anxiety, I don't know what is," Rent replied. "She got pretty defensive. Seemed a bit of an overreaction. Still, you grilled her pretty good."

"Just doing my job. Which brings up a related topic."

"Oh, yeah? What's that?"

"What are *you* not telling me?"

"Me? You think I'm involved in this?"

"Not directly. But one look at that photo and I have a pretty good idea who Rachel's daddy is."

"What are you saying?"

"Isn't it obvious?"

"What?"

"Either you're lying to me or you're thicker than you look."

Rent stared at her, then it hit him.

"You're saying I'm Rachel's father? No way. Hannah would have told me years ago, if for no other reason than to get child support."

"You better be straight with me."

"Swear to god."

"We're going back in there."

Velasquez flipped a U-turn and sped back to Hannah's place, where the PI confronted Hannah with the photo.

"I think it's time for a DNA test—for Rachel and this mug," she said with a nod toward Rent. "That girl has a right to know. And so do you."

Hannah let out a sigh of defeat. "Rachel's been wanting to do this for a couple of years. Begging me to do the tests so we can go on one of those genealogy websites and see if there's a match."

She turned and started toward the hallway leading to the bedrooms and motioned for the PI and Rent to follow.

"Come on. I think she's grown more suspicious. I'll show you."

She led them into Rachel's bedroom and pointed to a charcoal sketch on the bedroom wall.

"Holy crap," Rent said.

The PI looked at Rent, a wide grin creasing her face. "Nice likeness, Dad."

The drawing featured a bearded man playing a fiddle.

"Rachel loves to draw," Hannah said. "I think she did this from a photo she found online."

"She's been cyberstalking me?"

"Apparently. How's it feel?"

Rent shook his head, unable to stop staring at the drawing.

"When did she do this?" Velasquez asked Hannah.

"Just in the last few days, after he came into the bookstore."

"Now I definitely think it's time for that DNA test," the PI said, and cast her gaze on Rent. "Wouldn't you agree?"

He sighed in resignation.

Velasquez collected a toothbrush and strands of Rachel's hair taken from a hairbrush, and placed them in evidence bags.

IN THE CAR ONCE again, Rent tried to redirect the conversation. "What about that 'permission' BS at the start of the interview? You didn't need her permission to record it."

"Of course not," she replied. "But if the subject believes it, they are more cooperative. A little white lie. No harm done . . . Dad."

"Oh, puh-lease. Give me a break. She would have said."

"She really may not have known," Velasquez said. "It can take weeks before a woman realizes she's pregnant. That's why those highly restrictive abortion laws in red states are such a tragic fucking joke."

Rent did not reply as the PI pulled out of the driveway and onto Boulder Creek Road.

After a moment of silence, he asked, "Do you think Hannah's part of the scam, or just the victim as she claims to be? She doesn't come off as your typical welfare stereotype. She's articulate and seems well educated. Did you catch that reference to Freud and Chekhov? She did attend college, at least for a while."

"She could be an autodidact."

"A what?"

"Self-taught."

"Could be."

"And you do know it's no longer PC to call it 'welfare,' right?" Velasquez said.

"Yeah, yeah, I use all the current euphemisms in my stories," Rent replied.

"I'd like to believe she's just the victim, but it still has a noxious odor to it," the PI added. "If Mr. Magic Carpet Ride is up to no good, she's got to be suspicious. Or delusional."

"I hope she's suspicious, but some con men are super slick."

"You mean slimy."

"That, too."

"Speaking of slime," the PI said, "we may need to do a Dumpster dive."

"Davis mentioned that. Go through the trash. But why?"

"You might be surprised at what one can learn from the things people discard."

"Actually, I would not be surprised. But it could be difficult with that dog," Rent pointed out.

"Yeah. Might have to throw him a bone, literally."

"Speaking of . . . you didn't eat much this morning. You want to grab an early lunch and review what we've got so far?"

"Nah, I'm good to go for now," she said. "I need to get this recording transcribed and have some other things to attend to. But first let's see what lover boy is up to."

For the second time that morning, she turned up Pine Hills Road and drove slowly past Turner's house. A yellow banner hung almost limp from tall flagpole. A puff of breeze unfurled it to reveal a coiled rattlesnake and the slogan "Don't Tread on Me."

"Looks like he's got company," Rent said.

"You could do a bit more skulking after I drop you off at your truck."

"He's already seen me and my truck. At the store. And there's that little fracas at the restaurant."

"Okay, let's make it quick."

Velasquez pulled off the road, stopping by an oak that provided some cover, and left the engine running. "Stay here," she ordered as she got out of the car. She grabbed her camera from the back seat and found a spot where she had a clear view of the vehicles, aimed the telephoto lens, and whirred off a quick succession of photos. She returned to car, got in, and made a quick examination of the images.

"Good, I can read the plates," she said and handed the camera to Rent. "Jot down the numbers while I drive."

She put the car in gear and slowly drove off. "Normally, I'd have my dog with me for a situation like this," she said.

Rent glanced at her, his brow furrowed. "Your dog can read license plates?"

She chuckled. "Yep, smartest dog in the world. No . . . I'm just the lady walking the dog and no one thinks anything of it."

"What about the camera?"

"I become a birdwatcher."

ALICIA VELASQUEZ TOOK RENT back to his vehicle and, as he opened the door to get out, she stopped him. "Let's just get this over with," she said.

Rent frowned, genuinely puzzled. *Where is this going? Surely, she's not in lust.*

"The DNA . . . what do you think?"

Rent's face reddened. "DNA?"

"Yes, DNA," she replied and got a test kit from the back of her car, then returned to her seat.

"You really don't—"

"Shut up and open wide."

The PI swabbed the inside of Rent's cheeks and placed the samples in an evidence bag. "Now it's official," she said.

"You don't trust me?"

"Just being preemptive."

RENT DROVE TO THE Julian library at the other end of town. He began outlining his story and transcribed Hannah's comments from his recording of the interview, working until check-in time at the Rainbow Hill B&B.

Once checked in, he treated himself to a well-deserved nap, then grabbed an early dinner at the Rongbranch family-style restaurant.

Afterward, he stopped by the real estate office, where the Realtor reminded him that it was Abby's day off. He returned to the B&B, settled into the bed, and read about the structure, designed and built by Julian's renowned artist and visionary designer James Hubbell. To Rent, its otherworldly design looked like something out of a sci-fi movie or a Tolkien novel.

This place doesn't have a single square corner above the foundation.

Rent then turned to the G.M. Ford novel until he could no longer keep his eyes open. What with the early rise that morning, he wandered off into dreamland shortly after 8 p.m.

11

Wednesday, Day 11

The next morning, Rent, having slumbered in the bed portion of the hospitality, partook of the breakfast, a sumptuous feast comprising pumpkin soufflé, blueberry/apple muffin, apple juice, and Jamaican Blue Mountain coffee.

A couple from Montana joined him at the table, along with the hosts, a married couple who said they were retired schoolteachers. The gray-haired out-of-towners, who had recently sold their ranch and "moved to town," admitted to be escaping their home state's brutal winter, but praised the region's opportunities for hunting and flyfishing, and outdoor activities in general. Rent told them he and his sister had stopped at the Stockman's Bar in Missoula on their way to Lolo Pass and traversing a portion of the Lewis and Clark trail.

"Ah, yes, the Stockman," the man said, with a conspiratorial glance at his wife. "Liquor up front . . ."

". . . and poker in the rear," she said, completing the notorious notice posted on the wall behind the fabled establishment's bar.

The pair then laughed at their ribald humor and gave each other a high five.

Rent smiled and shook his head at the memory. He and his sister had had a good chuckle themselves.

He exchanged further pleasantries with the Montana couple, promising to return to Big Sky Country, but he withheld anything about his purpose for being in Julian other than to look at property for sale.

Afterward, he thanked the hosts, then patted his belly and remarked with a laugh, "I think I might have to climb Volcan Mountain to work this off."

He returned to Pine Hills and drove past Gabe Turner's place, but not so slowly as to arouse suspicion, in case the man happened to notice. He spotted the carpet-cleaning van and Bronco but not the Land Cruiser. "Crap, is he back at Hannah's?" he uttered aloud.

Rent continued on to Boulder Creek Road, where he turned left and proceeded downhill toward Hannah's abysmal abode. Again, he slowed, but not so much as to attract attention. He could only see a Jeep Cherokee, which he presumed to be Hannah's, it having been parked there the previous day.

He hadn't planned on stopping, then thought, *what the hell*, and turned into the driveway. He parked beside the Jeep and debated whether to get out.

The caterwauling canine in the kennel had alerted the household. The front door opened and Hannah peered out, shading her eyes and this time dressed in jeans, flannel shirt, down vest, and Ugg boots.

Rent guessed that due to the reflection off the windshield, she couldn't identify the occupant. Feeling safe from the dog, at least for the moment, he opened the door and exited the vehicle.

Her shoulders sagged. "Not you again. What the hell do you want now?"

"Just a couple of more questions. Please?" he replied.

"For the love of god, this is the third time in less than a week. If you think you're going to lure me back into the sack with you—"

"Hannah, I just want to ask you about the mine. Turner's . . . or whatever the hell his name is . . . gold mine. I meant to yesterday but forgot."

She sighed and stepped back, motioning him in. Rent shut the door to his truck and followed her into the house. She looked deflated, defeated, as if she had fought the law and the law won. The boy, Samuel, again cowered in the hallway. Still no sigh of Rachel, although he hadn't expected any.

Hannah motioned toward the kitchen, where breakfast dishes remained on the table.

"Coffee?" she offered.

"No, thanks," he answered. "Had more than enough at the B&B."

"Oh? Which one?" she asked as she refilled her cup.

"Rainbow Hill. You know it?"

"I know of it. A little out of my league. Hubbell house, isn't it?"

"Yeah, that it is," Rent said, with a shake of his head.

"Something wrong with it?"

"Oh, no. It's great. But the architecture is like nothing I've ever seen. A lot of peaks and swirls and vaults. When I got to my room, I checked under the bed for hobbits."

Hannah smiled. "So I've heard."

The two then stared at one another for an awkward moment.

She spoke first. "So? What's so important you couldn't have just called me?"

"I was in the area and swung past Gabe's place to see if he was around. His Land Cruiser was gone, and I—"

"Thought he might have spent the night here. That's where you're going with this."

"It did cross my mind, but, no, I'm glad he's not here. However, my question does have to do with him."

Hannah motioned to a chair. "Might as well sit down." She sat across from him and picked up her coffee cup, staring at him, eyebrows raised in a questioning posture.

"Have you ever been to Turner's gold mine?"

She and her kids had been there once, but they didn't actually go into the mine. He told them it was dangerous, but she didn't believe he actually worked the mine.

"Do you remember how to get there?"

She shook her head. "I don't. There are no road signs or notable landmarks out there. Just sand and rocks and chaparral and the occasional ocotillo. All I remember is turning off by the store and going up that rutted road, which practically gave me whiplash."

"Any idea where he might be?"

Again, she shook her head. "He could be anywhere and has never told me much about what he does when he's not cleaning carpets, which I suspect is most of the time. Maybe he's at the mine, although I doubt it. Maybe he's with a woman. Or he could be with those thugs he hangs out with."

"What do you know about them?"

"Not much. They're a bunch of bad asses," she said, adding that she had overheard some phone conversations. "I think Gabe was showing off, like I was some kind of trophy he could brag about.

"One of them was from Fallbrook," she continued. "He talked like a neo-Nazi, white supremacist, and I got the impression he may be involved with a militia group of some kind. He said something about the attack on the Capitol following Trump's loss. But I doubt he had the guts to actually show up there. I think he just wanted people to believe he was there."

She went on to say the guy even tried hitting on her. "Male chauvinist pig. Expected me to wait on him as if this was the Hard Rock Café."

Rent nodded, sympathetic. "And what about Rachel? She back home now?"

Hannah, who had been staring into her coffee cup while speaking, jerked her head up, her guard raised. "Uh, no. My parents are bringing her back this afternoon."

"She seems like a good kid."

"Yeah, she is. Maybe a bit wise beyond her years. And a bit obstinate at times, now being a tweenager."

"Like her mother?"

Hannah chuckled. "Maybe just a little."

Rent checked the time on his phone. "I'd better get going."

"Can I read your article before its published? I don't want to be misquoted or quoted out of context."

"We don't normally do that."

"But you'll do it for me?" She fluttered her eyelashes. "For old time's sake?"

Rent stared at her for a moment, a slight smile creeping into his otherwise unexpressive countenance. *Is she now flirting with me?* he wondered before replying.

"Yeah, okay. For old time's sake. I'll be in touch in a day or two."

Rent started to rise from the chair.

"Wait," she said. "I was going to call you anyway."

"Oh? The DNA test?" he replied and dropped back into the chair. "It takes a while to get the results back."

"That too. But—" She hesitated.

"But?"

"That may not be necessary. I mean, it's necessary, yeah . . ."

"What are you saying?"

Hannah sighed. "I think you probably are her father."

Rent stared at her for a long moment and swallowed hard. "And you're just telling me this now?"

Hannah stared back at him before answering, as if trying to read his face. "What was the point? You were a lousy prospect, a poor college student like me. We would have made a great married couple . . . *not*. After you so unceremoniously dumped me."

"Yeah, I could have handled that a little better."

"You think? Anyway, I had a short fling with a guy, an older guy, married with children. Met him at a party. I didn't know he was married at first. But even when I found out, I didn't care. I guess I felt like I was getting even with you. Proving to myself that I was a worthwhile human being. He wined and dined me, and bought me presents. But I knew it wasn't going to last, school was getting out for the summer. By then, I knew I was pregnant, and I told him he was the father. He called me every name in the book, so I threatened to tell his wife."

Hannah paused.

Rent waited for her continue. When she didn't, he said, "And?"

"And I did a despicable thing. I told him he could buy me off and I would disappear. He had a ton of money and liked to flash it around. He was some kind of muckety-muck at one of those tech outfits. I could have gotten an abortion, but my parents would have disowned me if they found out, and I had no where to go. I figured I was better off taking his money and having the kid. I didn't put his name on the birth certificate. That's why her legal surname is Powell."

Rent sighed. "Got anything stronger than coffee?"

"I don't do that anymore, remember?"

"Just as well—a bit early in the day." Pause. "We still need the DNA results, just to be sure."

"You don't believe me?"

"It's not that. If I am going to become a part of Rachel's life, then I want it to be legal and above board."

"You want to be certain."

Rent shrugged. "Well, yeah."

"I get it. But don't get me wrong. I love that girl. I would do anything for her. That's why I sent her to stay with my parents until I can get Gabe out of my life."

"And that's why you agreed to talk to the PI and me."

She nodded. "But I need your help. I wasn't totally up front with you and that woman."

"We suspected as much."

"I didn't lie," she replied, then, in a more subdued tone, added, "I just didn't tell you everything."

"I'm listening."

She told him how Gabe had introduced her to a man at the San Diego County Health and Human Services Agency who would help her get CalFresh and CalWORKS benefits.

"I don't remember his name," she said. "He helped me complete the application and personally walked it through the system so I would get benefits right away. Then the amount went up, which was great, except Gabe would take my card and use it to buy beer and booze, when that wasn't allowed under the program. There's a store in Ramona where the owner turns a blind eye."

"Do you remember what the HHSA guy looks like?"

"I never actually met him. I only talked to him on the phone."

"So, what is it you need help with?"

"Can you check this guy out? See if he's legit? I don't want to be blamed for something I didn't do, like that third child the private investigator asked about. I don't know anything about that."

Rent agreed to follow up, then thanked her and left. As he drove away, he wondered: *Could it be that the EBT hackers are white supremacists selling the account info on the dark web and using the cash to finance their illicit activities? Where do the Eastern Europeans fit in, if at all? And where does this HHSA dude enter the picture? Is he the one Rod Davis suspects of being complicit with fraudsters?*

RENT RETURNED TO THE B&B. He updated Rod Davis at HHSA, then reworked his story while seated in the common room. The hostess treated him to a cup of coffee.

"Big plans for tonight?" she asked.

"You could say that. I'm meeting a . . . uh . . . friend . . . for dinner."

The hostess flicked her eyebrows. "A little romance in the air?"

Rent blushed. "I don't know about that. We've only just met."

"Ah, early days is it? Well," she said with a wink, "don't do anything I wouldn't do," and sauntered off.

Rent shook his head. *Jeez, these old folks are worse than teenagers.*

Rent checked his email, and he updated his editor on his interview with Hannah and her comments about Gabe and his associates. He closed his laptop and returned to his room, where he called Abby.

"What, you're afraid I might welch out on you?" she asked with a laugh.

"Not exactly," he replied. "But I do need to know where and when."

"Yeah, about that . . ."

"So, you are welching."

"Sorry, but a last-minute change of plans has thrown the proverbial wrench in the wringer. My boss wants me to attend a town council meeting tonight. It has to do with zoning regs and how that could impact us."

"Sounds like a real yawner."

"How about we meet for lunch instead? There's a Mex place just around the corner from my office."

"I'm not really hungry, thanks to my overindulgence at breakfast . . ."

"Then let's go to my place and just have dessert."

"Now you're talking."

RENT AND ABBY LAY snuggled together in bed, their lustful passion expended, again.

"I could make up for welching on you by making a nice dinner for you on Friday—unless you're already booked," she said.

"Already booked? No contradance, if that's what you mean. It's on Saturday."

"No, silly. It's Valentine's Day. And . . . I don't want you to feel pressured, it having such romantic implications. We don't have to make a big deal about it."

"No pressure. I would like that. I guess that means you're not going out with what's-his-name."

"You had better be joking."

"Yes, and I might as well tell you, because you need to be careful."

She raised up on one arm, a look of alarm drawing her features taut. "Be careful?"

"I can't go into details, but he may be involved in this thing I'm investigating."

"Which is?"

"As I said, I can't go into details at this point. Just be careful."

"Hmm. That may explain some things. There is something about him. Secretive."

"Care to elaborate?"

"Not right now. I don't want to ruin the mood. But if you know that, why hasn't he been arrested?"

"The authorities are still gathering evidence, and they believe he will lead them to bigger fish they can fry."

Abby sighed. "This world is so screwed up."

She rolled away from Rent and stared at the ceiling, flickering candlelight reflected on her face, which had acquired a contemplative expression.

"Uh-oh," Rent said, breaking their silence. "Having second thoughts?"

Startled, Abby stuttered her reply. "No . . . um . . . nothing about you. It's just that . . ."

"Something's troubling you?"

"Yeah, kind of."

"Let's hear it."

Abby stared at the ceiling. "Okay, I guess the mood has been ruined. So . . . there's this girl . . . she's twelve . . . and I've sort of become friends with her. We were supposed to go get a goat yesterday, but her mom told me she had gone to stay with the grandparents in Arizona for a few days. But it all sounded a bit fishy to me. Hannah, that's the mom, seemed real defensive and didn't want to talk about it, and got all weird when I asked her if Rachel, that's the daughter, was okay."

"Hannah from the bookstore?"

"Yeah, do you know her?"

"I stopped by there last week and spoke to her, and to her daughter. The day I met you."

"Did Rachel ask you if you were her father?"

Rent did a doubletake. "What?"

"She does that with a lot of men. At least that's what Hannah said."

"Really?" Rent asked, feigning ignorance.

"Yeah, it's kind of sad. Rachel doesn't know who her father is, but she wants to know. Hannah won't tell her."

Rent remained silent for a long moment before saying, "So, what's with the goat?"

Abby rolled onto her side, again propped up on one elbow, and examined Rent's face. "Hmm . . . blue eyes . . ."

"A blue-eyed goat?"

"No, silly. You. I see some resemblance there, minus the beard, of course."

"Don't all goats have beards?"

She feigned a slap to his bicep. "Don't be silly. I'm talking about Rachel and her blue eyes, and your blue eyes, not the goat."

"Back to the goat."

She studied his face for a few seconds. "Yes, I'll try to make it short," she began. "Gabe had been dating Hannah . . ."

"Hann—" Rent started to say, then cut himself short. "Sorry, I interrupted you. Please continue."

Abby frowned, then went on. "It seems Gabe had been dating Hannah for a while. That was before I really knew either of them. But she broke it off, and then we—Gabe and I—went out a couple of times. I didn't know anything about Hannah at the time. He suggested we take Rachel, calling her his daughter—which she's not—on a picnic. In hindsight, he was just using her as a prop to impress me. Part of his con game to lure me into his spiderous web. But at the time, gullible me believed him."

She paused and took a deep breath. "I'm talking too fast. . . . Anyway, as it turned out, it also involved taking Rachel to a 4-H Club meeting in Ramona, where she, like all young girls, hoped to get a pony. Hannah said no to the pony but said Rachel could get a goat. Rachel sulked for a while but finally gave in. We were supposed to go get the goat yesterday. I didn't want to go, because of Gabe, but I had promised Rachel that I would. Then, when they didn't come pick me up, I called Gabe and got no answer, so I called Hannah. That's when I found out that Rachel was at her grandparents."

"But now you think something else is going on."

"Yeah. Because . . . I forgot to mention this other bit. Last week, after leaving the 4-H Club, we came back here. Rachel tripped and fell, and hurt her arm. So I wondered if she was okay. But when I asked Hannah about it, she tried to change the subject. I asked her if Rachel had been seen by a doctor, and she got all pissy about it. She practically shouted at me. She said, 'Rachel's fine. Now mind your own business.' And she hung up on me. Totally weird. And now I'm more worried than ever."

Rent weighed this new information, silently agreeing with Abby, but needing to withhold his knowledge of the situation.

I need to contact Hannah's parents, much as I'd rather not.

Abby poked him in the ribs. "Now you're the one who seems troubled."

"Uh, no. Just thinking about how screwed up things can get between people and the toll it can take on the children involved."

"Yeah, it is sad. I just thought maybe you were worried about Gabe and me. As I said, I'm done with him. Especially after the way he treated Rachel."

"Oh?"

"She seems wary of him. That's why she fell. Trying to get away from him. I wouldn't be surprised if he's tried messing around with her. That could be why Hannah dumped him."

"Could be, but why would she let him take her to 4-H?"

"Good question. Maybe I was to be her chaperone?" She shook her head. "Why do men have to be so . . ." She stopped and glanced at Rent. "Present company excluded. Then again, I'm partly to blame."

"For what?"

Abby confessed to being attracted to 'bad boys.' "My grandmother says it's because I think I can reform them."

Rent thought: *Apparently, she has never read Anne Brontë's The Tenant at Wildfell Hall.* Then he wondered aloud, "What makes you think I'm not a bad boy? That I don't have a dark side?"

She laughed. "You may have a dark side. Who doesn't? But you seem like a decent sort. Maybe not a goody-two-shoes, which would be no fun, but someone who respects others, and I've read some of your stuff in the newspaper, exposing corruption and all that. Alice got it for me at the library."

"So you've been spying on me?"

"Well . . . just a little. Truth be told, you're probably too good for the likes of me."

"Abby, come on. Don't be so hard on yourself."

"Yeah? Well maybe you should be a little hard on me, if you catch my drift." She tickled him.

"You are a naughty girl."

"I know. Isn't that what you like about me?"

Serious for a moment, Rent said, "You have a sharp mind. I like that about you."

"Perhaps, but right now we're just being slaves to our bodies, you know."

"I know. Hormones running rampant, leading to poor judgment."

"Disgusting."

"But it's beyond my control. I hate it," Rent whispered.

"I love it. Mmmmm," she murmured and snuggled closer, as if it were possible.

The "L" word startled Rent. For an instant he thought she was about to say she loved *him*. When she didn't, he silently sighed in relief. Yes, he liked Abby. He enjoyed her company, her wit, and, obviously, her body. And she apparently felt the same. But love? Love meant caring and devotion. Responsibility. Commitment. He'd been through that with what's-her-name. He'd settle for lust for the time being and nuzzled her breasts one more time, delighting in the pleasure that the pressure of a hardened nipple against his cheek gave him.

"I'm like a bonobo, that's my problem," she said, rolling away from him and staring at the ceiling.

"Bonobo?"

"Yeah. Their motto is 'make love, not war.' "

Rent raised himself on an elbow. "Aren't they a type of chimpanzee or something?"

"Oh, no. Not in the least," she replied. "Well, yeah, they are both great apes, along with gorillas and orangutans and humans. But bonobos are not like the other species. They're not patriarchal; they're matriarchal. Instead of fighting, they make love. They have lots of sex, and that's how they maintain peace among themselves. They welcome newcomers, and if the males get possessive and out of line, the females gang up on them and set them on the straight and narrow."

"Amazing. I did not know that," Rent said. "Sounds like 'petticoat government,' as Charlotte Brontë might say."

"Charlotte Brontë?"

"Yeah, the eldest of the Brontë sisters. *Jane Eyre, Wuthering Heights, Agnes Grey.*"

"Oh, yes," Abby replied. "I had to read them in high school. Heathcliff. Now there was a bad man. How that woman ever fell for him, I don't know. Of course, I should talk."

"No, you shouldn't. Let's change channels and go back to bonobos."

Abby sighed and snuggled closer. "Too bad humans aren't more like bonobos instead of chimpanzees, which treat each other horribly. The males can be so vicious. Even commit murder. If you want to know what's wrong with the human race, you have to look no farther than chimpanzees. Did you know ninety-eight percent of the human genome is identical to that of the chimpanzee?"

Rent nodded. "Yeah, and humans have one less chromosome than chimpanzees—twenty-three. Maybe that's the fatal flaw. We share a lot of our genome with rats as well. Even the lowly amoeba."

Abby kissed him. "So let's you and me be bonobos, not chimpanzees or rats or lowly amoebas."

"Works for me. But does this mean I have to share you?"

She half-closed her eyes and assumed a thoughtful expression. "I'll get back to you on that. Meanwhile, I'm all yours," she said as she ran a finger lightly over his bare abdomen.

He shivered in response to her light touch. "Does this mean you're still in lust with me?"

"Oh, yes. More than ever."

He put an arm around her shoulders and pulled her close.

"I'm wondering," he mused.

"Yes?" she replied, an air of trepidation to her voice.

"What follows the lust phase?"

"The Like phase. The getting-to-know-you phase. We can't just spend all of our time making lust."

"If you say so. And after the Like phase?"

"Let's not go there. We're still in lust. But I do like to do other things. I'm sure you do too."

"Such as?"

"Outdoorsy stuff. That's what I like about living in Julian."

"You mean like having sex outdoors?"

She mock slapped him. "You have a one-track mind. I mean hiking, camping, star gazing, birding . . ."

"Birding?"

"Birdwatching," she explained. "Serious birdwatchers call themselves birders, and they turn that into a verb: birding."

She went on to tell him that San Diego County has excellent birding opportunities because of the several climatic zones: coastal, inland, mountains, and desert. The county has more than 500 species on record, although a number of those are migrants or vagrants and not often seen.

"Still, the number of indigenous species is quite high," she concluded. "Your eyes are glazing over. TMI?"

Rent shrugged. "I'm listening."

"You should go out birding with me," Abby continued. "The coast is good now, what with so many waterfowl that winter here. Even Rangeland Road in Ramona. Did you know there's a big flock of Canada geese in a cow pasture? And eagles. There are nesting pairs of bald eagles and golden eagles. Red-tailed hawks, falcons, kestrels, meadowlarks, red-winged blackbirds, and maybe yellow-headed blackbirds. We even had an endangered spotted owl at Heise Park one year."

"I play a fiddle tune called *Red Wing*."

"A song about the bird?"

"Actually, it's about a Native American girl named Red Wing who falls in lust with a young warrior." He began singing, "Now the moon shines tonight on pretty Red Wing, the breeze is sighing, the night bird's crying . . ."

"I'm Native American. Well, one quarter."

"Kumeyaay?"

"Cherokee. My grandmother is from Oklahoma. But I powwow with the Kumeyaay here and the Nez Perce in Idaho. I even made my own outfit."

"And do you adorn it with feathers of the birds you watch?"

"I know you're being sarcastic, but, yeah, some, if I find them on the ground. But we digress. There's a hawk watch in Ramona we could go to. It's really cool. You can see raptors up close. Owls, too. I took Rachel there. She loved it."

"Could be interesting. I like seeing hawks and eagles soaring overhead. I've seen a bald eagle flying over Lake Cuyamaca."

"See? You're a closet birder. The spring migration is coming up, so we'll get a lot of songbirds coming through on their way north to their breeding grounds. You should get the Merlin app for your phone."

"Merlin? Like the magician in King Arthur's Court?"

"No, the magician's bird. It's a merlin, a small raptor. The app listens to bird songs and calls, and tells you what bird you're hearing. It's free. You can download it from the Cornell University website."

"I'll check it out."

"You should. Do you have binoculars?"

"Yeah, but I don't know how good they are. My dad gave them to me. Probably military surplus."

"They might be a bit clunky. I have a spare pair you can use. Besides, if you're going to go on a stakeout with that PI again, you'll need a good pair of bins."

"Bins?"

"Short for binoculars, silly."

"Ah, of course. Birder jargon."

"See? You're getting the hang of it already."

"All this talk about birds is making me hungry."

"Oh, yeah? I'm not enough to satisfy your *raven*-ous appetite?"

"I could go for some hard-boiled spotted owl eggs."

"Watch it, buster, or you'll be eating crow."

Abby snuggled closer to Rent and tickled him. "But enough punny stuff."

"Are you being naughty again, young lady?" he teased.

She rolled on top of him. "Haven't you figured that out yet? I'm no lady."

Abby kissed him lightly on the lips, then glanced at the clock/radio sitting on the bedside nightstand. "Oh, crap, I have to get back to the office."

"And I have a deadline to meet."

RATHER THAN GO STRAIGHT back to the B&B, Rent returned to the store at the foot of Banner Grade. He asked if Gabe Turner had been in recently. The storekeeper shook his head.

"Not this week, but I caught a glimpse of a Land Cruiser turning up yonder, headin' into the canyon. Pretty sure it was him. I ain't seen him come out, but I coulda missed 'im."

Rent pulled his wallet from a pants pocket, withdrew a business card, and handed it to him. "If he does come in, could you give this to him? If he's willing, I'd like to talk to him about gold mining. A human-interest sort of thing."

The storekeeper stared at Rent for a moment. "What am I, your messenger boy?"

Taken aback, Rent looked away before responding.

"Tell you what. I'll buy another bag of that delicious peanut brittle. I took the last one into the office, and it all mysteriously disappeared."

"In that case, I suppose I could manage it."

Rent extracted a five-dollar bill from his wallet and handed it to the man, along with the business card. "Keep the change," he said.

The storekeeper reached under the counter for the bag of sweets and handed it to Rent. "Nice doin' business with ya. Oh, hang on a sec."

"Something else?"

"If you're writing an article about the mines, you might look into Golden Chariot. Rumor has it that mine is going to reopen."

"I'll do that."

"In town for long?" the man asked.

"Just a couple of days. Staying at Rainbow Hill."

"Well, la-di-da."

12

Rent awoke to a knock at the door. "Yes?"

"Last call for breakfast."

"I'll be right there," he said and checked the time. "Oh, crap."

The previous evening, Abby had texted him, saying the meeting ended early and invited him over. He accepted and didn't get back to the B&B until later than he had planned. He dressed quickly and went to the dining room, where the other guests were just leaving.

"Coffee?" The hostess asked as she gestured toward a clean place-setting on the table.

"Please," he said and parked his knees under the polished redwood planks.

The hostess filled Rent's cup and winked at him. "Late night. Got lucky, did you?"

"Margie . . ." her husband reprimanded. "Be nice."

"Just being sociable," she replied as she retreated toward the kitchen.

"Looking for gossip more like it," he retorted as he turned his gaze toward Rent and shook his head. "She and her co-conspirators."

"No harm done," Rent said. "People accuse me of the same."

"Goes with the territory, I suppose. You being a newspaper reporter."

"It does. Indeed, it does."

"Ever get threats of violence?"

Rent took a sip of coffee and looked at the man over the top of the cup. "Occasionally," he replied. "One time a guy threatened to kill me."

"You might want to check the windshield of your truck before you leave."

"Oh?" Rent set down his cup, pushed back the chair, and rose to his feet as the hostess appeared with his breakfast tray. "I'll be right back."

"I hope it was nothing I said," the hostess directed at Rent's back.

"I told him about the note on his windshield," her husband replied.

Rent returned a moment later. "Do you have a large mailing envelope, or even a plastic bag that I can put the note in? And a pair of tongs. I don't want to touch it."

The hostess set down the tray. "Coming right up."

Rent remained standing, picked up his coffee, and took a sip while he waited.

The woman returned with a letter-size manila envelope and kitchen tongs. Rent thanked her and went back to his truck. The note had been placed on the windshield on the driver's side, held in place by a windshield wiper. It read:

Back of or your DED MEET!!!

"Oh, fuck. Not another one."

He pulled his cell phone from a pants pocket and took several photos for context. He lifted the wiper blade and picked up the death threat with the tongs, then slid it into the envelope. As he returned to the dining room, he wondered, *Does this have to do with me seeing Abby? Or the investigation? Or both? Judging by the bad grammar, this puts Gabe Turner, or one of his goons, at the top of the list as being the author.*

He took the envelope to his room and laid it on the bed, then went back to the dining room. The host and hostess were seated at the table and glanced up at him with expectant expressions.

"I imagine you were tempted to edit the misspelled words and poor grammar," Rent said.

They both chuckled.

"Oh, yes. I was tempted to get out my red pencil," the hostess answered. "I saw it when I went out to get the morning paper. My husband and I both prefer the real thing, rather than reading the news on a computer or our phones. Call us old fashioned. I also like doing the crossword."

"But you didn't—"

She shook her head. "Heavens no. I figured you would want the cops to see it and dust it for fingerprints. So I didn't touch it."

"Thank you. I appreciate that."

"Well, you better eat up. You want a warmup on that coffee?"

"Yes, please. I fear it's going to be a long day."

"I can imagine," the hostess said. "You're not actually in Julian to look at real estate, are you?"

"Why do you say that?"

"We recognized your name. You're a reporter for the newspaper, and you probably poked your nose into something suspicious and someone is obviously not too happy about it."

Rent raised his arms in mock surrender. "Guilty as charged."

She grinned at him. "I knew it. Go on, tell!"

Rent shook his head. "Sorry, I can't divulge any details at this time. But I will have a story about it in the Sunday edition. You can read all about it then."

"We'll look for it."

"Meanwhile, please keep this death threat to yourselves. You'll probably get a visit from the cops, wondering if you heard or saw anything last night."

She shook her head. "Not a thing. He could have parked down the hill a ways and walked up."

Rent nodded and turned to his breakfast as the hostess refilled his cup. He had to force himself not to wolf down the bowl of yogurt, granola, and fresh fruit. He saved the muffin for a snack later on.

Back in his room, he called Alicia Velasquez and told her about the death threat and his suspicions.

"We obviously touched a nerve there, and I think you're right, but how would he know about you and how to find you?" she said. "Even if Hannah told him who you are, how would he know where you're staying?"

Rent sighed. "I told him, at least indirectly."

"How'd you manage that?"

He told her about leaving his business card at the store and having mentioned where he was staying.

"And you thought you were being so clever. Oh, well, what's done is done. You need to give that note to the cops."

"Got anyone particular in mind? I do have a contact at the sheriff's office, but she's PR."

"She would know who talk to, or you could just stop at the substation in Julian and they'll know how to handle it. Better yet, call your Deep Throat at HHSA. He can put you in touch with the detective he's working with."

"I'll do that."

"You need a gun? I have a spare pistol I can loan you," she said.

"Uh . . . I don't think that's a good idea," he replied. "I'd probably end up on the business end of it. But Turner sure as hell has one. I saw him shoot at a coyote at the store on Banner Grade."

"Well, there you go."

"Oh, yeah, I can see it now—the shootout at the O.K. Corral."

"If you want to go to the range and fire off a few rounds, let me know. I go in once a month just to keep sharp," she said.

"Have you ever actually needed it?" he asked.

"I've had it out during a few apprehensions. Never fired it. But as Archie McNally says, 'One never knows, do one?' "

"Archie McNally?"

"Fictional PI. Funny. I think you'd like it. Google it."

"Thanks, I will. But first the cops. I'll be in touch."

He disconnected and called Rod Davis at HHSA with an update. Davis said Alicia Velasquez had briefed him, but he was still waiting for her formal report and transcript of the meeting with Hannah Stapleford.

"And there may be a further development in this case, but I need to do more checking around," Rent said.

"Oh?"

Rent told him about the daughter, Rachel, and that he could not confirm her whereabouts. "Hannah insists that she's with the grandparents, but they aren't returning Alicia's calls," he said." So it leaves me wondering if they are complicit in this fraud."

"Or maybe she ran away," Davis said.

"Possible, but I don't want to get the cops involved unless we think the girl's in danger. I just hope Turner hasn't abducted her."

"Why would he?"

"Hannah is concerned that he may have tried to molest her, or has molested her. The guy is not exactly on any short list for the model citizen award."

"Shit, just what we need."

"Actually, it could work in our favor."

"How's that?"

"Gives us leverage to get him to squeal on the not-so-honorable thieves he's consorting with," Rent said.

"Yeah, if he's done anything to that girl, he will be in a whole load of shit," Davis replied.

"Two more things."

"I'm all ears."

Rent told him about the death threat.

"You have to call the cops, if you haven't already," Davis said.

"I will. That's one of the reasons I called you. You work with someone in the sheriff's office, right?"

"Yeah, a detective, Financial Crimes. You'll like this. His name is Abraham Lincoln Washington, but most people just call him 'Al.' Don't call him Abe."

Davis gave Rent the detective's phone number, then said, "And the second thing?"

"Hannah told me about a guy within HHSA who helped her get her CalFresh and CalWORKS benefits. Turner referred her to him, but she never met him, only talked to him on the phone. But she's concerned that he may be the reason her application says she has three kids, not two."

"He could be our Charlie Oscar," Davis said.

"That sounds like military-speak," Rent replied.

"Cop-speak, actually. Stands for Corrupt Official. The HHSA guy we suspect is in cahoots with the bad guys. Did she give you his name?"

"She couldn't remember it."

"Maybe she still has his phone number?"

"She said she'd try to find it. I'll get back to you on that."

They concluded the call. Rent then phoned the detective and got a recorded greeting after several rings. He left a message, identifying himself, his work with Rod Davis at HHSA, and the death threat, and asked him to call back.

Rent exhaled a heavy sigh as he sat staring at his phone. *Time to make the most dreaded phone call of them all.* He went through his notes and found the names and phone number for Hannah's parents.

"I wonder if they'll remember me?" he muttered.

He sighed again, then punched in the number. The call went directly to voice mail and he left a message, asking them to call him. "It's urgent," he said and ended the call.

He took a quick shower and packed his duffle bag, then checked out. On his way through town, he stopped at the real estate office. As he stepped through the door, Abby smiled.

"Ah, Dr. Watson, I presume," she said. "Still looking for that big ranch, are we?"

"Yeah, something like that."

Abby turned to her co-worker. "Nancy, this is the guy I told you about. The renowned investigative reporter."

Nancy stood and offered her hand. "How do you do? Nice to meet such a celebrity."

Rent shook her hand. "Hardly, but thank you. My pleasure to meet you, I'm sure."

"Oh, a gentleman, too," the woman said and grinned at Abby.

Abby shot her a crinkled funny face, then turned back to Rent. "If you've got time, I could show you that property I mentioned."

Rent shook his head. "Sorry, something's come up. I need to talk, outside."

"Now you're scaring me."

"Please, outside. It will only take a minute or two."

"My, a lover's tiff already? Tsk, tsk," Nancy muttered.

Abby scowled at the woman, then followed Rent outside.

"You had better not be dumping me, buster. I'll kick your balls so hard you won't be out of bed for a week."

"Abby, no, trust me, it's not that. Of course I want to keep seeing you."

"Then what's so important that—"

"It's Turner."

Her expression turned to ice. "What's he done now?"

Rent told her about the note.

"Holy crap. Are you sure it's him?

"Who else would it be?"

"That means I—"

"Not necessarily. It could be just about the investigation. The woman that the PI and I interviewed probably called him as soon as we left."

She sighed. "I haven't told you everything. He's been sending me threatening texts, and maybe he saw my car at the restaurant last night. He would have seen you follow me back to my place. You're right, it probably was him that drove past the house."

"You need to be careful. Do you have someone you could stay with?"

"I own a shotgun. And I know how to use it."

"You, too, huh?"

She shot him a quizzical look, and he told her about the PI's offer to loan him a pistol.

"I agree with her. And I need to get back inside. I'm freezing."

"Yeah, go. I'll call and let you know what the cops say."

She gave him an air kiss and went inside. He got in his truck and headed for his office in Mission Valley.

RENT'S PHONE CHIMED AND the caller's name appeared on-screen: Detective Al Washington. His truck being pre-Bluetooth, he answered manually.

"Hi. Thanks for calling back. I'm driving, so hang on a minute while I pull over."

He had just reached a large pullout adjacent to the egg ranch and veered left, crossing the opposite lane and coming to a stop on the gravel lot.

"Okay, go ahead."

The detective identified himself and asked, "What's this about?"

"Like I said, I'm working on a story about welfare fraud, and I found this threatening note on my windshield. Rod Davis suggested I talk to you."

"Yeah, he called me. You think this involves Gabe Turner, as he likes to call himself?"

"That would be my first guess, but I don't know for sure. I can bring it to you."

"It would have been better if you had left it there and let a deputy collect it as evidence. We have a substation in Julian."

"Sorry, but I don't have all day to be sitting on my ass, waiting for cops to show up. I have not touched the document itself. I put it in a virgin, letter-size envelope, handling it with tongs, and I can drop it off, or you can come to my office in Mission Valley and pick it up. I also took photos of it on the windshield. And if you're involved in this investigation, I'd like to speak with you."

The detective did not immediately reply.

"Hello?" Rent said.

"I'm here," Washington replied. "I'm at the main office on Ridgehaven Court, off Ruffin Road, between Balboa and Aero. You can't miss it."

"Yeah, I've been there. I'll swing by when I get back to town. About forty-five minutes."

"Roger that," the detective said and disconnected the call.

"Ungrateful sonofabitch," Rent muttered.

RENT ENTERED THE MAIN office of the San Diego County Sheriff's Department and told the receptionist Detective Al Washington was expecting him. The receptionist told him to take a seat and the detective would be out shortly. Ten minutes later, a large man with chocolate-colored skin stepped into the reception area, and Rent rose to greet him.

Rent held out his hand and said, "Sorry if I came off as combative on the phone. This thing has me a bit rattled, and it's totally screwed up my day."

The detective shook Rent's hand, then turned his hand palm up. "Let's see it."

Rent gave him the envelope and the detective peered inside, then motioned for Rent to follow him. Washington led him to Interview Room 1. *Just like the murder mysteries on TV*, Rent thought as he entered and saw another individual sitting at a table, waiting for them.

Washington handed the envelope to the man. "Check the note inside for prints, and we'll need his prints for elimination," he said, with a nod toward Rent.

Rent protested. "I told you I didn't touch it."

"Even so, it's protocol. We don't want some bleeding-heart judge tossing it out over a technicality."

"Yeah, okay, I understand," Rent replied.

The man left the room.

"Have a seat," Washington said.

Rent pulled a chair out from the table and sat down as Washington sat across from him. Rent gave him a statement, detailing why he had been in Julian, the ride-along with the PI, his run-ins with Turner, and what had transpired at the B&B. He showed the detective his photos and texted them to the man. The detective then took him to another room, where a technician fingerprinted him.

Washington refused to discuss the county's investigation into the welfare fraud, other than to confirm that they had Joshua Gabriel Turnbull, alias Gabe Turner, on their radar.

"For now, you'll have to get a statement from my lieutenant. And if Turner pulls any more shenanigans, I want to be the first person to hear about it."

"Got it," Rent said. "And, again, I apologize for coming on so strong earlier. It won't happen again."

"It had better not," Washington said, then flashed a glimpse of gleaming teeth through a slight smile. He extended his hand as a peace offering. Rent shook it.

13

Thursday, Day 12, afternoon

Rent sat at his desk in the newsroom, reviewing his notes, then opened a new document on his computer and began typing. Two hours later, he saved the file and went to the break room for coffee, hoping there may be a donut or two remaining.

As he entered, Greg turned away from the counter, taking a large bite from a doughy snack. He grinned at Rent as he passed. Rent stared at the empty box, then licked a finger and dabbed at the loose sugar littering its bottom.

"The Meal Machine strikes again," editor Janis O'Connor said as she entered the room.

Rent patted his belly. "Yeah, just as well."

"Nice of you to grace us with your presence," she said.

"I just came from the sheriff's office," he fired back. "I have not had a pleasant morning."

"Oh?" she said as she opened the refrigerator and took out a soft drink.

Rent told her about the death threat and having to give a statement to the detective and being fingerprinted.

"Interesting. Get any insight into the state of their investigation?"

"Nah, his lips are sealed for now, but he wants me to stay in touch. So it's another foot in the door."

"What have you got so far?"

"I just finished my piece, laying out more of the big picture and setting up what's to come. I'll give it another read, then send it over."

She nodded. "Sounds good."

Rent filled his mug with hours-old coffee, a burnt odor fouling his nostrils, and returned to his desk. He opened the file and began to read:

SAN DIEGO—Jane Jones couldn't believe it. She had swiped her electronic benefits transfer (EBT) card through the slot on the card reader at the grocery store, as she had done several times before. But this time the cashier told her there were insufficient funds in the account to pay for the items he had just rung up and bagged.

"That can't be," she said. "My card was reloaded just this morning and this is the first time I've used it."

"I'm sorry, ma'am, but that's what I'm being told," the cashier replied. "There's nothing I can do. You will have to contact the card issuer and get it straightened out."

"But that's not fair! How am I supposed to feed my kids?"

Jones, a single mother of two children, said she didn't want to be receiving public assistance, but her husband had run off, and she only works part-time. She went to her local Family Resource Center, operated by the San Diego County Health and Human Services Agency, and learned that her account had only $9.45 remaining. There should have been in excess of $700 in her account. When told how the money had been spent, she said she had not purchased any of those items.

"I don't know how I'm going to pay my bills or my rent," lamented Jones.

She isn't alone. Another victim, who asked that her name be withheld, said she had to go to the food bank in order to feed her children, and a third victim learned that her account had been debited with a large purchase at a Costco store in Ohio.

For those relying on public assistance to make ends meet, this troublesome scenario is playing out more frequently, not just in San Diego, or even California, but nationwide as unscrupulous fraudsters steal the funds within hours, if not minutes, of the EBT cards being reloaded with benefits on the first of the month.

Law enforcement agencies have reported an uptick in this brazen and insidious form of fraud that impacts some of the most vulnerable groups in America, not just a single parent with children, but senior citizens and disabled persons as well.

Jones is just one of thousands of people in San Diego County who have had their EBT card hacked in recent months, according to county officials.

"This is being conducted by a sophisticated crime ring," said Michelle Berkman, San Diego County spokesperson. "This crime activity is most frequent at the beginning of the month, after public-assistance benefits are loaded to the EBT cards."

According to the California Department of Social Services, low-income Californians reported $29.7 million in cash benefits stolen and $4.7 million in food aid stolen in the 14-month period ending last September.

California has seen substantial increases in EBT theft of CalFresh and CalWORKs benefits via electronic means. Cash benefit theft has nearly doubled from less than one percent of total cash benefits distributed last year to a projected 1.7 percent for the coming year. Nationally, the fraud is estimated to amount to billions of dollars a year.

The theft of EBT card data is a rapidly growing problem, according to the U.S. Department of Agriculture (USDA), which oversees the federal Supplemental Nutrition Assistance Program (SNAP) and distributes funds to the states. In California last year, EBT data theft increased by 4,000 percent compared to the prior year. In Los Angeles County alone, $25 million had been lost to stolen benefits in the first six months of last year.

It's not just California. According to statistics released by the USDA, the agency spends $5 million annually to fight fraud, which rises into the billions due to card skimming, card cloning, phishing, retailer fraud known as "trafficking" (allowing benefits to be exchanged for cash or non-food items), and false applications for benefits.

In Massachusetts alone, more than $1.6 million in SNAP benefits were stolen from more than 5,000 households from June to November, according to the Massachusetts Department of Transitional Assistance.

The USDA states that: "Although we are aware of reports of benefit theft in some states, USDA does not have comprehensive data on the number of incidents for each state."

In California, the state reimburses the recipients who have their benefits stolen, but it can take ten days or more to reinstate it. The state then gets reimbursed by the federal government, leaving federal taxpayers on the hook for the loss.

"The criminals stealing this money may see this as a victimless crime, that for a corrupt, wasteful government it's barely a drop in the bucket. But that's not the case," said Jennifer Mitchell, spokesperson for the California Department of Social Services. "When a single parent is not able to feed their children, it's the innocent children, who through no fault of their own happen to live in poverty, who suffer. Ultimately, it's the law-abiding taxpayers who foot the bill for this fraud."

Mitchell went on to point out that in California, the recipients are fortunate in that the state issues new cards to fraud victims. But not all states do this, so those victims are out of luck and have to rely on friends and family for their assistance and generosity.

The largest form of public assistance, formerly known as food stamps, is awarded under SNAP, which is authorized by Congress and the benefits are distributed in California by individual counties through the state's Department of Social Services.

Once qualified, beneficiaries receive a card that resembles a typical debit card, although the cards are not affiliated with banks or credit unions. This is an important distinction, because financial institutions in the private sector have improved security in their electronic-payment systems by placing microchips in their millions of credit and debit cards.

"We're seeing large-scale phishing attacks and account takeovers in the government sector by cybercriminals," said Amanda D'Amico, Vice President of Government Solutions at the research firm Thomson Reuters. "Bad actors continue to innovate and look for opportunities to exploit vulnerabilities in government programs."

There had been a tremendous increase in applications for government benefits during the COVID pandemic. Thieves swooped in to take advantage through account takeovers and also started filing fraudulent applications, most often through identity theft fraud, according to Thomson Reuters.

These fraudsters get their information mostly through phishing schemes and social engineering. It works like this: A victim gets a text message or email from a person claiming to work for a government agency, stating that fraudulent activity occurred on the victim's account and that they need to click on a link to reset their password. When they do that, the fraudsters have direct access to the funds in that account.

In addition, according to CalMatters, a nonpartisan and nonprofit news organization, thieves may install skimming devices onto card readers at retail stores to steal identification information and account numbers from the cards' magnetic strips, then the thieves go "phishing." Sometimes the thieves use hidden cameras to capture the cardholders entering their PINs. Either way, the thieves then create counterfeit cards to access the funds.

The skimming devices are often plastic keypad overlays that look nearly identical to the card reader terminals themselves. Security expert Ed Maxwell said these devices harvest data from every person who swipes a card. Later on, the thieves return and extract the data file from the device.

Law enforcement officials in Los Angeles County recently arrested 16 men for the theft of private account information of California EBT card holders, the creation of illegal, cloned cards with victims' account information, and the withdrawal of large cash amounts from those accounts at ATMs.

Officials also seized $130,000 in cash and more than 300 cloned EBT cards with an estimated value of $400,000, according to the county DA's office.

Similarly, San Diego County has ramped up its efforts to root out cases of EBT fraud, saying that crime rings based in Eastern Europe may be involved.

A spokesperson at the regional office of the Federal Bureau of Investigation acknowledged the agency's interest in the involvement of neo-Nazi groups and Eastern Europeans working at the bidding of Russians trying to disrupt American governmental operations and political activities. However, the spokesperson declined to provide specific details, stating that such information could undermine the ongoing investigation.

San Diego County's Berkman said one of the problems is that the EBT cards lack the high degree of security of credit cards because the EBT cards don't have a microchip in them as do credit cards. The reason for this is the higher cost of implementation. But when comparing the cost of incorporating the security chips to the loss to fraud, doesn't it make sense to do it?

Government agencies are looking into it but say it's not just the cost of upgrading the cards. The entire computer system has to be upgraded, and that's where the big expense lies.

"This past June, Card Verification Value, or CVV, functionality for all EBT cards was recently enabled, which would add an additional layer of security to help mitigate EBT theft," Social Services spokesperson Mitchell said in a statement.

However, she acknowledged that adopting and implementing that microchip technology could take years. Asked why the government doesn't use direct deposit, Mitchell said many of these people don't have bank accounts. So the most efficient way of distributing the funds is through EBT cards. But these cards also make it easier for scammers to steal the money.

Mitchell also pointed out that thefts amount to less than 1 percent of the $3.2 billion in CalWORKs allotments and just 0.04 percent of $11.2 billion in food assistance over the 15-month period.

"Incorporating CVV chips in the EBT cards would go a long way toward combatting fraud. They add another layer of verification," security expert Maxwell said, noting that elected representatives lack the political will to invest in the technology, in part because in their minds the loss ratio is low, even though the actual dollar amount may seem exorbitant to the average citizen.

"Unless the citizenry raises a ruckus about it, it's unlikely they're going to do anything near term. The sad part is that it's the most vulnerable that get hurt by this.

"Whenever a government entity begins handing out money, scammers and fraudsters step up to rake in a percentage of that money," Maxwell continued. "Look at the COVID relief program: billions of dollars went to undeserving or fake businesses. But that money has dried up, so now the fraudsters are going after EBT."

Maxwell added that, in his opinion, government officials don't take the fraud problem more seriously because in their minds it's akin to "shrinkage" in the retail sector. "They just shrug it off like it's a cost of doing business. But unlike retailers, they can't pass the cost along to their law-abiding customers in the form of higher prices. Now, with the percentage of theft expected to skyrocket this year, maybe that will get their attention. Unlike retailers, they can't put the product in locked display cases, which we're seeing more of in the retail industry."

At the local level, San Diego County is also conducting an internal investigation regarding fraudulent applications, according to sources familiar with the investigation who were not authorized to speak publicly about it.

Meanwhile, Jane Jones, who asked that her actual

name be withheld, worries that the EBT theft will happen again. "How am I supposed to tell my children they won't be getting any dinner tonight?"

Satisfied, Rent sent the nearly 1,900-word file to his editor. He also emailed it to Hannah and left the building to get some lunch. When he returned, O'Connor waved him over to her office. Rent entered and took a seat in front of her desk.

"Are you going to hand out Kleenex along with this piece?" she asked. "And the word 'welfare' no where to be found. How generous of you."

"Yuk, yuk, thou soulless cynic."

"Just kidding, Rent," she responded. "Jesus, you and your righteous indignation."

"We need more righteous indignation. While the powers that be dine at three-star restaurants and discuss their next Lindblad cruise through the Caribbean or to Antarctica, innocent kids and senior citizens go hungry."

"Okay, seriously. Good work on laying out the issue and the amount of money involved. Now get more details on what's actually being done to catch these crooks. Maybe your new friend at the sheriff's can feed you some tidbits as an unnamed source. This will make a good series."

"I'm on it."

"See you at the party on Sunday?"

"Is that a joke too?"

"You are allowed to climb down from your high horse and have a little fun with us mere mortals once in a while, you know."

Rent rose from the chair. "Yeah, yeah. Maybe I'll see you there."

Back at his desk, he called Abby and updated her, then apologized for his hasty exit.

"I'm going to be in Julian tomorrow," he said. "Maybe meet for dinner and . . ."

"Aaaaand," she teased.

"Make a lusty evening of it?"

"Cupid come calling?"

"Cupid?"

"Do you even know what day it is?"

"Yeah . . . it's . . . oh, right, February thirteenth."

"Which makes tomorrow . . .

"Valentine's Day . . . Cupid. And I'm Stupid."

"Come to my place. I'll cook."

"You think it's safe?" Rent wondered.

"You can be my knight in shining armor."

"I think Gabe is mostly bluster."

"Maybe so, but he has friends who are more than bluster."

"Keep the shotgun handy."

14

R ent dropped in at the office to check in with his editor before heading back to Julian, waiting for the morning traffic crush to dissipate and for the library to open.

Naomi Clark, crossing the newsroom, stopped at his desk. "You and your tootsie have romantic plans for the evening?" she asked, eyebrows raised and her face creased with a devilish grin.

He looked up and stared at her for a moment. "Maybe."

"Or are you not celebrating such things these days?"

"I have no idea what you're talking about."

Janis O'Connor joined them and winked at Naomi. "What are you two talking about?"

"I was just asking lover boy here if he has a hot date planned with his new girlie friend tonight, but he feigns ignorance."

"And you're surprised? He is a man, after all."

They both chortled.

"What is this, Petticoat Junction?" Rent retorted.

"Naomi, I need to talk to you about that embezzlement story," O'Connor said.

Naomi nodded and they moved off, toward the editor's office.

"Jeez, Louise," Rent moaned. "Can't a guy get a break once in a while?"

He called Hannah but got voice mail. He left a message saying he'd be in the area soon and would stop by. He stood, put on his coat, grabbed his phone, and left the building. With most of the traffic headed down-mountain toward the San Diego suburbs and the city proper, he made good time. The weather forecast had called for an overcast sky and possible rain showers, but nothing like the deluge from the atmospheric river expected to hit the following week.

He drove to Hannah's house, but found no one there, so he continued on to Turner's place. He saw what he thought to be Hannah's Jeep parked next to the carpet cleaner's van. He pulled into the gravel-strewn, weed-infested yard, then turned his truck around and parked facing out in case he needed to make a quick departure.

He went to the front door and knocked. When no one answered, he pounded on the door with his fist. He heard a muffled voice respond inside and a moment later the door opened. Turner stood there in his underwear, appearing to be suffering from a hangover.

"What the fuck do you want?"

"I need to speak to Hannah."

"She ain't here."

"Why is her car here?"

"Electrical problem. Told her I'd fix it."

"Then where is she?"

"How the hell would I know? Try her place."

"I did. She's not there. Where's Rachel?"

"She ain't my kid neither."

Rent overlooked the man's questionable grammar. "I want to see for myself."

"Be my guest," Turner said and took a step back. Then, after glancing to his right, he thought better of it and held out an arm to block Rent. But Rent shoved past him and looked around the room, which looked as if it had hosted a frat party the night before.

He caught a glimpse of what he took to be EBT cards scattered on the kitchen table, but when he made a move in that direction, Gabe grabbed a pistol from a small table behind the door, stepped in front of him, and grabbed Rent's arm. "Out!"

Rent eyed the pistol, then looked toward the back of the house. "Hannah! Rachel! Are you here?"

Turner shouted at him a second time. "I said out!"

Rent heard the pistol being cocked and stared directly into Turner's eyes. "You stay away from Abby Wilburforce and stop sending her threatening texts."

"And if I don't, what're *you* gonna do about it?" Turner said, implying that as a lesser man than he, Rent would be powerless to do anything.

"Restraining order."

Gabe snorted. "You just want to fuck her. Good luck with that tight-assed bitch."

Rent stepped out of the house and heard Turner shout at him: "And don't come back!"

Without turning around, Rent raised a hand, middle finger extended. He flinched when he heard the gunshot, but felt nothing and continued walking, albeit a bit shakily. He then heard the door slammed shut.

He reached his truck, got in, and looked in the rearview mirror. No sign of Gabe Turner.

"Fuckin' psycho," he muttered.

He started the engine and drove off, headed toward Julian. When he rounded the last corner, leaving a straight shot up the final ascent to Main Street, he could see that the weekend crowd had already begun to drift in. Several cars were backed up at the stop sign, most of them with turn signals blinking, indicating they would make a right turn toward the shops.

When Rent reached the head of the line, he went straight, past the sheriff's substation, and took a right on Second Street to bypass the congestion on the main drag to get to the library, which sat adjacent to the high school. As he approached it, he recognized the green building with its gray metal roof and signature cupola crowning the entranceway.

He pulled into the parking lot, finding plenty of empty spaces. Inside, he went to the front desk. A woman straightened up behind the counter. The woman from The Nugget restaurant.

"How may I assist . . ." she began. "Oh, it's you, Mr. Investigative Journalist."

"Hello, Alice. Nice to see you again," Rent said. "You wear multiple hats."

"I volunteer here a few days a week. What can I do you for?"

Rent chuckled at her old joke. "I'm doing research on Chariot Canyon and the gold mines there. Just wondering if the library has a specific section or items I could look at."

"I'm sure we have something, but I'll have to get one of the people who actually get paid to be here. But before I do . . ." She leaned across the counter and spoke in a low voice. "Meet me in the parking lot, but first I need to grab my coat. It's blustery out there."

"I'll wait for you at the door," he said, wondering what was so important that they had to go outside.

A moment later, she joined him and they stepped out.

"We can sit in my truck. The engine's still warm."

"Good idea."

Rent unlocked and opened the passenger side for her, then walked around to the driver's side, opened the door, and got in.

"I was going to call you, and then you show up. The world works in strange ways at times."

"Indeed it does. What's going on?"

"I'm worried about Abigail and I think you should know this."

"Has something happened to her? I just spoke to her yesterday, and we're meeting for dinner tonight."

"Good, that's good. She mentioned that she had a fun date the other night," Alice said with a wink.

"But now?"

"Yesterday, late afternoon, as I was going to the restaurant for my shift, I saw that man, Gabe Turner, threatening her outside the real estate office. I was on the other side of the street, so I didn't hear precisely what he said, but he shook a finger at her and shouted something to the effect of, 'Keep your mouth shut or you will be sorry!' "

"But you didn't hear what this was about, specifically."

She shook her head. "All I know is that man is up to no good. I'd bet good money it's something illegal because I doubt he makes enough carpet cleaning to make ends meet."

"Well, he does have the gold mine in Chariot Canyon. Maybe he found a new vein and told Abby about it, and he doesn't want her blabbing it around town."

"Oh, shush," she replied. "That lazy lout. He talks a good game, but he can't live up to it. He can be a real charmer, especially with the ladies, but he's alienated a number of folks with his sudden outbursts, like at the restaurant that night. He brags about his winnings at the casino, but unless he's a world-class poker player—which he's not; you can bet your bottom dollar on that—he can't be winning much, if anything. How he could afford that Land Cruiser is a mystery. No, he's taking in money on the side. I just haven't figured out where it comes from."

"Do you know anything about EBT fraud?" Rent asked.

"E-B-T? Never heard of it."

Rent explained that it stood for electronic benefits transfer, public assistance for those who can't make ends meet. He went on to tell her how crooks ripped off unsuspecting people dependent on that assistance, and that it hurt innocent children, senior citizens, and disabled people the most.

"You mean poor folks on welfare, on the dole."

"They don't call it 'the dole' or even 'welfare' anymore."

"Yeah, yeah, all that political correct nonsense. Where I come from, we call a spade a spade."

"Regardless of what you want to call it, it's a serious matter. Millions of dollars in benefits are stolen every year in California alone."

"And you think that's what Gabe Turner is doing? And somehow Abby found out about it?"

"Possibly, but don't go shouting that from the rooftops just yet. The authorities are looking into it, as am I. In fact, on Sunday I'll have a story about it in the paper. I lay out how these EBT cards—they're like debit cards from a bank, or those COVID relief cards we all received during the pandemic—are being cloned and used to drain the unsuspecting recipients' accounts before they have a chance to spend it."

"Maybe that's what happened to me," Alice exclaimed. "During the pandemic, some of that COVID money mysteriously disappeared from my benefits card. I accused the storekeeper of overcharging me, but he denied it. Maybe somebody hacked my card."

"It's possible. It appears now that's how this EBT fraud escalated so quickly. It carried over when the COVID money dried up. I'll ask around, although there's not much that can be done about it now."

Rent got the information from her, saying he would talk to the storekeeper.

Alice looked at her watch. "I need to get back, or they'll think I've gone to meet my maker."

They returned indoors and Alice introduced Rent to Ken Wilson, one of the library's staff members. Ken said they didn't have a lot of material on Chariot Canyon specifically, but he'd do his best.

"It might take a while, because I'm helping some students with their research papers," the man said. "Can you come back this afternoon? Plenty of shops and eateries in town, if you want to wander around."

Rent thanked him and left the library. From there, he went to the convenience store Alice had mentioned and asked the storekeeper about the incident. He remembered it, because Alice got so upset.

"But I had nothing to do with it, and I had no idea how that could happen," he said. "That card worked like a debit card. She used it to buy a coffee and Danish, but when she wanted forty dollars cash back, it came up insufficient funds. She claimed that she should have had more than a hundred dollars remaining on the card and left in a huff."

"Scammers have a number of tricks up their sleeves. Alice wasn't the only one. Not by a long shot," Rent said. "Do you mind if I try something?"

The storekeeper shrugged. Rent took a close look at the card reader next to the cash register and ran a finger along an outside edge. He looked up at the storekeeper. I think you may have a card skimmer on here."

"A what?"

"I'll show you."

Rent pulled a Swiss Army knife out of a pants pocket.

"Whoa, what's going on?" the man exclaimed.

"Just watch."

Rent gently pried at a corner of the card reader, loosening a thin layer covering the top of the device. Slowly, the card skimmer came loose. Rent grabbed a napkin so as not to leave any fingerprints and continued to pull upward, loosening it further, but not removing it entirely.

"What the hell? I've never seen that before."

"That's because the scammers distract the employee behind the counter and put on the skimmer when the person is not looking. It only takes a few seconds and most people can't tell the difference. Then scammers are able to get the account information and drain the account of its funds. Sometimes the stores are in on it and get a piece of the action."

The man shook his head. "No way. I had no idea."

Rent had another thought. "Has a technician been in recently for maintenance on these devices?"

"Now that you mention it, yeah, about a month or so ago," the storekeeper said. "A guy came in to upgrade the card reader. I didn't pay much attention. He even installed a little video camera to increase security."

"Do you think he was legit?"

"He showed me a work order. It all seemed above aboard."

"Can you describe the man?" Rent asked.

The storekeeper looked up, toward the ceiling. "Let me think . . . big guy, carrying a clipboard and a toolkit. He was dressed in white coveralls; even had his name embroidered on them."

"Anything else?"

"He had a lot of tattoos, but who doesn't these days? Wore a stocking cap. It was cold that day, but I think he was bald underneath."

"Remember his name?"

"John? Or Joe?"

"Doesn't matter. I doubt it was his actual name."

"So you think he was one the crooks?" the man asked.

Rent responded with another question. "How often do you get a maintenance guy in here?"

"Not often. Usually only when there's a problem and one of us calls it in.

"But you did not call it in, right?"

The man shook his head. "No. Like I said, he just showed up."

Rent told the storekeeper he could not use the device any longer and called Detective Al Washington at the sheriff's office to report what he had found. Rent agreed to remain there until a sheriff's deputy arrived to investigate. After the call ended, he used his cell phone to take several pictures of the device.

While waiting for law enforcement to arrive, Rent asked the man if he ever did any business with Gabe Turner, the carpet cleaner. The man pointed out the store didn't have carpet, but said he had Turner to his house once. However, he didn't think Turner did a very thorough job.

"I wouldn't use him again," the man said.

"Does he ever come in the store?"

"Off and on, but he's not a regular. He stopped by the other day with a couple of other fellas. They bought some beer and snacks."

"Did they use an EBT card or maybe a debit card?"

"Come to think of it, yeah, one of them guys used a debit card. At least I think it was. It wasn't a credit card, because he had to enter a PIN number to complete the transaction."

Number is redundant. That's what the "N" in PIN stands for, Rent thought, but kept it do himself. "But it was not an EBT card?"

"To be honest, I didn't notice. They all look pretty much the same to me. And it all happens so fast. They swipe, enter the PIN, and they're done. I don't really pay attention, as long as the transaction goes through. I have my eye on the screen on the cash register. Money goes straight into the store's account. I prefer it to a credit card. The banks these days and all their fees. I'm lucky to make any money at all, thanks to those lousy money grubbers—legalized thievery.

"There ought to be better usury laws, but nobody ever listens to a little guy like me. The bigger stores, they got more clout, and get better rates. But what do the politicians do? They're in on it too. Why last year . . ."

Rent's phone rang. He excused himself and stepped outside to take the call. His editor. She needed a clarification on a fact check regarding his fraud story. They agreed to a slight rewording for clarification.

"Anything going on up there in the mountains other than blue sky and apple pie?"

"Funny you should ask," he said. He explained what had just happened and said he could knock out a sidebar to his story.

"Go for it," she said and disconnected.

A sheriff's patrol vehicle arrived; a deputy got out and approached the entrance to the store.

Rent waved and called out, "I'm the one who phoned in."

The deputy, a woman, walked up to him. Her name badge read: Smith-Jones. "Hi. Something about a card skimmer?"

"Yeah. I was talking to the storekeeper about scammers stealing account information from people using benefits cards, and I discovered a skimmer on the card reader."

"Let's take a look."

They went inside and Rent pointed at the device with the partially removed card reader. "I used a knife blade to pry the corner loose. I haven't touched it, although I imagine it's already covered in prints."

"Are you the guy who got the death threat?"

"Word gets around."

Smith-Jones nodded. "Okay, I'll take it from here."

"I'd like to write a short piece for the newspaper about this. Can I get a comment from you?"

"You'll have to go higher up the chain of command for that. You talked to Washington, correct?

"Yeah."

"Give him a call back later on and he can help you out, or talk to his lieutenant.

"Thank you, I appreciate it."

"I need to get your full name and a brief statement for my report."

Rent showed her his driver license and gave her a business card, then told her about his investigation and the article that would appear in Sunday's paper, which led to the discovery of the card skimmer. Rent then thanked the storekeeper and left the store.

He got into his truck and, as he put the key in the ignition, his phone rang. He looked at the ID and sighed. *Here it comes.*

He swiped the phone and put it to his ear. "Hello?"

"You scumbag. Why are you torturing my daughter again? After all these years and all the shit she's been through."

"Hello, Mrs. Powell. Nice to hear from you."

"Cut the crap. You know what this is about."

"It's about your granddaughter. Is she with you? People are worried about her."

"Rachel's fine. People should mind their own darned business."

"Would you be so kind as to put her on the phone, please?"

"She's not with me at the moment. She's walking the dog."

"How convenient for you. But if so, why didn't you return the calls you got from Alicia Velasquez, the private investigator?"

"I had to talk to Hannah and find out what this business is all about. Accusing her of fraud and being an unfit mother."

"Neither I nor Alicia nor anyone at the HHSA has accused your daughter of fraud or of being an unfit mother. She is being treated as a victim of fraud and, thus, a witness for the prosecution."

"A witness against whom?"

"The authorities have their eyes on number of people, but that boyfriend of hers is certainly on the short list."

"He's not her boyfriend; not anymore. I don't know what she ever saw in that bum. She's always made poor choices when it came to men, present company included."

Rent sighed. "Dredging up ancient history, are we?"

"What do you want?"

"I'm just trying to find out if Rachel is with you and if she's okay."

"Like I said, she's here with me and Sam and she's fine."

"When are you bringing her back to Hannah's?"

"That remains to be seen. I don't trust that carpet cleaner."

"Wise move, but if Rachel stays with you, Hannah will have to report that and her benefit will be reduced accordingly. If she doesn't report it, then that will land her in hot water."

"What business is it of yours? You certainly didn't give a damn about her all those years ago."

"Jesus Christ—"

"Don't you take the good lord's name in vain."

"I apologize. But I'm not going to relive the past. What's done is done. We were teenagers, barely out of high school; we had a fling and it didn't work out. It happens. Get over it."

Silence.

Rent waited a moment. "Mrs. Powell, are you still there?"

"I'm here. Anything else?"

"Did Hannah tell you why I went to see her? That I didn't even know she would be the one I was meeting until I arrived at her door? This is my job; it's what I do. I'm an investigative journalist. I ended up interviewing her purely by happenstance."

"You're a muckraker, that's what you are. Giving my girl a bad name."

"I'm keeping her name out of it. She's not being identified in any way, other than the fact that she's a single mom whose deadbeat ex-husband is behind on child support and she needs public assistance to feed her two kids."

"Then what's this fraud crap have to do with it?"

"Hannah is a victim of scammers who stole money from her account . . . twice . . . and left her penniless until she could be reimbursed. Of which I'm sure you are well aware. This is a nationwide tragedy costing taxpayers billions of dollars, and I'm doing my bit to see that the bad guys are identified and put behind bars."

"Gee, how noble of you. You could start with the carpet cleaner. I have no doubt he's involved somehow. He's also a pervert and ought to be arrested for that, but Hannah refuses to do anything about it."

"As far as I know, he is a person of interest," Rent said, but I can't say anymore about it."

"Is that all?"

"Hannah said you're camped somewhere along the Colorado River. I'm in Julian. I could be over there in a couple of hours."

"Why do you want to come here?"

"To confirm that Rachel is where you say she is, and that's she's in good health."

"You come right on over—and your welcoming committee will be led by Mr. Glock."

"Well, you and the carpet cleaner have that in common, at any rate."

"What's that?"

"Goodbye, Mrs. Powell. Nice talking with you."

Rent disconnected the call. "Fuck me," he muttered. "I need to eat something." He rummaged through his duffle bag and found the muffin left over from his stay at the B&B.

A bit stale, but it will tide me over.

Rent returned to the library, where Alice had laid out a few items regarding Chariot Canyon and the gold mines. It consisted of historic black-and-white photos of mining equipment and old news articles.

"Gold wasn't just about the mines, though," she said.

"Oh, yeah?"

"A local guy offered to clear the manzanita stumps to level the football field for nothing, but he got to keep any gold he found. The school board thought it was a great deal for them." She huffed a sardonic laugh. "Until they found out he pocketed fifty thousand from the gold he gleaned from the roots of the manzanita."

"Clever man," Rent said.

"I'll leave you to it," she replied.

He thanked her and took down some notes as he went through the material. He learned that in its heyday, the hastily constructed town of Banner City boasted of 78 saloons, three stamp mills, a freight station, a cemetery, and a school. Floods in what had been charitably named San Felipe Valley—its canyon-like walls were so steep mining equipment had to be lowered by ropes during the gold rush—had wiped out the town. Twice.

When he had finished, he called Detective Washington and got a bland statement he could use to give credibility to his story: "No arrests have been made . . . we have identified persons of interest . . . and the investigation is ongoing." He completed the sidebar and sent it to his editor.

Rent checked the time. "Oh, shit." He called Abby, apologized and formulated a white lie. "I got waylaid by the cops again. On my way."

"You do remember what day it is, yes?"

"I haven't forgotten," he said, fingers crossed to negate his lie.

He disconnected and found Alice, who had just put on her coat.

"Make it quick," she said. "I'm due at the restaurant."

"Is there a flower shop or card shop in town? I need to get a Valentine—"

"You wait until the last minute? Try the Warm Hearth. Better yet, the Juliantla Chocolate Boutique on B Street."

15

Friday, Day 13, evening

Rent knocked and heard a faint "door's open." He let himself in and strode across the living room to the kitchen. On the way, he set a small gift bag on the coffee table. Abby was standing at the stove, spatula in hand. Rent stopped beside her and started to speak, but she cut him off.

"I hope you like chicken cordon bleu," she said. "Although it's probably cordon black by now." She nodded at a bottle of Mark West pinot noir on the dining table. "You could open that. Corkscrew in the center drawer. I would get it for you, but I might be tempted to use it on you."

Rent sighed. "I know I messed up. I'll make it up to you. It's just that . . . this job . . . unexpected things happen and I have to—"

She stepped up to him and placed a finger on his lips. "Save your breath, boyo. I'm just glad you're here and . . ." She choked up for a moment and cleared her throat. "Not dead. At least not yet."

She kissed him lightly and stared into his eyes for a moment. "The wine."

"On it," he said.

Rent found the corkscrew and went to the dining table, which had red hearts scattered over its surface and three red candles yet to be lit. Small green salads sat next to the dinner plates, and a dish of candy hearts sat next to the wine. He opened the wine and poured a splash into each of the two glasses at the place settings.

Abby stepped to the table holding a baking dish in one hand and used the spatula to serve the main course. She returned the dish to the stove.

"I hope you like smashed potatoes and broccoli with cheese sauce."

"Yes."

She set two serving dishes on the table. "Then dinnah is served. Have a seat."

Abby removed her apron and sat opposite him. She raised her wine glass and Rent followed suit.

"To lust," she said.

"To lust," he repeated.

"And maybe like," she added with a wink. "Although being on time would have been a nice gesture."

"I—"

"Shush. Just eat, or it'll get cold."

Rent took a sip of wine, set the glass down, and picked up a fork and knife. "Smells delicious. Thank you for going to all this trouble. I would have been happy to—"

"The last place I want to be on Valentine's Day is in a crowded noisy restaurant playing crappy music."

"I hear ya there," Rent said over a mouthful of chicken. "Mmmm. This is great. You really know the way to a man's heart."

"I hope you don't forget that."

They ate in silence, and Rent refilled their wine glasses.

"Seconds?" Abby asked. "I made plenty."

"As much as I'd like to . . ."

" I also made dessert."

"In which case I will save room for that."

Abby lifted her glass and took more of a gulp that a sip, then stared at Rent with an almost fearful aspect.

"I hope you don't think I'm putting the cart before the horse, so to speak . . ." She waved her hand over the table. "I know we barely know each other, but I haven't celebrated Valentine's Day in several years, and I just thought it might be fun. But I don't want to scare you off."

"No, it's fine. I haven't either. And the last one ended in disaster. She actually made me a 'break-up cake.' Can you believe it?"

"I've heard of that, yeah." Abby stood up. "Let me clear these dishes, then we can have dessert."

Rent started to rise, saying, "I'll give you a hand."

"No, stay there. Have some more wine."

"Plying me with liquor, are you? Like the old saying, 'Candy's dandy but liquor's quicker.'"

She grinned and flicked her eyebrows. "Something like that."

The table cleared, she sat down and picked up her wine glass, taking a sip.

Rent told her about his phone call to Rachel's grandmother, omitting any mention that they had met before.

"Well, I hope what she said is true, that Rachel's with her," Abby said. "I feel sorry for that poor girl."

"Yeah, the shit some kids have to go through."

"But I'd rather we—"

"I tracked down Turner, but he denied knowing anything."

"You're crazy. He threatened to kill you."

"We don't know that it's him, and even if it is, I suspect it's all bluster."

"You said that before, but I'm not so sure. You get him cornered and he might just coil up and strike. . . . And as I started to say, I'd rather we talked about something else."

Rent nodded. "Okay, just let me finish this thought. Hannah's mother tore me a new one. I couldn't believe it. I asked her where she was staying and said I could drive over to the river and confirm Rachel was there. She refused, saying it was none of my business. I tried to explain that I was only interested in Rachel's welfare, and she said if I showed up, I might get shot. Maybe she left that death threat."

"Just drop it, will you?"

"I'm just sayin'. A twelve-year-old girl disappears and . . ."

Abby slammed a flat hand on the tabletop. "Shut up! I don't want to hear about it right now. Let's not spoil a romantic evening." Tears glistened her eyes. "Let's just talk about something else, okay?"

They sat, silent, staring into their wine glasses. Finally, Abby shoved her chair back and stood. "I'll get the dessert."

She went to the refrigerator and returned with a sumptuous-looking concoction of cake, strawberries, and whipped cream.

"Voila!" she said. "Behold chocolate strawberry cake."

"My god. I'm going to have run another five miles after this."

Abby served them each a slice and they dug in. After several bites and uttering sounds of pleasure, Rent spoke, keeping the topic neutral.

"Weather forecasters are saying there's a big atmospheric river approaching. Could deliver three to five inches of rain in twenty-four hours. That's more than the entire month, on average."

"Yeah. I hope it's on my day off. I don't want to have to leave the house. We might get snow at this elevation."

Rent silently chided himself: *My god, that's what strangers in elevators talk about when they're uneasy with the strained silence.*

The fire popped and startled them both.

"Throw another log on, will you?"

Rent restocked the wood stove while Abby cleared the table. She brought the wine glasses to the living room and they sat together on the couch, enjoying the warmth of the fire.

Rent apologized for upsetting her. She apologized for her outburst.

"I obviously touched a raw nerve, but I didn't realize it was something that would upset you. I thought you would be concerned about what's become of Rachel."

She stared silently into the fire, tears welling in her eyes again.

"Were you abused as a child or adolescent?" he asked tentatively, stepping onto what he knew could be thin ice.

"What makes you think that?"

The fire gave off another frightening pop and they both flinched, as if they had heard a gunshot.

"Your vehement reaction to the subject for starters," Rent replied, a bit peeved that she was getting so angry about it. Still, he had to remind himself that he was not interviewing someone for a story. He was having a frank discussion with a woman with whom he had become romantically involved. Always treacherous territory at such an early stage . . . at any stage. They were bound by passion—hot, wanton passion—being "in lust"—and damn any rational thoughts. But if the passion cooled, the relationship might end. Rent didn't want to lose that. Not yet.

I am enjoying being with a woman. Again.

Still, if things were to progress, they had to get beyond just being sexual partners and learn more about each other. Was it worth investing more time? Would the price of the sexual rewards become too high to pay? He believed the relationship had potential. Nor was he thinking of just himself. He knew she had to be thinking along the same lines. Unless she was living in a total fantasy world—her bonobo world. *It's possible, but not likely for someone as bright as Abby.*

Abby remained silent as she reached for a tissue and wiped at the tears rippling below her eyes, then stared into the fire.

"I hate it when I get like this," she said. "A weak female who can't control her emotions."

"It's not weakness," he countered.

"Then what is it?" she said, reaching for another tissue and wiping her nose.

"Fear. You're feeling vulnerable and that scares you. I get that."

"You think you're so smart."

"No, I think I'm a bit fearful too."

"What are you afraid of? That I might stop seeing you?"

"Yeah, sort of. Are you?"

She shrugged. "A little, but that's not why I shouted at you."

"Obviously, my question touched a nerve. I did not mean to sound critical, or meddlesome. I asked out of concern for you, trying to be understanding and supportive. I'd guess you or someone close to you suffered a traumatic incident of some kind?"

"Something like that."

Rent hugged her tightly. "I'm sorry. It must be painful for you. If you want to talk about it sometime, I'd be happy to listen."

Abby sat wooden, unresponsive. Rent turned her shoulders and looked intently into her eyes. "I mean it. I'm not trying to be judgmental. It seems like it might be good for you to talk about it."

Abby pushed him away and stood up. "You're not my fucking shrink! Just let it go, will you?" She stepped up to the fire and stared into the dancing flames, her back to Rent.

"Look, Abby, I'm just trying to be the sensitive male of the new millennium. I'm trying to show you that you mean a bit more to me than a just a little roll in the hay. That I care about you and don't like to see you hurting, which you obviously are."

Abby spun around and faced him, her face consumed with fury. "Well, maybe that's all I want, just an occasional roll in the hay. Maybe I don't need . . ." and her tone became decidedly sarcastic ". . . a sensitive male of the new millennium."

Rent's shoulders drooped as he felt her icy demeanor encase him. "Maybe not." He turned away, grabbed his jacket, glanced at the gift bag but strode past it and headed for the front door.

"Besides," she shouted after him, "if you want to be a sensitive male, try reading Anton Chekhov, or better yet, Alice Munro, instead of Fyodor Dostoyevsky—you ungrateful biped!"

Ouch.

He opened the door and stepped out onto the porch and started to slam the door. Then thought better of it and closed it gently. Before he descended the short staircase, he dared a glance through the front window. Abby had returned to the couch and sat with head in hands, sobbing. Rent felt his chest tighten. He wanted to go back and hold her, console her, comfort her. Yet, he hated himself for even thinking it. *The ungrateful bitch. I tried to be understanding, to show some compassion. And what do I get in return? Kicked in the balls.*

He spun gravel as he pulled out of her driveway and began the 60-mile drive back to San Diego. He drove hard, angry. A close call with a live oak at a tight corner brought him back to his senses. *This isn't a descent in Le Tour de France.* He slowed to a sane pace, forcing air into his lungs in deep breaths. At the egg ranch, he pulled over and parked until he had calmed down.

May as well get back to San Diego under my own power rather in an ambulance. Or worse—a hearse.

16

Saturday, Day 14

Rent called Abby the next morning. She didn't answer. He left a message, asking her to call. He started some laundry, then went for a long run in Tecolote Canyon. He knew the nature preserve had been named for an owl, but he had never seen one there.

Maybe Abby could help me find one.

For the first time, he noticed the birds singing, wondering which species were the noisiest. He thought he heard an owl hooting.

Back home he put the clean clothes in the dryer, then practiced fiddle tunes for the dance that night. He added *Red Wing* and *The Girl I Left Behind Me* to the tune list, both in the key of G. Then he doodled, playing folded scales and arpeggios, his mind wandering back to the investigation. The PI's comment about "skulking" popped into his mind and he played an E minor chord. Twenty minutes later he had a new tune: *Skulking*. He made a quick recording on his phone for future reference, then put the instrument away.

Before heading off to the dance, he folded his laundry and fixed a grilled-cheese sandwich while watching a Six Nations rugby match between his favorite, Wales, and arch-rival England. Wales got whacked. "The bloody Poms cheat," he muttered.

Sunday, Day 15

Rent slept in after a late night at the dance and winding down afterward with what he had dubbed a "Mel Bay"—cheap gin and diet grapefruit soda, served in a repurposed frozen orange juice can. His poor man's Greyhound. He watched SNL, until the skits got too silly for him to take anymore of it. "This show just ain't what it used to be," he muttered. "I swear the writers are all twelve-year-old boys sequestered in a locker room."

He set coffee to brewing and retrieved the morning newspaper. As expected, his story ran on page A1, above the fold, and continued inside on A6. His sidebar also appeared on the inside page. He sipped his coffee while briefly thumbing through the rest of the paper.

Rent called Abby and again no answer. He disconnected and texted her:

I'm sorry. Please call me back.

He made an omelet and caught the latest news from National Public Radio. More dire predictions of the atmospheric river laden with moisture, rain of biblical proportions, and possible "bomb tornadoes" dominated the weather forecast.

He looked for four-wheel drive rentals available through the Turo car rental service.

None of these are cheap, but it's only for a few days.

He saw a Jeep Wrangler Rubicon that looked like Abby's gold metallic model, the same year as his pickup.

Did I cross the Rubicon with Abby? I hope not.

He settled on a late-model Toyota 4Runner TRD in army green. When the owner delivered the vehicle, he looked at Rent's aging Toyota Tacoma and chuckled.

"Man, you're going from the horse-and-buggy days to the space age."

Rent shrugged.

The man gave him the run-down on the vehicle's features, including the touchscreen interface, Bluetooth cell phone connectivity, panoramic view, and multi-terrain monitor.

Rent shook his head in amazement.

"The owner's manual is in the glove compartment in case you're having trouble falling asleep tonight."

Back inside, he prepared for yet another trip to Julian, which would include driving into Chariot Canyon.

Maybe I do need a place of my own, if I'm going to spend so much time there.

He vacuumed the carpet, wondering if he could lure Mr. Magic Carpet Ride off the mountain to clean it. *Nah, with gas topping five bucks a gallon, it wouldn't be worth it.*

As he reviewed his plans for the coming week, he was reminded of the co-worker's birthday barbecue. He sighed. *What's the point? We just drink too much and whine about politicians who fail to live up to their campaign promises, and how the San Diego Padres, having made some expensive trades, promise to be contenders once again.*

With nothing better to do, Rent showed up at the party. Several of the attendees congratulated him on his piece on the EBT fraud. "Your series could be an award winner at the Press Club, even Best in Show," one said.

"Actually, he's got his eye on a bigger prize," Naomi said with a smirk. At questioning looks from others, she added, "Pulitzer."

Rent rolled his eyes. "I could use a cold one."

"Over there, in the cooler," the birthday boy said.

Rent opened the ice chest and extracted a Modelo Negra beer. He twisted off the cap and raised the bottle. "Happy birthday, Greg." Then added in a sing-song voice, ending on flattened seventh note, "And many more."

Greg tapped the bottle with his own. "Thanks. Glad you could make it. We have shrimp on the barbie and the usual munchies. Help yourself."

Rent nodded a thanks and grabbed a handful of tortilla chips, then surveyed the scene. As usual, most of the people had separated into small groups, an occasional laugh cutting through the banter.

He felt an elbow in the ribs. Naomi Clark.

"Nice story," she said. "I didn't realize welfare fraud was such a big deal. It sort of flies under the radar."

He eyed her with a look of skepticism.

"Seriously. I'm offering you a compliment."

"Thanks," he said and took another sip of beer.

"I'm amazed that you showed up. Or did your other plans get cancelled."

"And those plans might be?"

"Your little mystery miss in Julian. You did take her out on Valentine's Day, did you not? Or has that gone south already."

"Do you actually want an answer? Or are you looking for a way to humiliate me?"

"Oh, so it has gone south. What's it been, barely a week?"

"It hasn't gone south. Just a little misunderstanding."

"Uh-huh."

"What is it with you women?" he asked. "You claim to want a man who's sensitive and caring, yet when we try to do that, it's suddenly none of our damned business, punctuated with a kick in the balls."

"You can't just start grilling her as if she's a politician you suspect of corruption."

"Something's troubling her. Threatening texts and worries about a twelve-year-old girl being molested by her mother's boyfriend. I thought maybe she'd want to talk about it."

"Sometimes all you can do is hold her hand and say nothing."

Rent shrugged.

"Do you think she's involved in the fraud scheme?" Naomi asked.

"I don't see how, although this guy she went out with a few times is one of the targets of the investigation. I just assumed it's because she told him to get lost and he keeps hassling her. What about you? Getting any action?"

She offered a sly grin. "Maybe."

"Don't want to talk about it, eh? Would you like me to hold your hand and say nothing?"

She scoffed. "As if. A bit late for that." She then turned and waved at a new arrival. "Good luck," she added as she walked away.

One of the party-goers tapped a fork against a glass and shouted, "Okay, everybody, time to cut to the chase and cut the cake. But first, we have to sing. Happy Birth . . ."

"I hate that insipid fucking song," Rent muttered. He drained his beer, placed the bottle in a cardboard box with "recycle" hand lettered on its side, and left.

17

Rent stopped at the Kitchen Kountry restaurant for coffee and breakfast. The same girl as before greeted him.

"Welcome back," Lindsey Helstrom said. "Sit anywhere you like. Coffee?"

"Please," he said and took a seat near the window.

She returned with a cup and coffee pot, set the cup down, and filled it.

He thanked her, then congratulated her on her recent award as editor of her school's newspaper and her contributions to the local commercial newspaper. He'd seen a write-up about it in Sunday's paper.

"Have you thought anymore about interning at the *Herald*? I could put in a good word for you."

"As *your* intern?" she inquired, her voice laced with skepticism.

"No, that's not what I meant. I don't even know how it works. You'd probably be working with my boss. She's sharp. One of the best. And you could shadow some of the reporters."

She lifted her eyebrows. "Like you, you mean?"

"No, that's not what I'm getting at. . . . What? You think I'm some dirty ol' man?"

She smirked. "Are you?"

Rent stared at her for a beat, a smile creasing his face. "You didn't really spit on my eggs last week, did you?"

"A girl never tells," she replied and sauntered off.

Rent stared at his cinnamon roll, hesitating before partaking. Not seeing any evidence of sabotage, he torn off a chunk and stuffed it in his mouth, savoring the sweet cinnamon flavor, then washing it down with coffee.

A few minutes later, she returned with the coffee pot and topped off his cup.

"Sorry if I sounded unappreciative. Thanks for the suggestion," she said. "I'll look into it."

Still chewing the roll, he nodded and gave her a thumbs-up.

After leaving the restaurant, he followed up with Detective Washington, who told him they had found partial prints on the card skimmer, but no match. The detective also said the security video at the store was limited and so far they had found nothing relevant.

"The skimmer could have been there for weeks, if not months," Washington said.

Rent took notes but didn't have enough to justify a follow-up piece.

RENT DROVE TO PINE Hills, slowing down as he neared Abby's house but not stopping, and went on toward Gabe Turner's place. He passed the house, noting that both the van and Land Cruiser were parked there, along with an old Bronco. He proceeded another 100 yards before turning around and heading back. He pulled over at a wide spot and parked the 4Runner, hoping he wouldn't have long to wait.

He cracked a window and hunkered down behind the wheel. A slight breeze rustled the leaves of the flora surrounding him. Birds sang and chirped, and he heard a woodpecker hammering a tree. A bobcat sprinted across the road and disappeared in the underbrush. He used his binoculars to try to spot the birds, but mostly he just saw silhouettes flitting about. "Those might be ravens or crows," he muttered. "And those in that bare tree look like pigeons. Otherwise, I don't have a clue."

Motion up the road caught his eye. A vehicle nosed out of Turner's driveway, then pulled out onto the road, churning gravel and turning away from Rent.

His van. Does he actually have a job to go to?

Once the van rounded a corner and went out of sight, Rent followed, backing off whenever he caught a glimpse of it. The van slowed slightly as it passed Abby's place, then Rent saw a puff of exhaust as the driver put the pedal down and accelerated. It continued on Pine Hills Road until it reached the 78, where it turned left, heading west toward Wynola.

Rent stopped at the intersection and sighed with relief as another vehicle came from the direction of Julian, following in the van's wake. Rent pulled out and maintained a safe distance from the vehicle. He could see the van farther ahead.

The van barely slowed as it passed through Wynola and raced down the steep grade toward Santa Ysabel. Rent increased his speed but had no way to get around the vehicle between them, the driver of which seemed intent on obeying the 55-miles-per-hour speed limit. After passing through Santa Ysabel's tiny cluster of businesses, the road straightened out for nearly a mile.

With no oncoming cars, Rent gunned it and passed the slower vehicle, then eased off once around it, not wanting to get too close to Turner's van. Turner would be unlikely to suspect a 4Runner of following him, but Rent didn't want to take any chances.

The van continued on to Ramona, where the amount of traffic increased and the speed slowed, and came to a stop at a red light. Rent closed up on the van but kept another car between them.

When the light turned green, the van shot ahead, moved into the right-hand lane, and turned into the parking lot of a commercial center, coming to a stop in front an office unit with a For Lease sign in the window. Rent turned into the parking lot and continued on to the other end, where he pulled into a parking space. He watched as Turner got out of his van and went to the door of the building. There must have been someone waiting for him, because he paused only a few seconds before going in. A few minutes later, he came out, opened the back of his van, and began moving his equipment into the building.

Rent had seen enough. *He's going to be busy for a while. Chariot Canyon, here I come.*

RENT BOUNCED AND WEAVED on the poorly maintained road, thankful he had a rental. He encountered a group of mountain bikers and waved to them.

Farther along, he spotted four men target shooting. They had lined up a series of beer and soda cans in front of an embankment above a small ravine. He stopped and, claiming ignorance, inquired about the legality of the shooting. They told him that because they were on BLM land, it was lawful as long as they didn't destroy property.

Two of the men had flintlock rifles and were pleased to show Rent how they worked. He'd seen the weapons depicted in Hollywood movies, but had never actually witnessed the entire procedure of loading and firing. He remarked on how they poured black powder from a powder horn into a measuring device before pouring the powder down the barrel.

"You can't believe that shit they show in the movies, like that lame one starring Leo DiCrapio," one of the men said.

He held up the powder measure, which appeared to have been carved from the tip of a deer antler. "Fifty grains," he said.

The shooter then pulled a lead ball from a pouch on his belt, wrapped it in a piece of cloth, and thumbed it into the open muzzle of the barrel. He then used a barrel-length wooden rod to ram the ball the down the barrel, which Rent judged to be at least three feet in length.

"Got to seat it good on top of the powder, otherwise it doesn't shoot properly and could cause a problem. Want to take a shot?"

Rent declined.

"Ah, come on. Once in a lifetime."

Rent thought about it, and the possibility of getting a story about these throwbacks to the Old West.

"Okay, I'll give it a try."

"Ever shot before?."

"Yeah, my dad had a couple of rifles that we shot occasionally when I was a teenager."

"This is similar, but not quite the same, because there's a fraction of a second between when you pull the trigger and the gun goes off, so you have to hold 'er steady even after you pull the trigger."

The man took off his safety glasses and handed them to Rent. You need to wear these, just in case."

"In case of what?"

"In case the gun explodes," one of the other men said, and his companions laughed.

"Never mind them," the instructor said, and handed the gun to Rent. "This gun's in perfect working order, but it will throw off sparks."

Rent hefted the rifle. "Wow, this is heavier than I expected."

The man nodded. "A lot of iron and a lot of maple in that baby. Made it m'self." He took the stopper out of his powder horn. "Now prime it. Pull the hammer back to half cock, then lift the frisson to expose the pan."

Rent thumbed the hammer back until it clicked, then looked at the man expectantly.

"Like this," the man said and flipped the frisson forward. He poured a small amount of powder into the shallow pan, then pushed the frisson back to encase the powder.

"Now, here's what's goin' to happen," the man continued. "You're goin' to pull the hammer back to full cock . . . No, not yet. See this piece of flint in the hammer?"

Rent nodded.

"When you pull the trigger, the hammer will snap forward, the flint will strike the frisson, creating sparks, which ignite the powder in the pan, which in turn sends a bigger spark through a tiny hole into the barrel and ignites the powder in the barrel, and . . ." The man slaps his hands together, creating a loud pop. "Wham, the gun fires, shooting that lead ball out the barrel and at your target."

Rent looked from the man, down at the gun, and back at the man, shaking his head in wonder.

"Put the butt tight against your shoulder. This baby can kick. And pull the hammer back to full cock."

Rent lifted the gun to his shoulder and raised the barrel, trying to hold it steady, and cocked it. "This is a lot harder than it looks. It's a wonder anyone can hit anything with it," Rent said.

"Once you get the hang of it, you can be dead on with one of these things," the man said. "Just hold it steady, line up the sights on the barrel with your target and squeeze the trigger."

Rent did as instructed. The gun fired and a puff of dirt lifted from the embankment.

"I missed."

"Not by much," the man said. "Try it again."

"Nah, I don't want to waste any more of your powder and lead."

"Oh, come on. Do it," another urged.

Rent gave in and slowly loaded the gun himself. He primed it, flipped the frisson down, and began to raise the gun to his shoulder.

"Stop!" the instructor commanded.

Rent did. "Something wrong?"

The man held up the powder horn. "Notice anything?"

Rent looked at it for moment, then his shoulders sagged. "The stopper."

The stopper dangled from a cord tied to the powder horn.

"Correct. Always, always put the stopper in before firing. This powder horn is a bomb waiting to explode. A flintlock gives off sparks, and if one goes into the horn— Bam! Big explosion. Trust me, it has happened and it ain't pretty."

The man jammed the stopper into the end of the horn and nodded at Rent. "All clear. Go ahead and shoot."

Rent took aim, feeling more confident, and squeezed the trigger. One of the cans spun away.

"You see? You did it. Not bad for a greenhorn."

"Yeah, but I was aiming at the one next to it."

The men laughed as Rent handed the gun back and thanked them, then exchanged contact information with the gun owner and started to turn away.

"We have a mountain man rendezvous in the spring," the man said. "You should come out. Lots of folks show up in period attire and re-enact the rendezvous of the beaver trappers back in the eighteen twenties and thirties. They'll be wearing buckskins and be camping in canvas tents and tipis, or some just lay out on the ground."

"Do you know a guy named Strummer? He keeps telling me to come."

"You mean the guitar and banjo player?"

Rent nodded. "I sometimes make music with him. I play the fiddle. One of my favorites tunes is *Leather Britches.*"

"Then you should definitely come. That'll get the Buffalo Gals a dancin'. And someone's bound to give you a jug of pie."

"Pie?"

"Booze. Alcohol flavored with fruit, like peaches and pears and such."

Rent agreed to consider it and again started to leave.

"Say, you know what you call a muzzleloader after you've taken your shot?" one of the other men said.

Rent stopped and shook his head.

The man flipped his gun around and grabbed it by the barrel, then swung it back over his shoulder like a baseball bat. "You call it a club!"

All the men guffawed.

"Good one, boys," Rent said. "Thank you for the demonstration. Oh, one more thing. Do you know anything about the Golden Eagle Mine?"

They all eyed one another for a moment, then shook their heads. They knew nothing about it or any of the mines or miners, although they cautioned him to be careful. "Those guys don't like strangers poking around. And it may not be just gold mining they're involved in," one man said.

Rent drove a little farther, then realized he could spend hours being tossed back and forth in his seat as he traversed the rutted backroads of the BLM land and find nothing. Or maybe worse: encountering another man or men—or women—toting guns, but not being as friendly as the ones he'd just met.

He returned to Ramona, where he found Turner's van still parked outside the vacant office. He parked at the opposite end of the parking lot and walked to a convenience store for a coffee and corn nuts, then hunkered down in the 4Runner. He scrolled through the news feed on his phone, checked Instagram—the usual dogs, cats, kids, and selfies —then X, fascinated by the conspiracy theories and other lunacy from the fringes of society.

After an hour, Turner appeared and began packing up his equipment. He spoke to a woman dressed in business attire, accepted an envelope from her, then drove off. Just outside of Ramona, he pulled into a gas station.

Rent followed, but he drove to the store, not wanting to get stuck at a pump, or be recognized. When Turner had finished refueling, Rent trailed him, allowing two other cars to get between them. There were a lot of folks on their way home from work, making it easier for Rent to remain anonymous.

The carpet genie turned off at Pine Hills. Darkness had settled in, but Rent could still recognize the van and its taillights. The road led past Abby's place and on to Turner's, but the man pulled into Abby's driveway and parked next to her Jeep.

"Fuck!"

Rent continued on without slowing so as not to draw attention. The narrow road offered no place to pull over and few opportunities to turn around. Rent turned off at an intersection and pulled as far off the road as he dared. He could hear the screeches of branches scraping along the side of the vehicle.

I'm glad I bought the insurance.

He walked back to Abby's and crept as close to the house as he dared. He flinched when a neighbor's dog barked, but nothing came of it. He could hear loud voices from within. Through the window he could see the two standing in the living room.

Turner shouted, "Who is he? He's the same guy who was at Hannah's the other day, asking about me and Rachel, isn't he?"

"I don't know what you're talking about," she yelled in reply. He raised a hand as if to slap her. "You hit me and I'm calling the cops."

Turner dropped his hand but began shouting again. "You say anything to that reporter asshole and it'll be the last thing coming out of that big yap of yours, you little two-bit whore. And he'll be next."

Rent moved toward the steps leading to the front door, but the door swung open and slammed against the side of the double-wide. Turner stomped out and drove off, leaving Abby standing in the doorway. As she began to close the door, Rent called out and joined her. She collapsed against him, between sobs saying, "I'm so scared. I'm so scared."

"What happened to your shotgun?"

She shoved him away. "Fuck you!"

"Sorry, that was uncalled for."

"He burst in, unannounced. I guess I forgot to lock the door. And I keep the gun in my bedroom."

Rent consoled her and offered to stay in case Turner came back.

"I don't feel safe, but I don't want to involve you."

"I am involved," he said. "And you heard him. I know I said earlier he's all talk, but now I'm taking his threat seriously. I'm staying at the B&B again. Join me there."

She fell silent for a moment and sighed. "All right. I'll go. But I don't feel too lustful right now."

"That doesn't matter. As long as you're safe."

She hugged him and murmured, "Thank you for the nice card and the chocolates. I'm sorry I shouted at you. It's just that . . ."

"What?"

"You were right. There's more going on than I told you. With Gabe and his threats. It's not just you."

Rent put his hands on her shoulders and looked directly into her eyes. "I haven't told you everything either. Not because I was trying to keep it secret. I just didn't think it concerned you. But maybe it does."

"Let me pack an overnight bag."

"Okay. While you're doing that, I'll go get my car. I parked down the road a ways."

When he returned, he called the B&B and explained that he would have a companion with him, and agreed to the additional charge. Abby emerged and joined him. She threw her bag on the back seat, then settled into the front passenger seat.

"Nice wheels," she said.

"It's a rental. Have you eaten?" Rent asked. "I haven't had much since breakfast and I'm famished."

"Let's get some takeaway. I'll call Alice at The Nugget," she said.

At the restaurant, Rent had no trouble finding a place to park, it being a Monday evening. He went inside for the meals and paid.

"What's going on with that girl?" Alice asked. "She sounded terrified."

"She is."

"It's that galoot Gabe Turner, isn't it."

"Something like that. I'm taking her with me to the B&B for the night."

"You keep her safe."

"Will do."

Rent returned to the car and they did not speak on the short drive to the B&B. Rent checked in and led Abby to the same room he had before. The hostess offered them the dining room to eat their meal, but Rent said they'd prefer the privacy of the room.

"We'd prefer you didn't eat in the room."

"Look," Rent said. "This is not a spur-of-the moment romantic tryst . . ."

"Is she the one you—"

"Yes, but she has just been traumatized by a crazy man threatening physical violence—the same guy I suspect left the death threat—and I brought her here as a safety precaution. She needs her privacy."

"Okay, I'll let it go, if—"

"If there's an extra fee for cleaning, just add to the bill," Rent said and returned to the room.

Abby had lighted candles and laid out the meals on a small table. Next to one of the covered dishes sat a red envelope and gift-wrapped package. She handed him a bottle of wine.

"Here, open this," she said and offered him a corkscrew.

"Wow," he replied. "When you pack an overnight bag, you really pack."

She smiled at him. "Maybe we can rewind a bit and have a do-over."

"Good idea. What's for dinner?" he asked and began to twist the corkscrew into the bottle's cork.

Abby uncovered the dishes, exposing their contents.

"Sorry, but it's the only thing they could put together quickly on such short notice."

Rent looked at the dishes—the Miner's Special he had passed on earlier: pork and beans with crusty sourdough bread.

"Perfect," he said and poured the wine.

They ate without speaking, devouring their meals in short order. Abby cleared the containers and placed them in a waste basket.

"Open them," she said with a nod at the card and gift.

"If you insist."

"I insist."

Rent ripped open the envelope, removed the card, and read the message. Then he smiled and said, "Yes, I'll be your valentine." He then opened the gift: *Sibley Field Guide to Birds of Western North America*. "Aw, thank you. I could have used this this morning when I was staking out Turner's place."

They both chuckled, then stared at each other for a long moment, neither wanting to go first. The candles flickered, as if prompting them, one of them, to say something. They began speaking at once, stopped, and uttered an awkward laugh. Abby took a large gulp of wine.

Rent took the lead. "Okay, I'll tell you what's going on, on my end, but it cannot leave this room. I'm only telling you this because you need to be very careful."

"I read your story in yesterday's paper. Is Hannah Stapleford the Jane Jones?"

Rent nodded. "That's why I couldn't tell you. Her identity has to be protected. She's in enough danger as it is."

"Is she involved in the fraud? Using the counterfeit cards you wrote about?"

"Maybe. I don't know. But I have no doubt Gabe Turner is involved. The authorities suspect him, but they need hard evidence, and they hope he will lead them to bigger fish."

Abby took another sip of wine, as did Rent.

"That poor woman," she said.

"Yes," Rent replied, "and I hope she's not involved in Gabe's scheme, or if she is, she's being coerced. Otherwise, she may be looking at jail time, and her kids . . . well, who knows?"

"She's still being cagey about Rachel and her whereabouts. I tried talking to her last week, but same as before, she just said to mind my own business."

Rent told Abby about calling Hannah's parents and getting the same runaround.

"I hope nothing has happened to them. Rachel's such a sweet kid. All she wanted was a goat."

"Yeah, you mentioned that."

"I didn't tell you the whole story, though."

Rent gave her a sidelong glance. "Oh?"

Abby mimicked Rent with a deep breath and exhale.

"This may take awhile."

"I've got all night."

"No, on second thought, not tonight. I'm frazzled and this wine is making me drowsy. Sorry, I want to take a shower and go to sleep."

"Good idea."

She gave him a seductive look. "Join me?"

18

After breakfast, Rent took Abby home. Being her day off, she offered to show him some properties. Rent resisted, claiming he needed to keep going on his EBT fraud investigation.

"What about me?" Abby said. "What if Gabe, or whatever his name is, comes calling again? Just this morning, okay? Then you can work from here this afternoon. Besides, you can't spend all your time tailing him. Eventually, he's going to get suspicious, unless you change cars every day."

"Yeah, you're right," Rent replied. "And you can tell me the rest of the goat story."

While she changed into her clothes and did her makeup, he checked in with his editor, followed by a call to Detective Washington. Rent told the detective about Turner's latest threat to Abby.

Abby offered to drive, but Rent said he didn't want to leave the 4Runner at her house, in case Turner dropped by again. As they got into the vehicle, Rent asked her about the cabins at Mt. Laguna. She knew of one on Los Huecos Road that was on the market, but she explained that he wouldn't actually own the land, only the structure. The land is owned by the federal government, which also places restrictions on what can and cannot be done to the historic cabins.

Rent pulled onto Pine Hills Road and headed toward town.

"Even so, how much are we talking about?" he asked.

"This one is listed for $150,000, cash," she said. "No bank loans."

"Holy crap, the price of real estate in this county has gone nuts."

"On your budget, about the best I can do is get you into a place at the Golden Nuggets mobile home park for about fifty grand. It's just up the hill from the sheriff's substation."

"Golden Nuggets? That sounds like something served at a fast-food joint."

She suggested a wooded half acre. "*Only* forty-five thousand, but it has no dwelling on it."

"I could always pitch my Clam tent."

"It's south of town, off the 79, in a subdivision."

Rent scowled. "Subdivision? Julian has subdivisions?"

"Sorry, but it's the best I can do—until you win the lottery."

"Yeah, as if."

Rent's phone chimed. His editor. He pulled over at the intersection with Heise Park Road and answered the call. She asked him if he was still in Julian. Rent confirmed it.

"Good. A body has been found near there. I want you to cover it."

"That's not my beat. What about Clark?"

"She's on another story, and since you're already in the area, you can be the first journo on the scene. A photographer has already been dispatched."

Rent sighed. "I need to call you back. Give me five minutes."

He disconnected and said to Abby, "Sorry, I have to take you home."

"Damn. I don't want to be home alone, shotgun or not."

He retraced his route. At the house, she leaned over and kissed him.

"Good luck," she said.

"You take care of yourself. Lock the doors and windows, and keep your phone handy."

"I have a better idea."

"Oh, yeah?"

"Shopping."

She exited the 4Runner and waved goodbye.

Rent called his editor back. "And this body is where, exactly?"

"A place called Chariot Canyon. Isn't that the place with the abandoned gold mines you mentioned?"

"Yeah, I was just out there yesterday."

"All the more reason for you to cover it," she said. "The two stories may be related. You know what they say about honor among thieves."

"Any ID?"

"Not yet. You'll have to get that from the watch commander."

Rent called the sheriff's office and the receptionist put him through to Sergeant Diana Alvarez. She was not at the scene but gave him the GPS coordinates and said she would meet him there. He thanked her and punched the numbers into the 4Runner's navigation system.

"It's near where I saw those shooters. Maybe it's at Turner's mine," he muttered.

As he pulled onto Pine Hills Road, he could hear a siren wailing in the distance.

RENT STOMPED THE BRAKES as he went into a corner too fast.

What's your rush? The guy's already dead.

He obeyed the speed limit into and through Julian. As he began the descent down Banner Grade, a sheriff's patrol vehicle raced up behind him, lights flashing but no siren. Rent moved onto the narrow shoulder to let it pass, then followed it down the grade to the turnoff into Chariot Canyon.

He stayed well behind the sheriff's vehicle to avoid the dust cloud in its wake, but had no trouble finding his way. Helicopters had joined the turkey vultures circling overhead. He began humming the melody of the fiddle tune, *Boys, Them Buzzards Are Flying.*

Nice double entendre.

Rent retraced his route from the previous day, then turned off at a fork in the road. "Looks like I'm taking the road less travelled."

After another half mile, he could see multiple sheriff's vehicles parked randomly and uniformed deputies moving around the scene. He also noted a Chevy Silverado with the BLM logo emblazoned on the side. A shelter had been set up to create shade and block the activity from looky-loos. Off to the side, he noticed three horses and their riders standing next to them, holding the reins. Rent parked and exited his vehicle, notebook and recorder in hand.

A plainclothes man recognized him. "That was quick. That new 4Runner of yours must have wings," said Detective Washington.

"It's a rental, and I was already in town," Rent replied. "Coincidently—or not—I was near here yesterday."

"Brave man. Or just foolish." The detective grinned. "I guess that makes you a suspect."

"Yuk, yuk. I was just poking around, hoping I might find the carpet guy's fabled gold mine."

"Did you?"

"Nah, I ended up talking to a bunch of target shooters."

"I'll need their names, if you got 'em."

"I have one guy's contact info. You don't think—"

The detective shrugged. "Guys with guns and a dead body. Gotta check it out, although from the look of things, this vic's been here for a while."

"Days? Weeks? Months?"

"Not months. Days, more like it. Looks like a coyote might've uncovered it and gnawed on it, and that in turn attracted the other scavengers. The foot's on the small side, so it might be a woman or an adolescent boy. Whoever did it was in a big hurry. Maybe intended to come back and do a better job later on. Or, like most crooks, just stupid." He scoffed. "They always believe they're smarter than everyone else and never gonna get caught. Fuckin' idiots."

"Got an ID yet?"

"We don't have shit at this point. And, no, you cannot quote me on that." The detective motioned toward the shelter where a group of deputies and technicians had gathered near the body. "Still diggin' 'im out. Someone buried 'im in that pile of mine tailings over there."

"You think it's a 'him'? Maybe our carpet guy?"

"I'm just speaking in generalities. Odds are, considering the location, it's a white adult male, or possibly an illegal immigrant. Oops, I mean 'undocumented' immigrant. We'll find out soon enough. I just hope it's not another Chariot Canyon massacre."

Rent frowned. "Massacre?"

Washington nodded. "A bit sensational, but that's the media for you."

Rent rolled his eyes. "Yeah, yeah . . . but what do you mean?"

"Two guys got killed in a squabble over a mine, back in eighty-nine."

"Eighteen eighty-nine?"

"No, nineteen eighty-nine. Still before your time."

"So you think there might be more bodies here?"

"As I said, right now we don't know much. But we have to check out the possibility. We've called in a cadaver dog."

"Tire tracks?"

"We made plaster casts, but good luck finding a match."

"What's with the BLM dudes?"

"This is BLM jurisdiction, but they mostly deal with disputes over mining claims, and search and rescue. In cases like this they defer to us."

"So, who called it in?" Rent asked.

The detective tilted his head toward the riders. "The horsey set over there."

"Do you mind if I talk to them?"

Washington thought for a moment, then offered a half shrug. "I got preliminary statements from them, so, yeah, be my guest."

Rent walked toward the riders, who were staring toward the activity at the mine tailings, talking among themselves: two women, one older and the other closer to Rent's age, and an adolescent boy. They each wore black helmets, matching T-shirts, tan pants, and knee-high boots.

"Hi," Rent said and identified himself. He handed business cards to the two women.

"Can I have one?" the boy asked, and Rent gave him a card as well.

Rent turned back to the women. "Mind if I ask you a few questions?"

The two looked at each other, shrugged, and the older one spoke. "Not much we can tell you. We just saw a lot of turkey vultures and ravens circling overhead and some landing on the ground, and thought we'd check it out. Figured it would be a dead animal, a deer or bighorn sheep carcass, or possibly a hiker who got lost, and then we saw the birds pecking at something. But instead of a hoof we discovered a human foot sticking out from that pile of rubble. So we called nine-one-one."

"You got reception out here?"

"Barely one bar, but it was enough."

"Do you mind if I get your names and ages?"

The women again glanced at each other, then the elder of the two said, "Don't you know it's impolite to ask a woman her age?" Then she cracked a broad grin.

Rent chuckled. "Yeah, well, under the circumstances . . ."

"I'm Emily," the woman said, "and this is my daughter, Charlotte, and her son."

"What's his name, Branwell? Heathcliff? Rochester?"

"Ha, ha. Definitely not Heathcliff. It's more biblical in nature."

"Thomas, like Saint Thomas," the boy blurted out.

Emily shot him a look of admonishment. "Shush, grownups only," she said, then turned back to Rent.

"Last names?" the reporter asked.

"We'd rather not," Charlotte answered.

Rent sighed. "Okay, but if the cops publish your names and ages, it's fair game."

"We've asked them to keep our names out of it. We like our privacy."

"Do you live around here?"

"In Ramona," Emily said.

"Is this a place you ride often?"

"Not often. A few times a year. It's too hot much of the year, and there's very little water out here."

"Any idea what this area is called, or the road we came in on?"

The mother shook her head and nodded toward her daughter. "She's the navigator. I'm hopeless without GPS."

The daughter answered: "This is the Rodriquez Spur Truck Trail, which splits off from the California Riding and Hiking Trail that begins at Banner. The one you drove in on."

"So you were just out for a ride and stumbled across what appeared to be a dead body in a pile of rubble and notified the authorities."

"Yep, that's about it," Emily said. "Just doing our civic duty. But we don't want to be involved."

"You live in Ramona. Ever have your carpets cleaned by the Magic Carpet Cleaner?"

"We don't have carpets," Charlotte replied. "They collect dust and dirt, and my son has allergies."

"So you have no idea who this dead person might be?"

"Are you suggesting we buried the body?" Emily asked with a teasing twitch of her eyebrows.

Rent backed up a step, his face reddening. "No, not at all," he said. "It's just a question I have to ask."

Emily grinned. "Just giving you a hard time, Mr. . . ." She paused to look at his business card. ". . . Rent Beacham, investigative journalist."

"So, no idea who this might be? Missing person?" Rent asked.

"Not a clue," Emily said. "God rest his, or her, soul."

"How about a phone number in case I have any follow-up questions?"

She thought about it for a moment. "Okay, but you have to guarantee it goes no farther than this."

"I'll just write it down and not put it into my phone," he replied.

She gave him the number.

"Okay, thanks. I appreciate your taking time to talk to me." He paused, then said, "One more thing."

"Yes?"

"Okay if I pet your horse?"

"Oh, Kitty would love that. Do it like this," Emily said and gave her mare a solid pat on the shoulder.

Rent grinned and did as instructed. The mare swung her head around and nuzzled Rent's chest, knocking him off balance.

"Whoa," he said.

"She's thanking you," Emily said.

Rent patted the horse a second time and said, "You're welcome, Kitty."

He thanked the women again, wished them "happy trails," and rejoined Detective Washington.

"Gettin' a bit warm out here, especially for this time of year."

"No shit. No fuckin' shade in this place. I'm going to go sit in my vehicle with the doors open. Maybe a little breeze will come up."

Rent followed him to his county-issued SUV, and the detective motioned for Rent to get in.

"Any progress? Rent asked.

"Not yet. Takes a while to uncover a body."

"Sort of like an archeologic dig, is it?"

"Something like that. Can't just drag the body out. Gotta preserve as much evidence as possible. We'll be here for a while."

"You get many cases like this?"

"Nah. Out here it's usually search and rescue." He shook his head. "Dumb fucks from the city, wearing flip-flops, don't carry enough water, and get lost, thinking their iPhone's GPS will save them."

"That doesn't seem to be the situation here though. Dead people generally don't bury themselves."

Washington snorted a laugh. "Generally not."

"So you're thinking homicide."

"It's certainly suspicious, although cause of death has yet to be determined. That's up to the ME. And ID could be a problem, depending on the condition of the body."

"Possibly a missing person?"

"Again, who knows. It's all speculation at this point. It could be hours. You're probably wasting your time here."

"My editor wants a story. But I think I'll go to the store at Banner and get some water and something to eat. Can I get you anything?"

"Yeah, something cold and something crunchy."

"You got it."

"By the way, I'm now with the Homicide Detail. Just so you keep your facts straight."

Rent drove to the store, grabbed a few items, and asked the storekeeper about Turner.

"Gabe hasn't been here since that time you were here," the man said, "and I ain't seen the Land Cruiser or that old Bronco of his but maybe once since then, and that was over a week ago."

Rent thanked him, paid for his items, and drove back into the canyon. He encountered the remounted horseback riders and waved as he passed. He arrived at the incident scene with four chilled cans of Dr. Pepper and two individual packets of Cheetos and shared them with the detective.

"Perfect," Washington said. "Now put your hands out. I have to cuff you for offering a bribe to a law enforcement officer."

Rent, a look of concern creasing his face, began to protest.

Washington grinned. "Just shittin' you, my man." He popped open a can and took a long gulp, then ripped open the packet of Cheetos. "Nothing like a healthy diet to keep a guy on his toes."

Rent chuckled and followed suit, then stepped out of the SUV and tried to call his editor, but had no signal, even after aiming the phone at every point on the compass. Another sheriff's vehicle arrived and a female officer emerged. She checked in with the others, one of them pointed at Rent, and she approached him.

"Off the fraud case and now on the violent crime beat, huh?" she said, extending her hand and introducing herself.

Rent shook hands with her and explained his presence at the scene. He then told her about the stakeout and interview with Hannah Stapleford.

"I don't believe she told us everything, and she may be lying," he said. "She seemed anxious and scared. Not just about the investigation, but something else."

The deputy acknowledged that the sheriff's department had run checks on the two vehicles seen at Turner's place. "One guy lives in Fallbrook, the other near Temecula, which is in Riverside County, so that complicates the matter further. I have to liaise with the Riverside sheriff's office. They arrested a couple dudes last week, so maybe these other guys are involved. Hard to say at this point."

The newspaper's photographer arrived, but Detective Washington would not allow her to get close to the body.

Just then, shouts caught their attention. Members of the forensic team had lifted the body and placed it into a black body bag. The sound of the zipper startled Rent, as if adding a note of finality to the individual's unfortunate demise.

Washington walked over and sighed, shaking his head. "This never gets any easier. It's a female. We're not sure how she died. No visible signs of trauma, other than a lump on the back of her head. Could have been struck or maybe she fell and hit her head. Even if she died by accident, burying her out here is a crime, not only legally, but against her humanity. And somebody's got to be missing her."

Rent felt a chill run through his body. "How old do you think she is?"

Washington shrugged. "Hard to tell at this point."

Rent sighed, then asked, "Adult? Adolescent?"

"Adult, judging by the size of her," the detective replied.

Not Rachel, Rent thought, then muttered, "Fuck."

Washington and Alvarez glanced at each other.

Alvarez asked, "Do you know who this is?"

"Maybe, but I sure as hell hope I'm wrong," Rent answered. "Meaning no disrespect to this woman, whoever she may be."

Washington stepped closer to Rent. "Well? What's going on?"

Rent looked up and stared at the sky, where vultures, natural and mechanical, continued to circle below cotton-ball clouds polka-dotting the eternal blue. He took a deep breath, then exhaled.

"It may be the woman we interviewed last week, Hannah Powell . . . er . . . Stapleford. At first, when you said female, I thought it might have been her daughter, Rachel, who seems to have disappeared. Hannah said she sent Rachel to stay with her grandparents in Arizona, but I spoke with the grandmother and found her evasive, not credible."

Alvarez broke in. "I spoke with Alicia Velasquez, the PI, about that. She left a message for the girl's grandparents but never heard back. Arizona cops tracked them down to one of those RV parks that cater to snowbirds, but the manager said they'd left for a few days, maybe to Quartzsite. He couldn't be sure."

Alvarez went on to say that, according to the La Paz County sheriff's office, the grandparents belonged to a camping club and went to a different place every month. Neighbors had seen the grand-daughter a few times before but didn't recall seeing her recently, and couldn't say one way or the other if the girl was with them or not. Or the boy either, for that matter."

"Yeah, but if this is an adult woman, then it's not Rachel," Rent said. "But it could be the girl's mother. Let me see the body."

"Negative," Washington replied.

"Look, I'm just trying to help out. It could save you a lot of time, even as a preliminary ID. Obviously, if it is Hannah, you're going to have to track down her parents to confirm it, but it would be a start."

The detective thought it over, then lifted the perimeter tape. "Okay, come with me."

Rent ducked under the yellow tape and followed the man to the shelter, where the body lay. Sgt. Alvarez joined them. One of the deputies partially unzipped the body bag, exposing the head and shoulders. Rent looked, then turned and stepped away. He leaned over and vomited.

"I'll take that as a yes," Washington said.

Alvarez shook her head in disgust. "Al, you can be so heartless at times."

"How do you think I maintain my sanity in this thankless job?"

Alvarez grabbed a sterile wipe from the forensics table and handed it to Rent. She then consulted Washington, but Rent couldn't hear what they said. They both glanced at him and Alvarez motioned for him to rejoin them.

Washington spoke. "So, you have no idea where her kids are?"

"No clue," he replied. "I thought Rachel was with her grandparents, and when I stopped by Hannah's place last week, Sammy was there with her. But if she's been dead for a few days, surely the kids can't be at the house by themselves. I'm going there now, just in case."

"No," Alvarez said. "You stay out of this. I'll send a couple of deputies to the house. Meanwhile, we have to contact the woman's parents."

"I have their phone number," Rent said.

Alvarez glared at him. "Do you want me to slap the bracelets on you?"

"No, I only meant—"

"We will contact them. Let us do our job. Now, what's the number?"

Rent dug out his phone and brought up the number for her, and she entered it into her phone.

"Got it. Now, largarse."

Did she just tell me to fuck off?

"You're welcome," Rent countered and turned to go.

"Imagine meeting you here," came a voice from behind.

A female voice that Rent recognized. Pamela Berringer, fellow musician and head of forensics for the sheriff's department.

Rent turned to face her. She held an evidence bag in one of her gloved hands. "Hey, Pam." He nodded at the bag. "Find anything incriminating?"

"Won't know till I get back to the lab and run some tests. And you know I couldn't tell you, even if I did. That being said, have you checked your email recently?"

"Uh . . . I glanced at it before coming here."

"Do more than glance at it. See you at the old-time jam on Thursday?"

"Yeah, unless this situation blows up even more than it already has."

"So sad, cases like this. And you knew her."

"Sort of."

"Sort of?" She sounded skeptical.

"We had a fling—"

"Uh-huh. As I said, check your email. Diana will let you know if we can release anything to the public about this death. Now, I need to get back to work."

"Yeah, see ya later," he replied and waved a hand to get Alvarez's attention.

Alvarez sighed. "What now?"

"One last question?"

"Make it quick."

"Anything from the cadaver dog? I'd hate to think her daughter might be buried here too."

"Nothing so far."

"Let's hope it stays that way," he said and began walking toward the 4Runner.

"Stop!" Alvarez ordered. "I know you want your scoop, but if this is Hannah Stapleford, we will need formal identification by a close relative. By the way, how well do you know this woman? You've only just met her, right?"

Rent paused before answering and Alvarez stared at him, her face as stoney as her immediate surroundings.

"I knew her in college, so it was quite a surprise—for both of us—when I showed up at the house last week," Rent said.

"Sweethearts, were you?" she asked.

"We dated briefly; lasted only a few months. We were both young."

"And what was it like after you reunited? Got a bit out of hand?"

Rent's jaw dropped. "You don't think—"

"You'll need to come to the station and answer some questions."

19

Rent followed the sheriff's vehicles and the vehicle from the medical examiner's office containing Hannah's body, forming a parade as they left the canyon. He began singing in a mournful tone: "I was standing . . . by my window . . ."

When they reached Banner Grade, he pulled off to the side and called his editor, Janis O'Connor. He tapped the Speaker icon.

"It's about time," she greeted.

"I had no reception while I sat on my ass, hoping for an ID on the victim," he retorted as he put the vehicle in gear and pulled out onto the road.

"You got a story for me or not?"

"Not. At least not yet. The cops need to confirm the ID. They're on their way to the morgue right now."

"Any clue as to who it might be? The carpet guy maybe?"

"Not the carpet guy," Rent said as his throat tightened and his eyes watered.

"You still there?"

Rent inhaled deeply. "Yeah, I'm here. Just trying not to drive over a cliff. I'm on Banner Grade, heading into Julian."

"So, man, woman, child?"

"It's the woman I interviewed last week, but this is unofficial and off the record at this time."

"Holy crap. So we now have a murder tied to the fraud case."

"I don't know that yet. They may not be related."

"Yeah, and the tooth fairy may be real."

"The cops are trying to contact her parents, who are in Arizona. They'll have to go to the morgue for the formal ID."

"Shit, that will take hours."

"I'll crank out the story and send it as soon as I get confirmation."

"We do have a deadline," O'Connor said and disconnected.

AS RENT REACHED THE top of the grade, he weighed his options. Would it do him any good to go to the morgue? *Waste of time. I could be there all night, waiting for Hannah's parents to show up.*

He went to the library instead. It would be a while before he heard from Alvarez, so he opened his laptop and checked his email as Pam had ordered. Among the more than a dozen new messages in the Inbox, he spotted the one from her, which she had sent that morning using her personal email. The Subject read: **DNA test results.** It had not only been sent to him, but also to the PI, who had collected the DNA samples, and Hannah.

Hannah? She's . . . of course, Pam didn't know that when she sent it. But when she spoke to me at the mine, she already knew about our relationship.

Rent swallowed hard, then clicked on it.

> Hey Alicia, Rent, Hannah,
> Sending this to give you a heads up. The formal DNA report will be released in another day or two, but I thought you should know what to expect so you're not blindsided. The lab found a match: As you suspected, Rachel's biological father is Regent Beacham.
> Congratulations, Dad. It's a girl.
> Pam

Rent felt the blood drain from his face. *Holy shit.* Even though he had anticipated it, the reality had not settled in. Until that moment.

He stared at the computer screen, trying to comprehend the implication of those few monumental words. He then noticed a reply from Alicia. She offered to go with Rent to break the news to Rachel. Rent clicked Reply and keyed in a quick response:

Hi, Alicia,
Two things: First off, I am sorry to have to report that Hannah is dead. Her body was found this morning, buried in rubble at an abandoned gold mine. This is off the record for now. The cops are waiting for a formal ID from her parents.
Second, thank you for the offer, but this is something I need to do myself. But first I have to find her. No one seems to know where she is. I'll let you know as soon as I learn anything new. Presumably she doesn't even know her mother is dead.
RB

Rent clicked Send, then hammered out a preliminary draft of the story and saved it to disc. If the cops didn't get an ID before his deadline, he'd have to keep Hannah's name out of it.

His phone beeped, announcing the arrival of a text message. He didn't recognize the number. He tapped the screen to open the message, which read:
Drop it or your a ded man

Christ, just what I need. Another death threat. He scoffed and muttered, "So when did Neanderthals learn to text? But I demean Neanderthals."

"What about Neanderthals?" a voice questioned.

Rent looked up. "Hey, Alice."

"You got a scoop on what all the commotion down the grade is about? Rumor is they found a body at one of the mines."

Rent nodded. "It's true."

Alice pulled out a chair and sat at the table beside the reporter. She leaned toward him and whispered, "Spill it."

"I don't have much at this point. It's the body of a female. Her identity has not been formally confirmed."

"They must have some idea, surely."

"They do, but they're not releasing any details until family members have been notified."

"Yeah, that makes sense," she said, then lowered her voice even more. "I was hoping it had to do with that carpet guy. Good riddance to bad rubbish." She straightened up. "How are things with you and Abby?"

"Good," he replied. "In fact, I think I'll go say hello right now."

"You two make a nice couple," she said with a wink. "Don't blow it."

Alice rose from the chair, pushed it under the table, and walked off. Rent closed his laptop and returned to the 4Runner. He wanted to see Abby, but he had to make another stop first.

He drove to the bookstore, parked, and went inside, seeking out the proprietor. She stood at the cash register, dealing with a customer.

When she finished, she greeted Rent and said, "Hannah's not here. She—"

Rent held up his hand. "I know, but I need to ask you something."

A look of concern crossed the woman's face. "Has something happened?"

Rent considered how to phrase his response. He looked around. Only two others in the store, and they were engaged in browsing the shelves.

He leaned across the counter and spoke in a low voice. "This cannot go any farther, for now."

The woman nodded. "Come around."

He joined her behind the counter and continued to speak in a hushed tone. "You probably heard the sirens."

She nodded.

"A body was found down the grade, by a mine in Chariot Canyon."

"Oh, my god. Not Hannah?"

"The body has not been formally identified, but it's possible."

"Oh, god, no," the woman exclaimed. Her eyes watered and tears began to streak her cheeks. She reached for a tissue in a box below the cash register and dabbed her eyes, then leaned against the edge of the countertop. Rent helped her into a nearby chair and squatted beside her.

"You cannot repeat this," he said. "The cops will not confirm it until family members have been notified. In a town like this, we don't need baseless rumors flying around like trucks in a tornado."

She sniffed and said, "I understand."

"But here's the thing and why I need your help. No one seems to know where her children are. Do you have any idea?"

She sobbed and shook her head back and forth in rhythm with her speech. "Oh, no, no, no, no!"

Rent took one of her hands in his and held it, remaining silent. With his empty hand, he offered her a clean tissue. After the woman had composed herself, she let go of Rent's hand and began to speak.

"Hannah told me that if something happened to her, to contact certain people. She was sending Rachel and Sammy to friends for safekeeping. As far as I know, she hadn't told anyone else."

"Not even her parents?"

"No. She was afraid they would be Gabe Turner's first stop if he somehow managed to track them down. She said she would explain it all later. That's the last time I heard from her."

"When was this?"

"Three days ago."

"And you have those names and phone numbers?"

She nodded. "Hannah said you were one of the people I should contact if something hap—"

The woman's voice cracked and she broke into sobs again. Rent took her hand in his but said nothing.

After taking a few deep breaths, she said, "I'll get it for you. It's in my desk in the office."

She rose and steadied herself with a hand on the checkout counter, then approached the two patrons. She explained that a family emergency had arisen and she was closing the store. They muttered conciliatory comments and made their way to the front door. She closed it behind them and locked it, and reversed the OPEN sign hanging in the door's window. She then motioned for Rent to follow her to the office.

She opened a desk drawer and withdrew an envelope, then extracted a piece of folded foolscap, which she handed to Rent. Written on the paper were the names, phone numbers, and addresses of two people, whom he judged to be women, based on their names. Below the first, Hannah had written "Rachel," and below the second, "Samuel."

"Do you know these people?" he asked.

The woman nodded. "Not well, but they come into the store occasionally. "The one has a son who is a friend of Sammy. The other, Martha, is older and she fosters kids and horses."

Rent set the paper down on the desk and took a photo of it with his cell phone. "I'll text this to the cops, and they'll get in touch with them," he said.

"What about Hannah's parents? I think they're—"

Rent held up a hand. "If the cops haven't notified them yet, they will soon and, presumably, her parents will soon be on their way to the morgue in San Diego to formally identify the body."

"Those poor people," the store owner said. "Such a sad situation. I hope they put that guy away for life."

"That guy?"

"That lowlife Gabe Turner. It's got to be him who did this."

"Why do you say that?"

"Who else would want to hurt her? She's the nicest person, but she got caught up in one of his schemes and . . ." Sobs blocked any additional words from the grieving woman.

Rent produced a business card and laid it on top of the message from Hannah.

"I'm sorry to be the bearer of such sad news. Do you have someone who could come and be with you so you're not alone?"

She nodded. "My husband; he works from home."

"And you think you can get home okay? Or do you want to call him?"

"I'll be okay. We just live over by the winery."

"All right," he said. "Again, I'm so sorry."

"I'll let you out," she said and led the way to the front door.

RENT GOT INTO HIS truck and stared at the bookstore, the CLOSED sign prominently displayed in the door window. He shook his head at the irony, then pulled out his phone and brought up the image of Hannah's message. He wondered if it was the last thing she had written before her life had been snuffed out. Apparently, Turner's threats were not just bluster after all, he being the presumptive perpetrator.

He knew he should forward the information to Washington immediately. But what if it wasn't accurate? He called the first number and a woman answered.

"May I speak with Rachel, please?" he said.

"And you are?"

"I'm a friend of Hannah's and I'm just checking on her daughter's whereabouts and to know she's safe."

"Has something happened? Has that S-O-B hurt Hannah?"

"There's been an incident. The sheriff's department will be in touch with you shortly. I've been assisting them in trying to locate Rachel, since no one seems to know where she's been for the past few days. Not even her grandparents."

"She's safe, I can assure you of that. But you still haven't told me who you are."

"It doesn't matter. As I said, someone from the sheriff's office will be in touch shortly. Thank you for your assistance."

With that, he ended the call and tapped in the second phone number. When a woman answered, he repeated what he had told the first woman. He then texted Detective Washington, attaching the photo of the names and contact information to his message. He also forwarded the death-threat text to the detective, then pondered his next move.

As he started the engine, his phone dinged. Alvarez:

We need to talk. 5 minutes.

He texted back, then drove to the four-way stop and turned right onto the 78, and a mile later turned onto Pine Hills Road.

I hope he's not home.

When Rent reached Gabe Turner's place, he did not see the Land Cruiser, so he parked a hundred yards down the road and waited for the phone call. He answered immediately.

"This is Sergeant Diana Alvarez," she stated formally, "with Detective Al Washington."

"Double teaming me, are you?" he replied.

"We have a few questions if you've got a minute."

"Absolutely."

"Do you have any idea who Rachel's father is?" she asked. "Hannah's mother said it's not Turner . . . or Turnbull. Whatever the heck his name is."

"Why are you asking me?"

"On the off chance. You did ID her, after all."

Rent thought for a moment. *Surely, they've heard about the DNA by now and want to see if I'll take the bait.*

"Hello? Are you there?" the sergeant asked.

"Yeah . . . sorry. Uh . . . no. Still waiting on the DNA test as far as I know." Only a half lie, he told himself, then continued. "Hannah mentioned some married guy she had a fling with, but I have no clue as to who he is. You've obviously talked to Hannah's parents. Maybe they know who it is."

Washington answered. "They're on the way to the morgue now. We're meeting them there."

"Are you picking Turner up?" Rent asked.

"Do you know something we don't?"

"He's ostensibly Hannah's boyfriend . . . was her boyfriend . . . and has told people he's Rachel's stepfather, although that's not actually the case. He must know something. And the fact that the body was found in the vicinity of his mining claim ought to raise some mighty big red flags."

"No shit, Sherlock," Washington said. "We have an APB out on him. We sent a deputy there. And he ain't."

"Yeah, I know. I'm parked just down the road."

"Don't try anything stupid."

"Don't worry. I know he's packin'. You got my texts, yes?"

"I'm contacting those people as soon as I'm done talking to you, and I'll get the geeks on the death threat. You've become quite popular."

"Apparently so," Rent replied. "Look, I'm going to file my story on the body found in the canyon as soon as you get a confirmation from Hannah's parents. Anything else you can tell me?"

Alvarez answered. "Only that the investigation is ongoing, and if anyone has any information about this to please contact the sheriff's office, either by phone or through the website. And if you could include the phone number and Web address, that would be helpful."

"Will do," he said.

"I know you won't wait, but we'll be issuing a formal statement as soon as we get confirmation on the ID. It'll include a comment from the sheriff. Or you can just make that up . . . as usual."

Rent groaned. "Give me a break. The entire news release will be the usual pedantic boilerplate. All you're going to do is change a few details regarding the victim."

Alvarez scoffed. "I'm off. Al, he's all yours."

Washington spoke. "You better not be holding anything back, Beacham, or I'll have your sorry hide. Bribe or no bribe. Capiche?"

"Al, you have everything I know, which is not much as far as this death goes. I hadn't seen Hannah since we were in college, and I sat in on the interview with the PI. I met Rachel for the first time at the bookstore two weeks ago and that's it. I have no idea where that girl is, if she's not with that woman. I suspect Turner could shed more light on that."

"Possibly," the detective replied. "I want you at the station first thing tomorrow morning. Maybe you can shed more light on the death of this woman as well, and your whereabouts at the time."

"This statement is just a formality, right? For elimination purposes."

"That remains to be seen. Meanwhile, you hear anything else, I wanna be the first to know about it.

"Understood."

"And make sure you spell my name right."

"Would that be your full name or will Detective Al Washington be sufficient?"

"Don't be a wise ass."

TIME FOR A DUMPSTER *dive.*

Rent grabbed a pair of gloves, got out of the 4Runner, and began walking to Turner's house. He stopped in his tracks and spun around.

Fuck it. I need to go see Rachel. Cops be damned.

He returned to his vehicle, then checked the time and changed his mind.

This shouldn't take long.

He put on the gloves as he went to Turner's place. He did a quick scan of the area, then lifted the lid on the trash bin.

I think I might puke.

He dropped the lid and looked about the yard. He spied a narrow piece of discarded lumber and used that to poke through the trash, periodically raising his head and turning away for gasps of fresh air.

"What have we here?" he muttered.

Using the stick, he moved some items and uncovered what looked like an EBT card. He pulled out his phone and clicked a few pictures, then dropped the lid and tossed aside the stick. He texted the photos to Washington and Alvarez.

He returned to his vehicle, put it in gear, and spun gravel as he accelerated onto the pavement. He drove up Pine Hills Road, not expecting Abby to be home either, which proved to be the case, but he parked in her driveway in the dappled shade of an oak.

He moved to the passenger seat, opened the draft of the story on his laptop, and banged out the rewrite in 15 minutes. He filed it, then called his editor, who already had the photos, although she said they weren't worth even a hundred words, let alone a thousand.

"Like I said in my text, I'll let you know about the ID confirmation as soon as I hear from the sergeant. Hopefully, it won't be much longer," Rent said.

"What about the fraud story? Any connection or anything new?" O'Connor asked.

"Jeez, I'm working on it. Or are you going to dump something else in my lap?"

She laughed and disconnected.

Rent returned to the driver's seat, started the engine, turned the vehicle around, and got back on the road, headed for Julian, destination Descanso. Rent called Abby while driving.

"I just left your house. How was the shopping?"

"Grand. I found a cute dress at the thrift shop. I don't think it's even been worn. I'm still at the Carmel Mountain mall and was about to go through the drive-thru at In-N-Out and I need to stop at the dry cleaners in Ramona and I need to do some laundry. Join me. You never did get to fondle my unmentionables. You just ripped them off me."

"Listen, this is serious. I need to talk to you, in private."

"Is it dead serious? Like having to do with the dead body?"

"This is no time for puns. What have you heard?"

"Alice texted me."

"No surprise there."

"She said someone found a body near Julian and she hoped it was Gabe Turner."

"It's not Turner, and that's the problem. You're gonna have to be careful. That's why I need to talk to you."

"Now you're scaring me."

"Just bear with me."

"Okay. My laundry can wait. I should be home in less than an hour, if I don't get stuck behind some pokey old fart in an RV on his way to the desert."

"Actually, you don't have to rush. I have an errand to run first. It could take me a couple of hours. If I'm not there by the time you get home, go wait at your office, and keep the door locked, or go to the library and stay with Alice until I get back."

"What the hell is going on?"

"The shit has hit the fan, that's what's going on. I just want you to be safe. I gotta run."

"Wait—"

20

Rent disconnected and tossed the phone on the passenger seat as he approached the four-way stop at Julian's Main Street. He turned right and had to force himself not to speed through town.

Damn it, I don't know where the hell I'm going.

He grabbed his phone and pressed the number he had called earlier—Martha Flanagan.

"Descanso Equine Rescue, may I help you?"

Rent hit the brakes. "You dumb ass," he muttered.

"I beg your pardon. Who is this?"

"Um . . . sorry, a jaywalking tourist just stepped out in front me. I'm Rent Beacham. I called you earlier about Rachel."

"Oh, yes. The sheriff's office called as well. They wanted to know if Rachel was here. I told them she was, but they didn't tell me anything else. Just that Hannah's parents were on their way. Has something happened to Hannah? We're getting worried because she hasn't been answering Rachel's calls."

"I'm on my way as well. Just leaving Julian," he said as he turned right onto SR 79. "But I need directions. I'm not familiar with Descanso."

"Are you sure this is okay?"

"I've known Hannah since we were in college together. We were more than just friends, if you catch my drift."

"She did mention you. You're the newspaper reporter, right? What's this all about?"

"I'll explain when I get there. Rachel's still with you, correct?"

"Rachel is out at the barn, talking to the horses."

"That's great. Directions, if you don't mind?"

"Take the 79 from Julian toward Cuyamaca . . ."

"On it now."

She gave him a few more details. He thanked her and said, "I'm driving a dark-green Toyota 4Runner."

Rent disconnected and pressed his foot harder on the accelerator, driving as fast as he dared, and hoping no slow-pokes got in his way. Only one vehicle slowed him up, and he crossed the double yellow to pass on an open space near Lake Cuyamaca, arriving little more than 20 minutes later.

He parked and approached the house. The front door opened and a woman stepped out. Rachel then burst through the doorway and ran up to Rent, her left arm in a sling. With her right hand, she held up her cell phone, the screen facing away from her so Rent could see it.

"Why didn't you come to see me before, you dirty bastard?" she shouted.

"Rachel, language," Martha scolded.

Rent looked at the screen. The email from Pamela Berringer regarding the DNA match.

"How did you—"

Rachel shoved the phone in a back pocket of her jeans, took another step forward, and wrapped her arms around Rent. He grasped her and held her tightly.

The woman stared at them, as if to say, what the hell?

"I knew it," Rachel said. "I knew you were my dad. We have the same eyes, the same nose, the same chin . . . I think. It's hard to be sure because of the beard. But I knew it. That's why I drew that picture. But my mom wouldn't . . ."

"Rachel," Rent said as he released her and slumped to a knee before her. "About your mom."

"Where is she? I've been trying to call for two days but she doesn't answer."

"There's no way to make this easy for you . . ."

Rachel stepped backward. "She's dead, isn't she? That bastard killed her, didn't he? That's why Grandma and Grandpa are coming to get me."

Rent stared into the girl's tear-filled eyes, then shifted his gaze to the woman, who stood frozen, her face horror stricken. He introduced himself and she identified herself as Martha Flanagan as they shook hands.

He then looked back to Rachel. "I'm so sorry to have to tell you this, but your mother has died. Some people found her body this morning. That's where I've been, and why I didn't get here sooner."

Rachel collapsed into Rent's arms again, her body wracked with sobs. He held her until her body went limp and she sagged to her knees.

"I hope he gets bit by a rattlesnake and dies a horrible death," she said.

Martha stepped up to them, placing a hand on a shoulder of each.

"Let's go inside where it's warm and get some refreshments."

She turned and walked toward the front door.

Rachel spoke again as she stood up, her words coming so fast they ran together. "I saw him do it. I saw him knock her down. Abby tried to stop him but she couldn't."

Rent interrupted her. "Wait. You were there? And Abby too?"

She nodded. "Uh-huh. He pushed my mom and she hit her head and I thought she was dead but then she woke up. She said she was fine. The next day she brought me here to keep me safe from that pervert, and she gave me the password to her email and your business card. Now I know why. He must have come back and finished her off, that dirty bastard."

"Is that when you hurt your arm?"

She looked at the arm in the sling. "No, this happened before. He did that, too. He pushed me down. It's not broken, just a bad sprain."

Rent stood, hugged the girl again, and said, "I'm glad to hear that. You can fill me in on the details later. Come on. Let's go inside."

As they walked toward the house, Rachel kept talking. "I was so happy when I saw that email and found out you were my dad, and now I'm so sad because my mom is dead," Rachel said. "Now she'll never know for sure."

"She knew," he said. "We discussed it when you were with your grandparents. That's when we agreed to do the DNA test. But when did you return home? And why?"

"The day before, so I could go to 4H and get the goat. But then she said I couldn't go because she was going to tell that private investigator everything and make sure Gabe was gone for good. Then he came to the house and—"

Rachel began sobbing again. Rent held her tightly until her body stopped quivering, and they resumed their walk. They entered the house and Martha beckoned them into the kitchen. She had homemade chocolate chip cookies on a plate, and a glass of milk poured for Rachel. The girl sat on a chair and picked up a cookie.

"Coffee?" she asked Rent. "Or something a bit stronger?"

"Actually, a glass of water would be fine," he said. "I can't stay long. I have to get back to Julian."

"Don't go. Please don't go . . . Dad," Rachel cried out.

Rent had reached for the glass of water, then froze for an instant at the word "dad," realizing his world had taken a sharp turn into uncharted territory.

"I'm sorry. I'll be back as soon as I can," he said, then added without hesitation, hoping he wouldn't regret it. "Tomorrow."

"Take me with you."

"Rachel, I wish I could, but I can't. I'm not officially your dad yet. I could be charged with abduction or kidnapping. I don't want to be an Amber Alert."

Rachel pouted for a beat, then offered a faint smile. "You'll come back tomorrow? You promise?"

"I promise."

"Pinky swear?"

He nodded and held out his right hand, extending his little finger. She did the same, and they locked their fingers together. "I swear," they said in unison.

The sound of car doors slamming shut drew their attention and a feeling of dread coursed through Rent's lanky frame.

Martha greeted the two visitors, a man and a woman who appeared to be in their mid- to late fifties, and invited them in. They introduced themselves as Fred and Agnes Powell, Rachel's grandparents.

Rent stood up as they entered the kitchen.

The woman stopped mid-step when she saw Rent. "What the heck are you—"

Rachel jumped out of her chair and stood next to Rent, as if protecting him, even though her head didn't reach his shoulder. "Grandma, he's my dad," Rachel said.

Agnes Powell, arms akimbo, looked at Rachel, then Rent, then back to Rachel. "No, he's not. I won't hear of such nonsense."

Rachel pulled her phone out of her pants pocket and expertly tapped the keyboard on its screen. She then stepped forward and showed the email to her grandparents. Agnes reached a hand into her purse, fumbling for her reading glasses.

"Darn it, they're here somewhere," she said.

She found the glasses and put them on, then bent over to view the screen. Her husband peered over her shoulder. She read the message in silence, her lips moving slightly, then straightened.

"It says it's only preliminary. I don't believe it. We'll get our own test."

Rent began to explain. "The preliminary refers to the email message, not the test—"

"You stay out of this," she said, cutting him off. "You've caused enough trauma to this family as it is."

He tried to protest, but Agnes again interrupted him.

"We already know who the father is, but as I said, we'll get our own test to prove once and for all that you are not her father." She then looked at Rachel and said, "You're coming with us, young lady, and no more of this foolishness."

"No, she's not," Martha Flanagan injected. Mrs. Powell stared at her in disbelief as Martha explained. "Hannah gave me explicit instructions, in writing, that Rachel is to stay with me until that Turner fella is behind bars, and the county has approved it."

Agnes tried to protest and Martha continued. "She was afraid that Gabe would track you down and take Rachel and possibly—probably—kill her if something happened to her. Which it now has."

"What?" both grandparents uttered in union.

Rent explained. "Rachel is a witness. She can incriminate him in Hannah's death. Without her testimony, the cops would have a harder time proving their case."

"Well, I never . . ." Mrs. Powell replied. "I'm going to call that detective back right now." She turned away and left the house.

The grandfather spoke. "Rachel, honey, do you feel safe here?"

Rachel ran to her grandfather and put her arms around him. "Yes, Grandpa, I do. Hardly anyone knows I'm here. And she's going to let me ride her new pony. I want to go riding with my dad." She turned at looked at Rent. "If he knows how to ride."

Rent's face flushed. "I suppose I could learn."

"No problem. I'll teach you, won't I, Martha. As soon as my arm heals."

Martha offered a dim smile and nodded. "I'm sure you will."

Agnes Powell returned and scowled. "This is not the end. We're going to initiate custody proceedings immediately. Come on, Frank, we've got phone calls to make . . . and a funeral to arrange, in case any of you have forgotten."

They said goodbye to Rachel and Martha, ignoring Rent, and left the house. As they drove off, Rent said he should go as well. He needed to wrap up and submit his story. And, keeping it to himself, thought, *and break the bad news to yet another person.*

Rachel, rivulets of tears again streaking her cheeks, gave Rent a long hug before letting go, then demanded his phone number. He recited his number and she entered it into her own device.

"That's a pretty nice phone you have there."

"I got it for my twelfth birthday."

Rent realized he didn't know her date of birth, but did a quick calculation in his head. "That wasn't long ago."

"January eighth."

"I play a fiddle tune called the Eighth of January. It—"

"It's about the Battle of New Orleans," she said. "I know all about it because I saw the YouTube video of you playing and singing it."

They began singing together Jimmy Driftwood's hit song: *In eighteen fourteen, we took a little trip, along with Colonel Jackson down the mighty Mississipp . . .*

Rent ran a finger across his lips as if zipping them closed. "I have to go, but we'll sing the whole song another time."

She hugged him again and made him reiterate his promise to return the next day.

As darkness descended, Rent texted Abby saying he was on his way. She responded, saying she was at the office. He drove back to Julian, again driving as fast as he dared.

As he entered the town, he glanced around, looking for any sign of Turner. Not seeing anything suspicious, he found a parking space near the real estate office and went to the door. He got no immediate response and raised a hand to bang harder when Abby appeared, creeping toward the glass door. Rent nodded to indicate it was safe. She opened the door and Rent stepped inside, then she closed and locked it.

"Let's go in back so no one can see us," he said.

Rent followed her into the back office, then she spun around.

"What, no hug?"

He hugged her and lightly touched her lips with his, then guided her to an office chair, where he motioned for her to sit as he leaned against the desk.

"You're scaring me," she said.

"Good. You need to be scared."

"So, no pillow talk."

"Not at the moment. That body they found? It's not just any dead body."

"Not Rachel—"

"It's not Rachel."

She exhaled in whoosh. "Thank god."

"It's Hannah."

The color drained from her face and her eyes glazed. Rent knelt and grabbed her before she slid out of the chair, and held her until she recovered. He found a bottle of water, opened it, and handed it to her. She swallowed a large gulp and stuttered a thank you.

After a moment to catch her breath, Abby shook her head. "It can't be."

"I couldn't believe it either, but it's true. I saw her for myself."

"Oh, how awful. Was she . . .?"

"Her body had been buried in a pile of mine tailings in Chariot Canyon, and with the cool weather, it had not decomposed a great deal. I recognized her immediately."

"Oh, my god, Rent! You identified the body? Does Rachel know? Her parents?"

He nodded. "The parents have been to the morgue and did the formal ID."

Abby put her face in her hands and began to weep. Rent pulled a tissue from a box on the desk and handed it to her. She dried her eyes and asked, "How did she die?"

"They won't know for sure until the pathologist does an autopsy and the medical examiner releases the report," he said, then paused, weighing how to respond. "She may have fallen and hit her head, or maybe someone struck her."

"Oh, shit. He must have come back. Was she . . . you know . . ."

"Raped?"

Abby nodded.

"She was fully clothed, so it doesn't appear so, but we won't know for sure until the autopsy is done. Some horseback riders saw turkey vultures gathering and investigated, and saw her foot sticking out of a pile of mine rubble. The sheriff's forensic team dug her out."

Abby sat staring straight ahead, struggling to breathe. He paced the floor as she regained her composure. She straightened up.

"So where's Rachel? Do you know?"

He nodded. "That was the errand I had to run. I just came from there. She's safe. She's with a friend."

"Who?"

"I can't say."

"Can't or won't?"

"Both. I've notified the sheriff's department and it's in their hands. The boy is safe too."

"Thank goodness for that. I feel so sorry for them."

"Why did you think it might be Rachel? And what did you mean when you said he must have come back?"

Abby sighed and again cradled her head in her hands. "That's what I've been wanting to tell you, but Hannah made me promise not to. She was afraid you'd go after Gabe and get yourself killed. It all goes back to the goat. Something happened," she said, then paused.

"And . . ."

"I could use a glass of wine, and it's a long story. Let's go to my place."

"Okay, but not for long. It's not safe." Abby gave him a puzzled look. "That's why I told you to come here. I thought Turner might come looking for you. Rachel told me what happened that night."

"But Hannah was alive when I left, and I spoke to her the next day."

"Yeah, I know. But she ended up in Chariot Canyon a day or two later. Only Turner can explain that, assuming he put her there. Come on. We need to get out of here."

Rent left the office and scanned the street again. No sign of Turner, so he motioned for her to come out. She locked the door, and he helped her into the 4Runner, then got in himself.

He drove at an even pace, still on the lookout for any sign of Turner. When they reached Abby's place, Rent found what remained of the wine from the previous night and poured her a glass. They seated themselves on the couch.

Abby sipped the wine, then inhaled deeply and began.

"A few weeks ago, not long after I met Gabe and still found him charming, I ran into him at Stater Brothers in Ramona. He had Rachel with him and introduced her to me as his daughter, and explained that it was his custody visit. This surprised me, because Gabe had never mentioned having any children. She's a cute kid and I complimented her on her hair and outfit. Rachel murmured a thank you but didn't say much, acting guarded. Gabe made a quick exit and I finished my shopping."

Abby had been speaking rapidly and became breathless. She drank more wine and a took few deep breaths before continuing.

"Later, after I'd gone out with him a couple times, I suggested that the three of us go on a picnic or an outing of some kind on Rachel's next custody visit. At first he said no, but I bugged him about it, and he finally agreed. I wondered what we could do. For sure not shopping—not with him along—so I mentioned the wolf sanctuary or the hawk watch, something outdoorsy. That's when he told me about the 4-H Club and that Rachel wanted a pony."

Another sip of wine and more deep breathing before continuing.

"So we went to a meeting. Gabe told her she couldn't have a pony, but she could get a baby goat. If she showed responsibility for the animal, then later on they could talk about a pony. She wasn't happy about it, but she reluctantly agreed and she selected a goat. She couldn't take it home that day, so we'd have to come back the following week. That was the day they never showed up."

"So something happened between those days," Rent said.

Abby nodded, then drank the rest of wine in one gulp. "Oh, Jesus, this is partly my fault. I should have . . ."

She choked up and began sobbing again.

Rent opened another bottle of wine and refilled her glass. He began to mix himself a gin and tonic, then thought better of it and made coffee instead.

We're gonna be at this for a while.

He rejoined her and handed her the wine. She readily took another big sip.

His phone chimed and he returned to the kitchen. Sgt. Alvarez following up. She formally confirmed the ID on the body.

"Yeah, I heard," Rent said.

"You heard?"

"I ran into the grandparents not an hour ago at Martha Flanagan's house."

"What—" She sighed and said, "I'm not even going to ask."

"I am curious how they got there so quickly."

"Turns out they weren't in Arizona after all. They were at the Oakzanita campground, which is between Julian and Descanso."

"That answers a number of questions."

"It doesn't answer one question."

"Yeah? What's that?"

"Where did you get that information about the kids?"

Rent remained silent.

"We need to know."

"Yeah, okay. I got it from the bookstore owner in Julian."

"And then you called them before sending us that information."

"I just wanted to confirm the information was accurate. It was virtually simultaneous."

"Uh-huh. You got anything else you're not telling us?"

"Not yet, but maybe. I'll know more later on. Right now I have a deadline. Are you issuing a statement?"

"Yeah, we'll have something soon, once it's been approved."

"Please send it to me soon as."

"You're on the distribution list and so is your boss."

"Thanks."

"Gotta go."

The call dropped. Rent poured himself a cup of coffee and rejoined Abby. "That was Sergeant Alvarez. It's now official," he said.

Abby shook her head. "This is so heartbreaking. I didn't know Hannah that well, but I love Rachel. Now, with her mother's murder, that will scar her for life, and she has no father to turn to."

Crap! How am I going to explain that? "Um . . . yeah, it's a sad situation. I haven't finished my story. Just give me a few minutes."

He had already brought in his laptop, which he opened up on the dining table. He did a quick scan of the draft, made some minor changes, and sent it to his editor. He then called her.

"I just sent you the story," he said when she answered. "The sheriff will issue a statement within the hour. If they say anything worth repeating, we can drop that in at the last minute."

"I'll handle it from my end," she said. "But keep your phone handy in case I have any questions."

"Will do."

"Thanks for the quick turnaround."

"I aim to please."

O'Connor chuckled. "That's not what I hear. Where are you?"

"I'm still in Julian."

"Give her my best."

Click.

Rent looked at his phone and shook his head.

He topped off his coffee, rejoined Abby, and prompted her to continue. "So that day at 4-H," he said. "What happened after Rachel agreed to take the goat?"

"She was all grumpy and in a pissy mood, and she didn't say a word on the way back here to drop me off. When we got here, Gabe got a phone call. It was a bit mysterious, because he moved far enough away that we couldn't hear him, so I'm pretty sure it wasn't about carpet cleaning. And I don't think it was his regular phone."

"You think he has two phones?"

Abby shrugged. "Maybe? I don't know."

"That would explain the anonymous death threats."

"Yeah, it would. Anyway, Rachel got out of the car and was standing by me. Out of the blue, she blurted out that Gabe was not her father, and not even her stepfather, that she didn't know who her father was, but that Turner spent a lot of nights at their house."

Abby went on to explain how she had started to pry more information out of Rachel but stopped when Gabe returned. Rachel stepped away, crossed her arms, and turned her back on Gabe. He looked from one to the other and his jaw tightened. Abby stiffened but remained silent. Gabe said something had come up and they had to go. Abby suggested Gabe leave Rachel with her and Gabe could tend to his business, then pick Rachel up afterward, or Abby would take her home.

"Gabe yelled at me," Abby continued. "He said, 'No, Rachel will do as she's told and go with me.' And he called me an 'interfering bitch.' Rachel refused to get back in his Land Cruiser, so Gabe yelled at her, demanding to know what she had said to me. He said, 'You better not be telling more lies!' "

Abby paused for a beat, then said, "Oh, god . . ."

"Did he hit her?" Rent asked.

Abby shook her head and went on, saying Rachel became defiant.

"I think she thought I couldn't hear her, and she said, 'What do I get this time if I keep my mouth shut?' "

Abby further recounted how Rachel told him she hadn't said anything, she and Abby were just talking girl stuff, because she had gotten her period. Gabe didn't believe her and he reached for her. She stepped away and shouted at him, saying that she knew what he was doing with those other men and that if he ever so much as laid another finger on her or her mother, she would call the sheriff.

Abby took another sip of wine before continuing. She said Turner grabbed Rachel by the arm and reached for her throat. Abby tried to get between them and get Rachel out of the way, but Rachel fell backward and screamed.

"I went to see if Rachel was all right," Abby said. "Gabe told me to stay out of it. He slapped me! I couldn't believe it."

"Oh, Christ," Rent replied.

She pulled a fresh tissue from the box on the coffee table and dabbed her eyes. He went to the kitchen and refilled his cup, then rejoined her and she continued.

"I got out my phone to call nine-one-one and he grabbed the phone and tossed it aside. He shook a finger at me and said, 'Don't you breathe a word of this to anyone or else.' I couldn't believe what had just happened. He was like Jekyll and Hyde."

Abby put her face into her hands and began crying again.

Rent consoled her, then asked, "That's when Rachel hurt her wrist?"

Abby nodded as she reached for another tissue to dry her eyes and wipe her nose.

"She said her wrist hurt and when I touched it, she cried out in pain."

"And then what did Turner do?"

"He just stood there, swearing at both of us, as if we had done this on purpose. I helped Rachel sit up so I could examine her. I told Gabe she needed medical care immediately and begged him to call nine-one-one. But he said, 'Fuck it. I'll take her to the fire station.' There's a fire station on Boulder Creek Road not far from Hannah's place. So, I helped her into the back of his SUV."

"And that's it? He drove off?"

"What are you saying, I should have done more?"

"Abby, I'm not blaming you for any of this. This is all his doing."

"It doesn't sound like it."

"I'm sorry, I can't help it."

"So, what, this is just another front-page story for you?"

"What? No. Not at all. I'm just trying to make sense of it and figure out what happened and how her mother ended up being treated like a piece of garbage by that piece-of-shit slimeball."

"Gabe took off down the road with her. The next day, in the evening, I went to Hannah's house to see if Rachel was all right. She had a soft cast that went from her hand to her elbow, and her arm was in a sling. She said her wrist wasn't broken but badly sprained."

Abby sobbed again.

"What is it?" Rent asked.

"Gabe was there and it got ugly. He started yelling at Hannah, accusing her and Rachel of telling lies about him and if they didn't stop, they might not live to tell about it."

"Rachel was there?"

She nodded. "He then made fists and acted like he was going to punch Hannah. I tried to intervene and push them apart. Hannah stepped backward. I guess she tripped, or maybe Gabe pushed her and she fell. She hit her head on the corner of the kitchen counter. It knocked her out and I ran to her. Thankfully, she regained consciousness. She got up and then sat down at the table. I got her some water and told Gabe to get the hell out of there."

"Did you offer to take her to—" Rent began to ask.

"Of course, I did," she said, defensive. "What do you take me for, some heartless nincompoop?"

"No, I just—"

"I wanted to take her to urgent care in Ramona, but she refused. I told her I'd check in with her the next day and left. That was last time I saw her or spoke to her. The only call I got was from Rachel, a couple of days ago. She wanted to know if I'd seen her mother. I was with a client, so I couldn't talk."

"Abby, you have to tell this to the authorities. They're going to ask you more questions than I am. But it sounds like that incident led to Hannah's death, if not directly, then indirectly."

"I'll be arrested . . . as an accessory or something."

"No, you're a witness," Rent said. "But to be credible, you need to tell them what you saw and heard, clearly and distinctly. You got in a scuffle with Turner while trying to protect Hannah; she fell and hit her head. It's not your fault. It's that slimeball's fault. And you had no involvement in what happened after that."

"But I didn't say anything when they went missing. I just believed the bullshit Gabe was shoveling. Or at least I wanted to believe it."

"What about the other night?"

"What do you mean?"

"When Turner was yelling at you? Alice told me that she saw him confront you at your office. What was that all about?"

"Have you been spying on me too?"

No, I've been worried about you, and so has Alice. Worried that that psycho would hurt you. Or worse. He's been threatening you, hasn't he?"

She nodded. "He told me he would kill all of us if—"

"You, Hannah, and her kids?"

"Yeah. And I believed him. He has a pistol, you know."

"I am well aware of that."

"But I didn't know what happened. He said they had gone away to stay with Hannah's parents in Arizona. But I thought maybe he kidnapped them and was trying to extort money from Hannah's parents. They had been wanting both Rachel and her brother to live with them, but especially Rachel, until Hannah could get her shit together and get that asshole out of her life. I can't believe I got suckered by him. Then he held all that stuff over me. Threatened to kill me if I didn't keep my mouth shut."

She began sobbing again. Rent put an arm around her and pulled her to him. She leaned her head against his chest.

"That's what guys like him do," he said. "The man's a sociopath. Maybe a psychopath. He preys on vulnerable people, and once they're involved, like Hannah and this fraud scheme, he holds that over them so they don't go to the cops. Then Rachel gets hurt and that compounds the situation. Rachel said her mom changed her mind and was going to tell the PI what Turner was up to. That's why you need to be careful. And so do I for that matter."

"The death threat on your windshield," she mumbled.

"That, and today I got another anonymous text."

"Have they arrested him?"

Rent shook his head. "The sheriff has an APB out on him, but as far as I know he's still at large. They're probably ransacking his place right now, or they will be as soon as they get a warrant. The EBT fraud is one thing; murder and disposing of the body is something else entirely."

"Murder?"

Rent drank from his coffee cup before replying. "Well, it might be manslaughter. Even if it's ruled involuntary it will mean jail time for the perp, if that can be determined. Who knows what Turner will say to explain away what happened. He will no doubt try to blame you and Rachel. That you were still there after he left."

Abby straightened up and glared at Rent. "Me?"

"Look, I'm not accusing you. I'm just saying the cops will look at it from every angle. Everyone somehow involved is a person of interest, if not a suspect, until they can provide a viable alibi. Hell, I might even be a suspect. And you know that if Turner did this, he will try to weasel out of it. That means pointing his finger at anyone he can. Me, you. Who knows, maybe he got those goons he hangs out with to do his dirty work. But until the cops have turned over every rock, they're not going to rule out anyone."

Abby began sobbing, head in hands. Rent again put an arm across her shoulders and pulled her close. "I'll do everything I can to help you. But you really need to talk to the authorities and tell them what you know. If you need an alibi for any time we were together, I will provide that. I'll give a statement to the cops about the incident at the restaurant. And I'm sure Alice will tell them all she knows."

She sat up, fear etching her face. "You're not going to splash my name all over the front page like you do for your other articles, are you?"

He shook his head. "No. Besides, I doubt I'll be writing any more stories about Hannah's death. I probably will have to recuse myself, as the saying goes. It's not my beat anyway. One of my co-workers will handle it. But I will stay on the fraud story, at least as long as they are treated as separate investigations."

"I need another drink. How about you?"

Rent glanced at his nearly empty coffee cup. "Wouldn't hurt."

Abby went to the kitchen and set out bottles of liquor. When Rent joined her, she said, "Pick your poison."

Abby mixed herself a martini, Rent a gin and tonic.

"Here's to nothin'," she said and raised the glass to her lips. "Mmm, just what I needed."

She set down the glass and opened a bag of tortilla chips and a jar of salsa, and set them on the dining table. They sat down, sipped their drinks, and devoured the hors d'oeuvres.

"I suppose we should be having margaritas with these chips. Or tequila shots," she said.

"I've got a long drive on a road that has more twists than a pretzel."

"No, you don't. You're staying here . . . as my bodyguard."

"I don't know that you're safe here. Come with me."

"I have a shotgun. And I know how to use it."

"You have to sleep sometime."

"We'll take turns."

"Then we'd better cork these bottles and make more coffee."

21

The near-sleepless night passed without incident. Rent called Sgt. Diana Alvarez to tell her about Abby's encounter with Gabe Turner.

"I'm coming in to give a statement anyway, and she can come with me. But I think its apparent that this is all Turner's doing. He threatened to kill Abby, and Hannah and her children, if she said anything."

"That seems to be his MO, threats of violence and death," she said. "But we can't jump to conclusions. We need evidence. That's why we need to talk to everyone who had any involvement with Hannah Stapleford, including you and your girlfriend."

"I understand, but we will not put up with any bravado from Washington or others using the Reid technique, trying to wring confessions out of us. I have a lawyer on speed dial."

Alvarez laughed. "Why does that not surprise me in the least."

"Do you think Hannah may have been involved in the fraud, but only due to coercion?"

"That remains to be seen. Right now we're focused on her death. Meanwhile, I want you and Abby here A-sap."

"See you in about an hour. Abby's getting cleaned up."

Rent disconnected, then called his editor.

"So the wayfaring stranger lives," Janis O'Connor said in greeting. "How're things out there in the land of woe?"

"I'm on my way to the sheriff's office."

"Good. Maybe they will give you something more than that bland boilerplate they gave us yesterday."

"That's not why I'm going there. I'm being questioned as a material witness."

"What the—"

"I'll fill you in later. It's all a formality, but it also involves the woman I've been seeing, so . . ."

"Oh, for Pete's sake."

"On the bright side, this could break the fraud case wide open."

"How's that?"

"I have a hunch Turner is going to get desperate and do something really stupid, and I suspect the cops are going to find the evidence they need when they tear apart his place and Hannah's."

The editor sighed. "Okay, come see me when you're done at the sheriff's."

RENT TOOK ABBY INTO town to retrieve her Jeep, and they drove in separate vehicles to the San Diego County Sheriff's Department headquarters in its namesake city. While they sat in the reception area, waiting to be escorted to interview rooms, Rent gave Abby the number of his lawyer acquaintance, A.J. Hawke, Esq.

"Andrew is the best defense attorney in town. If these guys start giving you a bunch of shit, or especially if for some reason they Mirandize you, you zip it and call him."

Abby looked horrified. "Mirandize me? I haven't done anything."

"I know, but when they catch up with Turner, he will no doubt feed them a bunch of BS and try to implicate you and even me."

"But wouldn't that be hearsay? I watch *Law & Order*, you know."

Rent chuckled. "Yeah, you and millions of others. Forget that. This is the real world, but I doubt they're going to give much credibility to what Turner says at this point."

A deputy entered the reception area and directed them to separate interview rooms. Abby gave Rent a baleful look as she entered Interview Room 1.

"You'll do fine," Rent said, as if trying to reassure himself as much as Abby.

He entered the next room on the corridor and took a seat as directed. While he waited, he looked at his phone, wondering if he should make a pre-emptive call to the lawyer.

Nah, he's probably in court. No point in bothering him unless things get dicey.

Nearly thirty minutes passed before Detective Al Washington entered the room, accompanied by a man Rent had never met, and they both sat opposite Rent.

"Well, well, well," Washington began. "How's it feel to have the shoe on the other foot, Mr. Interrogative Journalist?"

"Cut the crap, Al, and get on with it. We should be out of here in a matter of minutes. Who've you got riding shotgun?"

"This is Detective Dick Ogilvy. He's one of our FNGs."

"FNG?" Rent inquired.

"Fuckin' New Guy," Washington said with a grin. "Dick, meet Mr. Regent Beacham, investigative journalist par excellence. Or so he would have you believe."

Ogilvy gave only a slight nod of acknowledgement.

"Can we cut the charade and get on with this?" Rent said.

"What's your hurry? We've got all day. Oh, that's right you probably have a deadline. In that case, I guess we'd better get started."

"Anything new on Hannah's death or are you still waiting on the ME?" Rent said.

Washington leaned forward, resting on his elbows. "You're forgetting that I ask the questions in here, not you."

"As I told Alvarez, I have a lawyer on speed dial. Do I need to make that call? Where is she, by the way?"

"As if it's any of your business, she's next door, observing and no doubt handing out Kleenex to your weepy-eyed girlfriend."

"My weepy-eyed girlfriend, as you so eloquently phrase it, also has my lawyer on speed dial. You treat her nicely, or she's going to sic A.J. Hawke on you."

Washington rolled his eyes. "Okay, enough tit for tat. Remind me, why are you even here?"

"As if you don't recall. You instructed me to come in and make a formal statement about how I know the deceased and provide any material information I may have regarding her death. In addition, I am romantically involved with the weepy-eyed woman in the next room, who is also making a statement about her relationship with the deceased and her daughter, as well Mr. Magic Carpet Cleaner Gabe Turner, a suspect in the EBT fraud case you and I have been investigating."

Washington nodded at his companion, who started the recording device and said, "Please state for the record your full name, age, address, and occupation."

Rent did as instructed and told the detectives about how he had met Abby Wilburforce, Gabe Turner, Hannah Stapleford, and Rachel Powell. He also told them about the coyote incident and the confrontation at the restaurant, followed by the death threats. He did not tell them about his confrontation with Turner at the man's house, but he did summarize Abby's account of Rachel's injury and how that may have precipitated Hannah's death.

"And that was an accident, at least where Abby's concerned. You want to pin an assault on Turner, be my guest," Rent concluded.

Washington flicked his eyebrows. "That may be up to a jury to decide."

"Oh, for chrissakes, Al, you're not even close to putting this anywhere near a jury, so don't lay that shit on me. Until you bring in Turner, this case is going nowhere. How's that going, by the way?"

"You're forgetting something."

Fuck. Does he know about me going to Turner's place? Rent thought before asking, "And that would be?"

"Your relationship with Hannah Stapleford," Washington said. "You've got two girlfriends in the middle of this oh-so-tangled web. And we found your business card in the dead woman's back pocket."

Rent breathed a shallow sigh of relief. "You know damned well—"

"For the record," injected Ogilvy.

"For the record . . . Hannah, then Hannah Powell, and I dated briefly while we were in college. That was years ago. I never saw her during the intervening years. Not until I ran into her at the bookstore in Julian two weeks ago."

"And?" Washington asked.

"And I saw her again the morning that I and the private investigator, Alicia Velasquez, interviewed her as part of the county's fraud investigation. An interview in which her identity was not disclosed to me until I arrived on her doorstep and she wanted to know what the hell I was doing there. So now who's being obfuscational?"

"Is that even a word?" Washington asked.

"Oh, for fuck's sake, Al, you're not just grasping at straws here, you're breathing noxious fumes, which obviously have clouded your otherwise sound judgment."

"Flattery will get you nowhere. Where were you on the days following the altercation between Hannah Stapleford and the man known as Gabriel Turner?"

"Is this a joke? I have any number of people who can provide me with an alibi for those days, including you and other members of the sheriff's department staff." Rent pulled out his phone and said, "Lawyer time?"

Washington sighed. "Look, I'm just doing my job here, okay? You know the drill."

"Actually, I don't know the drill. I've only seen it on *Midsomer Murders*, which, according to cops, is the least accurate crime show on TV. And in that show and others like it, the first arrest the cops make is always the wrong person."

Washington looked at Ogilvy and rolled his eyes again as Rent continued. "As far as I'm concerned, you're just confirming the negative stereotypes hyped up by the defund the police mob."

"All right, you can go," Washington said. "But don't go far."

"Oh, I'll be heading straight to my office from here. You know where to find me."

"Raking muck, no doubt."

Detective Ogilvy leaned close to Washington and whispered into the man's ear. Washington nodded and said to Rent, "One more thing. It'll only take a minute."

Rent glared and motioned with his hands, palms up, as if to say, what now?

"D-N-A," Washington said and gave a sideways nod to his partner, who left the room.

"For what purpose?"

"For elimination purposes. You were close to the body, practically touched it, and you visited her, possibly on the day she died. There could be DNA residue on her clothing, or even her body," he said, raising his eyebrows for emphasis.

"Jesus Christ. I already gave DNA to Alicia Velasquez, the PI, and you've probably seen the report by now."

"That's a separate investigation. Just humor me."

Rent sighed. "Whatever."

Ogilvy returned with a DNA kit and swabbed the inside of Rent's cheek.

"See, that wasn't so difficult was it," chided Washington.

"Are we done?"

Washington nodded. The men stood and moved toward the door.

"Question," Rent said.

"Back in reporter mode now are we?"

"Always. What about Abby?"

"What about her?"

"How much longer you gonna to keep her? I can't imagine she has much more to say."

"That's not for you to decide."

"Well, as I said . . ." Rent held up his phone. "Speed dial, if it comes to that . . ."

Washington humphed in reply and said, "Go on, get outta here, Br'er Rabbit."

"I'll take that as compliment," Rent said and returned to the reception area. A middle-aged woman and young man sat in a corner, the woman weeping and the man consoling her. He took a seat at the opposite end and drummed fingers on a thigh as he glanced around the room.

Even my dentist has better reading material than this place.

He went outside and called his editor with a brief update. "I'm going to hang around here a little longer, then I'll be in."

He went back inside, took a seat, and scrolled through a news-feed on his phone, ignoring the never-ending tittle-tattle of presidential politics. The Associated Press had repurposed his story about the discovery of Hannah's body, and it had been picked up by news outlets nationwide.

"Makes for sensational headlines: Mystery surrounds death of 32-year-old white female in remote area of San Diego County," he muttered.

His phone chimed, alerting him to a new email. For an instant, he felt as if he were staring at a ghost. The sender's name read: Hannah Stapleford. He shook his head to clear the thought, realizing it had come from Rachel, using her deceased mother's account. It read:

When are you coming to see me?

He replied, explaining that he was at the sheriff's office and would come to see her as soon as possible.

Forty minutes later, the interior door opened and Abby stepped through, red-eyed, followed by Sgt. Diana Alvarez. Rent stood up and Abby ran to him, collapsing into his arms. They embraced for what seemed like an interminable moment. Rent looked over her shoulder and caught the sergeant's eye, arching his eyebrows in a silent question.

Alvarez nodded and said, "Take her home."

Abby released her grip on Rent and took a step back. "They're letting me go, for now, but will likely question me again, once they have Gabe in custody."

"Okay, let's get outta here," he said and flicked a nod at the sergeant. Then he noticed Washington standing in the doorway. Their eyes met, but they exchanged no words.

Rent led Abby out the main entrance and into the parking lot. She began breathing heavily, gasping for air.

"You're hyperventilating," he said. "Come sit in my truck."

"I need to go home."

"You're in no condition to drive to the nearest In-N-Out, let alone to Julian. Besides, your home is not safe."

He grasped her arm and led her to his truck, opened the passenger side door, and eased her into the seat.

"Buckle up," he said and went to the opposite side and got in.

"What about my car?" she wondered.

"What, you don't think it'll be safe parked at the sheriff's office for a few hours?"

She glared at him. "You don't have to be a smart ass about it."

"Yeah, sorry. Just trying to lighten the mood."

"It's not helping. Where are you taking me?"

"To my place. I live just a few minutes away. You can unwind there, take a nap, whatever, while I go to the office. When I get back, we can decide what to do from there."

She inhaled deeply, then exhaled in a heavy sigh. "Okay." She shook her head. "What a fucking ordeal. You'd think I caused that poor woman's death, the way they bullied me. They even made me give a DNA sample."

"Yeah, me, too, but let's not dwell on that right now."

"I did learn something new."

"Oh, yeah?"

"Gabe's name is not Gabriel Turner. It's an alias. His real name is Joshua Gabriel Turnbull."

Rent said nothing as he put the truck in gear. Abby cast him a questioning look.

"You don't seem surprised," she said. When he didn't reply, she added, "You already knew that."

Rent nodded.

"But you couldn't be bothered to tell me?"

"I could not divulge it because it might jeopardize the investigation, and because I was afraid it might get you killed."

"So, you were going to tell me this when?"

"Look, if word got back to him that we knew his true identity, he'd skedaddle, causing a big setback in the investigation. And if you confronted him, who knows what he might have done. You need to keep this to yourself until he's in custody. I'm glad you heard it from them first. They're probably trying to scare you."

"They succeeded."

Rent drove to his condo at the North Rim complex off of Linda Vista Road and parked in the garage. He led Abby up the stairs to the main floor and into the kitchen.

"Sorry about the mess," he said. "I wasn't expecting company."

Abby glanced around. "It looks better than I expected . . . for a bach pad."

"Now who's being the smartass?"

"Tit for tat, Jack Sprat."

"See? You're feeling better already," he said and led the way through the L-shaped kitchen to the living/dining area and motioned toward the couch.

"Have a seat. Do you want anything? Water? Coffee? Something stronger?"

"Water's fine."

"Hungry?"

"Maybe."

Rent put ice cubes in a glass and filled it with water from a gallon bottle in the refrigerator, then handed it to Abby, who thanked him.

"There's stuff for a sandwich, or scramble some eggs, if you want something to eat."

"I think I'm just going to curl up here and die," she said, then shivered, as if a gust of frigid air had passed through the room.

Rent reached for a fleece Sherpa blanket sporting a Native American motif lying over the backrest of the couch. He shook it out and put it around Abby's shoulders.

"This'll keep you plenty warm. The heating system sucks in these units."

She lifted her face and, with a pleading tone to her voice, said, "You're leaving right now?"

"Yeah, I need to get the office. It's a daily grind, so to speak."

"Can't they give you a break for one day after what you've been through?"

"Who's says I want a break? I live for this."

Abby stared at him for a long moment, then shook her head. "Okay, go. Get out of here. I'll try to sleep."

RENT WENT STRAIGHT TO his editor's desk and she motioned for him to pull up a chair.

"How'd it feel to be on the other end of the interrogation," O'Connor asked.

Rent shrugged. "I gave as much as I got. They put Abby through the wringer though."

"Abby?" she questioned, her fingers framing the word in air quotes.

"Abigail Wilburforce, with the real estate office and of the scene at the restaurant."

"Oh, yes. How is she involved?"

"She had befriended the twelve-year-old daughter, who went missing, and there was an incident involving the dead woman's sometimes boyfriend, who also just happens to be the prime suspect in the woman's death."

"And this is the same Abigail with whom you are just a wee bit romantically involved, if the office gossip has any merit to it."

"Naomi Baloney whispering behind my back again, is she?"

"I'm no snitch."

"Yes, we've seen each other a few times."

"And you were once romantic with the dead woman."

"What are you driving at? I came in to follow up with the sheriff's office and see what the ME has to say about the cause of death, and any revelations from the forensics."

"Naomi Baloney, as you so eloquently phrased it, is taking care of that. It's her beat anyway. The TV stations are all over the story and now want interviews. You've become part of the story."

"Yeah, I've been getting texts."

"You can't be writing about it, too."

"All I did was make the preliminary ID."

"And how could you do that? Because you had played tootsy-wootsy with her."

"More than a decade ago. Jeez. Why does everyone make a big deal about that?"

"Besides, you have your hands full with the fraud story, as long as this Abby woman has no involvement in that."

Rent shook his head. "No, she does not."

"Naomi will want to talk to her if what you're saying is true."

"No."

"What do you mean, no? Do you hear yourself? You'd be all over this if you weren't so close to it. That's why I've given it to Naomi. You know how it works in this biz."

"Yeah, yeah, save the sermon for the choir."

"Do you think she'd be willing to talk to Naomi?"

"I doubt the cops will like it. Their prime suspect is still at large, and they're treating her as a person of interest."

"Okay, but if the cops clear her, she's open game."

"I want to be there."

"Oh, for chrissakes, grow up," the editor said. "What's the status of the fraud story?"

"I need to catch up. I got sidetracked by this other thing."

O'Connor waved him off. "Hop to it."

Rent went to his desk and checked the messages on his land line and email. Rod Davis from HHSA had called several times, as did a few TV reporters. He blew off the TV folks but called Davis with an update.

He opened an email from the PI. She invited him to go on another stakeout, this time to Fallbrook, "tomorrow morning."

Crap. Another early start. I'll take the bird book to look authentic.

She also wrote that, based on the license plates, the guys with the vehicles at Turner's place were possibly neo-Nazis suspected of criminal activity, but she gave no details. He replied with a "Yes!"

Naomi Clark entered the newsroom and beelined to Rent's desk.

"I want to talk to your girlie friend. What's her number? I'm sure you have it memorized by now," she said.

"With cell phones, we no longer need to remember phone numbers," he replied without looking up.

"Okay, smarty pants, FAVORITES then."

Rent swiveled in his chair and faced her. "My 'girlie friend' is off limits."

"Says who?" Clark snapped back.

"Says the cops. They've got her on a short leash. Go talk to O'Connor, if you want."

"What about Washington?"

"He's all yours, and I imagine he'd prefer it."

"Oh, yeah? Burn that bridge, too, did you?" she said.

"Actually, no," Rent replied. "We're best buds these days. Going over to Nate's for beer and barbecue any day now."

"Not what I hear."

"'Oh, yeah?"

"I hear you spent the better part of an hour across the table from him getting grilled like shrimp on the barbie."

"So what?" Rent responded. "I have no involvement in that woman's death other than making the preliminary ID. End of story. It's the magic carpet guy you should be talking to . . . if you can find 'im. Because . . ." Rent snapped his fingers. "Shazam . . . he's flown away."

"Very funny," she countered. "Any word on who the father of the daughter might be? The cops are trying to track him down."

Rent hesitated before answering and she looked at him askance.

"Yeah, I know, but why?" he replied. "Rachel doesn't know who he is and Hannah refused to say. Maybe she didn't even know."

"I doubt that," Clark said. "What is it you're not telling me?"

Rent stared at her. "They're doing some DNA testing. That's all I can tell you at this point."

"Well, at the very least the guy has a right to know. And you know how the cops work. Cast a wide net for elimination purposes. What if the guy found out and approached her, and he and Hannah had a scuffle and . . ."

"That's a very big *if*," Rent replied. "The most likely perp is Gabe Turner, the carpet cleaner and con man extraordinaire. Plus the fact that that those horseback riders found the body in a pile of mine tailings near his mining claim."

"It wasn't at his own mine then?"

Rent looked at her in disbelief. "He's not *that* stupid."

Clark shrugged. "Crooks generally are not the sharpest tools in the toolchest. Many a dull chisel out there. Any idea where he might be?"

"I have a pretty good idea where's he not. I imagine the cops have his place in Julian pretty well under wraps. I suspect he's with his pals in Fallbrook or Riverside County somewhere. I'm going on a stakeout with the PI again tomorrow. Try to connect a few more dots."

"If you get anything relevant to the murder, let me know."

"Do I hear a 'please'?"

She sighed. "Please! And you do the same . . . please!"

"You got it. But it's not a murder for certain, is it," Rent said. "Or has the ME released his report?"

"Not yet," she said, spun away, and crossed the room to her desk.

Rent grabbed his cell phone and laptop and headed for the exit, giving a wave of goodbye to his editor. As he exited the building, he caught movement in his peripheral vision.

Oh, shit.

A man strode toward him at a rapid pace, an object held out before him in his right hand, followed by a second man holding a larger black object, aimed at Rent.

"Fuck me," he muttered and continued walking toward his truck, knowing he could not get there before being intercepted.

"Rent, Rent Beacham," the first man called out

Rent sighed and stopped as the man drew near. Rent reached into his coat pocket and turned on his recorder. The first man pushed a microphone toward Rent's face as the second man arrived with a video camera aimed at Rent.

"Mr. Beacham, isn't it true you're now being investigated in the death of Hannah Stapleford, the woman whose body you identified this morning in Chariot Canyon?"

"I'm on deadline," he replied and, looking directly into the camera, added, "and don't have time for your bullshit." He then continued on toward his truck.

"Why do you bother? No one reads newspapers anymore," the TV reporter yelled at Rent's back.

Rent stopped and did a pirouette. "You do."

The man caught up with Rent. "What do you mean?"

"Everyone morning in the newsroom, you and your producers go through the morning papers looking for stories to sensationalize that evening. Why don't you go back to selling used cars?"

Rent heard the cameraman chuckle at his retort.

"And you never watch TV news," the reporter insisted.

"I like watching the Barbie dolls in low-cut, skin-tight dresses giving the weather forecasts," Rent replied.

The reporter extended his arm, again holding the microphone close to Rent's chin. "Isn't it true, Mr. Beacham, that you are now considered a suspect in the sheriff's murder investigation? And isn't it true that you had a prior relationship with the deceased woman and may have even fathered her child? Isn't it true that you're a deadbeat dad?"

Rent looked directly into the camera. "Isn't it true, Mr. Fuckwit, that you've been cheating on your wife and fathered a bastard child?"

"You motherfucker!"

Rent pulled the recorder out of his pocket. He showed it to the reporter and the cameraman. "Caught on tape. Exclusive: News at Ten."

He turned and continued walking toward his truck. He could sense the camera recording his every step, and he heard the reporter say, "We got what we needed. Let's go."

As Rent pulled his keys out of a pants pocket, he heard another voice calling his name. He sighed and ignored it.

"It's me, Dan," the voice called again.

Rent stopped at this truck and turned around. Dan Rowland joined him.

"You can't get a break, can you?" Rowland said. "The feminine faction in the newsroom and rabid TV reporters in the parking lot. You need a calm sail on the bay. Join us this weekend."

"Us?"

"Me and Greg."

"Greg doesn't go near the water. He practically lives at Rose's Donuts."

Dan shook his head. "You'd be surprised. He's actually a pretty good trimmer."

Rent flicked his eyebrows. "Who knew?"

"Join us? It'll do you good to relax, have a few beers. Tune out the big bad world for a few hours."

"I'll let you know. Right now, I'm up to my eyeballs in muck and it needs some serious raking to clean it up.

RENT STOPPED AT THE Roundtable Pizza on Friars Road for takeout and continued on home. There he parked in the garage and sprinted up the stairs, then stopped abruptly as he entered the kitchen.

"Oh, fuck."

He took it in at a glance. The sink sat empty of dirty dishes and cookware, and the dishwasher hummed. The spotless countertops gleamed. Only one object drew his attention. *Is that wine bottle half empty or half full?*

He set the pizza box on the countertop and continued on through to the living area. Abby lay blanketed on the couch, her breathing barely audible. The paper clutter on the dining table had been straightened and stacked neatly, leaving a clear space for working or eating. He set down his laptop and phone.

Welcome to domesticity. I dread what I might find upstairs.

He tiptoed across the room and up the stairs in measured steps. He checked the bedroom. *Thank god.* The bed looked as he had left it:

unmade. Dirty clothes remained on the floor, in a corner by the closet. In the bathroom, a toothpaste tube still sat on the edge of the sink.

Surely, she took a peek though.

He descended the stairs as quietly as possible, but as he crossed the living area toward the dining room table, his phone chimed and Abby stirred. He picked up the phone, the screen displaying "PI."

He swiped it to answer and said, "Alicia, hi," as he stepped into the kitchen and spoke just above a whisper. "Can we make this quick? I'm in the middle of something here. Or I can call you back in an hour or so."

"Regarding the stakeout tomorrow, Davis got a tip from Riverside. Come-to-Jesus meeting at Fallbrook. Be at my place at five a.m."

"Text me your address."

"On its way."

He disconnected as he heard a voice from the living room.

"Rent? Is that you?"

"Hi, honey, I'm home," he sing-songed and went to join Abby.

She laughed as he approached her. She threw off the blanket, sat up, and rubbed the sleep out of her eyes.

"I guess I nodded off. What time is it?"

"Time to eat. I brought a pizza. And thanks for cleaning up, but that wasn't necessary."

"What else was I going to do? And I helped myself to some wine. I hope you don't mind. Then everything just sort of overwhelmed me and I collapsed on the couch."

Rent returned to the kitchen, grabbed a pair of plates and eating utensils, and took them to the table. "Come on, while it's still warm." He fetched the pizza and set it on the table.

Abby joined him and lifted the lid on the box. "Oh, yum. You remembered."

"More wine?" he offered.

She shook her head. "Water's good."

He refilled her glass with ice and chilled water, and poured himself a glass of the Syrah. They sat down and each one selected a slice of pizza. Abby asked him about his office visit. He told her he's no longer on the story about Hannah.

"And as I left, I got ambushed in the parking lot."

"Oh, no. Are you all right?"

He told her about the TV reporter trying to bait him with leading questions. "I can just imagine how creative the editing will be," he said.

Abby nodded as she raised another slice to her mouth, then blurted out, "Oh-my-god, my car. It's still at the sheriff's."

"Eat first, then I'll take you. You can stay here. I'll change the sheets."

"I . . . go . . . ome," she mumbled over a mouthful of dough, pepperoni, and cheese.

"It's not safe."

She swallowed and replied, "I have a shotgun."

"And that went so well last time."

"Besides, I have to feed the deer."

"Oh, yes. Your pet deer."

"And I have to go to work. I'll keep the shotgun within reach at all times. I'll be prepared."

"I thought your boss said you can have the rest of the week off."

"Yeah, and I lose out on a potential sale."

"Money's more important than your life?"

"Without money, I have no life."

"Abby, please. I'll help out."

"I'm not a charity case."

"No, you're a stubborn mule."

She shot him an alluring glance. "You could be my bodyguard."

"I have a stakeout in Fallbrook tomorrow. Leaving before dawn."

"What's goo . . . for . . . goose . . ." she said around another mouthful of pizza.

"Oh, shit," he muttered. "Rachel."

"What about Rachel?"

"Oh . . . uh . . . I need to check on her. Make sure Turner hasn't tracked her down.

22

After eating, Rent drove Abby to the sheriff's office and she retrieved her car.

"You're sure you won't change your mind," he said.

"I'm sure. I'll be fine. He'd be a fool to try anything now. If he's smart, he's long gone. Back to Arkansas, or wherever the hell he's from."

"How'd you meet this guy, anyway?"

"Gabe came by the real estate office one day, not long after I started working there, and gave me a flyer about his carpet-cleaning business. Very polite, very charming, a real southern gentleman. I told him I would hang on to it in case a client needed that service. I'd see his van around town and maybe wave or say hi, and one day he asked me out, after my boyfriend dumped me. We went out a few times, no big deal."

"Until . . ."

"Yeah, until it became a big deal, at least for him. I gotta go."

She hugged Rent, then gave him a soulful kiss. "Thank you. I don't know how I would have gotten through this without you."

"I think you would have managed just fine."

She got in her car and drove off. Rent checked his phone for the time: 3:37. *Damn it!*

As he returned to his truck, the door to the sheriff's headquarters opened. Detective Washington stepped out and veered right. Rent stopped, keys in hand, not sure if Washington had seen him or not. The detective continued on, fronting the building, and spoke without looking at Rent.

"I see'd you, Br'er Rabbit, skulkin' behind that briar patch of a vehicle of yourn," said the detective, uncharacteristically feigning dialect.

"Not skulking. I just brought Abby back to retrieve her car, and I'm about to go home."

"Got some news, if you're interested," he said and continued walking at a slow pace.

Rent shoved his keys back in his pants pocket and jogged across the pavement to join the detective. Washington continued on until he reached the corner of the structure, then stopped to allow Rent to catch up.

"The ME has reached a preliminary decision on cause of death. This is just on the QT, not for newsprint. He'll release his official report tomorrow."

"I'm off that story anyway. Naomi—"

"Yeah, she rang. I couldn't give her much she didn't already have and referred her to Alvarez for the canned speech."

"The ME?"

"Intracranial hemorrhage, or in layman's terms, brain bleed. Death occurred two or three days after the head injury."

"Oh, shit."

"Yeah, poor woman. If she'd gone to ER, they might have caught it in time."

"Does this make it murder?"

He shrugged. "Maybe, but not necessarily. Depends how she sustained the initial head injury. Could be manslaughter, or just plain ol' accidental death."

"You have Abby's testimony, and Rachel can corroborate it."

"The DA won't want a twelve-year-old on the witness stand if she can help it."

"What about negligent homicide if Turner caused it and refused to take her to a doctor?"

"Yeah, possibly, but how would we ever prove that? However, there is that little matter of how the body ended up in a pile of rubble next to an abandoned mine shaft."

"There is that," Rent replied.

The detective continued. "We still don't know the whole story, and even then that will be up to the DA's office. Your lady friend gave us a peek at some of what happened, but even assuming she's telling the truth, it's he said, she said. We need to talk to the girl."

"Don't forget her brother."

Washington stared at the reporter for several beats before answering. "You know where they are, but I recommend you keep your snout out of it. They have a lot of shit to deal with."

"What about the grandparents?"

"Ditto."

"I understand, but the kids are potential witnesses, if not suspects, right? I mean, if they were adults, you'd be questioning them as we speak."

"Children's rights laws in this state have changed since that do-gooder attorney got involved. We can't ask 'em a single question without a qualified adult or a lawyer present."

"As it should be. You're referring to the Stephanie Crowe case, when three teenage boys were nearly sentenced to life in prison for a murder they did not commit. And that ambitious prosecutor is our current district attorney. Then there's the Central Park Five. Total miscarriage of justice."

Washington looked away and sighed. "You might as well know."

Rent stared at the big man, almost feeling sorry for him.

"They've lawyered up," the detective said.

"Hannah's parents?"

Washington nodded.

"What for?"

"They're talking about suing everybody in sight for wrongful death, abducting their grandchildren. You'll probably get caught in their net."

"Oh, Christ. Do you know who the lawyer is?"

"Probably some dude they saw an advert for on TV."

"You get a name?"

"Mmm, Tucker, maybe. Or am I confusing that with 'fucker'?"

Rent chuckled. "Alan Tucker?"

"Could be."

"Oh, shit."

"Friend of yours, is he?"

Rent snorted. "As if. Ambulance chaser. He also just happens to be the president of the homeowners' association where I live. Had a run-in with him a while back over a CC&Rs technicality."

Washington turned away. "I gotta go or the wife's gonna give me a brain bleed."

"Thanks for the update, Al. Much appreciated."

"You learn anything new . . ." the detective said and raised a hand up to his ear, thumb and little finger extended to mimic the shape of a telephone handset. "Quid pro quo."

"Got it. Oh, by the way, you may want to watch News at Ten tonight."

The detective gave Rent a quizzical look.

"I do believe you may have a tattletale telling stories out of school."

The detective's eyebrows nearly joined above his nose.

"Just sayin'."

Rent returned to his truck and called Martha Flanagan.

"It's about time; she's pulling her hair out," the woman said. "You'd better hit the road soon; the nightly crush hour has begun."

"Just leaving the sheriff's office. Stopping by the house, then on my way."

Rent went to his truck and headed for home. He smiled as he recalled his run-in with Alan Tucker six months earlier. Rent had collected his mail from the bank of mailboxes in a kiosk and sifted through the contents as he returned to his unit. Mostly political propaganda for the upcoming primary. Then, *What's this?*

He noted the return address on a business-style envelope—his homeowner's association. As soon as he got inside, he ripped open the envelope and extracted the letter.

"Oh, for chrissakes, they're fining me thirty-five dollars?" he shouted as he threw the letter at the far wall of the living room. The piece of paper didn't go far before it shot upward, then feathered to the floor a few feet in front of him. He sighed heavily, leaned over, and collected the letter to finish reading. It said that if he wanted to appeal the fine, he would have to appear in-person at the next board meeting, that coming Thursday. An association board primarily made up of a bunch of self-important lawyers and bean counters.

Humph. I wonder who narked on me.

According to the details, the infraction had occurred two weeks earlier, at 5:13 p.m., less than hour before the time of day specified in the association's covenants, conditions, and restrictions for setting out one's trash bag. CC&Rs, the bane of condo existence, which also dictated the style of his screen door and the color of his front door. Never mind that the doors were not even visible from the street.

He checked his calendar. *What the . . .* Then slapped his forehead. *Of course . . . I set it out early because I had to go the airport and would be out of town for a few days. The bastards!*

He mixed himself a "Mel Bay" and tipped the orange-juice can to his lips for a large gulp, then switched on the TV.

Two evenings later, he appeared before the all-male board, airline ticket in hand, and pleaded his case. It being his "first offense," the board agreed to let him off with a warning. "But don't let it happen again," they admonished him.

"One more question," Rent said.

"Yes?" the president inquired.

"How did you did know it was my trash bag?"

The man looked at the other members and hesitated before responding. A voice from the audience filled the momentary silence. "From Ralph, the security guy."

Rent turned to look at the speaker, then back at the board members, and said, "So, Ralph poked through my trash, looking for anything with a name on it to identify the poor sod who had committed this heinous crime against humanity?"

The president, Alan Tucker, replied, "We have rules to maintain a cooperative living environment for the good of all our residents, Mr. Beacham. You of all people should under—"

"Oh, so now I'm a hypocrite as well, am I? Spare me your sermon," Rent said and stalked out of the room. He started for home, then took a detour and walked toward the pool enclosure, where he found Ralph, the security guard.

"Hey, Rent, how's it goin'," the man greeted.

Rent liked the man. He had an easy-going manner, and he dropped an occasional tidbit about Rent's neighbors. But Rent being the subject of the gossip changed his tenor toward the guard. He sighed and tightened his lips, eyes narrowed.

"I'm sorry, Ralph, but I have to ask." He handed Ralph the letter from the board. "Do you know anything about this?"

Ralph looked at the letter and blushed. "Umm, yeah . . . I'm really sorry, but I had no choice. I could lose my job if I don't report it."

"Yeah, I get it. I don't blame you. I had no idea those assholes were such sticklers over a fuckin' trash bag on the curb a few minutes early."

"It's that new guy, Tucker. He's real by-the-book. He actually goes around checking up on me, making sure I identify all the offenders."

Rent offered his hand to shake, which Ralph accepted as he said, "I'll be more careful from now on . . . for your sake, not his."

"Thanks, Rent. Truly, I am so—"

"Forget it. Water under the bridge. I hope you have a very uneventful evening."

Ralph saluted. "Thank you, sir."

Back in the present, Rent turned off Linda Vista Road and drove down the short hill into the condominium complex situated on the north rim of San Diego's Mission Valley.

"How ironic," he muttered as he passed the pool enclosure: Alan Tucker having words with Ralph, the security guy.

Rent hit the brakes, stopped, and got out of his truck.

Tucker looked at him and said, "You can't park there, Beacham. Either park in your garage or—"

"Shove it, Tucker," Rent said. "I want a word with you when you get a minute."

"You want to put your trash out early again?"

"No. About the death of Hannah Stapleford. Rumor has it you're—"

"The word's getting around already, is it? If you're looking for an exclusive, forget it."

"No, that's been assigned to one of my colleagues."

"Then what, man? I've got association business to attend to."

"More trash-bag infractions?"

The security guard tried to suppress a grin.

Tucker wagged a finger at Rent and started to reply, but Rent cut him off, saying, "It's a more personal matter."

"Yeah, it's personal all right. It's so personal, you're gonna be the person at the top of my witness list."

"That so?" Rent replied. "Well, in that case, send me a letter. I believe you have my address."

Rent returned to his truck, parked it in the garage, and took the stairs two at a time. In the kitchen, he started a cup of coffee in a travel mug and attacked the leftover pizza while the coffee brewed. He checked the time.

Abby won't even be to Ramona yet.

He called his editor.

"This better be good," she said. "I'm up to my ass in copy, as if you wouldn't know."

"I'm just calling to give you a head's up about the woman's death. I just ran into a person at the sheriff's office, and this person said— off the record—that the ME will release his report in the morning, so Clark should anticipate that. I don't know if they're holding a presser or not."

"But we'll have cause of death?"

"Yeah."

"Well, that's something. Did this person whisper that to you as well."

"Again, off the record until the report is official."

"I got that."

"Brain bleed; she died two or three days after she fell and hit her head, or was struck by the proverbial blunt instrument."

"That sucks. Poor woman. Are they going after the boyfriend?"

"Remains to be seen. And the kids will be treated as witnesses."

"I'll call Naomi. Maybe she can get an unnamed source to confirm that, and we can put something in tomorrow's paper, ahead of the TV mob."

"If it bleeds, it ledes," Rent said.

"Goodbye, Mr. Beacham."

"Oh, one more thing."

"Make it quick."

"Make sure you catch the News at Ten tonight."

"I generally make it a rule not to."

"You might want to make an exception. I got ambushed in the parking lot when I left this afternoon."

"Oh, shit."

Rent ended the call and checked the time. *I gotta get a move on.*

On the road again, he joined the workday commuters driving home on the Interstate 8 freeway, headed toward East San Diego County. The traffic putted along well below the speed limit, and it got slower the farther east he went, through La Mesa and on to El Cajon. He turned on the radio and tuned into KPBS. The approaching atmospheric river once again topped the region's weather news. Expected to pummel Southern California and northern Baja with several inches of rain, triggering flash floods and mudslides, especially in the mountains and deserts.

His phone dinged, alerting him to a new text message, which appeared on the 4Runner's dashboard screen:

Where iz the girl UR both so ded!!!

Rent shook his head. *Moron.*

Not knowing eventually got the better of him and he called Abby, but the call went to voice mail. He left a message, disconnected, and mentally began a list of what he'd need for the stakeout—dark clothing, snacks, binoculars, and the bird guide.

A few minutes later, his phone dinged. A text message from Abby:

Home. Call me.

He switched to phone mode and tapped the icon next to her name.

"I ain't dead yet," she chirped.

"That's supposed to be funny?" he replied.

"You don't have a monopoly on gallows humor."

"I was beginning to worry about you."

"I stopped at In-N-Out on the way home, and I had a ton of cars ahead of me."

"The pizza wasn't sufficient to sate your ravenous appetite for junk food?"

"I barely had one slice. Besides, it's comfort food. And ketchup is a vegetable, you know."

"I ran into Washington right after you left."

"Oh, yeah? I can imagine what he said, the big brute. He scared the crap out of me."

"His body mass can be intimidating."

"And insensitive."

"That's his job."

"He practically called me a liar."

"That's his basic assumption, that people lie to him, or withhold information. He has to separate fact from fantasy and fiction."

"Don't make excuses for him."

"He fed me some confidential information."

"Do tell."

Rent told her about the cause of Hannah's death and possible implications.

"I hope they string him up by his balls."

"Hopefully, you'll be in the clear."

"Why wouldn't I be?"

"Gabe Turner is as big of a liar as they come. He might well try to implicate you in her death, or even Rachel."

"And I thought you called to cheer me up."

"Sorry 'bout that. I just wanted to know you got home okay, and let you know about Hannah."

"I do appreciate it. I'm going to watch a rom-com and tune out the real world for a few hours."

"Which one?"

"Does it matter? I'll just turn them into you and me."

"So we live happily ever after?"

"Of course. Sweet dreams, my lusty lover. Oh, wait."

"Yes?"

"On the way home, I remembered something Rachel told me."

Rent waited for her to continue.

"Are you still there?" she asked.

"Yes, I'm listening."

"So, Rachel said that sometimes on weekends, when Hannah worked at the bookstore, Gabe would come to the house to keep an eye on the kids, to see that they did their chores and so on. However, he spent most of the time playing video games on Hannah's computer. Or at least that's what Rachel thought he was doing. And sometimes he would talk to people on his phone. She figured it was about carpet cleaning or just talking to friends. But she didn't pay that much attention."

"Interesting," Rent said as he slammed on his brakes amid honking horns.

"Where are you?"

"I'm creeping through El Cajon, on my way to see Rachel."

"Why?"

"I promised. I'll ask her about the computer."

"You think that's important?" she asked.

"Could be. Let me cogitate on it. Gotta go."

He ended the call and pressed harder on the accelerator. The traffic had begun to thin out once he got through El Cajon and drew closer to Alpine.

"How do these people do this day after day?" he muttered. "I think I'd shoot myself."

Once he passed through Alpine, he attained the speed limit and arrived at Martha Flanagan's place 15 minutes later. Rachel rushed out and stood waiting for him as he stepped out of the 4Runner. She held him tightly, her head against his chest. He embraced her and remained silent.

"I miss my mom," Rachel said.

Rent gave her a squeeze. "I know you do. Just remember that your mother loved you with all her heart."

Martha joined them. "I don't imagine you've eaten," she said to Rent.

"I had some pizza a while ago," he replied.

"I was about rustle up some grub. Care to join us?"

"Yes," Rachel said. "You have to."

Rent looked from Martha to Rachel and back to Martha. "I passed that café as I drove in. How about I treat?"

"Yes, can we?" Rachel cried.

"Do we dare risk it?" Martha responded. "The deputies were quite adamant about keeping her location a secret as long as that Turner guy is on the loose."

Rent nodded. "Good point."

"I have some meatloaf I can thaw out, and we can make a nice green salad, can't we, Rachel," Martha added.

Rachel gave them a pouting look.

Rent patted her shoulder. "We'll go once they have him in custody."

"Promise?"

"I promise."

As they returned to the house, Rachel said, "I hope they catch him. I know he did it."

"Yes, I'm pretty certain he did it, too."

"You don't understand. Just like the cops. They wouldn't listen to me. They told me I had to wait and talk to a detective."

"Are you two coming?" Martha shouted from the front door.

Rent waved in acknowledgement. "Be right there." He turned his eyes back to Rachel. "After dinner, I want you to write down everything you remember, okay?"

She nodded.

"Let's go," he said.

Rachel, using her good hand, took Rent's hand in hers as they continued on to the house. Inside, Martha led them into the kitchen. She took a container of meatloaf out of the freezer and placed it in a microwave oven to thaw. Then she set out the makings for the salad.

"How can I help?" Rent asked.

She handed Rent two carrots and a peeler. "Start with these. Something to drink? I have cerveza, vino, or?"

"A cerveza would be great," he said.

She opened the refrigerator and pulled out a bottle and held it up. "Modelo okay?"

"Perfect," he said as he took the bottle of Modelo Negra and twisted off the cap. He took a big swig, then set the bottle down and began peeling the carrots.

When Martha turned to the sink to rinse the lettuce, Rachel picked up the beer and took a quick sip, then sent it down.

Rent lowered his head, closed one eye, and shot her a reprimand with the other.

Her back still turned, Martha said, "Young lady, in this house you may have iced tea or lemonade. Help yourself."

Rachel's face flushed as she pursed her lips.

"Busted," Rent said in almost a whisper.

Rachel rolled her eyes and went to the fridge.

Martha turned, winked at Rent, and set out a bowl filled with tortilla chips and a bowl of salsa. To Rent, she said, "Help yourself, but don't spoil your appetite." She then handed Rachel three potatoes. "Scrub these and we'll nuke 'em. Then set the table."

The carrots peeled, Rent took another sip of beer and ate a few chips.

"I guess I shouldn't just assume, these days," she said. "You haven't mentioned it. Are you a vegemite, or vegan?"

Rent smiled and shook his head.

"Martha?" Rachel said as she set out three plates and utensils.

"Yes, honey?"

"After dinner, can I show Mr. Beacham . . . I mean my dad . . . the new horse and pony?"

"*May* I show, not *can* I show."

Rachel made face. "You're just like . . ." Then her voice broke. She began crying and ran from the room.

Rent started to rise from his seat at the table.

Martha waved him back into his seat. "I'm sorry. Can't get the ol' schoolmarm out of me. Let her go, son. She's trying to put on a brave face, but inside she's hurting. It will take time."

The microwave oven dinged, but Martha left the meatloaf inside. "I'll go check on her," she said and left the room.

Rent stood and went to a window that overlooked the corral. In the fading light, the horses stood together, occasionally turning their heads at a sound or movement. He returned to his seat at the table and finished off the remaining beer.

A few minutes later, Martha returned. "She'll be out soon. . . . I understand you're a fiddler. Ever played at Vaquero Days?"

"Yes. Good fun."

"Then I have heard you. Your band is good."

"Thanks."

"You even played my song."

"Your . . . oh, you mean *Old Mother Flanagan*."

She grinned. "But don't you dare call me old. It may be true, but you don't need to rub it in."

Rent smiled in return. "Wouldn't think of it."

He extracted his phone from a pocket, brought up Turner's latest text, and showed it to Martha. She read it, then looked up at Rent, exhaling heavily.

"We've got to keep her safe," she said.

Rachel returned and stood beside Rent. "I'm sorry. I just couldn't help it."

He put an arm around her. "You have nothing to apologize for. You've lost your mother. You have every right to be upset and feel sad. You can shed a bucket load of tears if that's what it takes to feel better."

"Okay. At least now I have a dad."

Rent's eyes teared up and his throat tightened. Martha handed him a paper napkin. He dabbed the moisture from his cheeks and said, "Now look at what you've started."

They held each other for another long moment, and Rent could hear Martha sniffling as well.

Martha cleared her throat. "Dinner's getting cold. Let's eat."

They ate in silence. When they had finished, Rachel helped Martha clear the table.

"Let's go check on the hay burners, then we'll have some dessert," Martha said. "How does that sound?"

Rachel smiled. "Yes!"

They walked to the corral and the horses came to the fence, anticipating a handout. Martha had brought along carrots. Rachel showed Rent how to feed them without risking a finger or two in the process.

"Hold your hand out flat with the carrot in your palm."

Rent did as instructed, and the big mare snapped it up, then stared at him, waiting for another. They gave each of the three equines two carrots.

"Now pat them on the neck. They like that," she said.

Rent did as instructed, and the pony poked its head over the fence, sniffed Rent's arm, then opened its mouth and softly bit his forearm.

Martha looked on in amazement. "Did he just bite you?"

"It wasn't much of a bite. I think he was trying to give me a hickey."

Martha shook her head. "Usually, if they bite, it hurts and you get a nice bruise out of it."

"He must like you," Rachel said.

"Apparently so. Or he just wanted another carrot," he replied, then asked her about Turner using Hannah's computer. "Abby said you told her about it."

"He played video games. But he's not very smart. I had to show him how to play a dumb game."

"Did you ever see him use it for anything else?"

"Like what?"

"Send emails, business sort of things?"

"I saw him searching for porn. He didn't think I knew about it, but I told my mom. I asked him to help me with a school assignment, about the gold rush, but I knew more than he did. He's no gold miner. He doesn't know schist from slate."

"Rachel, language," Martha said.

"I'm not swearing. I'm saying *schist*, not sh— . . . er, poop. It's a type of rock, spelled s-c-h-i-s-t, and it can contain quartz veins that also have gold in it, especially blue quartz. I did a science report on it and got an A-plus. The Julians—they were cousins—and the Baileys got rich off of their mines near Julian, in Chariot Canyon. And that's how the town got its name, from Mike Julian, because he was famous."

"Wow, you're quite the scholar," Rent said.

"Alice at the library helped me find the books, and I found stuff online too," she said.

As they returned to the house, he asked Martha about her equine rescue operation. "Basically, I save them from the meat wagon. From becoming dog food south of the border. For example, that mare and the pony came from the res, the reservation. It seems that they had taken a liking to the tribe's marijuana crop, so they had to go. When I heard about it, I bought them."

Rent chuckled. "I hear a good story in this."

"Well, there's not much to it. But it does have an element of humor, I'll give you that."

At the house, Martha set out cookies and ice cream, and served Rent fresh coffee.

He glanced at the wall clock. "I hate to be a party pooper, but I have to hit the road pretty soon. I have a busy day tomorrow."

"Nooooo," Rachel said. "Spend the night. Please?"

Rent sighed. "As much as I'd like to, I can't. I'm going on a stakeout tomorrow."

"Can't it wait?"

"I'm sorry, Rachel, but no, it can't wait. We're going to try to track down Gabe Turner and his henchmen. This is very important."

"I hope you catch him and put him in jail."

"That's the sheriff's job, but if we can tell the sheriff where to find him, that will help speed things up."

"Then you'll come back here and we can celebrate."

"Absolutely."

BACK AT HOME, RENT organized the items on his mental check list, then mixed a Mel Bay and turned on News at Ten. As he had predicted, Hannah's death led the broadcast.

The news hosts said the body discovered in Chariot Canyon had been formally identified, and the sheriff asked members of the community to come forward with any information they might have that would help the department's investigation.

They ran a clip from Sheriff Paula Clifford's news conference, with the sheriff stating that Joshua Gabriel Turnbull, also known as Gabe Turner, was wanted for questioning and anyone with information as to his whereabouts should contact her office immediately. She then took questions.

The reporter who had ambushed Rent that afternoon asked, "Sheriff Clifford, is Rent Beacham, a reporter for the *San Diego Herald*, a suspect in your investigation? It has been rumored that he had a relationship with the dead woman."

The sheriff took a deep breath before replying. "Rent Beacham is not a suspect—"

"Is he a person of interest? It's my understanding that—"

The sheriff raised a hand. "If you will let me finish. Mr. Beacham is not a suspect. It's our understanding that he knew the deceased, but that their relationship ended more than a decade ago. We have spoken to him, and he is cooperating with us in our inquiries. Next question."

"Gotcha, asshole," Rent said and turned off the TV.

23

Thursday, Day 19, morning

Rent met private investigator Alicia Velasquez at her house in Rancho Peñasquitos, one of San Diego's sprawling subdivisions, and she headed north on the I-15 freeway toward Fallbrook, a rural town located just south of the county line.

"So," Rent asked. "Where'd this hot tip come from?"

"I don't know," the PI answered. "Davis said he got it as an anonymous text but it seemed genuine because of the amount of detail in terms of where and when and who might be there."

"I hope we're not being set up."

"That's why we're going so early."

They arrived before full daylight and located the house in question, then found a place to park. The house sat well back from the road, nestled among a grove of oaks. Bright yard lights illuminated the area in front of the house.

Rent and the PI exited her Honda CR-V, Rent with binoculars and the bird book Abby had given to him, the PI carrying binoculars and a digital camera with a telephoto lens. Raucous bird calls filled the air, along with quieter melodies and chits. They walked slowly, craning their necks to mimic birdwatchers.

"The woodpeckers help give us some cover," Velasquez said.

"Woodpeckers?" Rent wondered.

"That loud annoying racket you're hearing, acorn woodpeckers. Noisy little buggers."

"Oh, yeah, I've heard them at Abby's house," he replied.

They stopped to observe the driveway from the opposite side of the road. A Stars & Bars Confederate battle flag had been painted on a garage door. Atop a flagpole, a black-and-white American flag—give no quarter—and a Don't Tread on Me rattlesnake banner fluttered limply in the light morning breeze. A corral contained two horses that eyed them with curiosity. Somewhere a dog barked.

Rent chuckled and said, "Check it out." He gestured toward a sign nailed to one of the trees at the head of the driveway:

Protected by Smith & Wesson
Glock Winchester Colt
Remington Beretta
Mossberg Ect.!

The PI took a few photos, then started moving again.

"We don't want to linger long and arouse suspicion," she said. "They doubtless have security cameras as well."

The pair continued walking along the shoulder, pretending to be looking for birds, pausing periodically and keeping an eye on the driveway.

"So, tell me about the dead woman," Velasquez said. "That's a truly sad, unfortunate case."

Rent filled her in on what had transpired in Chariot Canyon, including his identification of the body.

"So, you think it has anything to do with us and this EBT case?"

"Possibly," Rent replied, "along with your garden variety domestic abuse, and perhaps Turner not wanting to risk taking her to a doctor, where she says something that the medicos think needs to be reported to the cops. She may have confronted him about molesting her daughter."

"Oh, shit."

Rent nodded. "Abby told me that after he had taken Rachel to a 4-H Club event the week before, Rachel got quite upset and had told Turner that she knew what was going on, and if he touched her again, she would call the sheriff. I'm assuming that relates to the fraud, and possibly molestation. If Hannah confronted Turner about that, he could have smacked her good."

"Yeah, well, it's now coming full circle to bite 'im in the ass."

After about 100 yards, they retraced their route, giving the property another lookover before returning to the car.

"There are some shrubs we can skulk behind as well," the PI said. "We need to get set up while it's still on the dark side. Then we can have some refreshments."

She went to the back of the SUV, opened the liftgate, and took out a conical-shaped object attached to a tripod, which she handed to Rent, along with two folding camp stools.

"Listening device?" he guessed.

"Spot on," she said and extracted a second tripod. "Let's get these in place."

They returned to the tangle of shrubs and moved behind them, where the PI set up the parabolic listening device and aimed it toward the suspect house across the road. Then she set up the other tripod and attached her camera and telephoto lens to it.

"All set," she said. "Come on."

She led the way back to the vehicle. She opened a Thermos and poured each of them a cup of coffee. Rent grabbed granola bars from his knapsack and offered her one, which she accepted.

"Now, here's what we're going to do," Velasquez said as she unwrapped the granola bar. "Once we get more daylight, you're going to be the decoy while I hide behind that shrub. You go first and meander up the road looking at birds. I'll make my move a few minutes later."

They finished their coffee and snack, and Rent did as instructed. Once he had passed the entrance to the driveway, she moved into position.

Rent wondered how long it would take before anything of interest transpired. *I don't think I have the patience for this job.* He stopped and pretended to look up a bird in the book.

The sun's morning rays had begun to highlight the tops of the trees. Soon it would be full daylight. An occasional big pickup or SUV passed by but kept on. One driver honked at Rent and flipped him off.

"Neighborly of you," he muttered.

He kept on until he had lost sight of the driveway entrance, then turned around. His phone beeped, indicating a text had been received.

Damn it, I forgot to turn it off.

He pulled the phone from a jacket pocket. The PI:

Lights on. Creatures stirring.

Rent replied with a thumbs-up emoji. He put the phone on vibrate mode and returned it to the pocket as he headed back toward the driveway. When he drew even with the PI's position, he heard her hoarse whisper.

"Keep going, then circle back and keep out of sight."

Rent walked several more paces before ducking into the underbrush and making his way back to where Velasquez was sitting on one of the stools, peering through her binoculars, wireless headphones covering her ears. Rent opened the other camp stool and sat beside her.

Twenty minutes later, headlights appeared up the road and drew near as a vehicle slowed.

"Well, well, what have we here?"

Velasquez let her binoculars fall, suspended from a strap, and rotated the camera, then fired off a few quick shots. Rent's eyes focused on the vehicle as well and the sight registered in an instant: a magic carpet emblazoned on the side of the van turning into the driveway.

"Based on his direction, he probably came from the north, somewhere in Riverside County," the PI whispered.

The van continued up the drive and stopped, and they heard the toot-toot of a horn.

Velasquez adjusted a knob on the listening device. "Those damned woodpeckers are driving me nuts."

Rent lifted his binoculars and peered through the magnifying lenses as Gabe Turner got out of the vehicle, holding what appeared to be a plastic grocery bag. Turner slammed the door shut and stood beside the vehicle. A man approached Turner from the house and Turner handed him the bag. The man peered into the bag, then looked up at Turner and shook his head.

Rent could hear voices but could not make out what was being said. The PI adjusted the knob on the listening device again.

"Getting reception," Velasquez said, again whispering. "Now if only the damned birds would shut up. . . . My, my, a bit of dissension within the ranks."

"What are—"

"Shush!" she ordered and her camera began to whir. "Gotcha, scumbag."

Rent continued watching the verbal exchange between Turner and the man from the house. "That may be one of the thugs at Turner's place last week," he said in a low voice. "We can compare the license plates."

The PI nodded. "We'll know more once I get home and clean this stuff up."

"What now?"

Velasquez turned to face Rent with a devilish grin creasing her lips. "We wait."

"I don't know how you do this without going insane," he muttered.

She responded with a low cackle. "Maybe I don't."

The man returned to the house and Turner paced the yard, hands in his pockets, occasionally kicking a small stone out of his way. Once he reached down, picked up a stone, and threw it at the woodpeckers overhead. One of the birds emitted a loud squawk and several of the birds took flight.

"Thank you," the PI muttered as the entire area went silent for the moment and a light breeze began to rustle leaves.

"I'm going to need to pee before much longer," Rent uttered.

"Put a cork in it," the PI replied.

Another 10 minutes passed, then voices cut through the air. Two men joined Turner, who glanced at his watch and threw up his hands, as if to say, what's taking so long? One of the men had a cell phone to his ear.

"They're waiting for someone," Velasquez said, "and that someone is running late. I think one of them mentioned his name, maybe Johnson or Swenson . . . something like that. I couldn't quite make it out."

"One of the guys is wearing a vest that looks suspiciously like the one some of the January 6 insurrectionists had on," Rent replied.

She took more photos while the minutes passed and the ambient light grew brighter. The two men returned to the house, leaving Turner alone in the yard. He leaned against his van and studied his phone, occasionally thumbing the screen.

"I'm going to water a bush," Rent said.

He went farther back into the undergrowth and relieved himself. Not seeing any change at the house, he returned to the vehicle and took two apples from his knapsack. He pocketed them, then checked his phone.

A message from Rod Davis of HHSA, checking in. Rent texted back:

The clan is gathering.

He texted Abby:

Boring!

Then he worked his way back to the stakeout position. The PI had disappeared.

She must've had to pee after all.

Another few minutes ticked by and more vehicles passed without stopping or even slowing down. Velasquez returned, a bit breathless, and sat on her stool.

"Mission accomplished," she said.

Rent offered her an apple, which she declined. Rent took a big bite and chewed as quietly as he could manage.

Then a vehicle approached from the opposite direction as Turner's van had come, slowed, and turned into the driveway, parking next to the van.

Rent could see Turner say something, but the only word he could make out sounded a lot like "fucking." The driver got out of the vehicle, gesturing at Turner and shouting back it him.

"Come to mama," the PI muttered as she captured more digital images on the camera's 128GB memory card. "Gotcha!"

"Any idea who he is?" Rent whispered.

"No clue, but we will soon."

The man from the house, along with a companion, rejoined Turner and the newcomer. They huddled near Turner's van, talking among themselves.

"They're planning their next move," Velasquez said. "Get ready to haul ass."

Rent started to rise, and she grabbed his sleeve.

"Not yet."

They continued to watch as the four men separated. Rent took another two bites from the apple, then tossed the remainder into the brush behind him. *A little snack for the critters.*

Turner got in his van and the newcomer returned to his Silverado. The other two went to a Dodge Ram and its diesel engine roared to life. Turner led the way, followed by the others, turning left out of the driveway and going back the way he had come.

"Let's go," the PI said. "You get the listener."

She stood up, folded her stool and hung it on one arm, then grabbed the camera and tripod. Rent followed suit, bringing along the listening device. They hurried back to the PI's vehicle, stowed the gear, and spun gravel as they hit the road in pursuit.

"Finally, some action. This is what I live for," Velasquez said. "The chase is on."

"Any idea where they're headed?"

"North," she said. "Beyond that, I haven't a clue. But maybe Mr. Turner will keep us apprised of his whereabouts. Hold the wheel for a sec."

She let go of the steering wheel, placed her phone in a holder on the car's dashboard, and tapped the screen a few times. A map appeared on the screen, displaying a red dot. The vehicle veered off the road, the right-side tires churning gravel.

"Keep it on the road for chrissakes!" Velasquez ordered.

Rent rotated the wheel slightly to get the vehicle back on the road.

"You could slow down a bit, you know," he said as she retook charge of the steering wheel.

"Ha, you wimp. You need to get out more. Live dangerously."

"Easy for you to say. I'm the one getting the death threats. What's with the phone?"

"Tracking device."

"On the magic carpet?"

"Shazam."

"When . . . how . . ."

"While you were relieving the strain on your bladder, I saw my opportunity. I snuck up the driveway as Turner also went in the weeds to pee and stuck a tracker on the underside of his van. The woodpeckers, bless their little hearts, gave me cover. He didn't suspect a thing."

Rent shook his head. "You amaze me."

"You ain't seen nothin' yet, baby."

As expected, the road led to the freeway and Turner's van merged with the northbound traffic, which was relatively light when compared to the southbound lanes, which were crowded with commuters headed toward San Diego.

They trailed Turner and his companions, keeping a safe distance behind to avoid detection. The freeway climbed a high ridge, past the former border patrol station, then plummeted down the other side into Temecula. At the bottom of the slope, the vehicles turned southeast on SR 79 toward Anza. They drove through a developed commercial area, where a long string of traffic lights made it difficult for the trackers to maintain visual contact.

"Keep your eyes peeled. They could turn off at any time, although I suspect their destination is farther out."

The right-hand signal light on Turner's van began to blink. He turned into a parking lot and stopped in front of a convenience store. The other two vehicles continued on.

Velasquez followed Turner and parked a short distance away.

"They're probably all going to the same place," she said.

A few minutes later, Turner emerged from the store, carrying two half-cases of beer and a plastic grocery bag overflowing with bags of assorted items of junk food.

"Looks like he's the gofer in this outfit," Rent said.

Turner drove back onto the highway and continued eastward. Eventually, the road narrowed to two lanes as it meandered through increasingly rural farmland and traffic dropped off. After passing a sign that read Dripping Springs, the van's right-hand turn signal began blinking again. Turner veered onto a side road leading into an area with low population and structures spaced substantially far apart. In the distance loomed the north slope of Palomar Mountain.

After another two miles, Turner pulled up to a gate at a compound surrounded by a high chain-link fence topped with razor wire. As with the place in Fallbrook, the compound contained a tall flagpole with a black-and-white American flag and a Don't Tread on Me banner barely fluttering in the faint breeze. Rent noticed a Nazi-like swastika adorning the side of one of the outbuildings.

The PI continued on up the road until out of sight of the compound's occupants, then came to a stop. She pulled over and had Rent take the wheel as she got into the back seat with her camera. They returned to the compound entrance and drove past at a slow speed, the PI taking photos through an open window. All three vehicles were parked there side by side.

At the highway, the PI had Rent do a 180, then park.

"What now?"

"We give it a while. We'll make another pass up and back, then we go home and I get to work on the photos and audio files."

Rent poured himself more coffee and ate the other apple. The PI sipped some water and munched on a handful of sunflower seeds.

None of the vehicles they had followed drove past, and after a half hour, the PI signaled for Rent to get moving.

"One more pass and we're out of here," she said.

"Don't we have to come back this way?"

"Yes, but we won't slow down. Just act naturally."

Rent put the car in gear and moved onto the road, driving at a moderate speed.

"Ease up a bit while I take some more shots," the PI instructed.

As they passed the compound, Rent saw the men standing near their vehicles. Two of them turned to look at the PI's SUV but had no obvious reaction.

Rent continued on until they were out of sight, then stopped.

"I need to pee again. Long drive home from here," he said.

"You and your caffeine," she replied as she returned to the driver's seat.

While Rent stood behind the SUV, a vehicle approached.

"Oh, shit," Rent muttered.

"We've been made," Velasquez shouted.

He hurriedly finished his business and moved toward the CR-V's passenger door.

"Get in!" Velasquez ordered as she put the car in gear. She began moving before Rent could get in. He opened the door and ran alongside.

"Get in, get in!" she shouted.

Rent managed to fall into the seat, one foot hanging out the open door.

"You're going to kill me."

"No, they're going to kill you—and me—if you don't get your ass in that seat."

Rent twisted around, facing forward, and finally got his right foot inside. He slammed the door as Velasquez floored it.

The big diesel pickup bore down on them, straddling the lane divider. The PI had to swerve off the road to avoid being hit. Bits of weeds smacked the windshield as she struggled to get her vehicle back on the potholed pavement.

Rent turned to look behind them. "They're turning around."

"Damn. It's at least another mile to the main road."

They passed the entrance to the compound, where three men stood watching. Rent recognized Turner among them. The big truck gained on them, drawing closer until its bumper nearly touched that of the PI's SUV. The PI looked into the rearview mirror, seeing only a ram's head leering through the rear window.

"Can't this thing go any faster?" Rent asked.

"I'm going as fast as I dare. This road isn't exactly the Indianapolis Speedway.

"Well, the guys behind us seem to think so."

They approached the intersection with the main highway and Velasquez slowed. The truck veered into the oncoming lane as if to come abreast. Then a car on the highway turned onto the side road, on a collision course with the pickup. Horns blared as the pickup backed off and returned to its own lane. Velasquez looked left, then right, saw an opening, and surged past the stop sign.

She barely slowed down as she swerved left onto the highway, tires screeching in protest, ahead of an oncoming vehicle. Another horn blared as the vehicle had to slow down to avoid rearending the PI's CR-V. Velasquez crushed the accelerator pedal to the floor. The pickup followed, but had been forced to trail behind two other vehicles.

After a mile or so, the highway widened to four lanes and Velasquez kept up her speed, weaving around slower-moving traffic. A red stop light slowed their progress and allowed the pickup to gain on them. Moving again, the PI stayed to the right, hoping for an opportunity to suddenly veer off the road.

But the driver of the pickup chose to be more aggressive, blasting his big-rig horn as he wove in and out of other vehicles, amid blaring horns and one-finger salutes, to pull alongside the PI. The passenger brandished a semi-automatic pistol through the open window and fired.

Velasquez had seen the move coming in her peripheral vision and tapped the brake pedal just as the man fired three shots in rapid succession. The first shot cracked the windshield, and the next two ricocheted off the car's hood. She then saw her opportunity. She spun the wheel hard to the right, forcing her SUV onto the shoulder, and slammed on the brakes, the car skidding to a full stop. Rent shot forward against the restraint of the seatbelt, his head hitting the sun visor.

They both sat still, hearts thumping and breathless. The pickup had been forced to continue up the road to avoid a collision. It, too, had pulled over and the men got out, but they appeared to think better of any further action. They got back inside and drove off.

Rent watched the truck as it merged with the traffic, then moved left into a turn lane.

"They're coming back," he said.

"We're going to be long gone before they can get through this traffic and back here. There's an outlet mall up ahead. I think we can get lost in there," she said.

"Wait!" Rent said as she shifted into Drive. "When you hit the brakes, I saw something roll off the hood."

"An ejected shell casing maybe?"

He shrugged. "Worth a look." He started to open his door.

"Stop," she ordered and shoved the gearshift lever back to the Park position. "If we find anything, I have to collect it and put it an evidence bag. And don't you step on it!"

They got out of the car and scanned the ground under it and around it.

"Right there," she said and pointed.

Rent stood still as she got an evidence bag from the car. She used a latex glove to pick up the brass shell casing and place it in the bag. "Now, let's get the hell out of here. I'll label the bag later."

AT THE SHOPPING CENTER, Velasquez found an empty slot in the most congested area of the parking lot. She sniffed the air and turned to face Rent.

"Did you pee your pants?"

"What? No!" he answered.

She cast him a doubtful look as he ran his hand down a pant leg.

"Oh, fuck," he muttered. "I got in such a hurry back there, I think some splattered on me."

"Well, see that you don't get any on my seat."

She got out and went to the back of the vehicle. She grabbed her camera and the memory card from the audio recorder attached to the listening device, and placed the items in a canvas bag. She then opened a carrying case and removed a small revolver and added that to the contents of the bag.

Rent had joined her at the back of the car. "What the—"

"Just in case," she said. "Let's find a Starbucks or reasonable facsimile thereof." She chuckled. "And you can clean yourself up. Come on."

Rent rolled his eyes and stuck out his tongue at the back of her head, then followed in her footsteps.

They entered the main building, searching out the food court, and found an off-brand coffee shop.

"I don't need anymore coffee," Rent said, "so just water for me. And maybe one of those scones."

They placed their orders and found an empty table. Rent excused himself and went to the restroom. When he returned, he found Velasquez sipping a cup of tea and tearing off chunks of a blueberry muffin.

Rent opened his bottled water, took a sip, and began nibbling at the cranberry-orange scone.

Velasquez had her phone sitting on the table, and she peeked at it periodically.

"Turner's still at the compound."

"I think we should call the cops," he said.

"And tell them what?"

"That we got shot at by a couple of neo-Nazis."

"And what do they do? Take a statement and yawn," she replied.

"Not if we give them details on where to find them."

"If they go out there, it could totally fuck up our investigation."

Rent wrinkled his face and nodded. "But couldn't we be nailed for obstruction of justice or some such BS?"

"We'll cross that bridge when we come to it."

"Okay, but I'll talk to Washington. He wants to take down Turner, if he can find him. He can get in touch with the Riverside folks."

"Turner won't stay there long. Who knows what hidey hole he's going to crawl into."

"An abandoned gold mine, perhaps?"

She glanced at her phone again, then sighed. "The light's out."

Rent frowned. "The light?"

"They must've found the tracker, and it's no doubt now been crushed into a zillion pieces by some guy's bootheel."

"So, what now?"

"We'll check the parking lot periodically, then head for home. No point in hanging around here any longer than we have to. Unless you want to do some shopping. Maybe get another pair of pants?"

Rent just shook his head. "Doesn't bother me." He ate the rest of his scone.

"I'm going to call Davis and then Washington, bring them up to speed," he said. "I imagine with this escalation, they'll want to start planning the roundup. We can now definitively tie Turner to these other guys. And hopefully we can identify the fourth guy."

"Problem is, they're going to be super vigilant. They may even be destroying evidence as we speak," she said.

"Yeah, but they don't know who we are. For all they know, we're a rival gang."

"You sure about that?"

"Turner never got a good look at me, and I doubt he would recognize you. He's mostly looking out for cops coming after him. I think if the sheriffs hold off going after these other guys, they may get complacent, thinking they scared off whoever they think we are. Meanwhile, with any luck, we identify the fourth guy. That could be the key to unlocking this thing, or least take a big chunk out of their armor."

She nodded. "You may be right. Let's go take a peek at the parking lot."

They cleaned off their table and returned to the entrance doorway, where they stood behind the glass and surveyed the outside area.

"They could be standing right outside, waiting for us."

"Doubtful, but just in case, let's go shopping."

Rent groaned. "What the hell for?"

"Disguises, my man. Disguises."

Velasquez led the way to a Macy's store, where they each purchased nondescript hoodies, sunglasses, and hats, and he bought a pair of pants. They donned their new attire and exited through the doors on the opposite side of the building from where they entered. The PI went first and turned left. Rent followed five minutes later, going right. They would rendezvous at the car, if the coast was clear.

As Rent stepped out the door, he narrowed his eyes against the bright sun.

"It may be February, but it feels like July. So much for that atmospheric river the chicken littles are clucking about," he muttered. "Too bad that eclipse is still a few weeks off."

He found a place in the deep shadow and surveyed the parking lot, which was jammed with vehicles of every description. He scrutinized every large pickup but found nothing suspicious. He headed off, walking as nonchalantly as possible, and as if being unsure of where he had parked his car. He continued around the building, then drew up short at the sight of a large man standing in the shade and swiveling his head, as if looking for someone.

Rent approached the man, thinking he did not look like either of his pursuers.

"Lost your missus, too, eh?" the man said. "She said she'd only be a minute."

"Yeah, women," Rent said, shaking he head. "Can't live with 'em; can't live without 'em."

The man chuckled. "Ain't it the truth. Good luck to you."

Rent smiled at the man. "Thanks. And same to you."

Rent breathed a sigh of relief as he continued on and rounded a corner of the building. There he stopped and caught his breath, then continued on toward the next corner. He stopped and surveyed the area yet again, trying to remember where the PI had parked. His phone vibrated and he checked it. A text from the PI:

All clear here. Waiting.

He replied:

Almost there.

The sound of a diesel engine caught his ear and he froze, then glanced around with only slight movements of his head. The truck came into view and continued on, a middle-aged woman at the wheel.

"I may need another pair of pants before I get out of here," he muttered as he continued on. He returned to the doorway they had initially entered, then retraced his route to the PI's car. He rapped the window on the passenger-side door and waved to her. She unlocked the doors and he got in, and she immediately relocked the doors. She had the engine running and the air conditioning turned on.

"Phew," Rent said.

"We still gotta get on the freeway headed south," she reminded him.

VELASQUEZ ACCELERATED UP THE onramp and merged with the midday southbound traffic on the I-15.

"Thank goodness," she said as she pulled back the hood, then took off the hat and tossed it over a shoulder into the back seat. Rent followed suit.

"So, we got some excitement after all," she said and offered a quick smile to Rent.

"Yeah, some excitement," he replied with a shake of his head. "That kind of excitement I can do without."

"Me, too, now that I'm a PI. Had a few close calls as a cop, though."

"You were a cop?"

She told him she left the police force because it was a man's world. Her ex was still on the force. He didn't want a wife, a partner; he wanted a mom and maid at his beck and call; he tried to restrict her social life.

"Now I'm thirty-six years old and single. It gets a bit lonely at times, but mostly I'm happy just having a dog, a yellow Lab," she said. "A dog that flunked out of service training," she added with a laugh.

"I like Labs; they are so loving and lovable. But my mom likes boxers, not to say they're not lovable. The first dog I remember, Heidi, got hit by a car and it broke her spine, paralyzing her hind legs. That devastated the entire family.

"I was in junior high at the time, yet I still cry about this, twenty years later. My dad took me to the vet's to say goodbye before she was put down. I can still see the look of bewilderment on Heidi's face, unable to comprehend her fate and only wishing to escape that confining cage where she lay, helpless, and to go home with us. And I witnessed one of the few times I have ever seen my dad cry."

Velasquez looked at Rent, wide-eyed. "That is so bizarre. When I was fourteen, I had a black Lab named Heidi. She met the same fate. The only real difference in the two stories is that my 'loving' father let me make the decision whether to put her down, or try surgery, but she would never walk again. I chose to euthanize her. During the ride home, my father turned to me and said, "Well, you just killed your dog."

Rent stared at her disbelief. "Your father actually said that?"

She stared straight ahead, keeping her eyes on the cars in front of her. "Pathetic, isn't it? But enough about me. What do you think our carpet guy will do now?"

Rent thought for a moment. "I suspect he's been hiding stuff in the mine, and he's going to try to get it out ASAP."

"What kind of stuff? Stacks of counterfeit EBT cards?"

"That, too, but I'm thinking more along the lines of weapons and explosives."

"Hmm, that could be, considering the thugs we encountered this morning."

"We've got another presidential election coming up, and they could be stockpiling. And that woman's death has thrown a big wrench in the works, putting a spotlight on Turner and whatever high jinx he's been up to."

"Yes, but won't the sheriff have that area covered?" Velasquez asked.

"In theory, yes, but as you know, they're understaffed," he replied. "Alvarez told me they can't watch the mine round-the-clock, so they just check it out periodically. Ditto for the BLM crew. Also, I did some poking around the Web, chatting with some off-roaders, and one of them told me about a back entrance to Chariot Canyon, one that comes up from the desert, off the S-2, closer to Blair Valley. Rodriguez Canyon."

"You think Turner knows about that?"

"I'm sure he does. A rat like that is going to want an escape route. And they're likely to do it in the middle of the night, under the cover of darkness. Maybe even during a storm—like this atmospheric river they keep telling us about every hour, on the hour—so they're less likely to be discovered."

"That's a big risk. They could get stuck out there, or caught in a flash flood."

"These guys live with risk," Rent replied. "Dostoyevsky would argue they love the risk. That they believe two plus two equals five. That essentially they're gamblers and thrive on risk and danger and the adrenaline rush."

The PI shot a puzzled look at the reporter. "Huh? What the hell are you talking about?"

"*Notes from Underground.* One of Dostoyevsky's more brilliant works."

"I've heard of him. Ruskie, right? Never read a word of it."

"In essence, he says that even though humans are endowed with big brains, allowing them to be sensible, to be reasonable, and think rationally, and do what's best for themselves and society as a whole, they also are endowed with what one might argue is a fatal flaw, otherwise known as free will, and they have wants, or desires, and they choose to satisfy these wants and desires even when they know it could ultimately cause them harm—whether physically, emotionally, or financially—or even death."

Velasquez kept her eyes on the road as the traffic became more congested. "And that's news to anyone with even half a brain?"

Rent shrugged. "Well . . . he wrote that more than a hundred and fifty years ago, when science and mathematical principles began to make big strides over the dominance of religious beliefs and superstition: in the wake of Darwin and the theory of evolution, and the industrial revolution that transformed transportation, communications, and the mass production of consumer goods, not to mention mass destruction."

"Ah, I see. So, back then it would have been controversial."

"Very much so, and it remains controversial today. It's considered to be a rather cynical view of humanity."

"Yeah, well, in the business we're in, cynicism pretty much carries the day. It's that segment of society we deal with almost to the point of exclusivity. A confederacy of dunces, one might say. But enough of the philosophy lesson and cut to the chase, so to speak."

"I predict that Turner and his pals are going to attempt to move their stockpile away from the mine via that backroad in the next few days."

"That's for the cops to deal with. It's nothing to do with us and this EBT fraud case."

"The cases are intertwined, because the one finances the other," Rent responded. "And I feel that I owe it to Hannah, the dead woman, to see that this scumbag gets his just desserts."

"Okay, Sir Lancelot, you climb aboard your steed and charge the windmill."

"Aren't you mixing your metaphors a bit?"

"You get my point. I'm going home, taking a hot bath, and then getting to work on the evidence we collected this morning. I have a report to file with Rod Davis so I can collect a paycheck and finance my own wants and desires."

24

Rather than go to the office, Rent returned home following the stakeout. He had calls to make and didn't want the inevitable interruptions. He called Washington and reported on the morning's activities, including being shot at by Turner's companions.

"So that was you. Why am I not surprised," Washington said.

"What have you heard?" Rent asked.

"Just that there was a shooting incident near Temecula, no injuries reported, and the Riverside cops are investigating. We'll want forensics to inspect your vehicle."

"Not mine, the PI's."

"Whatever. Forensics needs to see it. Maybe recover a round. I need her address."

"We retrieved a shell casing at the scene. The PI has it in an evidence bag."

"Excellent, but we still want to examine her vehicle."

"This happened in Riverside County."

"Doesn't matter. We can send them the results, or they can send someone for a second look. Point is, we need someone on it before she drives it again."

"She said she'll be home the rest of the day working on her report for HHSA," Rent said and gave him her phone number. "They gonna pick these goons up?"

"On what grounds?"

"Gee, I don't know. Attempted murder by any chance?"

"At this point, we only have your say so. Besides, if some FNG looking for a hero's medal busts in on these guys, it could blow up the investigation. We might never see them again. There's only one person that I'm interested in right now, and that's Turner for the Stapleford death."

"You might try the mine. I suggest you put a couple of guys out there round-the-clock. He's bound to show up."

"Oh, so you're givin' us orders now?"

"Just a suggestion," Rent said. "This guy's dangerous. And the girl could be next."

"As you know, the girl, and her brother, are safe for now."

"Have you questioned them yet?"

"None of your business."

"And you expect me to be forthcoming with you."

"Obstruction of justice jingle any bells for you?"

"Have you turned over Hannah's place yet?"

"That's Alvarez's department. You'll have to talk to her."

"Will do. But what about the mine? You gonna send some uniforms out there?"

"Not more than we have at this time."

"I'm telling you—"

"We're short staffed, and now we have that shooting at the school to deal with. That's sucked up all our available manpower."

"Maybe I'll go out there."

"The school?"

"No, the mine."

"It's your funeral," Washington said and ended the call.

Rent tossed the phone on the table and leaned back in his chair, pondering his next move. He went to the kitchen, made coffee, and fixed a ham, cheese, and tomato sandwich with items purchased at Trader Joe's, for all practical purposes the only place he shopped for groceries.

With the sandwich half eaten and caffeine infused in his veins once again, he reached for his phone. He punched up the number for Sgt. Alvarez, got a recording, and left a message. He next called his editor and told her about the stakeout and the incident in Riverside County.

"That was you who got shot at? Holy crap."

"Yeah, I'm putting in for battle pay."

O'Connor laughed. "Good luck with that. But I'm glad you're okay."

"What have you heard?"

"Just that there was an incident out near Anza reported by motorists and the Riverside sheriff's department is looking into it. Right now they're suggesting it was a gang-related drive-by. I'm going to have Naomi look into it. I'll have her give you a call."

"Oh, please."

"Rent, like or not, you've become a story in and of itself, what with ID-ing the woman's body, and now being shot at. The two are obviously related and have raised the profile of this entire investigative piece you're working on."

"Yeah, yeah . . . great for the bottom line. It's always about the money."

"Where are you? I thought you'd be returning to the office after the stakeout."

"I'm at home. I have phone calls to make, and I didn't want to be bothered by any of this other shit."

"You got a story for me?"

"Nothing's really changed. Sure, we connected a few dots, but we need some hard evidence or an arrest. Right now it's still mostly speculation."

"What about the search warrant?"

"I'm waiting for Alvarez at the sheriff's to get back to me with an official tally."

O'Connor sighed. "Okay. I'll have Clark call you."

"Whatever," he replied and punched the phone to end the call.

Rent poured himself another cup of coffee and finished the rest of his sandwich. He then opened his laptop to record his notes from the day's events. He made little progress before his phone began vibrating. The screen identified the caller as Naomi Clark.

He swiped the phone to answer. "Hello, Lewis," he said.

"Yuk, yuk. You have a minute or two?"

"For you, maybe even three or four."

"You're being so generous with your time."

"How may I help you?"

"Wow, you are in a good mood. Get laid last night, did you?"

"I'm trying to be serious."

"Yeah, okay. That must have scared the crap out of you, getting shot at."

"You could say that. Although it happened so fast, it didn't really hit me—"

"So to speak."

"Poor choice of words. The realization of what had just occurred didn't really sink in until it was all over."

"What'd you do then?"

"Changed my underwear."

"Can I quote you on that?"

"O'Connor will rewrite it."

"Let's get back to being serious, shall we?"

"Works for me."

"Give me the nitty-gritty."

Rent related the incident, beginning with the stakeout and tailing Turner and his companions to the compound near Anza, then being chased and shot at.

"And this relates to the ongoing investigation into the EBT fraud?" Clark asked.

"It does, but you can't say that. It could totally fuck up the progress we've made. It would be better if you just left it for now; leave it for the Riverside rag to cover."

"That means I have to come up with something else."

"Or you could just continue working on your novel."

"Shush. No one needs to know about that."

"It's not exactly a state secret," he said and ended the call.

Rent checked the time. *A bit early for an adult libation. Then again, I did get shot at today, and it's five o'clock somewhere.*

He mixed a Mel Bay and got out his fiddle to help him wind down. "What shall it be? he wondered aloud. "How about *Booth Shot Lincoln*."

THE INSISTENT BUZZING OF his phone jarred Rent from his slumber on the couch. The sun had set, and only a bit of twilight remained.

He crossed the room to the dining table, rubbing the sleep from his eyes. By then the incessant rattling on the tabletop had mercifully ceased. He picked up the phone and switched it from vibrate back to ring-tone mode, then checked to see who had so rudely awakened him. Alvarez had returned his call.

He sighed, used the bathroom, then reheated the remaining coffee. He returned to the dining table and stared at the phone, debating whether to wait until morning to call her back. He picked up the phone. *Might as well strike while it's hot.*

His mind shifted gears and *The Merry Blacksmith*, one of his favorite tunes, popped into his consciousness. He shook his head to clear the thought. *Focus, Beacham. Focus.*

He called Alvarez and she answered on the second ring.

"Hello, there," she greeted. "I thought maybe you were in the hospital, getting your wounded pride sutured up."

"Yeah, yeah, make fun of my nearly getting killed."

"Well, nothing like a little first-hand experience to see what it's like being a cop," she said.

"You got me there. What's up?" he asked.

"First, I just wanted to see how you're feeling. That really was a close call. You're dealing with some serious bad asses. And you're not even in Oaxaca."

"Yeah, no shit."

"Washington said you found a shell casing next to the PI's car."

"It's a start."

"Yeah, but without a gun, we don't have anything to match it to."

"So, no arrests at this point."

"No, and just as well," she said. "The Riverside crew's just tightening the net, hoping these idiots'll to do something even stupider and they can reel 'em in."

"What about Turner? Anything new there?" he inquired.

"Actually, that's why I called. We finally got a warrant, thanks in part to the EBT cards you spotted in his trash, along with his possible involvement in the woman's death. We're going first thing in the morning. You can observe, if you want."

"I want. What time?"

"The usual crack of dawn."

"Two days in a row," he said. "I can't wait to get back to my usual routine."

"Oh, you poor man. Not getting your beauty sleep?" she teased.

"Not lately. Text me when you're on your way?"

"Will do. Sweet dreams, sleepyhead."

Rent disconnected and sighed. "Back to Julian. I might as well move up there . . . Oh, shit. Abby! And Rachel."

He brought up FAVORITES on the screen. *Better call Rachel first.*

"Hi, Dad. How was the stakeout?"

"Hi, Sweetie. That's partly why—"

"Oh, I'm Sweetie now?"

"Sorry, it just came out. It's a term of endearment."

"I know that. I'm twelve, not five."

"We can think of something else."

"No, I like it. It's better than what Mom—"

Rachel choked up for a moment.

"Rachel, I'm sorry. I didn't mean to—"

"It's okay. I'll be all right. What I was trying to say is that Mom called me Fusspot. I like Sweetie better."

"Then Sweetie it is. Is Martha there?"

"She's in the house. I'm with the horses."

"Okay . . . listen carefully. I want you to go to the house and stay there. Are you wearing a hoodie?"

"Yes."

"Is the hood up?"

"Of course. It's cold here. We're in the mountains, as if you didn't know."

"Good. But I want you to go to the house and get with Martha, and put the phone on speaker so she can hear what I'm saying."

Rachel complied and Rent explained that Rachel needed to stay indoors. He gave only the highlights of the day's events, telling them how they found Turner, but he discovered them and disappeared again.

"He's extremely dangerous. I'm confident you're safe because only a few people know where you are, but stay indoors and away from the windows."

Martha spoke. "I'll keep her safe. And I'll get the twelve-gauge out of the gun cabinet and keep it handy, just in case."

"Let's hope it doesn't come to that," Rent said, then added, "Rachel . . . Sweetie . . . I know this is a difficult time for you, but I want you to know I love you, and I want you safe so we can spend lots of time together. You got that?"

"Yes," she replied, then whispered, "and I love you too."

"I have to go, but I'll come see you tomorrow."

Rent ended the call, breathed deeply and exhaled, then dried his eyes before calling Abby.

"Hey, there. I was beginning to wonder if you were missing in action."

"I almost was."

"What do you mean?" she asked, concern lacing her voice.

He told her about the shooting incident.

"Oh . . . my . . . god. Are you okay?"

"Still a little rattled, but otherwise I'm all right."

"I wish I could give you a really big hug."

"Maybe you can."

"Are you in town? I'm still at the office, but I'm about to call it quits and go home."

"Not yet, but I could be if you don't mind."

"Why would I mind?"

"Well, we hadn't discussed it, but something's come up."

He told her about the warrant to search Gabe Turner's premises, and he needed to be there early in the morning.

"Oh, so now you're just using my place for a flop house, is that it?"

"No, I—"

"Can't you take a joke? Of course I want to see you, and I'll feel safer with you here."

"I can pick up some takeout."

"Make it Thai?"

"Thai it is."

"There's a good place in Ramona, Pinto Thai, just as you come into town. I'll call it in. What would you like?"

"A curry, not too hot."

She gave him directions.

"See you in about an hour."

"I'll set out a towel for you. I suspect you'll need a shower . . . and I just might join you."

As they ate, Abby again expressed her concern about Rachel losing her mother and not knowing the identity of her father.

"While Rent finished chewing a piece of pork, he considered his response. *No use putting it off any longer. That'll just make it worse.* He felt his throat tighten and he swallowed hard, then took a sip of wine before answering.

"Hannah's parents believe it's some rich married guy up in Washington who paid Hannah a chunk of money to disappear."

"Ah, the Aeschylian plot sickens."

"However . . ."

Abby cocked her head and eyed Rent directly. "So, there's more to this."

Rent swallowed and took another sip of wine.

Abby's face contorted from a Bacchus-induced Aphrodite to the mask of drop-jaw disbelief of Electra. "Don't tell me . . ."

Rent could no longer maintain his poker face. He met her gaze with a clenched jaw and pursed lips.

"You gotta be joking. It's you?"

Rent nodded. "Afraid so. Her parents are in denial."

"Aside from this being totally incredible—I mean, what are the odds—I don't know whether to congratulate you or tell you to get the hell out of my house."

"Look . . . I—"

"How long have you known this?"

"I only knew for certain two days ago, after the DNA test results came back, and that has not been announced officially. I didn't say anything earlier because—"

"You're a coward."

"No, it's not that. You've been dealing with a lot of crap yourself, and I didn't want to dump any more on you and totally stress you out. The cops are still waiting on the DNA test from the other guy."

Abby sighed and gulped from her own glass of wine.

"Does Rachel know?"

"She knew before I did, and when I went to tell her about her mother, the first words out of her mouth were 'you dirty bastard.'"

Abby laughed. "Good for her."

"Then she hugged me and said she'd known ever since she saw me at the bookstore."

"So, she's pleased."

"Yeah, she is. She even drew a nice charcoal sketch of me. It's hanging on her bedroom wall."

"Actually, it would give me an excuse to do more stuff with her. I could take her shopping."

"She might prefer to go horseback riding."

Abby snorted. "You men. You really don't get women, do you?"

"What do you mean?"

"She would prefer to go horseback riding, and then go shopping."

Rent sighed and shrugged in resignation.

Abby grinned and shook her head. "I guess you can stay, but you might be sleeping on the couch . . . Daddy-o."

25

Friday, Day 20, morning

The alarm on Rent's phone began playing the Arthur Smith tune *Walking in My Sleep*, quietly at first, then louder in an escalating sequence.

"Okay, okay," he muttered as he reached for the annoying device.

"You're on your own," came a voice in the dark. "I'm going back to sleep."

Rent rolled out of the bed, grabbed his clothes, and crept out of the room. He closed the door as gently as he could and tip-toed to the living room before getting dressed.

Brrrrr, it's freezing my balls off in here.

He put on his clothes, including long johns, finishing with a wool sweater pulled over his head and to his waist, adding a down jacket, and finally topping his head with a red stocking cap. He went to the kitchen and started the coffee, then opened the fridge and took out the container of leftover curry.

Might as well eat it cold.

Enough coffee had dripped into the pot to get him going, so he poured himself a half cup. He cradled the ceramic mug in both hands as he sipped the scalding brew, warming his hands as well as his innards. The furnace clicked on and he welcomed the warmth emitted from a floor duct. It reminded him of his mom, standing over the heat vent in the breakfast nook, coffee in hand, as the warm air billowed her nightgown as if it were a parachute, drifting her downward into a new day.

He ate a few more bites of the curry, returning the remainder to the refrigerator. He went out to his truck to retrieve his travel mug.

"Christ, this is a cold frosty morning," he muttered. "Maybe livin' up here isn't such a great idea after all."

Back inside, he filled the travel mug with coffee.

Abby came up behind him, still wearing a flannel nightgown, and circled her arms around his waist. "Save any for me?"

"A cup or two," he said.

He felt her tug at the hair on the back of his head.

"You could use a haircut," she said.

He twisted around to embrace her and said, "Thanks, Mom."

She grimaced. "I just want you to look your best, although that red stocking cap makes you look like Woody the Woodpecker."

"I'm going to observe a search warrant being served, not attend a dinner party," he retorted. "I thought you were going back to sleep. Sorry if I woke you."

"It wasn't you," she said as she released him and helped herself to the coffee. "I couldn't stop thinking about you being shot at. I hope no one tries it again today."

"I'll be surrounded by cops. I think it'll be safe there," he assured her. "Besides, he's probably no where near his place right now. Unless he's dumber than he looks already."

Rent's phone chirped and he checked the screen. Text from Alvarez:

On R way.

RENT WAITED IN THE 4Runner, engine running and the heat on full blast. The sheriff's vehicles passed by, and he fell in behind them. When they reached Turner's place, he parked on the side of the road.

He approached the operation on foot and kept his distance as the deputies encircled the house. Once everyone had stationed themselves, they announced their presence. After receiving no response from inside the house, they forced the front door open and entered the premises, again identifying themselves. A separate group began a search of the Bronco parked in front of the house.

A uniformed officer approached him. Sgt. Diana Alvarez.

"You made it," she said.

"Yeah. A bit early for my taste, but duty calls."

"We'll be here for a while."

"That's okay. I've never seen a search before, so it's all new to me. You might want to check out his trash bin. That's where I saw some EBT cards."

She stared at him for a moment. "Al mentioned it. You didn't touch them, did you?"

"No. I had gloves on, and I just lifted the lid and poked around with a stick," he said. "That thing stinks to high heaven. Figured I'd leave the dirty work to you pros."

"Kind of you."

"Looking for anything in particular?"

She shrugged. "Anything relevant to the death or the fraud."

"Any idea where Mr. Carpet Cleaner might be?" Rent asked.

"He's evaporated into this thin mountain air," she answered. "I hear it was you who lost him."

Rent held up a gloved hand in a defensive posture. "Whoa, so now it's on me, is it? The PI put a tracking device on his van, but they apparently found it because it went dead shortly after we were shot at."

She chuckled. "Just joshing you. At least we know he's working with the dudes in Fallbrook and Anza. I'm sure there are others. Now we need to lay our hands on him."

"Have you checked his mine?"

"Not in the last twenty-four hours," she said. "We'll send a patrol over there after we're done here. We're not entirely certain which one is his. I've been waiting to hear back from the BLM folks in El Centro."

"I have an idea about that," Rent said. "I've been studying the claim diagrams on the BLM website and matching that with Google Earth's satellite imagery. I think it's between the Redman and Ready Relief mines, which are near the head of the canyon, and the Golden Chariot, which is about three miles farther south."

"Clever lad."

"I try. I'm thinking of going over there while you guys trash this place."

"And, why, exactly? To actually get shot this time?"

"I plan on keeping my distance."

"Famous last words."

A shout from a forensic technician interrupted them—his friend Pamela Berringer. Alvarez strode over to the Bronco, and Rent followed a few steps behind. She turned and held up hand. "Not so close."

Rent stopped and cupped his ears. The technician told her they had found blood on the back seat.

From Hannah's head wound?

The search continued as the sun breached the eastern ridge, providing some direct warmth to Rent's back. He went to his truck for his coffee, which had cooled to lukewarm. He started the engine and enjoyed the heat while he finished his infusion of caffeine. Abby had texted him, and he replied, saying he would call her later. He then returned to the graveled yard and resumed his observation of the search.

Periodically, one of the forensics team members emerged from the house with bagged items and placed them in one of the sheriff's vehicles. At one point, Alvarez looked through the boxes of items, then rejoined Rent.

"Finding anything incriminating?" he asked.

"We struck gold, so to speak," she said. "But this is just FYI for now. I will try to get you specifics this afternoon."

"Got it."

"So far the search has turned up EBT cards, skimmers, wads of cash, and a number of firearms."

"Nice work."

"We also found a computer. The geek squad will give that a thorough going over."

"About that."

Alvarez froze. "Don't tell me . . ."

Rent raised his hands, palms facing forward. "Nothing bad, just to let you know. Offering a bit of gossip in trade."

"Like what?"

"This is third-hand stuff, but it may be useful."

"I'm all ears."

"Rachel told Abby—"

"These would be the unimpeachable wits that include a twelve-year-old-girl and the Abby of Pine Hills with whom you slept last night?"

Rent rolled his eyes. "You're going to make detective any day now."

"Working on it. This had better be good."

"As I said, it's third hand, but Rachel told Abby that on days when Hannah was working at the bookstore, Turner would come to the house to keep an eye on her and her brother."

"By 'her,' you're referring to Rachel."

"Correct. But he spent most of his time playing video games on Hannah's computer. Or that's what Rachel thought. But it occurs to me that maybe that's when he did his phishing, using her computer, rather than his own."

"Talk about covering your ass."

"Do you have her laptop?"

"That's our next stop. But that's helpful. Thanks."

"You're welcome. You think maybe she was in on it? The fraud, I mean," Rent asked.

Alvarez shrugged. "We have to check it out. I'll talk to Washington."

"Where is he, by the way?"

"He's up to his ass in that school shooting."

Rent shook his head in disbelief. "What kind of society have we created . . . kids shooting kids . . . I'm gonna take off. I'll call you this afternoon."

"Don't do anything stupid . . . or illegal."

Rent grinned. "Who, me?"

RENT DROVE TO HANNAH'S house, but a pair of deputies motioned him away. He backed out of the driveway, intending to return to Pine Hills, then thought, "Screw it. I need to eat something."

He continued on Boulder Creek Road, proceeding south toward Descanso, then veered left onto Engineer Road and wound his way up the steep grade into the Cuyamaca Mountains. As he crossed over the ridge, the road dropped into a broad valley, where he spotted Lake

Cuyamaca glistening in the midday sun. The iconic Stonewall Peak provided a scenic backdrop with its lingering patches of snow on the north slope, along with the more mundane Cuyamaca Peak, its summit sprouting a grove of unnatural structures—microwave relay towers for wireless communications.

Rent turned right onto SR 79 and drove to The Pub at Lake Cuyamaca. He hadn't been inside since new owners took over and renamed the venerated café.

"Oh, shit," he muttered as he veered into the parking lot and spotted a Subaru Outback with a Washington license plate. He parked and sat there for a moment.

Of all the luck . . .

He went inside and saw them immediately, seated at a table next to an expansive window that overlooked the lake, a lake littered with wintering waterfowl. He approached the table and Hannah's parents turned their heads. Frank Powell eyed Rent with a blank expression, while Agnes Powell's shoulders sagged and her lips pursed.

"And we were having such a pleasant meal," Agnes said.

"Trust me, I didn't plan this," Rent said. "But since I'm here, mind if I join you?"

She sighed and waved at an empty chair. "Might as well."

Rent pulled out the chair next to Frank and sat down, facing Agnes.

A man about Rent's age, sporting shaggy hair and a beard, along with a prominent nose ring, set down orders at an adjacent table, then stepped over to the Powells' table.

"Everything okay here?" he asked.

Both Powells nodded, and Frank said, "Yes, the fish and chips are very good."

The server glanced at Rent. "Would you like a menu?"

Rent nodded.

"You got it," the man said and turned away.

Agnes leaned forward and spoke in a low voice. "I hate those stupid nose rings. Especially in men. Disgusting."

Rent lifted one shoulder in a half shrug.

"So, what news?" she asked as she picked up a French fry and dabbed it in ketchup.

"I just came from Hannah's place," Rent answered. "The cops are about to conduct a search. They will take her computer, so who knows what they may find on it."

"Hannah may have made some bad choices in her life, but she's not a criminal," Agnes said.

"The cops think it's possible that Turner used her computer for some of his illicit activities."

"That wouldn't surprise me," she said.

"Nor me," Frank added.

The server returned with the menu, then looked at the Powells. "Any dessert?"

"Maybe," Agnes said.

"Just let me know," the server replied.

When the man had left, Agnes said, "We've hired a lawyer."

"So I heard," Rent responded.

"We're taking custody of the kids. They belong with family, not some foster parent. And we don't want you anywhere near our grand-daughter."

"It's a bit late for that, I'm afraid."

Agnes scoffed. "Her father is that rich guy who paid Hannah off. It's nothing to do with you."

"DNA doesn't lie, and the official test results will confirm it. Besides, if Turner tracks her down, it will be a moot point. She's safe with Martha. Once Turner's been taken into custody, then, yeah, they should be with you. But until then . . . has he contacted you?"

Agnes grimaced and glanced at her husband, then shifted her gaze back to Rent. "He keeps sending us threatening texts, and he's figured out where we're staying, just down the road at Oakzanita Springs."

"He was there?"

"We found a note on the RV's windshield, threatening us. Had to be from him."

"Did you notify the cops?"

Frank nodded. "A deputy came by and took it with him."

The server returned and Rent ordered the Pub Burger and a Stonewall Stout.

"What about a funeral or memorial for Hannah?" Rent asked.

Agnes answered.

"It's being handled by a mortuary in Ramona, but no date set pending release of the body. We thought about having her taken back home to Washington, but we may end up staying here, with the kids. We're doing a cremation rather than a burial, so . . ." She shook her head, then added, "How'd you know about the lawyer?"

"Detective Washington told me. I know the guy, Tucker. Ambulance chaser. I recommend finding someone else. I know one of the best lawyers in town. He does criminal defense, but he could recommend someone."

The server returned with the stout and a napkin. "Your burger will be right up."

Rent thanked him, took a long pull at the beer, and wiped his mustache with the napkin.

"We like this place," Agnes said. "And we love all the birds, snowbirds, just like us."

I do believe it's the other way around, Rent thought but kept it to himself.

He looked at Agnes, then Frank. "Another thing . . ."

"What now?" Agnes said in an accusatory tone.

Rent urged them to get some professional help in dealing with the grief, especially for Rachel. "A violent death like this carries with it much deeper emotional scars than a death of natural causes, knowing that another person caused the death of a loved one."

He recommended they get in touch with a therapist named Connie Saindon. "She specializes in dealing with survivors of violent loss and the Restorative Retelling model of therapy. She's nationally, even internationally, recognized for her work in this field."

He explained that she lived in San Diego and offered group sessions so survivors know they are not alone, where they help each other to process the grief and deal with their loss. "She knows there is never any 'closure' in situations like this, but you learn to live with it better."

He further pointed out that she is the author of two books, *The Journey: Learning to Live with Violent Death*, and the award-winning *Murder Survivor's Handbook: Real-Life Stories, Tips & Resources*.

"I wrote a piece on her and her methods after she helped a friend of mine deal with the violent deaths of his parents, and he helped her write and publish her books. I will get you her contact information."

"We have spoken with a person with victim's assistance at the sheriff's department, a woman named Sally Johnson," Frank said.

"That's good," Rent replied. "I'm sure Connie's on their list of referrals."

The server returned and placed the mammoth burger on the table in front of Rent. Again, he asked if the others wanted any dessert.

Agnes shook her head. "Maybe next time."

Rent began the awkward task of getting his mouth around the burger and bun.

Agnes said to her husband, "We should be going," and he nodded. She then turned to Rent and wagged a finger at him. "You stay away from our granddaughter."

Rent set the burger down. "And if I don't?"

"You'll be hearing from our lawyer."

"As I said, before you rack up too many billable hours with Tucker, I suggest you find a different attorney."

She and Frank stood and left without another word.

Rent shook his head and downed a large gulp of stout, then attacked the burger again.

After finishing his lunch, he strolled along the lakefront. He recognized the multitude of Canada geese, and a Bald Eagle took a low pass over the lake, scattering the birds amid a cacophony of protests, but he knew nothing about the many species of ducks and other waterfowl populating the lake's surface and its shoreline.

I'll have to bring Abby out here.

Feeling chilled, he returned to the 4Runner and contacted Alvarez, who said they had not caught up with Turner. Rent inquired about the search of Hannah's house and the sergeant said they were still processing everything. But she had other news.

"Oh, what's that?"

"DNA results . . . Dad," she said, then chuckled.

"Great news. Rachel will be thrilled."

"Yeah? And here I thought you'd be in total denial and demanding another test."

"I already knew the results, and, as it turned out, so did Rachel."

"Someone leaked it."

"I wouldn't know."

"Humph. This place is a bloody sieve. But there's still a lot of paper shuffling to do."

"Whatever it takes. Hannah's parents aren't gonna like it though."

"Trouble with the in-laws already, eh?"

"They're not exactly my in-laws, but, yeah, I just had lunch with them. Ran into them at the café at Lake Cuyamaca."

"I got volunteered to break the news."

"I don't envy you that. They're already in denial, and I imagine they'll be demanding a test of their own."

"Good luck with that. Gotta go."

RENT STARED THROUGH THE windshield.

What now? . . . Fuck it.

He started the engine and got back on the road, headed toward Julian, then down Banner Grade to Chariot Canyon, hoping to find Turner's hideout. This time Rent had armed himself with the BLM information, and he had GPS in the rented 4Runner. He didn't believe for a second the con man was actively mining. That would require back-breaking physical labor and expensive machinery.

While enroute, he turned on the radio and again heard the dire weather forecast: atmospheric river to drop several inches of rain and will cause flooding; flash-flood alert for the mountains and desert.

As long as I'm outta here and back home before the deluge arrives.

At the bottom of the grade, he turned onto the California Riding and Hiking Trail and proceeded southward toward Turner's Golden Eagle Mine. The poorly maintained road got worse the farther he went.

After a few dead ends and backtracking, he reached what he believed to be the mine. It had a ramshackle shed, a rusting shipping container, and weathered piles of mine tailings. He saw a few remaining timbers from the structures built during the heydays of the short-lived mining boom, then spotted what appeared to be the entrance to the mine.

He parked and began walking toward the opening, which had a faded sign above it. He could make out some of the letters:

LDE   AG.

Could be Golden Eagle.

A gate made of chain-link fence covered the opening, and behind it a rustic door made of wooden slats. A sign beside the opening read:

No Trespassing.
Private Property.
Violators Will
Be Prosecuted.

The gate had a shiny padlock dangling from a chain to keep out intruders, so he explored the area near the entrance. Rusting equipment and tools littered the grounds.

What's this?

Rent leaned over to inspect a piece of debris, then picked it up. A small tin box, its paint having peeled off long ago, but the embossed lettering on the lid remained clearly visible.

"Mail Pouch," he uttered.

He lifted off the lid of the tin and discovered a piece of folded paper, browned with age. He didn't want to risk crumbling the paper, so he didn't touch it. The writing on the paper had faded; he could barely make out the words defining, apparently, the boundaries of the original claim ". . . 660 ft North of Monume . . ."

A slight breeze drifting down from the ridge 1,500 feet above whispered in his ear as he attempted to decipher the faint marks on the hand-written document. Then another sound.

Not natural.

Behind him.

Rabbit? Coyote? Mountain lion?

26

Rent never saw him coming. His only warning the sound of a slight scuffle of gravel before he felt the sole of a boot in the middle of his back, which knocked him to the ground, followed by a hard kick to the ribs. Pain raced through his chest like a jolt of high-voltage electricity. He curled into a fetal position and moaned, trying to catch his breath. Every attempt at breathing sent a new spark of current coursing through his chest.

He waited for a kick to the kidneys, but it never came. Only a surly male voice.

"If you want to live, leave it alone."

Turner's voice? He couldn't be sure.

Rent heard footsteps fade as the man strode from the scene, then the sound of a diesel engine starting and a vehicle driving away. It had been hidden behind the shipping container.

After several minutes of short, shallow breathing, Rent slowly stretched out, then tried sitting up. Another jolt. He rolled slowly onto his stomach and in a series of deliberate movements got to his knees. He spotted the Mail Pouch tin and its lid lying nearby, the paper document having spilled out but miraculously still in one piece. He crawled over to it and gently returned the document to the tin and put the lid on the box.

He then used a nearby boulder to unfold his body and extend himself to full height. For a moment. Out of breath, he sat on the rock. His lungs refused to fill with air. He felt as though he were being suffocated.

He knew he had cracked, if not broken, ribs. He'd been through it once before after a bicycle accident left him with a punctured lung. He had regained consciousness only to find a homeless man staring down at him, looking as if he were disappointed in not being able to steal the bike.

Rent had endured the pain for more than a month. He did not wish to repeat the experience. Later, he realized he would have welcomed a mere month of discomfort.

Taking cautious baby steps, he made his way back to the 4Runner. Even at his snail's pace, he became short of breath after a few yards of stutter-stepping. The vehicle appeared unharmed, although the possibility of sand or sugar in the gas tank, or some other form of sabotage crossed his mind. Recalling the words of the shopkeeper of the store on Banner Grade, he checked the tire valves. All clear.

As he passed through Julian, he stopped at the real estate office, but Abby was out with a prospective buyer. Rent said he'd call her later.

From there, he drove himself to urgent care in Ramona. An X-ray assured him that he had not punctured a lung, but he definitely had two cracked ribs.

Still, it hurts like hell.

He asked for Vicodin, but the nurse practitioner told him to go home, take some Tylenol or Aleve and get some rest. At home, he opened a container of ibuprofen and washed down four of the red, 200-milligram tablets with a double-shot of gin. He called Washington and left a message, then located his dog-eared copy of Charlotte Brontë's *Shirley* and fell back into his recliner.

Incubus!

RENT AWOKE WITH A start. He'd been dreaming. A dark place. A moving shadow. Terror.

He glanced at the wall clock in the kitchen: 4:27.

Crap! Still light out, so it must be afternoon.

The book lay on the floor. He started to get out of the chair, then groaned and fell back. Deep breaths, then in one fluid motion he pushed himself up and out of the chair and onto his feet. He put a hand on the back of the chair to steady himself. He made his way to the kitchen for a glass of water.

Gotta call . . .

As if by psychic communication, his phone chimed. O'Connor. He tapped the Answer icon.

"Where the hell's your story? I'm laying out the Sunday edition."

"I'm . . . working . . . on it."

"You sound out of breath. Has something—"

"I got ambushed. Turner kicked the crap out of me. Cracked a couple ribs."

"What the—"

"At the mine. I found his mine. I didn't know he was there until he hit me from behind. He warned me off, then split."

"Oh, Christ. What about the searches? Anything come of that?"

"I put a call into Alvarez but haven't heard back."

"I need an update today, tomorrow morning at the latest."

"I'll call Alvarez right now."

"Are you sure you're up for this? You sound like you're at death's door."

"I feel like I'm at death's door, but, yeah, I'll get you something."

"I can put Clark on it if—"

"No! I'll do it."

He disconnected. *Polly, put the kettle on. Gonna be a long night.*

He called Deputy Alvarez and left a message, then called Rod Davis at HHSA and sighed with relief when Davis answered.

"Give me a minute. I'm on my way to the parking lot," Davis said and ended the call.

Rent brewed a cup of coffee and eyed the bottle of gin. *Nah, you're gonna have to wait.*

He managed one sip of the hot brew before the phone lit up.

"Rod, thanks for calling back."

"You just caught me. Heading off to TGIF."

"Any joy from that photograph Velasquez sent you, the one from the stakeout?"

"Yes and no."

"Enlighten me with the 'yes' bit."

Davis confirmed that man was the county employee suspected of authorizing fraudulent claims, but the cops haven't acted on it as far as he could tell. He had not shown the photo to anyone else.

"I don't know who I can trust," Davis said. "I don't know if he's a lone wolf or running with a pack."

"Talk to Washington," Rent replied. "If nothing else, he'll scare the crap out of the guy, maybe get him talking."

"You okay? You sound like you're having trouble breathing."

"I ran into Turner. He cracked a couple of my ribs. I'll be—"

"What?"

Rent's phone dinged. Incoming call from Alvarez.

"Rod, I gotta go. Talk to you next week."

Rent ended the call with Davis and tapped the Answer icon.

"Sergeant, thanks for getting back to me."

"You okay? You—"

"Don't you start."

"Don't you be rude to me."

"Sorry, it's just that I've had a rough afternoon. I'm in a lot of pain, and my editor is jumping down my throat."

"Has something happened?" she asked, a note of concern in her voice.

Rent replayed, for the third time, his encounter at the mine with the man he believed to be Turner.

"Don't say I didn't warn you."

"Yeah, yeah, whatever."

"Any idea where he went?"

"Not a clue. But I do have some positive news."

"You gonna share that?"

Rent gave her the GPS coordinates of the mine and she thanked him.

"You turn up anything useful in the searches?" he asked.

"As I said earlier, we hit paydirt at his place."

"And Hannah's?"

"Not so much."

"What about their computers?"

"Off the record?"

"For now."

"So far, nothing that links them to the fraud."

Rent sighed. "Okay, what can you give me for the record?"

The deputy confirmed that the search at Turner's place had turned up several dozen counterfeit EBT cards and more than $100,000 in cash, along with skimming devices, a computer, and a number of unregistered firearms suspected of being purchased through private sales or from out of state, including ghost guns.

At Hannah's house, they found an EBT card, which appeared to be genuine, and a laptop computer. The malnourished dog had been turned over to the Humane Society.

"What can I say about the computers?" Rent asked.

"The forensic technicians are going through both of the computers, but until they've completed their work, no further comment will be issued by the department," Alvarez said.

"And Turner?"

"The department has a warrant for the arrest of Turnbull, a.k.a. Turner, in relation to the EBT fraud, and he's wanted for questioning in the death of the woman whose body was found in Chariot Canyon," she added.

She finished with a bland boilerplate statement from the sheriff.

"How'd it go with Mr. and Mrs. Powell?"

"They had nothing good to say about you."

"I had lunch with them today."

"Pouring gasoline on the fire, are we, Dad?"

"Totally by accident. I just happened to walk in while they were eating."

"And you wanted to gloat?"

"They said that?"

"Agnes did most of the talking."

"As usual."

"They have a lawyer."

"My neighbor. I told them they should get someone else."

"I gotta go."

Rent thanked her, disconnected, and grabbed his coffee. He sat at the dining table, fired up his laptop, and opened a blank Word document. He typed:

San Diego—A warrant has been issued for the arrest of a man suspected of being involved in the recent uptick in counterfeit EBT cards plaguing San Diego County officials. . . .

The predicted rain began to fall as Rent hammered out a draft of the story, the familiar rhythm of tapping the keyboard, combined with the rain splattering on the windows, created a syncopated melody as the alphabetic characters danced across the computer screen. Adrenaline diminished the pain in his chest and the pressure of the looming deadline resuscitated his flagging gray cells as he immersed himself in the news realm he called home.

His chiming phone broke his rhythm, but he had enough of the story outlined that he wouldn't lose all of his momentum. He saved the document and glanced at the phone's screen. The private investigator.

"Hey, Alicia. What's up?"

"Rod Davis called. How are you feeling?"

I know they mean well, but this is getting tiresome.

He repeated yet again the low points of his day.

"Have you eaten?"

"Not since lunch."

"Me either. How does Greek sound? I'll come to you."

"Are you sure?"

"No arguing. I insist."

He relented and gave her his address and directions, then returned to his EBT story, making tweaks here and there, and filling in the details about Turner being last seen in the vicinity of Chariot Canyon, near Julian, and that he was also wanted in connection to the death of the woman whose body had been found in the canyon. He repeated enough of the background from his previous pieces to give the new information sufficient context for the reader.

His editor called again, and he promised it would be in her Inbox in the morning. Then Abby called and he reiterated yet again his episode at the mine, as well as his chance encounter with Hannah's parents.

"I'll come see you."

"No, it'll be a wasted trip, and the atmospheric river has arrived. The roads will be slick. And I'm in serious pain. I have to finish my story, and I'm going to crash at any moment. Let's talk in the morning."

Abby expressed her disappointment and resigned herself to the postponement.

A loud banging on his front door, followed by shouts, interrupted the call.

"Someone's at the door. I gotta go," he said and ended the call.

Rent slowly made his way to the door, keeping his phone in hand in case he needed to call 9-1-1, at the same time wondering why he had not exactly lied to Abby, but certainly misled her.

At the door, Rent called out, "Who is it?"

"Alan Tucker. Open up, asshole!"

Rent peered through the peephole. He could see the lawyer glaring at the door, his hands balled into fists.

"Open up! I want to talk to you."

Rent sighed, unlocked the door, and opened it, but left the flimsy screen door locked and unopened as a barrier between them.

"You gonna let me in?"

"No."

The rain, increasing in intensity, had flattened Tucker's hair and wetted the shoulders of his jacket.

"Where do you get off calling me an 'ambulance chaser' to a client of mine?"

Rent snorted. "If the shoe fits . . ."

"You're scum. You're a lowdown muckraker. You'll regret this."

"If lawyers and their corporate cohorts and their bought-and-paid-for politicians didn't create so much muck, there would be no need for muckrakers."

"I could sue you for defamation."

"You're not familiar with the old adage 'Never quarrel with a man who buys ink by the barrel'?"

Tucker glared at Rent and opened his mouth as if to speak, but a woman's voice cut him off.

"Hello! Rent?"

Alicia Velasquez stopped a short distance away, holding an umbrella in one hand and a plastic shopping bag in the other. Tucker glanced at her, then back at Rent.

"You haven't heard the last of this, asshole," Tucker said and stalked off, stepping around the private investigator.

Alicia frowned at him, then looked toward Rent as she moved forward. "My, my . . ." she uttered.

Rent opened the screen door and motioned her in. "Never mind him. He's all bark."

She stepped inside and gave the interior a quick scan as Rent closed the door and took her umbrella. "Nice little bach pad you have here."

"It works for me. Kitchen's to the right."

"Two bedroom?" she asked as she set the bag on the counter.

"Yeah, upstairs."

"Good. You won't have to sleep on the couch."

Rent's brow furrowed. "The couch?"

Velasquez's dark eyes sparkled and her full lips profiled a mischievous grin. "When your daughter spends the night . . . Dad," she said as she removed her coat and handed it to Rent.

Rent's jaw fell. "Ah, that," he replied and draped her coat over the back of a chair.

"Yes, that. You have no clue what's in store for you, do you?" she added as she removed the take-out containers and a bottle of wine from the bag and placed them on the counter.

"What do you mean?"

"She's twelve, as I recall? Soon to be thirteen, as in teen . . . ager?" she stated as if it were a question, eyebrows raised.

Rent nodded.

"You're gonna be hit with a runaway freight train. Retsina?"

Runaway freight train? He stared at her for a long moment before shifting his gaze to the bottle of wine she had held up. "Isn't that the stuff that tastes like turpentine?"

"It can be an acquired taste," she said as she opened a cupboard door, closed it, then opened a second and, finding what she'd been looking for, withdrew two wine glasses. She handed the bottle to Rent. "Corkscrew?"

He took the bottle, opened a drawer, and took out a corkscrew. "Oh, what the hell. Can't be any worse than this day's been so far."

Rent started to remove the cork, then winced.

"Here, let me," she said and took the bottle from him. She popped the cork and poured the faintly yellow liquid into the awaiting glasses, then handed one to Rent.

He took a small sip and grimaced. "Acquired taste, you say?"

Alicia lifted her glass and tapped his. "To acquired tastes and better days."

Rent cleared the dining table of his laptop, notebook, and assorted paper items. Velasquez found plates and utensils and placed them on the table, along with the food.

"I hope you like gyros," she said as she took a seat at the table.

"Yes," he answered and joined her, easing himself slowly onto the chair.

While they ate, Rent retold her about Turner's painful assault and the earlier encounter with Hannah's parents, as well as his conversation with Rod Davis at the county's HHSA.

"So that dude we saw in Fallbrook is the insider on the take?"

"It seems like it, yeah, and he's probably the one who added the third child to Hannah's application without her realizing it. And Turner siphoned off the increase, and then some. But this guy may not be the only one. Even so, the walls are beginning to close in."

"By the way . . . and this is not for publication . . . that truck that chased us?"

"Yeah?"

"Registered to Beltz junior."

"Whoa!"

"Whoa is right."

"You think he was at the wheel?"

"No idea. I was too busy dodging bullets to get a good look at him," she said. "More vino?"

"Why not? I'm not going anywhere for two days. Let it rain, let it pour."

Rent started to rise, groaned, and dropped back onto the chair.

"Sit," the PI ordered. "Let me do the pouring."

She retrieved the bottle and refilled his glass, then splashed a little more into her own before retaking her seat.

"Anymore stakeouts on your itinerary?" Rent asked.

"Not on this case. Just a few more follow-up interviews."

They chatted for a while longer, then Velasquez looked at her watch.

"I'd better get going before the roads start washing out."

She insisted on tidying up while Rent remained in his seat, then held up the wine bottle.

"I'll leave this here . . . in case you've acquired a taste for it."

Rent grinned. "I may have."

He went to the door and opened it as she put on her coat and retrieved her umbrella.

"Drive safe," he called as she stepped off the porch.

She stopped, turned, and said, "And you stay out of trouble," before continuing on.

Rent watched her until she disappeared around the corner of his building, then closed the door. He returned to the kitchen and refilled his wine glass.

Maybe I have acquired a taste. And not just for the wine.

He lifted the glass to his lips, then froze.

Oh, shit. Abby!

He took a quick gulp of wine, went to the living room for his phone, and plopped into his recliner with an "oof!"

She answered his call with a question. "What the hell's going on?"

How could she know . . .

"What do you mean?"

"I thought Gabe had come to your house and finished what he started at the mine."

Rent relaxed and let his head fall against the back of the chair.

"Sorry, I should have called sooner. But I had to finish writing—"

"You and your deadlines. Is that all that matters to you?"

"It is my job."

"Yeah, tilting at windmills."

"Some windmills need to be tilted."

"So if it wasn't Gabe, what happened?"

He told her about the lawyer and his involvement with Hannah's parents and the situation with Rachel.

"So now you're being sued?"

"He's just thin skinned. What about you? Heard anything more from Turner?"

"Actually, no. No more threatening texts. He hasn't come here. He's probably crawled under a rock somewhere, waiting out the storm, literally and figuratively."

"Let's hope so. But don't get complacent. He's getting desperate. No telling what he might do next."

"If he shows his face around here again, I'm ready. Locked and loaded."

27

Saturday, Day 21

Rent awoke with a start. Then groaned as his cracked ribs reminded him of the previous day's events. Did his phone ring? Or had he just imagined it?

Where is the damned thing?

He threw back the covers and struggled into a sitting position, recoiled in pain, caught his breath, then reached for the Costco fleece and flannel items on the floor next to the bed. He dressed with deliberation, trying to keep the pain at a tolerable level.

He made his way down the stairs and located his phone, which he'd left on the coffee table, next to the empty wine glass.

Apparently, I did acquire a taste.

He checked the phone. New message from Abby. *What now?*

He went to the kitchen and started brewing coffee. As it began trickling into the awaiting carafe, he called her.

"Did you get my message?" she asked.

"I haven't listened to it. I just—"

"You have to come. Now."

"Where are you?"

"At home, where do you think?"

"Why aren't you at work?"

"I don't feel well. Besides, in this weather, why bother. But I had a coughing spasm and called in sick. It better not be COVID. Again."

"Abby, I—"

"It's Gabe. He's stalking me. I'm scared."

"Then call nine-one-one."

"I did, and they said they had so many calls already because of the storm, it would be a while unless I was in imminent danger."

"What?"

"Just come, please? I don't want to be alone in case he comes back."

"I thought you were locked and loaded."

"I guess I'm not so brave after all."

"I just want to stay home, recuperate, curl up with Charlotte Brontë," he muttered.

"I know you're hurt, but wouldn't you rather curl up with me? At least while I'm still alive," she said, her tone shifting from demanding to a girlish pleading. "I'll make chicken soup."

Rent sighed as he felt his willpower melting. He wouldn't mind curling up with her, as painful as that might be, but the thought of driving to Julian on that narrow, winding road in torrential rain and blustery wind did not appeal to him, not in the least.

"Please?" she begged again.

"On my way," he said.

"Thank you. I love you," she said and ended the call.

Love? Oh, fuck. What happened to "like"?

AT LEAST THERE'S NOT much traffic, but still plenty of assholes in a big hurry.

Rent felt relieved as he turned onto Pine Hills Road, having navigated the drive into the mountains without serious incident. He continued on to Abby's house, slowing at the low spots where runoff had the pavement underwater.

He turned into her driveway and pulled up beside her Wrangler, then looked through the windshield at the double-wide mobile home.

Shit!

The front door stood open, waving in the wind. As a precaution, he texted Sgt. Diana Alvarez, Detective Al Washington, and private investigator Alicia Velasquez:

At Abby's. Could be trouble.

He put his phone in the center console, got out of the 4Runner, locked it, and walked as quickly as he could manage to the stairs.

"Abby?"

When she didn't reply, he climbed the stairs and stopped on the porch. He grabbed the door to stop it from swinging and peered through the doorway. Abby stood facing him from across the room, forcing a smile.

Rent entered, closed the door behind him, and, as she took a step forward, he began crossing the room to embrace her.

Movement to his left caught his eye. He stopped and turned his head as the fugitive Joshua Gabriel Turnbull, a.k.a. Gabe Turner, stepped from the hallway leading to the bedrooms and bathroom, Abby's shotgun in his hands.

Turner pointed the barrel of the gun at Rent's chest. "So, Mr. Nosy-assed Journalist . . . we meet yet again."

Rent shifted his gaze to Abby, noting her bruised and swollen face and lips. "What the—"

"He forced me . . . caught me off guard . . . lured me outside by making a racket. I thought it was the deer, that one of them got hurt or something . . . he said he would kill me . . .," she offered, her voice pleading forgiveness.

Turner waved the shotgun at Rent, then used it as a pointer. "Have a seat, asshole."

Rent went to the dining table, pulled out a chair and sat down.

"Hands behind your back."

Rent did as told.

Turner then nodded at Abby. "Take off that bracelet and tie his hands."

Abby still wore the survival bracelet. She unfastened it and began unraveling the paracord. When she had it loose, she bound Rent's wrists behind his back.

Abby, her mouth close Rent's ear, whispered, "Please don't hate me." She then stepped a few paces away.

"See?" Turner said to her. "I told you that would come in handy one day."

Rent twisted his head to look at Turner over his left shoulder. "You will regret this."

The man sneered. "No, I will not regret this. Not after what you did to me. I had a good thing going here. Until you, Mr. Goody Two-shoes, stuck your big fat nose into something that was none of your business."

"Fraud is everyone's business."

"Shut the fuck up or I'll blow your brains out right here."

"What, one murder isn't enough for you?"

"You fucker. I didn't murder nobody. That was an accident. She fell and hit her head."

"And died two days later and you left her body for the buzzards at an abandoned gold mine. You gonna kill her daughter too? And maybe Abby? Eliminate all the witnesses?"

"You're gonna tell me where she is."

"I have no idea where she is. Try her grandparents. She's probably with them in Arizona."

"Oh, ha-ha. Shows what you know. Her grandparents are not in Arizona. They're at a campground not far from here. But they don't have the girl."

"You tie them up and torture them, did you?"

"Not yet," he said. "Meanwhile, me and you are takin' a little trip, down the Mighty Mississipp'."

Turner ordered Abby to help Rent stand and go out the back-door to a Land Cruiser that Rent recognized as Turner's. They put Rent in the backseat, and Turner ordered Abby to drive.

"Where're we going?" she asked.

"Where do you think?"

AT THE MINE, TURNER unlocked the gate and opened the wooden door. He had a lantern and he handed Abby a flashlight, then motioned with the shotgun for her to lead the way and for Rent to follow.

Abby entered the mine, taking cautious steps.

"Come on, get a move on," Turner ordered.

"I'm trying. It's dark in here," she retorted.

They continued on, going deeper and downward into the mine. They lost sight of the opening due to a bend in the mine shaft.

When they came to a large brown tarp covering objects beneath it, Turner told them to stop.

"Over there," he said to Rent as he motioned with the lantern toward the tarp. You're staying here, with my goodies."

"What is this stuff?" Rent asked.

Turner stared at him for a moment, then grinned. "I'll show you."

The man leaned the shotgun against the wall and pulled back the tarp to reveal eight cardboard boxes stacked two high on a pair of wooden pallets. He tapped one of the boxes with the toe of his boot. "This here's gunpowder, black powder. Enough to blow a real big hole."

He tugged at the tarp again to reveal what looked like four military foot lockers, also stacked two high on a third pallet. He set the lantern on one of the boxes of gunpowder and laughed.

"Don't worry, this lantern is battery powered. No flame."

Next Turner opened one of the foot lockers. Rent peered inside. "Ammunition?"

"Yep. Hundreds, thousands of rounds."

"Where are the guns?"

"Got some in here," he said as he again motioned with his foot, then nodded toward the mine entrance. "That container out there? A lot more inside it."

"What are you, one of the Proud Boys or something?"

"Or something."

Rent shook his head. "You are nuts."

"The revolution is coming. We're gonna stop the next steal and take our country back, make it great again. Get rid of all the mud people."

"Are you tied in with Beltz?"

Turner's smirk shifted to a look of worry. "How do you know about him?"

"I'm Mr. Nosy-assed Journalist, remember?"

"Not for long you're not."

"I know all about you and your fascist pals up north."

Turner shook his head in disgust. "Those idiots. Should've taken you and that nosy woman out when they had the chance. But they blew it."

"You're all going to be rounded up. You and your sidekick at HHSA. It's just a matter of time. You've got a lot more to worry about than a twelve-year-old girl."

Turner's eyes narrowed. "You're not going to live long enough to find out." He turned to face Abby. "Come on. We're outta here."

"You're leaving him? With no water or food?"

Turner guffawed. "He's not goin' to be here long enough to worry 'bout that. He can shit hisself for all I care."

"Do I detect a slight southern accent?"

"He turns it on when he's trying to charm the ladies," Abby said.

"You shut your yap. You've said too much already," Turner said, then smiled slightly as he looked back at Rent. "Yes siree Bob. I'm originally from Mountain View, Arkansas, home of Jimmy Driftwood. Dry county, thanks to all the damned Baptists. My daddy and his daddy made a little 'shine in their day. Now they make it legal after being on that Moonshiner TV show. Now, that's what I call justice."

"You're gonna see justice all right, but not in a jar of moonshine," Rent said.

Turner pulled the tarp back in place, covering the foot lockers and cases of gunpowder, then flicked his head at Abby. She moved toward the mine entrance, while he followed.

As the light faded, Rent noticed a pick and shovel lying near the foot lockers. He knew they weren't for mining, but for burying. First Hannah, then him. He wondered how many people actually stand in their own grave before they die. *Not many.*

He recalled firing the flintlock rifle the previous week. *If I could somehow use a piece of quartz to strike a spark on the cart rail on the floor of the mine, maybe I could blast my way out. No, that would be suicidal.*

The light from the lantern and flashlight faded and he heard the chain and lock being fastened to the gate. Then nothing.

Total darkness, and silence, set in.

28

Sunday, Day 22, morning

Rent awoke, lying atop the cases of gunpowder, with the tarp pulled over him. He had no idea how long he had slept or the time of day, the only sound the trickling of water. He recalled the weather report: torrential rain and flash-flood warnings.

Trickling water? Oh, shit.

He sat up and stared into the blackness that surrounded him, wondering what Dostoyevsky would make of this "underground."

No one knows I'm here, except Turner, who intends to kill me, or leave me here to drown, or to starve to death, and Abby, who . . . what? Also wants me dead? Or is she merely an unwilling accomplice just trying to save her own ass? I suppose I'll know the answer soon enough.

He shivered, as much from the anxiety as the coolness of the mine and his damp clothing. Clothing damp not only from the moisture dripping around him. Rent straightened up and used the gunpowder containers, then the wall of the mine shaft, to guide him as he moved deeper into the mine, although he wasn't sure why. He needed to relieve himself. What difference would it make how or where he did it?

Right. I don't want to contaminate the water anymore than it already is.

Earlier, he had managed to kneel on the ground and drink from a puddle of water to sate his thirst, noting that he had probably ingested any number of toxic chemicals.

With his hands still tied behind his back, he couldn't unbutton his Levi's. He had tried to cut through the paracord by rubbing it against a sharp-edged projection from the wall of the mine. But that had proved futile, causing more harm to his exposed skin than to the paracord, and jarring loose fragments of rock that could potentially cause a cave-in. Or so he imagined.

As he had done previously, he squatted and leaned his back against the wall of the mine shaft, every move sparking another jolt to his ribs.

Can a bladder actually burst if it gets too full?

As distasteful as it seemed, he had no choice and relaxed.

At least it's not running down my legs.

That taken care of, he retraced his steps and continued on, slowly making his way.

"I'm going up slope, so it must be toward the entrance," he muttered.

He rounded a bend and a faint light provided a small degree of illumination. He could see where the light reflected off the rippling of the steady stream of water entering the mine, along with the steady drip, drip from the ceiling.

At the entrance, he inspected the wooden door and the chain-link gate again, in case he had missed something previously, but the chain and lock were still intact. Even so, he kicked the fencing material as hard as he could, the frustration and anger overwhelming him. Then he lost his balance and fell backward, landing hard on his buttocks and back, and crushing his still-tied hands.

"Son of a bitch!" he shouted as he rolled onto his side, his cracked ribs telegraphing their protest in sharp jabs of pain. He lay motionless and took slow, shallow breaths while he let the pain subside. After several minutes, he struggled to get onto his knees, where he again paused to catch his breath. It took him several attempts to get back on his feet. Breathing hard from the exertion, he leaned a shoulder against the gate.

This was not in my job description.

A faint sound brought him back to the present. A motor. A motor vehicle. His savior? Or his executioner? Maybe Abby did the right thing and called the cops.

He turned around and peered out of the mine, his eyes focused on where the road came into the mine site. His shoulders sagged and he exhaled heavily, having stopped breathing in anticipation.

"Fuck!" he muttered aloud.

Turner's Land Cruiser skidded to a stop beside the shipping container. Turner appeared to be the only occupant. The man got out and slammed the door, looked around, then opened the rear door. He removed two items, then strode toward the mine entrance, stepping around the puddles of rainwater as best he could.

He held a lantern in one hand and a duffel bag in the other. And there was no mistaking the pistol in the holster attached to the man's belt, just visible underneath the open jacket.

When Turner reached the gate, he set down the lantern and duffel bag, and fished a set of keys out of a coat pocket, then opened the padlock and pulled the chain away, all the while softly whistling *Dixie*.

As Turner reached for the gate to open it, Rent kicked it again, slamming it into Turner's face and knocking him backward. Rent then attempted to sprint through the narrow opening. But Turner stuck out a foot and tripped his captive, who fell forward, landing on a shoulder, again groaning from the impact on his ribs.

"You motherfucker!" Turner said. "You're gonna pay for that."

"Then you might as well get it over with and shoot me right here."

Turner emitted a guttural laugh. "Oh, no. You ain't gettin' off that easy. You're gonna suffer first. Now get up and get back in the mine."

"And if I don't?"

Turner lifted his right foot and drew it back as if to kick Rent.

Rent's eyes opened wide. "Okay, okay, I'll go."

Again, he struggled to stand, moaning in the process. Once on his feet, he walked slowly, feeling as if this were his death march. He shook his head as the strains of *The World Turned Upside Down* wafted through his mind. *It sure as hell has.*

Turner switched on the lantern and picked up the duffel bag, and followed Rent into the mine.

"You smell like a urinal in a biker bar," Turner said.

"Imagine that," Rent replied.

Rent stopped when he reached the cases of gunpowder, but Turner ordered him to keep going until he had passed them and gone well beyond the foot lockers containing the firearms and ammunition.

"Now sit and keep your yap shut for once."

Turner then went back up the sloping floor of the mine and disappeared from view behind the gunpowder cases. Rent could not see what the man was doing, although he could hear him grunting and the sounds of some type of activity involving tools of some sort.

Rent couldn't help himself. "You will get caught, you know. You're just delaying the inevitable. They've already got your pals in Fallbrook and Anza, and they're singing like canaries."

A little white lie is appropriate at this juncture.

"Bullshit," Turner called out. "Even if it's true, so what? You're never going to see the light of day again."

"That'll just ensure you get the death penalty."

Turner scoffed. "This is California, not Texas."

"Nevertheless, you'll never get out, not even on parole. And when word gets out that you're a child molester, you'll wish you were on death row."

Turner laughed.

"How do you live with yourself, taking the food out of the mouths of babes and disabled folks?

Another laugh.

Turner returned to where Rent sat on the floor of the mine. "No one gets hurt. It's just guv'ment money they waste on welfare, Social Security, Medicare, Obamacare. It's the poor folk and the rich folk who get the governments handouts, while those of us in the middle get taxed to death. I might as well get my fair share. All they do is take money from me, tax me into poverty. Take my guns away. Take my freedom away."

"That's your world view, is it?"

"My 'world view'? What sort of highfalutin, libtard, progressive bullshit is that? I live by the Golden Rule."

"Oh? He who has the gold rules?"

"Exactly," Turner said and laughed again. "You know how it goes—do unto others before they do unto you. That's my motto."

"So you're sort of a Robin Hood in reverse—you steal from those who can least afford it while further enriching shameless, greedy, gun manufacturers."

He scoffed. "As I said, no one gets hurt."

"Except Hannah?"

Turner glared at Rent, a venomous look in his eyes. "That was an accident."

"Manslaughter at best."

Turner waved it away. "Besides, I have a way out," he bragged.

"Oh, yeah?"

"Yeah, I do." He smirked. "I have a little place in Baja. At an old surf camp, south of Ensenada, Camp Salvador. On the beach. My own little Margaritaville. I'll be livin' in the style to which I deserve, a dark-eyed señorita on my arm. No more fuckin' carpet cleaning for ungrateful childless cat ladies. I just head out through Rodriguez Canyon."

"I hope you have a whitewater raft."

"No worries. I know my way around those boulders."

"You molested the girl, then killed her mother. And Abby knows it. Or at least she suspects it."

Turner stared at him, hollow-eyed. All color in his face had vanished. The man looked as if he hadn't slept in days.

The trickle of water entering the mine had increased to a warbling stream as the torrential rain pounded the compound outside the mine entrance. Water dripped from the ceiling of the mine shaft at an urgent pace.

Rent looked down and the sight startled him. The trickling stream had begun to pool around his feet. His pants were already so soaked he hadn't noticed. The mine would become unhabitable before much longer if the rainfall fulfilled the weather forecasters' dire predictions.

"You think you have all the answers, Mr. Investigative Journalist. Well, you don't," Turner said with a sneer. "That little princess of yours isn't as innocent as you think."

Rent stared at the man as he scrabbled to his feet. "What are you saying? Abby is somehow involved in the fraud, or even Hannah's death?"

"That's exactly what he's saying. Or at least that's what he wants you to believe."

Abby's voice shocked him. He turned to see her silhouette approaching from the mine entrance. He couldn't see her features until she entered the pool of lantern light.

Her hair hung tangled, and a streak of dried blood coursed its way down the right side of her face, near her ear. Her split and swollen lower lip disproportioned her otherwise graceful mien and bruising purpled her left cheek.

She stopped as tears, keeping pace with the rain above ground, erupted from her red-streaked eyes. She began sobbing as she embraced Rent. "I'm sorry. I'm so sorry."

He writhed in pain as she pressed against his rib cage.

"Hold still," she whispered and began to untie the paracord around his wrists.

Rent glared over her shoulder at Turner and said in low, guttural voice, "You motherfucking, cocksucking son of a bitch!"

Turner yanked Abby away before she could finish untying Rent and pushed her aside. Then he kneeled down and began rummaging through his duffel bag.

Rent, in a compassionate tone, asked Abby, "What really happened?"

"I was trying to protect her—"

"From him," Rent said, finishing her sentence.

Abby nodded. "I—"

Turner straightened up and shouted, "Shut up!"

He backhanded her, knocking her into the wall of the mine shaft. A trickle of debris fell and an aging timber creaked. They all glanced at it in unison, realizing they could end up being buried together under tons of quartz-riddled schist.

Rent then saw a look of horror on Abby's face, her eyes on Turner. Rent rotated his gaze to the man, only to see the business end of a .44 Magnum.

"Gabe, don't!" Abby shouted. "You'll never get away with it."

"They'll never find his body. Or yours, for that matter. I'll do it right this time."

Abby scoffed. "You think you're so clever. I called the sheriff's office before I came here. They're on their way. Give yourself up, Gabe. It'll make things a lot easier for you."

"I ain't takin' the fall for you. You pushed her because she was going to rat you out too."

A puzzled expression creased Rent's face. "Rat you—"

"It was you," Abby screamed, as if trying to convince herself as much as the two men. "You're the one who got me involved. You're a

. . . a con man, sweet-talking me, saying it would be easy money. No one gets hurt. Pay off my all debts . . ."

The growl of a V-8 engine struggling to pull several tons of fabricated steel up the rutted road drifted into the mine, underlaid by the thump, thump, thump of a helicopter hovering overhead.

"Time to go," Turner said with finality.

He lifted the gun, pointing it at Rent's chest. Rent had no idea what it felt like to die. His ill-spent youth did not flash before his eyes. He just felt sorry. Sorry for Abby. Sorry for Hannah and Rachel. He hoped it would be quick. And at that range, Turner couldn't miss, not with that cannon he held in both hands, arms outstretched.

Turner, seeking a flair for the dramatic, cocked the pistol deliberately, savoring the moment as the flush of power coursed through him like a tsunami crashing ashore. However deluded he may have been in his perception of self, he commanded ultimate control. He held in his hands the fate of two people's lives. He milked it for a moment longer, a hateful grin shaping his lips.

"You're gonna make my day."

As his finger tightened on the trigger, Abby lunged, screaming, "Noooooo!" The explosion left Rent momentarily deaf as flying rock fragments stung his face. He winced and tried to blink the grit from his watering eyes.

Abby lay on the ground, moaning, the growing pool of water that had given Rent sustenance had begun to turn red as Abby's blood leaked from her wounded body. Turner stood frozen by the unanticipated turn of events. Rent Beacham was supposed to be lying, dying, on the floor of the mine. Turner looked defeated, deflated, his arms at his sides, the gun pointed at the ground.

That moment of indecision gave Rent the time he needed. He stepped forward with his left leg, trailing his right, planted his left foot, and followed through with his right. Turner screamed in pain as the reinforced toe of Rent's Merrill hiking boot struck squarely in the man's crotch. Turner sank to his knees, doubled over in pain.

Rent kicked again, this time at Turner's right hand, sending the gun spinning into the dark. As Turner struggled to rise, Rent kicked him in the gut, then followed through with a knee to the nose, knocking Turner flat. Then he readied himself to deliver the blow he'd been secretly planning while a prisoner in the mine.

Let this son of a bitch feel what it's like to have broken ribs.

A voice from the darkness stopped him. "I think you've done enough damage. We'll take it from here."

He raised his eyes to see two members of the sheriff's department coming toward him, one of them Sgt. Alvarez, both wearing rain slickers and with guns drawn.

Rent nodded toward Abby. "She's been shot. Help her, please."

Then his knees buckled and he collapsed to the floor himself, the subsequent activities around him passing in a blur.

The deputies cuffed Turner, then administered first aid to Abby and rushed her out on a stretcher to the waiting helicopter. As the chopper lifted off, they returned to lead the spraddle-legged Turner away, blood dripping from his chin and staining his jacket and shirt.

Rent struggled to his knees, groans again emitting from his lips.

Sgt. Alvarez knelt behind Rent and finished untying his wrists, then helped him to his feet. "I've heard of one-armed paper hangers, but that was some mighty fancy footwork."

"And my daddy always thought those hours I spent practicing penalty kicks a la David Beckham were a waste of time," Rent replied.

"Say, you're bleeding too," the deputy said.

Until that moment, Rent hadn't felt anything other than his aching ribs. He touched his left buttock and winced. Apparently, the bullet had ricocheted off the mine wall after piercing Abby, a piece of the shrapnel embedding itself in his backside.

He then sensed something. "Oh, shit!" he shouted and leapt forward. "Run for it!"

29

Sunday, Day 22, mid-morning

Rent sprinted toward the mine entrance, with Sgt. Alvarez close behind. Outside, he ran toward the steel shipping container.

"Take cover! Get down!" he shouted at the deputies standing nearby, guarding the handcuffed Turner. He dove to the ground as he rounded the corner of the container. Alvarez followed suit.

A thunderous explosion split the air as if lightning had struck a defenseless oak. The container rocked, teetering on edge from the force of the blast. Rent held his breath as he envisioned being squashed like a bug, then exhaled heavily as the container settled back in place.

"What the hell was that?" Alvarez asked.

"Turner set it off as his final, desperate act. He had two hundred pounds of black powder stored in there. Along with automatic weapons," Rent said.

They both stood, Rent groaning as he did so, rainwater cascading from his head and shoulders. He tried to brush off the mud from the front of his jacket, to little avail.

"Stay here while I check things out," Alvarez said. "That may not be the end of it."

Rent nodded, but after she rounded the corner of the container, he poked his head out for a peek of his own. Alvarez stood at the end of the container, peering out over the compound to assess the situation.

She spoke into her radio, asking the other deputies to report in. They responded that no one was seriously hurt, although a few had minor injuries from flying debris and their ears were still ringing. She told them to remain in place for a while longer, just in case there were more explosions.

Alvarez rejoined Rent, and they sat down, leaning their backs against the container. She opened her rain slicker and told Rent to move closer so she could share the garment as best she could.

"You try anything funny and you'll get what Turner got."

Rent looked at her wide-eyed. "Don't worry. I'm in no shape to try anything, even if I wanted to."

He groaned as he slid sideways until they were thigh-to-thigh. She pulled one arm out of its sleeve and Rent pulled that portion of the slicker around his back. It didn't cover much, but it was better than nothing.

"That was scary," she said.

"Yeah, no shit," he replied.

"Thanks for the head's up. That mine shaft could've been our grave."

Rent nodded. "I saw him doing something with stuff in his duffle bag before he tried to shoot me. Then, after you arrived, I smelled something burning and a low hiss drifted past my ears as if a rattlesnake lay coiled in his bag. I realized he had lit a fuse. I guess he figured he'd have plenty to time to get out, but his plan went all to shit."

"Lucky for you and your friend," she replied.

"And you," he said.

"Good thing you gave us the GPS coordinates. Otherwise . . ."

They fell silent as the implications of Turner's intent sank in.

A voice on the deputy's radio broke their reverie.

"Alvarez, you copy?"

She pressed the talk button and replied, "Roger that. I'll be right there." She glanced at Rent. "Vámonos."

They both stood and Rent relinquished his portion of the rain slicker. With slow, deliberate steps, they rounded the end of the container. She then sprinted across the open space to where the other deputies and Turner were hunkered down behind their vehicles.

Rent followed her, struggling to keep up, cursing all the while. They dropped down behind the closest vehicle and caught their breath.

One of the deputies offered Rent a thermal survival blanket that looked like a massive piece of aluminum foil.

"Thanks," Rent said as he wrapped it around his shivering body and sat on the dirt next to Alvarez.

The man then looked at the sergeant. "That was a bit too close for comfort."

She nodded. "This job never gets any easier."

"Aw, you love it," the man replied.

A slight smile crossed her lips. "As long as I survive it. Let's get the EOD guys out here."

"E-O-D?" Rent inquired.

"Explosive Ordnance Disposal."

"Ah, got it," he replied.

"I don't think all of it exploded. If it had, we'd be dead, if not from the blast, from the debris raining down on us."

"If that's the case, good thing Turner didn't know what the hell he was doing."

"We'll bring in Dexter to check things out."

"A robot?"

She chuckled. "No, Dexter is a bomb-sniffing dog. He'll let us know if he senses any explosive material remaining in the rubble of the mine."

A male deputy radioed headquarters, requesting assistance and asking for further instructions. When he had finished, he motioned with a thumb toward Turner, who sat nearby, also cloaked in a thermal blanket, his hands cuffed behind his back, and his chin on his chest.

"You guys can take him in. I'll hang out here until EOD arrives."

Alvarez turned to Rent. "You need to be examined. Do you want us to drop you off at urgent care or the ER?"

"I can take Abby's Jeep."

"Do you have the key?"

They checked it. The key fob had been removed.

"Crap. It's probably in one of her pockets."

"As I was saying . . ." Alvarez offered.

Rent thought for a moment before answering. "I think I can drive myself to urgent care, if you just drop me at Abby's place, in Pine Hills. My rental is parked there. It's not far out of your way."

"Okay, you ride with us," she said and stood up.

Alvarez spread a fresh survival blanket on the back seat. "I don't want you leaving blood stains . . . or anything else."

Rent blushed as he nodded and eased himself onto the seat, trying to minimize the pain in his rib cage, and being reminded of the new and literal pain in his ass. Alvarez and her partner got into their respective seats.

"You comfortable back there?" she asked.

"As much as I can be," Rent replied, noting the slight smile in her reflection in the rearview mirror.

How am I going to live this down?

Rent stared out the window as they worked their way out of the canyon. Every rut in the road had become a small stream, and every bump meant another jab in his buttock, not to mention his ribs.

"I hope the road hasn't washed out," Alvarez said to no one in particular.

"Yeah, we've had enough excitement as it is," her partner replied.

They rode in silence as Alvarez negotiated the rough road and rivulets cutting across it. At one point, a rivulet had become a good-sized creek, and she stopped to inspect it before proceeding.

"What do you think?" she asked her partner.

"Gun it," he said. "Or I can take over if you want."

"I'm sure I can manage," she replied and pressed a foot down on the accelerator.

The vehicle leapt forward and plunged into the water, then just as quickly rose up the other side of the small gully.

The remainder of the way to Banner Grade passed without incident, and Rent sighed in relief as the SUV powered up the smooth pavement toward Julian, windshield wipers working overtime.

The deputy in the passenger seat radioed a report into headquarters, apprising his superiors as to the status of the situation. He also got an update on Abby: She would be going into surgery in a matter of minutes.

After creeping through Julian's rain-sodden and vacant main drag, they headed downhill toward San Diego. Alvarez turned onto Pine Hills Road; the trailing vehicle transporting Turner honked as it continued on.

At Abby's place, Rent exited the SUV, taking the blankets with him, and got into his own after covering the seat. Alvarez waited until he gave her the OK sign before leaving.

He sighed heavily as he stared at Abby's front door, again flailing in the wind and rain. He retrieved his phone from the console and dictated a text message to his editor:

> Explosion at mine. I'm safe and Turner on his way to jail. Abby flown to hospital. Will call asap.

He switched off the engine and entered the house, closing the door behind him. Furniture had been overturned and magazines lay scattered on the floor.

Rent went to the bathroom and found some Aleve in the medicine cabinet above the sink. He limped to the kitchen and washed down two tablets with water, then went to the bedroom, which had a full-length mirror. He pulled down his pants and underwear for a look at his wound. The bleeding seemed to have been staunched by compression from his own body weight.

He returned to the bathroom and found hydrogen peroxide and a sterile bandage. He flinched as he cleaned his wound, then applied the bandage. He got dressed, found a mop, and cleaned up the water at the entryway, hoping for a letup in the rain that incessantly drummed the aluminum roof overhead.

He reheated the coffee remaining in the pot and raided the refrigerator before making the call to his editor, feeling as if he were an uninvited intruder in a stranger's home. He scrolled through the RECENTS and tapped the number for his editor.

"What the hell is going on?" O'Connor queried without a greeting. "The explosion is already a headline, but no one seems to know what happened. The sheriff's department is not commenting."

"Yeah, thanks for asking. I'm not well, but I am alive," Rent replied, making no attempt to hide his sarcasm.

"I'm sorry. Are you all right? Are you in the hospital?"

"I'm not in the hospital, but when I get off the phone, I'm taking myself to urgent care."

"Were you injured in the blast? What caused it?"

"Actually, I was injured before the blast. I, in effect, got shot—"

"Oh, no."

"It was a ricochet of the bullet that went through Abby Wilbur-force, so it's minor, but Abby's is major, life-threatening."

"Oh, my god. Is she going to be okay?"

"All I know is that the chopper took her to Palomar Medical Center in Poway, and she was headed into surgery. I'll go there after a stop at urgent care in Ramona."

"Where are you now?"

"I'm in Julian. I had the sheriff's deputy drop me off at my vehicle."

"You're taking yourself?"

"You want to come get me?"

"Why didn't you have the sheriff's take you?"

"Then I would have needed a ride back here."

"I want you to talk to Clark A-sap."

"Have her call me in five minutes, after I get on the road."

As he disconnected, he spotted Abby's laptop on the floor, underneath the coffee table. *Hmm, I wonder* . . .

He went to the kitchen and found a plastic grocery bag, and grabbed a dish towel hanging on the stove's oven-door handle. Back in the living room, he picked up the laptop, using the dish towel to avoid leaving fingerprints on the device, and placed it in the bag. He then left, ensuring he had locked the door. She had shown him where she kept a hideout key and he pocketed it.

THE CALL CAME AS Rent slowed to a stop at the intersection of Pine Hills Road and Route 78. He tapped Answer.

"Hello, Lewis."

"Would you please stop calling me that?" Naomi Clark replied.

"How may I help you?"

"What the hell happened?"

"Hang on. I'm turning onto 78. I can't see for shit in this downpour."

"That's why they call it an atmospheric river."

Rent gave her the Cliff Notes version so she could ask questions to fill in the blanks.

"How do you know it was two hundred pounds of black powder?"

"Because I was sitting on top of it while locked in the damned mine shaft, waiting to go out with a big bang."

"Do you always have to be a smart ass?"

"It's in my DNA," he said. "But I'm serious. He had eight cases of black powder stacked in there, twenty-five pounds to a case. You do the math. But all of it may not have exploded."

"But why were you sitting on it?"

"Because he didn't have a Lazy Boy in there."

"Oh, for fuck's sake. I'm trying to write a factual piece, not a dime novel."

"Yeah, yeah. Sorry. I was trying to stay dry, and that was the driest spot, on top of the gunpowder, under a tarp. It was a dark and stormy night."

"You said 'he.' You're referring to Turner? He owned the gunpowder?"

"Yes, Gabriel 'Gabe' Turner. But that's his alias. His real name is Joshua Gabriel Turnbull, resident of Julian. Under his alias, he had a legit cover through his Magic Carpet Cleaner business. "

"Age?"

"Thirty-something. You'll have to get the exact figure from the cops."

"Was he planning on blowing up something?"

"A government building or a power station somewhere, I imagine. Or maybe make grenades with it. He wasn't specific."

"What about the guns? Did you get a precise count on that?"

"Sadly, no. A: It was dark as a dungeon in there, and they were in foot lockers, but he bragged about it, and opened one of the lockers to show me—bragged about having close to a hundred semi-auto and automatic weapons, a mix of pistols and rifles, the so-called 'long guns,' which aren't long at all in historic terms. I suspect the muzzleloaders I met there a couple of weeks ago may have helped him acquire the black powder, guns, and ammo. Brought it in from Arizona."

"You know that for a fact?"

"He said as much, but speculation at this point. I gave the name of one of the guys to the cops."

"And your girlfriend, what about her? She was involved in this as well?"

"Girlfriend might be overstating it . . . oh, fuck. Hang on."

Rent tapped the brakes to get a big pickup to back off, then slowed as he descended the steep grade to Santa Ysabel, barely visible through the downpour. The truck sped past him with a long blast of its horn, leaving twin rooster tails in its wake.

"Asshole!" Rent shouted.

"What's going on?" Clark demanded.

"Some idiot thinks he can defy the laws of physics and was tailgating me, trying to get me to speed up or pullover. Where were we?"

"Abby what's-her-name."

"Right. Abigail Wilburforce, age twenty-nine, resident of Julian, real estate agent." He spelled out her surname.

"Any word on her condition?"

"Not yet. I'll stop by the hospital on my way home."

"What's her involvement?"

Rent told Clark that as far as he knew, Abby had nothing to do with the explosives and weapons, only the welfare fraud, and to what degree she was involved on that front he still didn't have the full picture.

"Why was she at the mine?" Clark asked.

"Good question," he replied. "But if she hadn't called the cops and showed up when she did, I'd probably be mincemeat scattered all over Chariot Canyon."

"But you can state for a fact that Gabriel Turner shot her when she tried to intervene, and you were wounded when the bullet that struck her ricocheted off the wall of the mine shaft."

"Yes."

"But Turner did not get hit by a bullet."

"No, I just kicked the shit out of him."

"With your hands tied behind your back."

"That's my story, and I'm sticking to it."

"No one's going to believe it."

"I have four witnesses, two of them from the sheriff's department. You can corroborate that with them, one of them being Sergeant Diana Alvarez."

"Any news on the girl? Rachel?"

"This is off the record, not for publication."

She sighed. "Whatever."

"Last time I checked, she's safe, under foster care with a woman in Descanso, but she has no involvement in this story."

"You said she might have witnessed Turner assaulting her mother, which ultimately led to the mother's death."

"Yeah, the operative word here being 'might.' Keep her out of it, at least for now. Washington has yet to formally interview her, and right now he's got Turner and Abby to deal with."

"Okay, that should do it for now. But keep your phone handy."

"I gotta go. This rain's gotten worse. I can barely see."

Rent disconnected the call and focused on the yellow lane divider as he continued toward Ramona.

30

Sunday, Day 22, late morning

Rent checked into urgent care for the second time in three days and had his wound tended to, amid snickers from the medical staff. An hour and a half later he left, bound for the hospital where he hoped for an update on Abby's condition.

As he passed Mt. Woodson, he spied a large red pickup that had spun out and lodged in a roadside embankment. The same truck that had sped past him earlier.

"Waiting for a tow truck, are we?" he muttered. He double-punched the horn button at the center of his steering wheel. As Rent passed by, the driver flipped him off.

At the hospital, he parked, donned his rain jacket, pulled the hood over his head, and fast-walked to the ER entrance, dodging puddled water as much as possible.

An ambulance sat outside the entrance, a patient on a gurney being wheeled inside. He entered the waiting room and found it overflowing with people in varying degrees of distress. He joined the line at the reception desk, willing the attendants to speed things up. Those immediately in front of him and behind him wrinkled their noses. When his turn finally came, he flashed his press pass and asked for the status of Abby and Turner.

"I honestly don't know," the woman replied. "You'll have to inquire up front."

Rent sighed and followed the signs and painted lines through the corridor maze to the front desk. He learned that Turner had been

released into the custody of the San Diego Sheriff's Department;
Abby had been moved to a room on the fourth floor. There he found
a deputy stationed outside her room, blocking the entrance.

Rent didn't know the man and flashed his press pass. The deputy
rolled his eyes and said he could not comment.

"Look, I've been in touch with Detective Washington and Sergeant Alvarez regarding an active investigation, and I will be following
up with them. But, off the record, what can you tell me about Abby
Wilburforce, the woman in this room? Is she conscious? Able to have
visitors? I'm not just a newspaper reporter. I'm also romantically
involved with her, so this is personal."

Rent felt his eyes begin to water, and for a moment he turned
away, blinking rapidly.

"As far as I know, she's still sedated, and we're not even allowed
in there. Doctor's orders," the deputy said.

Rent swiped at his eyes and turned back to face the man. "What
about next of kin? Anyone showed up claiming to be a relative?"

"Not that I'm aware of."

Rent nodded and thanked the deputy. "I appreciate your help."

"You're welcome. And take a bath. You smell worse than cat piss."

HE RETURNED TO HIS vehicle and checked his voice mail—more than a
dozen messages. The callers included local TV and radio stations, as
well as Rod Davis from HHSA and Sgt. Alvarez.

He called Alvarez first. She confirmed that they had Turner in
custody and he would be formally charged, but she had no details
beyond that.

"I imagine my colleague, Naomi Clark, has been in touch."

Alvarez chuckled. "Oh, yes. Her and at least a dozen others. It's a
circus around here. But it's going to be a while before we have a
formal statement beyond the obvious."

"What about the EOD crew? They find anything?"

"Off the record?"

"Yeah, for now."

"Yes. It looks like all the explosive ordnance was consumed in
the one blast."

"I'm surprised it wasn't worse."

"The EOD guy said black powder is a low-level explosive. If it had been C-4, or even ammonium nitrate, it would have been a different story."

"What about forensics?"

"Are you joking? In this weather? If the rain ever lets up, we'll get a team up there, but for now we've got the site cordoned off and a couple deputies stationed there to keep out the riff-raff."

"You mean riff-raff like me."

She chuckled. "Speaking of, we need you to come in and make a formal statement. Like right now. Where are you, waiting to see a doctor?"

"Been there, done that."

"I bet they found that entertaining."

"Don't you start."

"So where are you?"

He told her.

"Good. You're only a few minutes away."

Rent sighed. "On my way. But I'm warning you, one of your colleagues already told me I need a bath."

"As if I don't know that already," she replied.

Rent disconnected and drove to the sheriff's department head-quarters, the drive taking twice as long as normal, what with the heavy rain, slow traffic, and multiple traffic accidents on the freeway. He called Davis and left a message.

At the sheriff's station, he parked and checked in. Alvarez greeted him and said it would be a while.

"Hurry up and wait, is that it?" he said.

"If you don't play nice, the wait could get longer," she replied.

"I hear ya," he said and took a seat.

While he waited, his thoughts turned to Abby—and her laptop computer. The Doors' song, *This Is the End*, came to mind. *"I'll never look into your eyes . . . again."* Outside of a courtroom, at any rate.

He began to consider the possibilities for the password to her laptop. *It's got to have a keyword in it, along with some other bit of personal information. Not her birthdate; that's too obvious. A bird theme? Shit, it's going to be impossible. Or could it be so simple I'm overlooking the obvious?*

"Mr. Beacham?"

Rent looked up. An unfamiliar deputy stood at the door to the interior workings of the department. Rent stood up and crossed the lobby. *At this rate, I'm going meet everyone who works here.*

The deputy led him to the familiar Interview Room 2.

"Have a seat. Detective Washington will be right with you," the man said.

Rent did as instructed and drummed his fingers on the tabletop.

"Bonobo!" he muttered.

"What about bonobo?" the detective said as he entered the room.

"Oh, nothing. I was just thinking of a conversation I had recently."

"About monkeys?" Washington said.

"Bonobos are not actually monkeys. They're—"

The detective raised a hand as he sat opposite Rent. "Spare me the lecture. We have a lot to talk about. I just hope it doesn't take all night. I'm practically living at this place. And, by the way, you stink to high heaven."

"So I've been told, so let's get this over with. I'd rather be somewhere else as well. No sidekick today?"

"Ogilvy's on his way, but we can get started informally."

"Fire away . . . so to speak."

"What the hell were you thinking, going to that mine?"

"Rest assured that I did not go of my own accord. I had a shotgun pointed at me and my hands tied behind my back."

Ogilvy entered the room and the formal interview began. Rent told them everything he could remember, beginning with Abby's call, begging him to come to her place. Two hours later, Washington asked his final question.

"What's Abby's involvement in the welfare fraud?"

Rent stared at Washington for a moment before answering. "Honestly, I don't know. What's Turner saying?"

"I can't comment on that, but you said—"

"I know. Turner implied she was involved and that Hannah was going to blow the whistle and yada yada yada. But that doesn't make it true. He's going to point the finger at anyone within reach. I can only imagine what he's saying about me."

Ogilvy snorted. Washington reprimanded him with a sidelong glance.

Have you searched her house?" Rent asked.

"I can't comment on that."

"If not, it's inevitable. I have the key so you don't have to break down the door."

Rent retrieved the key from a pants pocket and handed it to Washington.

"Thanks. I think we're done . . . for now," the detective said. "But don't leave town. I'm sure we will have more questions."

"I'm not going anywhere. I have a story to write."

But first he had to know.

RENT DROVE HOME, PARKED in the garage, and carried Abby's laptop up the stairs. He set the computer on the dining table, then made coffee.

This may take a while.

While the coffee brewed, he took a shower and put on clean, dry clothes. He filled his largest mug, then put on sterile gloves left over from the COVID pandemic. He sat down carefully, trying to keep the pain in his butt to a minimum, and opened the MacBook Pro. He clicked on the email icon and, as expected, a window opened, demanding a password to unlock the device.

I wonder how many tries I get before it shuts down?

He entered *Bonobo* and got an error message.

He tried a second time: *BonoboLust.* Another error message.

BonoboLove

LoveBonobo

LuvBonobo

GottaLuvBonobo

Bonobo1Q2W

"Fuck. There must be a program that hackers use."

He poured himself more coffee and opened up his own Dell laptop, then his phone dinged. He sighed, located the phone, and glanced at the screen. Two missed calls and a text message, from Rachel. *The latest complication in my life*, he thought, then immediately chastised himself.

Rachel's text read:
Why aren't you answering my calls???!!!

He checked his voice mail: Rachel wanting to know if he was all right. He returned her call; she answered on the first ring.

"I thought were dead, just like Mom," she blurted, then he heard her sniffles and attempts to choke off her sobbing.

"Sweetie, I'm sorry. I should have called you sooner. I'm fine. Well, mostly."

"When are you coming to see me. I'm scared."

"I can't today. Everything's crazy. Tomorrow for sure."

"Is he dead?"

"Who?"

"Gabe. I hope he's dead."

"He's not dead, but he is in custody and being questioned by the cops. He's gonna spend the rest of his days behind bars. He'll never be able to hurt you again."

"Promise?"

"Cross my heart. Now, I have to go, but I will come see you tomorrow."

"You better."

"I love you, Sweetie. Bye for now."

He ended the call and sat silent for a long moment.

Life as I know it has changed forever. For the better? How can it not be.

Rent turned his attention back to his laptop.

Maybe I should call geeky Greg. Nah, that opens a whole new can of worms.

He opened a browser and brought up DuckDuckGo. He searched for password-hacking software and got hundreds of results regarding password crackers. But they were useless, since he first had to unlock the device to install it.

Catch 22.

He searched for a way to get into a MacBook when forgetting one's password. *There has to be a workaround.*

"Got it," he said aloud. "A YouTube video. Imagine that."

He returned to Abby's MacBook and followed the instructions step by step.

Ta-da! That was so easy, it's scary.

As directed, he set up a new administrator account and password: *BonoboLuv4U!*.

This gave him access to her documents and email accounts.

This is so illegal. But I gotta know.

He shut off Internet access before opening the email account. He found emails he had sent to her and emails she had sent to him. He then scrolled through and read the emails she had sent to others. Nothing struck him as out of the ordinary. Most of the emails were work related—responses to inquiries about property for sale. Others were of a personal nature, but nothing incriminating.

Wait! What's this?

He noticed an email from <sdcounty.ca.gov>. He didn't recognize the name.

Could this be?

He wrote down the address in his notebook.

He moved to the base level of the email client software, and there he discovered a second email account labeled *goldeneagle*.

What the ef? That's the name of Turner's gold mine.

Upon further examination, Rent uncovered the real "gold mine." Abby—or Turner—had used this account to conduct "phishing" online, tricking unsuspecting people into revealing their EBT account information. This, in turn, allowed Turner and his cohorts to create counterfeit EBT cards and drain the accounts of some or all of the funds. He also noticed an icon labeled CyberGhost. Using his computer, he searched for the name—virtual private network provider.

I'd bet dollars to donuts he used this VPN to mask the identity of the device and its user.

Rent opened up the address book for the account and found email addresses assigned to accounts on servers with Russian and Eastern European country codes, as well as U.S.-based dot-com addresses.

Bingo!

As he scanned these emails, he learned that Turner, or whomever, had been buying personal data from these foreign operators and sharing it with others.

So, he's buying data, not selling it. The question now is, how do I use this information in my next piece without revealing the source? And without me being arrested?

Rent expressed his thoughts talking to himself while pacing the living room.

"We thought Turner was using Hannah's computer to conduct his phishing scheme, but that proved not to be the case, clearing her from that aspect of the fraudulent activities. But this now implicates Abby. *Fuck!*"

Rent considered the possibility that she was being manipulated or blackmailed by Turner and his pals. Could Turner have done it without her knowledge? Unlikely. But was she coerced?

Or, what if she's the one behind this branch of the scheme, and she's also in cahoots with those thugs up north that tried to kill me? And is her job at the realty just a cover, like Turner's carpet cleaning business?

Have I been conned by this woman? But it's not as if she approached me. I just showed up at her office in Julian purely by accident. That said, once she found out what I was really up to, she got rather inquisitive and kept asking for more details.

What was it Turner said at the mine? "That little princess of yours isn't as innocent as you think." Still, that weasel will point the finger at her whether she's involved or not.

He went to the kitchen and refilled his mug.

Shit! What do I do now? I don't have anyone I can talk to without totally fucking things up. Do I need a lawyer? He considered calling A.J. Hawke.

Not yet. I have to talk to Abby, but the cops won't let me near her.

His phone chimed. O'Connor.

"Yes, boss?"

"Anything new on the fraud story? I need something to keep the series alive."

"You ran my latest piece this morning. What's the rush?"

"That was before the *New York Times* jumped on the band wagon."

"*New York Times?*"

"Yeah, they picked up portions of your story and are running it as a sidebar to theirs. It's going national. I thought I told you."

"No. In case you've forgotten, I've been imprisoned in a mine shaft. But that's great, I guess."

"They don't really have anything new; just localized it for their region. So . . . what have you got?"

"The sheriff has Turner, and he's probably squealing like a stuck pig. But they're not giving me one lousy morsel. Right now they're more concerned with the death than the fraud. And Clark's covering that."

"What about the folks in Riverside?"

"They're waiting to see what San Diego gets out of Turner, but they're keeping an eye on that compound in case any of those guys make a run for it."

"And your new friend?"

"She's in post-op at Palomar Medical and still sedated, last I heard. As soon as she wakes up, the cops will have her locked up, at least figuratively, if not literally. I went to her room, but they had a guy guarding the door."

"So, all we've got is the explosion and the arrest. I'm surprised you haven't been on the local TV news."

"I'm not returning their calls. I gave my exclusive to Clark."

"Good man. Let me know if anything breaks."

"Will do."

He then called Rod Davis and updated him.

"A lot of this depends on Turner and how much he reveals," Davis said. "If he fingers the insider, then it will break this case wide open."

"He's got a potential murder rap hanging over him as well, so I would not be surprised if he cops a plea on the fraud business."

"Let's hope so."

"I may have something for you. An email address from the county. I don't recognize the name."

"Where'd you get it?"

"I can't say, at least not yet. But I will send it to you. Maybe your insider got sloppy. It involves an application for benefits from someone unlikely to be eligible."

31

Rent sat at his dining table, working on a draft of his story about the apprehension of Gabe Turner, a prime suspect in the welfare fraud investigation. Clark had already written a piece about the explosion and its aftermath, having to quote Rent in the process, much to her chagrin.

His phone chimed. "Shit, what now?"

He didn't recognize the number and hovered a finger over the red Decline icon, then thought better of it and tapped the green Answer symbol.

"Why are you calling?" he demanded, making no effort to be friendly or welcoming.

"It's me. Why are you being so rude?"

"Abby?"

"It's not Beyoncé."

"Sorry, I wasn't expecting— Where are you? How are you? I tried to see you—"

"I'm still in the hospital, where do you think? There's a cop standing right outside the door. They read me my rights and this is my one phone call."

"You've been arrested?"

"Well, duh, Einstein."

"Normally, that one call is used to contact a lawyer, not a newspaper reporter."

"They gave me the number of the public defender's office, but you have a lawyer friend, right?"

"I do, but he normally handles murder cases, like the Sphynx murders, not—"

"Not little stuff like welfare fraud?"

"Well, yeah."

"He must know somebody."

"Okay, I'll give him a call. What's your number?"

"Just call the hospital and ask for my room, four thirty-seven."

"Got it. I'll call him, then come see you."

"I don't think they'll let you in. Basically, I'm in jail."

"He'll get you bailed. How are you?"

"I feel like crap, to be honest."

"You're alive."

"Yeah, they tell me I got lucky—if you can call getting shot lucky. The bullet grazed my spleen as it passed through my left side. They got me stitched up, but it hurts like hell."

"I'm just glad you survived. They've got Turner in—"

"I gotta go. The deputy is giving me the stink eye."

"I'll call you later. Bye."

Rent disconnected and called his lawyer friend A.J. Hawke. He learned that Hawke was in a meeting and would have to call him back.

"This is not a social call. Please tell him it's urgent. A friend of mine has been arrested."

Rent ended the call and leaned back in his chair. *What a fucking nightmare.*

He got up, stepped into the kitchen, refilled his coffee mug, and returned to his chair. "Now, where was I."

He began reading what he'd written so far, making a few tweaks as needed.

Minutes later, his phone chimed again. Hawke.

He tapped Answer. "Drew, thanks for calling back so quickly."

"No problem. What's so urgent? Make it quick, if you can. I'm just taking a break from a client conference."

Rent explained what had happened in concise terms.

"You're right, this isn't normally something I'd take on, or are you suggesting I represent this Turner dude."

"God no. I hope he hires Alan Tucker. I just want to get some legal counsel for Abby. Do you have any suggestions?"

The call went silent for a moment. Rent could hear the sounds of office noise in the background.

"Okay, here's what I'm going to do. I'll have Liz, one of my associates—I think you've met her—"

"Yes, at one of your post-trial shindigs at the Barleymash downtown."

"Yeah, that's right. Anyway . . . this afternoon I'll have her handle the preliminary stuff, and I'll make some calls to see who might be available to take over from there."

"I owe you."

"Ha! You can't afford me . . . and I won't let you forget it. Gotta run."

Rent next called Sgt. Alvarez, who confirmed the arrest of Abby and that a search warrant had been issued for Abby's home.

Our crew is on the way," she said. "You gonna come watch again? Or is this one just a bit too close for comfort?"

"As much as I'd like to, I'm trying to find her a lawyer and get her released on bail."

"From what I hear, she's not leaving that hospital for several days."

"True, but I can't even pay her a visit. She might as well be behind bars."

"You think she's in on it?"

"The fraud, you mean?"

"Yeah, the fraud."

"I don't know. I'd like to think she's not, but maybe I'm wrong. Maybe I've been conned."

Rent ended the call and returned to his news story, reluctantly having to add Abigail Wilburforce as a defendant in the fraud investigation.

O'Connor is going to love this. Not.

THAT AFTERNOON, RENT MET the lawyer at the hospital. She introduced herself as Elizabeth Bernquist and said, "Call me Liz." They sat in the lobby and Rent brought her up to speed on the situation.

"Wow. I saw that on the news last night," Liz said. "Close call. You're both lucky to be alive."

"Yeah, but now Abby's gone from being victim to perp."

"With any more luck, I think we can make this go away, or at least bring it down to a slap on the wrist. Shall we go upstairs?"

"One more thing," Rent said, followed by a deep breath inhale, then exhale, recoiling as his ribs protested. "Hypothetically speaking . . ."

Liz raised her eyebrows. "Yes? Hypothetically?"

Rent nodded, his lips pursed as he thought about how he should phrase his next statement.

"Suppose there's a laptop computer, and suppose that laptop possibly contains incriminating evidence of crimes committed by, potentially, a number of people, but that laptop does not turn up in a search of the home of the owner of said laptop because it's in the possession of another party."

"I'm listening, but I'm not liking what I'm hearing, and let me remind you, we have no privilege. Abby is the client, not you."

"I understand that, which is why this is hypothetical."

"I do not want to hear another word, especially if you just happen to be this hypothetical third party. Let's go see your friend."

At the door to Abby's room, the young lawyer, dressed in a pin-striped, navy-blue pants suit and carrying a leather-bound briefcase, showed her ID to the deputy and nodded at Rent. "He's clerking for me."

The deputy stepped aside and motioned for them to enter the room. Liz identified herself and began to explain her purpose, but Abby cut her off, addressing Rent instead.

"I hear you got shot in the ass. I want to see the scar."

Liz eyed Rent, grinned conspiratorially, and raised her eyebrows.

Rent's face began to redden. "I don't think so. I'd have to drop my pants for that, and I'm afraid a passing nurse might take the opportunity to jab me with a needle."

"Don't make me laugh," Abby replied. Then she began crying silently, tears snaking down both cheeks.

Rent handed her a tissue from a box on the bedside table, which she accepted gratefully. He didn't know how to comfort her. Telling someone who knows she may go to prison that it's going to be all right *. . . Somehow that just doesn't cut it.*

He took her hand in his and gave it a light squeeze, staring numbly. Tears began to well up in his eyes too. Seeing this, she grinned and handed him a tissue. "Look at us, blubbering like a couple of babies."

An "ahem" from the lawyer interrupted their reunion.

"I hate to be the party pooper, but I'm working pro bono for the moment, so let's get down to business, shall we?"

A look of fear contorted Abby's face. Rent pulled a chair close to the bed for Liz, and he took a seat nearby. The lawyer explained the situation in no uncertain terms. Abby had been charged with recipient fraud, a misdemeanor punishable by up to six months in jail, a fine not more than $500, or both.

"Six months in jail?" Abby wailed.

"That's the worst-case scenario," Liz replied. "I doubt you will serve any time, based on what I understand at this point, and assuming you cooperate with the prosecution of Gabe Turner."

Abby nodded. "I will."

"I'm going to make a motion for dismissal, since this is your first offense, and that you agree to pay back the money that you received. Furthermore, I will argue that you were coerced into committing these unlawful acts by Turner."

Abby dabbed her eyes again. "Thank you, thank you so much."

"We're not out of the woods yet, but we'll give it our best shot. One more question."

"Yes?"

"Do you own a laptop computer?"

"Yes."

"Does it contain any incriminating evidence, such as emails or other documents related to this fraud?"

"I wish you wouldn't put it that way."

"That's exactly how it will be framed by the prosecutor for the judge and jury. That you are a criminal who belongs behind bars because you stole money from the State of California under false pretenses."

"It wasn't like that."

"Maybe not, but that's how the prosecution will present it, in the most incriminating light possible. It's up to the defense to present evidence that rebuts and casts doubt on their case. So, does your laptop contain incriminating evidence?"

Abby began sobbing.

"Jeez," Rent said. "Can't you go a little easier on her? She almost got killed for chrissakes."

"I'm just being honest with her. This is not a trivial matter."

Abby composed herself and responded. "The last time I saw my laptop, it was sitting on my coffee table. Unless someone took it. Do you think Gabe took it? He has more reason to make it disappear than I do."

"Okay, that's enough for now. You need to rest and get your strength back," Liz said and handed her a business card. "If you think of anything else, give me a call."

Liz and Rent left the room and found a quiet waiting area at the end of the hallway where they could sit and talk. Rent agreed to put up the money for Abby's bail bond.

"Once that's processed, she will be allowed to have visitors," Liz said. "In the meantime, I suggest you address your hypothetical before it becomes antithetical."

The lawyer picked up her briefcase and strode toward the entrance. Rent watched her go, thinking she cut a fine figure, then shook his head in disgust.

What the hell do I do now? Surely, Turner will tell the cops about that laptop to make Abby out to be the ringleader behind the fraud.

BACK HOME, RENT PULLED Abby's MacBook from a file cabinet drawer where he'd put it for safe keeping. He stared at it, looking for inspiration. He checked the time. Nearly two o'clock. *If I go now, I can get ahead of the traffic. But first . . .*

He called the Julian library and asked for Alice. She came on the line sounding annoyed. He identified himself and said he a favor to ask.

"I'm helping a student right now."

"It involves Abby."

"I'm worried sick about that girl. I saw in the news that she's in the hospital. I called but they wouldn't let me talk to her."

Rent explained the situation and what she could do to help. He would be there in an hour. Then he called Rachel and said he was on his way, but had to stop in Julian first.

"Martha wants to know if you can stay for dinner."

"As long as it's not liver and onions."

"Ew, no. We're making chicken soup and dumplings."

"Excellent. I should be there by five."

He then called his editor.

"As I live and breathe, the exploding man has returned to Earth."

"Yeah, yeah . . . I called to let you know that Abby has been arrested and charged with recipient fraud, and one of A.J. Hawke's associates is representing her for now, and has no comment other than her client will enter a plea of not guilty. I'll send a quick draft in a few minutes."

"Whoa. You're now writing a piece about your girlfriend? I don't think so."

"She's not my girlfriend. She nearly got me killed."

"Send me your notes and Clark will handle this. You are compromised."

"This is my story. I've done all the work and nearly got blown to bits in the process."

"You're wasting your breath," she replied and ended the call.

Rent stared at the phone. "Well, fuck you very much."

He grabbed the MacBook and raced down the stairs to the garage. He opened the door of the 4Runner, then thought better of it. *I haven't driven the truck in a while. And I need to return the 4Runner before it costs me more than it's worth.*

On the road, he slid a David Surette CD into the slot and immediately reversed it to the last track to enjoy the soothing melody of *The Belle of Newcastle* waltz.

Just the ticket to calm me down. That and *Da Slocket Light.*

The commuter traffic had begun to build, but not to the point of impeding his progress. The rain had lessened, but not stopped, and he drove with caution.

He pulled into the Julian library parking lot 57 minutes later and texted Alice. After a moment, she stepped out. He flashed his headlights, and she joined him, climbing into the passenger seat. She held a small plastic trash bag.

He had the computer on his lap, also in a plastic bag. He lifted it up and held it toward her. "Hold open your bag, and as I slide the bag back, we'll slip the computer into your bag. Don't touch the computer itself. We don't want our prints on it. Otherwise, we could be sucked into this fraud mess."

They completed the exchange, and Alice pulled the drawstring tight.

"Is she in big trouble?" Alice asked.

Rent nodded. "She is, but we met with a lawyer today, and she— the lawyer—believes she can get the charges reduced, or even dismissed. But a lot depends on getting this computer to the cops."

"And that's what all this cloak and dagger is about."

"Exactly."

Alice leaned toward Rent. "It's actually pretty exciting stuff. I lead a rather boring existence."

"Believe me, Alice, sometimes boring is best. You remember your part in this drama?"

"Yes. I take this to the sheriff's substation and say that Abby gave it to me last Friday and said that if anything happened to her, I should take it to the cops. And if they ask why I waited so long, I tell them that I tried to talk to her first, at the hospital, but that they wouldn't let me talk to her."

"Perfect. Thank you, Alice. Really, this is critical."

"As I said, anything I can do to help her out, especially if it puts that smarmy carpet cleaner in the clink and they throw away the key. I'll put this in my car right now, check out, and take it to the sheriff's."

Rent watched her cross the parking lot, place the computer in the trunk of her car, and return to the library entrance, where she waved to Rent before going inside.

RENT ARRIVED AT MARTHA'S 28 minutes later. He had driven at a more sedate pace than previously, calmed by the dulcet tones of David Surette's guitar and the accompanying piano and, without question, the fiddle. And having Abby's laptop out of his hands lifted a great weight off of his shoulders.

As he came to a stop, Rachel ran from the house to greet him. "I thought you'd never get here."

"I had an important errand to run, to help Abby."

"Is she going to be okay?" she asked as they walked toward the house.

"She's in good hands at the hospital and will be out in a few days. But, she's in trouble legally, so that's a different story."

"Is she going to jail?"

"We hope not, but she could be fined and put on probation, and that would go on her record."

"I have news," Martha said.

Rent raised his eyebrows.

"The funeral, in case you haven't heard."

Rent shook his head.

"Agnes called. Hannah's body was released yesterday. The service is scheduled for next Monday."

"Thanks. Not surprised she didn't call me."

"You two need to get on the same page."

"Tell me about it."

Rachel grabbed Rent's hand in hers and tugged him away, leading him into the house and to the kitchen. Savory odors filled the warm air, and Rent felt his mouth begin to water. He hadn't eaten anything but an orange and a piece of toast all day.

The sight of an unexpected individual stopped him. The young woman standing next to Martha grinned and said, "We meet again."

"Lindsey, right?" he replied.

"You remembered."

"How could I forget?"

Martha and Rachel both looked back and forth at the two.

"You know everybody," Rachel said to Rent.

"She served me breakfast a while back," he said, then addressed Lindsey.

"What brings you here?"

"L-T-B."

Rent frowned. "L-G-B-T?"

Lindsey shook her head. "No . . . L-T-B . . . Lions Tigers and Bears, the wild animal sanctuary. It's just up the road from here."

Rachel explained. "She's a volunteer. She took me there this afternoon. It's totes amazing. When I get older, I can volunteer too."

"Rachel and I know each other from 4-H, in Ramona," Lindsey said. "She has a baby goat waiting for her."

"I don't want a goat. I want a pony, like Martha's," Rachel said and took his hand. "I'll show you."

Rachel led Rent to the back of the house and into her bedroom, where she stopped and pointed to a sketch of a horse pinned to the wall over the bed.

"Very nice. Do you have name for it?"

"Lakota. It's a Native American name."

"I know. And who's this good-lookin' guy?" he said, pointing at the drawing of himself that she had done earlier.

She shot him a look of admonition, then climbed onto the bed and took down the drawing. She stepped off the bed and handed it to him.

"I don't need it anymore. I want you to have it so you don't ever forget about me."

Rent took the drawing from her. "Thank you, but even without it I would never forget you."

Martha stood at the doorway. "Nice likeness," she said. "Dinner's ready."

Rent rolled up the drawing and set it on the bed. "Don't let me forget this."

While they ate, Rent answered their questions about the explosion at the mine, and Abby, and Gabe Turner. Dinner over and the table cleared, Rachel suggested they say goodnight to the horses. Rachel and Lindsey led the way, Martha and Rent walking at a slower pace.

"The sheriff's office called today while you were on your way here. They want me to bring Rachel in for questioning tomorrow morning."

Rent froze and stared at Martha. "What? Those bastards. They didn't say one word to me about this. What time?"

They wanted her there at eight-thirty, and I said there's no way I was going to sit in that log jam on the freeway. They agreed to ten."

"That's not happening. Who did you talk to?"

"Some guy . . . Ooplebee or something like that."

"Ogilvy. No way," he said and reached for his phone. "Crap, it's in the truck."

As he turned, Martha stopped him. "No. You need to be with your daughter. You can call him later. Get him out of bed, if you have to. But right now she needs you."

Rent nodded. "You're right. Have the grandparents been around?"

"They took her to the Descanso Junction for lunch and complained again about not having Rachel with them."

"Yeah . . . broken record."

AFTER RETURNING TO THE house, Rent excused himself, saying he would be back shortly. He went to his truck, got his phone, and called Detective Washington's cell phone.

The man answered by saying, "This had better be good."

"This is about you bringing in a vulnerable twelve-year-old who just lost her mother and turning her over to Ogilvy. No way, José."

"This has nothing to do with you. It's a legitimate, routine homicide inquiry."

"Routine? Bullshit. You want to interview her, fine, but you do it here, at Martha Flanagan's, and I'm sitting in on it."

"No way."

"Yes way. I have a right to be present, and I suggest you bring Alvarez."

"She's not a detective."

"She will be, and she would benefit from the experience. And maybe you macho dudes could learn some human decency."

"She hasn't been trained on the interview techniques."

"You mean the Reid Technique? So . . . what . . . you're going to wring a confession out of her? Like the Stephanie Crowe case? Like the Central Park Five? Like the more recent Thomas Perez in Fontana?"

"Yeah, yeah, heard it all before," Washington said. "We just want to talk to her. And Alvarez has too much on her plate as it is."

"Fine. But you're doing it here, not at the station. All that's gonna do is traumatize her. You bring Ogilvy and Rachel's gonna start waving a 'defund the police' placard."

Rent paused a beat.

"How about Alicia Velasquez? She's a former cop and a licensed investigator working for the county on the fraud case. She can ask Rachel questions about that."

"You never give up, do you? Remind me again what authority you have in this matter other than a glaring conflict of interest?"

"I'm her father. As if you don't know that. I'm surprised you haven't issued a press release on it yet."

"Not a priority. But if you want to make a big deal about it—"

"Are you coming here? Or do I call my friend A.J. Hawke again. I could conference you in right now."

"What I'm thinking right now is arresting you for interference and obstruction."

"Go right ahead. See how far that gets you. I've been nothing but helpful to you in this investigation. If it wasn't for me, Turner would still be on the loose and you'd still be looking for that mine."

Washington sighed. "I have to talk to my lieutenant. I'll let you know in the morning."

"Sweet dreams," Rent said and ended the call.

While he had been talking to the detective, Lindsey had come out, waved, and driven off. He returned to the house and explained the change in plans to Martha and Rachel.

"Are you spending the night?" Rachel asked. "Please, please."

Rent shook his head. "I can't. I need a good night's sleep, and I need to have my tools of the trade in case they do show up."

Rachel pouted for a moment. "But you are coming back, right? We could go to L-T-B."

"Remember when I asked you to write down everything you could remember about the day your mom got hurt?"

"Mm-hmm," she said with a nod. "Do you want to see it?"

"Not at this moment. But keep it handy, and if you remember anything else, write that down too. Now, I have to go. I'll let you and Martha know as soon as I hear from the detective in the morning."

"Wait," she said and ran to the back of the house. She returned a moment later and handed him her drawing.

32

Tuesday, Day 24

As much as he wanted a good night's sleep, Rent only managed a few hours of shut-eye. He rose early. The atmospheric river had moved eastward and the morning dawned under a cloudless but cold sky. He longed for a run in Tecolote Canyon, hopscotching around mud puddles, but his cracked ribs jabbed him in protest. After coffee and oatmeal, he showered, then entered notes on his laptop, keeping the phone close at hand.

I'll be damned if I'm giving up this story.

His phone chimed. *Clark. Shit.*

"What?" he demanded.

"Get up on the wrong side of the bed, did we?"

"I'm expecting a call from Detective Washington."

"Just a few quick questions regarding your girlie friend, since I'm not being allowed to speak to her. How you wrangled your way in I'm afraid to ask. Your effervescent charm, not doubt."

"She's not—"

"I could just write it without your input. That way you could whine about it later. Want me to bring the cheese?"

Rent sighed in resignation. "Fire away."

Naomi Clark questioned him about the incident at the mine, and how he had come to be held hostage by the most wanted man in San Diego County. Rent filled her in.

"So, in terms of Abby, friend became foe, is that it?"

"Your words not mine. He overpowered her and threatened to kill her. To kill us both."

"Those are his exact words?"

"Close enough."

At that moment, Rent's phone chimed.

"It's Washington. Gotta go."

He ended the call with Clark and answered the call from Washington.

"Al, thanks for getting back to me."

"You do have a way of twisting things around. No wonder you're a reporter."

"Right now I'm a dad trying to protect his daughter from police harassment."

"Very funny. If I didn't have a ten-year-old daughter of my own, I might be a little less forgiving of your smartassery."

"So, what's the verdict?"

"Interesting choice of words, but not the word of the day."

"Which is?"

"Postponement."

"You're shittin' me."

"No. A coupla things have come up. First off, we're going to be involved in a joint action with the Riverside crew first thing in the morning."

"Let me guess. You're picking up the thugs in Fallbrook and Anza."

"I can't go into details, but you're on track. It's actually going to be bigger than that."

"Is the PI, Velasquez, involved."

"Not directly, but the intelligence she provided—"

"We provided."

"Whatever. The point is, that gave us a line on these badasses and their cohorts up the ladder to get the warrants."

"Enjoy yourself."

"I plan on it."

"What's the other wrench in the wringer."

"More DNA."

"From me?"

"No, from some dude up in Washington State."

"What the—"

"The dead vic's parents. They're sayin' that this guy is the true father of the girl, not you, and their lawyer is making big waves. So we're waiting on those results. I think it's all BS and that lawyer is taking 'em for a ride, but the guy's cooperating because he figures he can get some of his money back if he's not the father. Apparently, he set up a trust fund or some damned thing."

"And that's why you haven't released the results of my DNA."

"Not entirely, but that's part of it. Supposed to know today or tomorrow. If he's eliminated, then we're on for the day after with the girl."

"At Martha's house as we agreed?"

"Yes, but it depends on getting a negative result on the DNA test."

"Jeez, just when I think it can't get anymore complicated."

"You and me both. Gotta run."

"Wait. What about Abby?"

"Oh, yeah, I forget to tell you. She's officially been bailed and she can have visitors."

The connection went dead, and Rent called Rod Davis at HHSA to ask if he had more details on the joint action with Riverside.

"This is so far off the record it's outta sight, you got it?" Davis said.

"I hear ya, DT."

"They're going to nab Charlie Oscar when he clocks in tomorrow."

"Is it the guy you think it is? The guy we saw at Fallbrook?"

"One and the same. That email you gave me belongs to him as well. We'll be investigating every application he approved. We've already determined that he's the eligibility worker who altered Hannah Stapleford's application, and he approved the applications filed under the name of Annabel Wilbur, a.k.a. your friend Abby, among others.

"What's more—and you didn't hear this from me either—Turner is cutting a deal and will testify against him. Apparently, that laptop that mysteriously turned up has a treasure trove of incriminating evidence. The sheriff's are salivating over it. You wouldn't've had anything to do with that now would you?"

"No comment."

"Figured as much. You coming down for the fun tomorrow?"

"Maybe. More likely going to be in Fallbrook."

Rent refilled his coffee mug and caught his breath, then called Martha and had her get Rachel so he didn't have to repeat himself. He told them of the postponement, but the good news was that the interview would be at Martha's house, not at the station.

"Are you still coming today though?" Rachel asked. "I miss you."

"I'm sorry, Sweetie. I miss you too, but I can't. I have to go see Abby at the hospital, and I have to go into the office and work on an update on the fraud investigation. And tomorrow I'm going to observe the arrest of some bad guys in Fallbrook, then back to the office and write about that. After the interview on Thursday, we'll do something really fun together, how's that?"

"Do what?"

"It'll be a surprise."

Rent ended the call and phoned Alicia Velasquez, wondering if she knew about the sheriff's department's action set for the following morning. She answered in the affirmative and said, "Wanna ride shotgun with me?"

"Are you in on the action?"

"No, but I'll have a front-row seat. Come on," she urged.

"You're twisting my arm."

"It'll be fun, and I doubt those thugs will be taking any potshots at us this time."

"We can hope. What time?"

"The proverbial. And you won't have to pretend you're a birder this time."

"Hurray."

"See you at five. Don't be late."

RENT CALLED ABBY AT the hospital. Would she like some company?

"Now that's a dumb question."

"You're obviously feeling better."

"This place is driving me nuts. It's claustrophobic; they have nothing on the TV worth watching—all the news channels are blacked out—and I can't get much sleep. They wake me every few hours to take my vital signs and—"

"Are you in the same room?"

"Yes, four thirty-seven."

"I'll see you in a few. Bye."

Twenty-seven minutes later, Rent knocked lightly on the half-open door and stepped into the room.

"I am so happy to see a friendly face," Abby said.

He went to her bed and leaned over, and they embraced lightly. He sat on the bed and they stared at each other for a long moment before looking away.

"Don't hate me, okay?" Abby said, breaking their silence.

Rent turned to face her and shook his head. "I don't blame you for what you did. I understand it. Besides, you took a bullet intended for me. I'm lucky just to be here."

"Oh, so you think this is a conjugal visit, do you?"

He chuckled. "Bonobo time?"

She offered a wan smile. "I wish. I'm so wiped out. I feel like I've been ambushed by a troupe of chimpanzees. I still want to see your scar though."

"Maybe if you're nice to me. In the meantime, I would like to know."

"Know what?"

"How you mysteriously arrived at the mine just in the nick of time to rescue your seemingly doomed lover like some Kathleen Turner rom-com."

She huffed a laugh. "Yeah? Well, this rom-com ain't gonna have a happily-ever-after ending."

"He beat the crap out of you."

"No shit. After we got back to my place."

"He try anything else?"

She eyed him for a moment. "You mean like . . . rape?"

Rent nodded.

She scoffed. "Tried, but couldn't get it up."

She told him how the following morning Turner made her write a fake suicide note and attempted to drug her with sleeping pills, but she never swallowed the pills. She just pretended to fall asleep. After he left, she followed him to the mine in her Wrangler.

"Foolish thing to do."

"I know, but I felt guilty for lying to you. I had to do something."

"The cops have your computer, and they know about the 'goldeneagle' email account and the phishing."

"Yeah, I'm still a bit puzzled about that. But, Rent, I swear I didn't know. Not at first. Gabe said there was a new computer virus, and he would do a scan to make sure my computer was clean. But then I'd wake up in the middle of the night to go pee, and he'd be using my computer. He'd say he couldn't sleep and was playing a video game. When I figured it out, he told me to keep my mouth shut, or I would be arrested and thrown in jail because it was my computer, and I had signed the false welfare application."

"How long has this been going on?"

She did not answer immediately, her face reddening.

"Several months."

"What? I thought—"

"Let me explain."

He shook his head in disbelief. "So you've been conning me? You're not bonobo, you're chimpanzee."

"No! That's not fair. I like you. I want to be with you. I just hoped . . . I don't know what I thought. Other than I had totally screwed things up."

She went on to tell him she had been desperate due to her ex moving out and having to pay full rent and utilities, and being saddled with student debt and credit-card debt.

"Gabe sweet-talked me into it, saying no one gets hurt by it, but he took a huge cut and started using my computer for phishing so if he got caught, I'd take the blame. He said if I breathed a word of it, I would regret it. And he meant it. We now know how far he was willing to go."

"Apparently, we should have been interviewing you, not Hannah."

"Don't be cruel. At first, he let me use the EBT card—not all of it but most of it—and I started paying off my debts, but then somehow the money started disappearing. I'd try to use the card and, suddenly, the money's all gone. I guess he hacked my card and kept the money for himself. I didn't know about Hannah, but I had begun to have my suspicions. It makes me wonder how many others got caught in his spidery web."

"There are many. And the cops are going to arrest his partner-in-crime at the county HHSA, along with those scary dudes in Fallbrook and Riverside County."

"Good, they can join the club."

"The cops been giving you the third degree?"

"They've tried, but Liz, the lawyer, has kept them at bay. But how did you find about that email account? The cops barely know about it."

He told her.

"You hacked into my computer? How—"

He told her how easy it had been, but he did nothing else, that he had arranged for it to be delivered to the sheriff's office without them knowing he'd had it in his possession when they searched her home.

"How'd you do that?"

"It's best that you don't know. Otherwise, I might be in the cell next to you. So don't go telling anyone, even that lawyer. She might feel obligated to pass that tidbit on."

They heard a knock at the door and a woman stepped into the room. "I hope I'm not interrupt—" She caught herself mid-sentence as she recognized Rent in the dim light of the room. "What are you doing here?"

"I'm whispering sweet nothings to my little girlie friend, as you are so fond of calling her."

Abby's face contorted into a puzzled expression as she glanced from one to the other.

"Let me introduce my colleague, Naomi Clark. You can call her Lewis for short."

Naomi stepped farther into the room. "No, you may not. I'm here for the interview. You agreed—"

"Yes, please come in. I think I've answered every possible question a thousand times, but I guess one more time won't hurt."

"I'd prefer just one-on-one."

"What, you don't want me hanging around?" Rent replied. "I'm deeply offended."

"Get lost. This is my turn."

Rent patted Abby on the arm and stood up. "I'll see you later."

Abby spoke as he walked to the door. "I'll call you."

He flashed a grim smile. "Yeah, that's what they all say."

RENT RETURNED HOME, FRESHENED up, grabbed his laptop, and went to the newspaper's Mission Valley office for the first time in days. O'Connor intercepted him before he even reached his desk.

"Parley-voo. Pronto."

"Oui, mio capitano," he replied, making a mock salute and marching behind her to her desk.

"I need to know what the hell is going on. You're all over the county, not returning my calls—"

Rent held up his hands in a defensive posture. "I have returned every one of your calls."

"Eventually."

"Doesn't being trapped in a mine shaft and nearly being blown to bits count for something?"

"Three days ago, yeah, but in case you've forgotten, we're a *daily* newspaper."

"I've sent you dispatches. And tomorrow I will have breaking news, as the saying goes."

"Oh? This had better be good."

He told her about the joint operation of the two counties' sheriff's departments.

"Okay, I'll assign a couple of photographers."

"By the way, I ran into Clark at the hospital. She's putting Abby's thumbs in the screws as we speak."

"She have anything we don't already know?"

"Not much as far as the big bang goes, but I learned a bit more about her involvement—or lack thereof—in the fraud scheme."

"So she was involved."

"Yes and no. I'll talk to Clark and we can compare notes."

"You're walking a very fine line here."

"She's more of a victim that a perp, although I suspect she will face consequences of some kind. Her lawyer said—"

"Lawyer? Does Clark know about him?"

"Her. One of Hawke's associates."

"I might have guessed."

"Clark will get that out of her and she can give Liz a call."

"Oh, it's Liz now?"

"I barely know her. I sat in when they discussed the case. She thinks Abby will come out of this with barely a slap on the wrist, assuming she continues to cooperate with the authorities. If it wasn't for her, they wouldn't have Turner."

"How's she doing, health-wise I mean."

"She'll be released from the hospital in another day or two, but recovery will take a while."

"What about the girl, the dead woman's daughter. Anything new on her? Have they tracked down her father yet?"

"About that."

O'Connor shook her head. "Why am I getting a bad feeling about this?"

Rent looked away, fully inflated his lungs, winced, and exhaled with a whoosh. *A little dissembling won't hurt.*

"It seems that it's entirely possible that I may be Rachel's father."

"What? Oh, for Pete's sake. Now, I've it heard it all. And you're just telling me this? This is as huge effing conflict of interest as . . . as . . . I don't have words for it."

"It has not been confirmed by the cops yet. They're still waiting on DNA results from the guy Hannah's parents believe, or want to believe, is Rachel's father. Washington said they hope to have the results today or tomorrow. But—"

"But?"

"But the preliminary result indicates a match between me and Rachel."

"I don't know whether to congratulate you or sack you. Or maybe I'll congratulate you and then sack you."

"Washington is going to interview her on Thursday, and, assuming I am her dad, I will be sitting in on the interview, along with the woman who's fostering her for now."

O'Connor stared at the ceiling. "Please, dear god, spare me from this tribulation. You are not writing a story that involves your daughter unless it's a letter to Dear Abby . . . oops, that's out of bounds as well."

"I'm sure Clark will do a bang-up job of it."

"She spoke to the girl's grandparents. They were complaining about not being able to take custody of their granddaughter, something about the county saying it's because they're 'itinerant' and

Hannah's house is still taped off as a crime scene, and that some dead-beat, who shall remain nameless, after all these years, now claims to be her father and gets to spend as much time as he wants with her and . . . yada, yada, yada."

"Yeah, I know. I inadvertently had lunch with them on Friday."

"And that deadbeat turns out to be you."

Rent shrugged. "I could do worse. She's precious and precocious."

"So, how did you break the news?"

"I didn't. Through a twist of fate, she found out before I did, and she had already put two and two together. For her, it merely came as a confirmation."

"Smarter than all the adults in the room."

Rent raised his eyebrows and nodded.

"So, what am I going to do with you? I should take you off anything even close to the this mess."

Oh, come on. I've been on this fraud story for weeks, and just when it's breaking wide open you're gonna take me off of it? Rachel has nothing to do with the fraud story. Well, almost nothing."

"What do you mean?"

"She may have seen something, but the cops have so much other evidence her testimony wouldn't even be frosting on the cake. Turner, or Turnbull, is already copping a plea and blowing the whistle on the insider at HHSA, and Abby will testify—"

"That's the other conflict of interest."

"I'm the one who discovered the email phishing account on her MacBook and turned it over to the cops, and she's none too pleased with that."

"You? I thought . . ."

"This doesn't go any farther than you, and if you do say any-thing, I will deny it, and there's no way anyone can prove otherwise."

"So you not only have major conflicts of interest, you have also interfered with a police investigation and obstructed justice."

"That about sums it up, yeah. The *New York Times* is gonna love it."

"The *New York Times*?"

"Yeah, didn't I tell you about that? I guess I forgot."

"Don't be a smart ass."

"A guy from the *Times* got in touch and wants to do a profile based on my near-death escape from the mine and the ultimate capture of Turner and bringing down this multimillion-dollar welfare fraud racket with ties to bad actors in Eastern Europe, and possibly Russia, intent on spreading fake news regarding the upcoming presidential election."

"You're bluffing."

"You want his phone number? Got it right here," he said and tapped the pocket encasing his cell phone.

"And you agreed to this?"

Rent looked at her in disbelief. "Hell no. I told him I . . . we . . . are quite capable of handling this ourselves, fuck you very much."

"Thank you. . . . Okay, here's what I think."

"I'm listening."

"You're still the lead writer, but I have to bring in Clark. She will cover the Abby angle and, if need be, Rachel, in terms of the fraud investigation. You're hands off."

"Will she get a byline, or a mention in a tagline?"

O'Connor smiled. "Worried about having to share that Pulitzer, are you?"

Rent shrugged. "Just curious."

"Remains to be seen. But she will continue to handle exclusively the homicide investigation, which includes talking to Abby, which she's doing as we speak, and Rachel."

"And I will sit in on the Rachel interview, assuming the DNA results stand as they do now."

O'Connor nodded. "I can't deny you that . . . Dad. . . . but I don't envy you. Having a teenage daughter can be a challenge as I well know."

"Taking it one day at time."

"You're seeing her?"

"Practically every day. So far so good."

"The honeymoon won't last. Let's just hope she doesn't become too rebellious."

"Speaking of, I met a student who's a senior at Ramona High, and she wants to major in communications. You ran a story about her a while back. She edits the school newspaper and the Ramona weekly, won an award . . ."

"Lindsey something?"

"That's her. Any chance of her interning here?"

"I'll look into it. Have her send me a résumé and clips."

"Thanks. Are we done? I have—"

"A story to write. You'd better hop to it . . . Dad."

33

Rent arrived at Alicia Velasquez's house at five as she loaded her equipment in her Honda CR-V, her movements illuminated only by streetlights and a single bulb in the garage.

"Are we skulking again?" he asked.

"Not necessarily," she said with a grin. "But 'One never knows, do one?' I was a Girl Scout. Hop in."

The I-15 freeway had little traffic, particularly in the northbound lanes.

"I love driving at this time of day," she said.

Rent nodded but did not reply.

"You're rather quiet this morning. Something bothering you?"

Rent waited a beat before answering. "It's this whole fraud investigation. It has taken on so many different dimensions and gotten so bizarre, I feel as if I've followed Alice into her surreal netherworld or Dorothy into the Land of Oz. It's left my head spinning, not to mention getting into deep shit with my editor."

"You're referring to Hannah and her death, and Rachel. That must have come as quite a shock."

"You could say that again."

"How's that going? Is she holding up okay?"

"Martha, bless her heart, is keeping her occupied, but Rachel has moments where she just gets overwhelmed and has to retreat from the world."

"The sudden death of a parent will do that, especially a violent death."

"Yeah, and as you know, tomorrow Washington's going to grill her about the altercation at the house. Thank you for agreeing to be there."

Velasquez touched Rent's arm. "I'm happy to help."

"At least we're doing it at the house, not the station, and Martha will be there. It's not as if Rachel's a suspect. But who knows what BS Turner has been feeding them."

Rent stared through the windshield as they passed Rainbow and began the climb toward Fallbrook. They arrived at the familiar scene a few minutes later and parked well down the road from where the excitement would take place. Velasquez handed Rent a tripod and folding stools, and she grabbed her camera and audio recorder. They had both already looped binocular straps around their necks.

"We'll set up at the same place as before. It shouldn't be long now."

Birds had begun their dawn songs, welcoming a new day, establishing a tranquil setting about to be shattered by a turbulent confrontation between good guys and bad guys.

Moments after Rent and the PI got settled, the sheriff's vehicles arrived, travelling at a languid pace and without flashing lights or sirens. The deputies set up roadblocks on both sides of the driveway. Several dark figures in helmets and bulky vests crept toward the house and took up positions as if they were commandos on a secret mission behind enemy lines on foreign soil.

As Velazquez turned on her audio gear and began taking photos, Rent again noted the upside-down American flag and that the Don't Tread On Me banner had been replaced by one touting the phrase An Appeal To Heaven.

"Here goes the entry team, the 'stick,' " she said. "They'll treat this as a hostage rescue first, in case there are children in the house, then take out the combatants, if necessary."

"The 'stick'?" he questioned.

"Before they enter, they line up single file, and it looks like a stick."

Rent watched through his binoculars as the six-member squad approached the front door. The breacher used a battering ram to smash it open, then stepped aside. The others rushed in, one after the other, weapons at the ready.

Rent heard a faint female voice cry out, "Don't shoot! Don't shoot!"

Seconds later, gunfire erupted at the back of the house, and Rent saw a figure burst into the side yard, firing a weapon in the general direction of the cops.

"Holy shit!" Rent muttered as bullets whizzed through the bushes near his head. He slid sideways off his stool and sprawled flat on the ground, groaning as the all too familiar protestations from his ribs sent a jolt of pain through his chest.

The deputies returned fire, and Rent heard someone cry out. He couldn't tell if it was one of the suspects or a deputy sheriff. More shouting followed, along with another exchange of gunfire. Then silence.

Rent raised his head slightly and peered through the bush. No one moved. The birds began to sing again. Then a voice from a bullhorn ordered: "Drop your weapons. You are surrounded. I repeat, drop your weapons."

One of the suspects, who had taken shelter behind a large pickup truck, ran back toward the house, again spraying bullets randomly. As he rounded a corner of the house and into the darkness, more gunfire rang out and the scream of a wounded creature chorused the air, followed by loud cursing.

The voice repeated its earlier command: "Drop your weapons."

The wounded man's moans and cursing continued from the dim light beside the house.

"Don't shoot. We surrender," a voice cried out.

Two other individuals rose to standing positions, their hands held over their heads, their weapons at their feet. Deputies rushed forward and took the pair into custody, cuffing their hands behind their backs.

Rent sat up but remained seated on the ground. Velasquez did the same.

"That was a bit too close for comfort," she said.

"No shit," Rent replied.

The day brightened as the sun peeked over the eastern ridge. Occupants of the house filed out. Rent counted two women and four children, the latter still in pajamas and rubbing the sleep out of their eyes. The deputies cleared the house and declared it secure. The entire action had taken less than 10 minutes.

Rent and Velasquez carried their gear back to her car as a deputy approached, stopping about 10 feet away.

"Let me see your hands," he ordered, weapon in hand but pointed at the ground.

Velasquez held up her hands and identified herself, as did Rent. The man stepped closer as they produced their identification, then called for a sergeant to join them. After a brief exchange, the sergeant waved them off.

"Go on, we'll deal with you later."

"Could I at least get the names of the people you arrested, and the wounded man?" Rent asked.

"Not my department," he said and began walking back to the huddle at the head of the driveway.

"Is Alvarez here?" Rent called out.

The man stopped and turned around. "She's around here somewhere," he said, then continued on his way as an ambulance, lights flashing, departed from the scene.

A woman carrying a camera and telephoto lens approached. "Good morning, Rent."

He recognized her as Charlene Starr, staff photographer. "Pretty exciting, eh?"

"A bit more excitement than I needed."

"So, this is what, the third time in recent days you've been shot at?" she said.

Rent nodded. "Don't remind me."

"Well, at least you didn't get shot in the ass this time, or did you?"

"You're a real comedian, Charli. But I think you should stick to what you do best."

"I got some good stuff, and I'd better get back over there for some closeups. See you back the office."

Rent shook his head. "I'm never going to be able to live that down."

Velasquez chuckled. "Count your blessings. You could still be in that mine under tons of rubble."

"I'm going to find Alvarez and see if she's got anything for me."

BACK AT HOME, RENT'S fingers danced across the keyboard as he recounted the events of the morning. In Fallbrook, five adults arrested and four children taken into protective care. A search of the premises turned up dozens of firearms as well as more evidence of fraudulent activity, including counterfeit EBT cards, skimmers, and tens of thousands of dollars in cash.

The raids in Riverside County had similar results, with sheriff's deputies making multiple arrests and recovering evidence of criminal activities at the outpost near Anza and the home of Tim Beltz, Jr., in Hemet.

At the San Diego County's HHSA, the "Charlie Oscar" insider had been arrested without incident and charged with "internal welfare fraud," as were two Riverside County eligibility workers—all three of them, allegedly, having "falsified applications" and "collected or distributed unlawful benefits" from their respective county agencies. The agencies operate under the aegis of state and federal aid programs for impoverished families with minor children as well as senior citizens and disabled individuals. In one instance, a woman had five separate false benefits accounts.

According to the charging documents for "Charlie Oscar," he had set up payments for ineligible and nonexistent children. These acts of internal fraud cost the county more than $900,000, the charges alleged. The defendant not only faced fraud charges, he could also face charges for embezzlement, said a representative within the district attorney's office. In a recent case in Los Angeles, the judge ordered the defendant to pay restitution of more than $1.4 million.

Sheriff's deputies also arrested a man living in Shelter Valley, a small community in the desert, southeast of Julian. Gabe Turner had been hiding out there, and the man was alleged to have assisted Turner in the acquisition of guns, ammunition, and explosive material.

On the same day, a federal grand jury in Prescott, Arizona, indicted a man on charges of selling guns to be used in a mass shooting to incite a race war ahead of the upcoming presidential election. It wasn't clear if he had any connection to those arrested in San Diego and Riverside, but an FBI spokesperson said they were looking into it.

Elected officials in both San Diego and Riverside counties held press conferences in an effort to take credit for the "Big Bust," as some had labeled it, and the two county sheriffs praised their officers for actions well executed.

Rent questioned the San Diego County supervisors, asking them why more wasn't being done to improve the security of the EBT cards, but they deflected his question, saying it was up to the state to handle that, and he should direct that question at the state legislators.

"We also identified an employee involved in this criminal enterprise, and, thanks to our crack team of fraud investigators, he has been arrested," Supervisor Tom Horn said. "This will translate into millions of dollars in savings of taxpayer dollars destined for these important programs created to assist those less fortunate."

Rent queried the man again. "Supervisor, why did the county stop having mandatory fraud investigations of every application? Wouldn't that policy have prevented much of this widespread fraud from occurring in the first place?"

The supervisor hesitated before he responded. "There are a number of factors involved, not only at our level, but at the state and federal levels as well."

"So you're absolving yourself from this?"

"Not at all. I'm just saying that there are factors over which we have little or no control—unanticipated budget shortfalls, the lock-down during the COVID pandemic, understaffing, to name a few. If there are no more questions, thank you for your time."

Rent shook his head and left the room. "Typical gladhanding politicians," he muttered, "taking credit where it's not due."

"Ain't that the truth," Clark said as she joined the exodus from the room.

"Hey, Lewis," he said.

"Would you—"

"Sorry, I should stop winding you up."

"Yes, you should."

"Get everything you need from Abby?"

"Yes, she was very cooperative. I feel a bit sorry for her. Got in over her head, made some bad choices when it came to men . . ."

"Hey, don't look at me. She—"

Clark grinned. "Now I'm winding you up for a change. She

actually had nice things to say about you, overall, although she's still miffed that you hacked her computer."

"I was trying to absolve her, not incriminate her."

"That's not what she's worried about."

"Oh?"

"She keeps a diary . . . on her computer."

Rent stopped and stared at Clark. "A diary? I guess I missed that."

"Yeah, right. See you back at the office."

Rent went to the newsroom to finalize his story and submit it to O'Connor.

"Great job this. Seriously. Those glaring conflicts of interest notwithstanding," she said. "This series is already having a ripple effect. I mean, just look at the *NYT*. Maybe we'll actually see something come out of all this attention. Those politicians will never give you any of the credit though, you being the 'enemy of the people' and all."

"Yep, that's me: 'Enemy of the People.' "

RENT MADE AN APPOINTMENT for the 4Runner to be returned, then again visited Abby at the hospital, after she phoned to tell him she was being released. She explained that the cops had contacted her parents, and her mother and sister were flying to San Diego.

"They're taking me back to Idaho so I have someone to look after me while I recuperate. The doctor says it could take four to six weeks before I return to some form of normalcy."

"You don't sound overly excited about it."

"I haven't seen them in years, after what they did to me."

"What did they do to you?"

Abby swallowed and her Adam's apple bobbed before she answered. "I tried to tell you before but couldn't. I felt ashamed. I thought you'd think of me as damaged goods."

"And that's when you got so upset with me, when I pressured you."

She nodded and stared at the far wall of the hospital room. "My older sister's boyfriend."

Rent fastened his gaze on her eyes. "He raped you?"

She shook her head. "No, but nearly. And when I told my mom and sister, he denied it, of course. And my bitch of a sister called me a little slut for coming on to him, and when nothing came of my 'flirting' and so-called 'advances,' I became vindictive and falsely accused him. And that asshole smirked."

"He was there?"

"Yeah, the next day, when he came to the house to pick up my sister. And my mother believed them."

"You were how old at the time?"

"Twelve, in seventh grade. Same age as Rachel. That's how I ended up in California. As soon as I graduated from high school, I took off. I've had nothing to do with those people since then. And that's why I got so upset about Rachel. Some men can be such bastards."

Rent gave her hand a gentle squeeze. "You can always refuse to see them."

"Men?"

"No, your mother and sister."

"They apologized. Turns out my sister divorced that asshole after she found child porn on his computer, and she admitted she lied about what he did to me, that she . . ." Abby waved her arms and rolled her eyes. ". . . was 'in denial' at the time."

Abby uttered a low groan and paused to catch her breath before continuing. "Besides, I don't have anyone else. After what I did, I certainly can't expect much sympathy from you."

"Abby . . ."

"Don't. What I did was wrong, and you were just doing your job. It could have been a lot worse. And we did have fun . . . while it lasted."

Rent smiled at the memories. "That we did. Our bonobo phase. What about your legal situation?"

"The judge is letting me go as long as I promise to return for the court appearance. It looks like I'll have to pay a fine, make restitution, and be placed on probation. No jail time, thank god. But that's weeks away. If I fail to appear, he'll issue a warrant for my arrest."

"Let's hope it doesn't come to that. Don't need you holed up in some shack out in the Bitterroots."

Abby shook her head. "Don't worry. It won't."

They stared at each for a long moment.

"One more thing," she said.

"Okay."

"I apologize for coming on so strongly about you not telling me sooner that you're Rachel's father. I understand your reluctance. It's not as if we were getting married, and I would be acquiring a step-daughter."

"I could have been more forthcoming. I know you care about her."

They were interrupted by a knock at the door and two women entered, the familial likeness apparent. The women smiled at Abby, then cast questioning looks at Rent.

"Mom, Debbie, this is Rent Beacham, the reporter I told you about."

"Ah, the notorious Mr. Beacham, who nearly got my daughter killed."

"Mom, he did not! I nearly got *him* killed," Abby retorted, then flinched from the effort.

"Nice to meet you both," Rent said. "I'd better be going."

"No," Abby said. "Wait in the lobby. I'll be down as soon as I get dressed."

THE ELEVATOR DOOR OPENED and Abby, seated in a wheelchair pushed by a male nurse, entered the lobby. Her mother and sister followed, carrying plastic bags containing Abby's personal items. The sister said she would go get the car and bring it around.

Rent stood and followed them out to the passenger loading zone. Abby rose from the wheelchair and spread her arms toward Rent.

"Hug?"

Rent stepped forward and they hugged lightly, each careful not to inflict pain on the other.

Abby, tearful, said, "I'll never see you again, will I."

Rent took a step back and shrugged. "One never knows, do one? There's always the courtroom."

"You know that's not what I meant."

"I may just surprise you and go to Weiser for the fiddle contest again."

As RENT DROVE HOMe, his phone chimed. Text from Rachel:

ru ok

He waited until he got home to call her.

"I heard there were gunshots," she said. "You didn't get shot in the butt again, did you?"

"Aren't you a laugh a minute."

"I got scared. Did you?"

"No, not shot in the butt or anywhere else. I'm fine, but the guy who started the shooting is now in the hospital after the deputies shot him."

"Are you gonna come see me? I like Martha, but she's strict, and Grandma and Grandpa took me to the wolf place, but I'd rather do stuff with you."

"Tomorrow, like I promised. It's too late now anyway; the traffic sucks. Besides, I've been up since three-thirty this morning and I'm wiped out. I'd probably fall asleep at the wheel. I need to be fresh as a daisy for the interview tomorrow."

"Ooh-kay."

Rent could hear the resignation in her voice. "Do you have some books to read?"

"I'm reading *The Cat Ate My Gym Suit*. Martha gave it to me. It's funny."

"Yes, an oldie but goodie. I'll see you in the morning."

34

As he brewed his morning joe, Rent's ringtone began playing Bob Marley's *I Shot the Sheriff*.

"Hello, Detective. You're up early."

"I'm catching worms."

"We're still on for this morning?"

"Yes, sir. Got the DNA results back. Negative."

"That'll put a smile on Hannah's parents' faces. Have you told them?"

"Oh, yeah. That woman gave me an earful. We'll be at Martha Flanagan's place at ten-thirty sharp."

"We?"

"Me and Velasquez."

"Wise man. See you there. And thanks."

The detective scoffed. "You might not thank me later."

Rent disconnected and called Martha; she said Washington had already called her to confirm. "Do you want to speak to your daughter?"

Daughter. That's going take some getting used to.

"I'll call on her phone."

"Good idea. See you soon."

Rent disconnected and called.

"Hi, Dad. When are you coming?"

"I'm leaving as soon as I get off the phone. Have your notes handy."

"I will. Bye."

"Goodbye, Sweetie."

Rent ended the call, set the phone on the table, leaned back in his chair, and heaved a heavy sigh. *What the hell have I gotten myself into?*

He looked at the clock: 8:13.

I can be there by nine.

Upstairs, he used the bathroom and brushed his teeth, then descended to the main floor and put on a winter coat and a stocking cap. He put his laptop in its carrying case, and checked to make sure he had a notebook and recording device.

All systems go.

RENT ARRIVED AT MARTHA Flanagan's house 42 minutes later. She offered him coffee, scrambled eggs, and toast, which he accepted. Rachel joined him, firing questions about the previous day's raid in Fallbrook. He gave her the executive summary.

"You heard the bullets go over your head?"

He nodded. "Nearly scared the s—"

"Ahem," Martha said.

Rachel giggled. "Scared the *schist* out of you?"

"Daylights . . . nearly scared the daylights out of me."

Martha winked at him.

"Then what did you do?"

"Do? I did nothing but lie as flat on the ground as possible and kept my head down. Fortunately, the whole thing was over in a matter of minutes. As soon as the deputies shot the gunman, the others gave up, being the 'patriot warriors' they are *not*."

Rachel gave him a hug and kissed his cheek. "I'm glad you're okay."

"Me too. Now, let's go over what's gonna happen when Detective Washington gets here."

He explained the process to Rachel and Martha, and told Rachel that if she didn't feel comfortable answering a question, that's okay. Don't answer it. And if she didn't know the answer, just so say: I don't know, or I don't recall.

"Detective Washington is big, like a professional football player, and he might look scary, but he's really a softie at heart. Alicia

Velasquez, the private eye, can be a tough interrogator too, but she has a soft side as well. Are you nervous?"

Rachel nodded.

"That's normal. I'm nervous too, but we'll get through this. You'll do just fine."

The law enforcement officer arrived precisely at 10:30, and the PI pulled in behind him. Rent introduced them to Martha and Rachel, and they took seats at the kitchen table. Martha offered coffee. Rent and Washington accepted, Alvarez declined. Rachel requested a cup of hot chocolate.

While Martha organized the beverages, Rachel asked the PI if she was the one with Rent when he got shot at. She confirmed it.

"I'll bet that scared the schist out of you," Rachel said with a grin.

Velasquez's eyes widened and she glanced at Rent, who rolled his eyes.

"Rachel, this is no time to be making lame jokes."

"You do it."

Rent sighed and faced the PI and said, "Sorry 'bout that."

"Welcome to fatherhood," she replied.

Washington intervened. "Let's get this over with."

Martha served them and set a box of tissues to the side. "Would you prefer it if I left the room, or even the house?" she asked the detective.

Washington shrugged.

"Please stay," Rent said. "You're her official guardian for now, and one more set of ears wouldn't hurt."

Washington set out an electronic recording device, as did Rent, and began by telling Rachel how sorry he felt for her, not only for losing her mother, but in such a violent manner. Velasquez seconded that.

"We will bring the man responsible to justice," he said. "You can help us do that by answering our questions truthfully and not holding anything back, no matter how insignificant or trivial you may think it is."

Rachel nodded, her eyes tearing up and her hands shaking such that hot chocolate slopped out of her mug. "Sorry," she said.

Martha got a paper towel and cleaned it up, then handed Rachel a tissue. After Rachel had dried her eyes, the detective asked her to tell them what she remembered from the night her mother got hurt.

"Here," she said and slid a piece of paper across the table. "I wrote it all down."

Washington read it, then said, "This is helpful, but I also need to hear you say it."

Rachel gave a reluctant sigh and rolled her eyes.

Rent touched her arm. "You're doing this for your mom."

"Okay," she replied.

She told the detective that she had been in her bedroom, and she heard her mom arguing with Gabe Turner. That was nothing unusual, but the shouting got worse, so she got up and went to the kitchen, where they were standing. Gabe was telling her to keep her big yap shut or else, and she was yelling back at him, telling him to leave her alone or she was calling the cops, and she would tell them everything, including the EBT stuff.

"That's when he slapped her in the face," Rachel said. "And she picked up a plate off the table and threw it at him. He ducked and it missed him, and it hit the wall, making a loud bang. I yelled at him to leave her alone, but he tried to hit her again. That's when Abby tried to get in between them."

"Abby?" the detective said. "Do you mean Abigail Wilburforce?"

Rachel nodded. "Yeah, she tried to separate them, but Gabe shoved her down."

"Why was Abby there?"

Rachel held up her bandaged arm. "She came to check on me, to see if I was okay. We were supposed to go to 4-H and get a baby goat, but Gabe wouldn't take me like he promised."

"How did you hurt your arm?"

"He did it. He pushed me down and I sprained my wrist really bad and I had to go to the doctor and get this cast put on."

"When was this?"

"The week before, when we went to 4-H the first time."

"Okay . . . just so I have this straight," the detective said. "You went to 4-H and Gabe Turner knocked you down and you hurt your arm. Then, the following week, you were supposed to go again but you didn't, so Abby came to check on you and that led to a fight between your mom and Gabe Turner."

Rachel nodded. "Uh-huh."

"So your mom was mad at Abby. She was jealous of Abby. And Abby pushed your mother away from Gabe Turner."

Rachel looked at Rent, puzzled.

"Where are you going with this, Detective?"

Washington ignored Rent and stared intently at Rachel. "Did Abby Wilburforce push your mother down, causing her to hit her head and cause it to bleed?"

"No!" Rachel cried out. "That's not what happened. I just told you, she was trying to stop Gabe from hurting my mom. He's the one who pushed my mom, and she fell and hit her head and . . ."

Rachel put her arms on the table and laid her head on her arms, sobbing. Rent put an arm across her shoulders and pulled her close to him.

"Why doesn't anyone ever listen to me?" Rachel said, her voice muffled.

Rent daggered the detective. "Happy now?"

Washington asked Martha if he could use the restroom, and she gave him directions.

Rent patted Rachel's shoulder. "We're almost done, Sweetie."

Velasquez spoke. "Rachel, he's not trying to be mean to you. We're just trying get at the truth as to what happened that night. We hear different stories from different people, so we have to figure out who's telling the truth and who's not. Okay?"

Rachel lifted her head and wiped her eyes, then looked at the private investigator, who smiled in return.

"I am telling the truth," Rachel said. "Why don't you believe me?"

"It's not that we don't believe you. It's just that we have to look at all of the possibilities."

"I didn't do it. Abby didn't do it. Gabe did it because my mom said she would call the you and the cops and tell everything about the EBT stuff and . . ." She hesitated for a beat. "That's why they were fighting. And because of what he did to me."

"What did he do to you?"

Rachel sat up, her shoulders sagged, and she looked to Rent, then Martha, her eyes pleading.

Rent hugged her again and said, "It's not your fault. You did nothing wrong. It's okay to tell them what happened so it never happens again."

"He touched me."

"He touched you?" Velasquez said.

Rachel nodded. "He would pinch my boobs and make fun of how small they are, and one time, when my mom was at work at the bookstore, he put his hand between my legs. I slapped him and he just laughed, so I kicked him, right in the nuts."

Rent stifled a laugh; Martha and Velasquez passed knowing looks.

Washington returned and took his seat. "What's this?"

Velasquez responded. "Rachel is saying that Gabe Turner molested her and that's why her mom was so angry with him."

"That's a serious allegation," Washington said.

"Oh, for chrissakes, Al, you're dealing with a twelve-year-old, not a woman twice her age."

"I'm telling the truth!" Rachel shouted. "He did that to me and pushed my mom down."

Washington's lips tightened and he nodded at Velasquez.

"Rachel," the PI said, I have some questions about the CalFresh program. Do you know what I'm talking about?"

The girl nodded. "That card my mom . . ."

"Yes, the EBT card. She used it buy groceries, didn't she?"

"He stole her card, many times."

"Do you mean the man who called himself Gabe Turner?"

"Yes, he would take it and spend the money, on beer, and he'd go to the casino. Sometimes he'd come back with a bunch of money and brag about how much he won, but mostly he lost. My mom got sick of all of it and told him never to come back. That's when they got in the fight. I tried to stop him from hitting her, but he shoved me out of the way."

"Did he push you into your mother, and then she fell?" Washington said. "Did you push your mother away, trying to protect her, but she fell and hit her head?"

Rachel stared at Washington for a beat, then shouted, "No. You're not listening to me, you dirty bastard!"

"Rachel, language," Martha said.

"Sorry, but why isn't he listening to me?"

Washington sighed and leaned back in his chair, then nodded at Velasquez again, who spoke softly, urging Rachel to continue.

"Like I already said, he hit her, and when she tried to hit him back, her grabbed her by the arms and shook her and he called her a stupid bitch and told her to keep her big mouth shut, and then he pushed her away, hard, and she fell backward and hit her head on the corner of the kitchen cupboard and she was knocked out. After a minute or so, she woke up and said she was fine. So Gabe left. Abby put a bandage on her head and told her she needed to see a doctor, but my mom said she was fine and she told Abby to leave. The next morning, my mom took my brother to a friend's house and she brought me here, to protect me in case he came back, and that's the last time I—"

Rachel shoved back her chair, stood up, and ran from the house. Rent rose from his chair to follow.

"Sit down," the detective said.

Rent remained standing, looking out the window as he kept his eyes on Rachel, who ran to the corral. The horses trotted over to the fence to meet her.

"I'll go," Martha said and stood and grabbed a handful of tissues.

"I'll join you," Velasquez seconded.

The two women left the house, leaving Rent alone with Washington.

"Proud of yourself?" Rent asked.

The man sighed and turned his hands palms up. "I'm just doing my job. I'm sorry if you can't see that."

"Don't apologize to me. Apologize to that poor girl you just traumatized."

"I have to get at the truth. Turner is telling us all sorts of BS, as you can imagine. I just want to have her rebuttal on the record."

"Yeah, I get that, but did you have to be so accusatory?"

Washington shrugged.

"You get what you came for?"

"For now. If it comes to it, she may be called as a witness."

"Yeah, I suspected as much. Hopefully, it won't come to that."

"So, you gonna turn me into the big bad ogre in your newspaper?"

Rent shook his head. "You're in Clark's hands now. I have nothing to do with the homicide story, and I filed my latest fraud story yesterday."

Washington rose from his seat. "I'll go talk to her."

The two men walked to the corral. Rachel eyed the detective with suspicion. He put one hand on a fence rail for balance and squatted so he had to look up at the diminutive girl.

"Rachel, I'm sorry I upset you. That was not my intent. I know it's no excuse, but I deal with a lot of bad people, the worst people, like Gabe Turner, and they all lie to me. But I can't refute those lies unless I get truthful testimony from witnesses who were there, and we can use their testimony to prove beyond a reasonable doubt that the bad guys lied and convict them and send them to prison. So, I want to thank you for helping us today. We're going to see that your mother gets the justice she deserves. Okay?"

Rachel, tears again cascading down her cheeks, nodded, then turned to Rent, put her arms around him and squeezed and leaned her head against his chest. He winced but didn't mind the momentary jolt of pain and kissed the top of her head.

"Just one more question and we're done," Washington said. "Okay?"

Rachel gave him a blank stare.

"What about your brother? Where was he during this commotion?"

"He slept through most of it. He could sleep through anything. He didn't wake up until it was almost over, after Mom—"

Rachel pressed into Rent again.

"Thank you, Rachel. You've been a great help," the detective said.

Washington straightened up and put a hand out. Rent took it and they shook. The detective nodded at Velasquez and thanked Martha for her hospitality, and began walking toward his vehicle.

Velasquez said goodbye to Martha and turned to Rent. "She's going through a tough time, but she's resilient. She's lucky you two got united, even if the circumstances are so tragic."

Rent, tears welling in his own eyes, nodded and croaked out a thanks. Velasquez jogged to catch up with Washington, and they disappeared around a corner of the house.

Martha handed Rent and Rachel fresh tissues and they dried their eyes.

"Can we go riding?" Rachel asked.

Rent looked at Martha, who said, "Not until that cast comes off."

"How about this," Rent said. "We go to the mine and you can see what's left after it went ka-blooey and nearly blew me to smithereens."

Rachel jumped up and down. "Yes, can we?"

Rent looked at Martha. She smiled and said, "First, let's get out of this cold. And how about some chicken soup before you go?"

35

Rent and Rachel got into his truck and drove north on the 79 toward Julian and Chariot Canyon.

"You have a cassette player?" Rachel mocked in disbelief.

"Yeah, you want to hear my granddad playing his fiddle?"

"Do you have Taylor Swift?"

"Is she a famous fiddler? I don't think I've ever heard of her."

Rachel shot him a look of disgust. "Da-ad."

"Sorry," he said, then added in a sing-song voice, "Mama don't allow no Taylor Swift playin' round here . . ."

Rachel shook her head. "There's no screen. How do I turn on the Bluetooth?"

"You can't. This truck is twenty years old."

"It's older than me."

Older than I am, Rent thought but kept it to himself.

"How about a CD of my band, or maybe the *Pandemic Sessions*?"

"Does it have that squirrel song on it? The one you play in the video?"

He nodded at the center console. She opened it, found the CD, and slid it into the slot.

The first song began and Rachel started tapping a foot to the rhythm of the music.

"This isn't the squirrel head song—"

"No, that's number four."

"But I like it. It's bouncy."

"It's a very special tune. I learned it from Jimmy Widner, a Montana fiddler."

"Why is it special?"

"Because it's called . . ."

Rent glanced at her and grinned, then looked back at the road.

Rachel made a face, then opened the console and took out the CD case. She turned it over to read the tune list on the back. She looked at Rent, wide-eyed.

"Oh, my gosh! It's called *Rachel*. Let's play it again."

When the tune ended the second time, she asked, "Are you going to write a newspaper story about me? I don't know if I want to be in the news."

"I can't write about you, at least not a news story. That would be unethical. In legal parlance, I have to recuse myself from the assignment because I'm too close to you as well as Abby and your mom. It's one news story someone else has to write—Naomi Clark. She wants to talk to you."

"Do I have to?"

"No, it's totally up to you."

"Is she nice?"

"I will insist on it."

RENT SLOWED THE TRUCK as they reached the bottom of Banner Grade, but instead of turning right into Chariot Canyon, he turned left into the parking lot of the store. Rachel cast him a critical eye.

"We need trail rations," he said. "You'll like it."

They entered the store and Rent went straight to the checkout counter, where Rafe the storekeeper stood vigil. He recognized Rent and said hello, then asked, "You wouldn't happen to know anything about that explosion up in the canyon the other day, would you?"

"Yeah, I might know a bit about that. But don't believe everything you hear."

"I heard Gabe Turner got arrested."

Rent nodded. "That you did hear right. I doubt you'll be seeing him again any time soon."

"Humph," the storekeeper muttered.

Rent glanced around the store, then leaned over the counter and spoke in low voice. "You still have some of Granny's treats squirreled away under there?"

The man's face softened with a grin. "I just might have some left. A treat for the young lady?"

Rent nodded as a puzzled look crossed Rachel's face.

The storekeeper produced two bags and set them on the counter. "I have more."

Rachel examined the bags. "Is that peanut brittle?" she asked.

"The best peanut brittle that'll ever tempt yer tongue," Rafe said.

As Rent extracted his wallet from a pants pocket, Rachel opened one of the bags and popped a piece of the candy into her mouth.

"Mmm," she said as she munched the sweet.

"I'll take a couple of bottles of water as well," Rent said and handed the man a twenty-dollar bill.

Rachel reached her hand into the zip-lock bag for a second piece and Rent admonished her. "Save some for Martha . . . and your grandparents, and your brother."

RENT SWITCHED THE TRUCK into four-wheel drive mode. "I hope the road has dried out a bit," he muttered. The frequent vehicle traffic over the previous days had carved out parallel wheel tracks, improving the road.

They arrived at the mine without incident, where two sheriff's department vehicles stood sentry. The ground had begun to dry out, and the temperature had warmed to nearly 60 degrees. As he and Rachel got out of the truck, a figure wearing a protective coverall waved and started toward them, removing a mask and pulling the hood back. Rent recognized Pamela Berringer, the lead forensic technician and fellow fiddler.

"Good afternoon," she said. "What brings you here, as if I have to ask."

"Just wanted to have a look around and show her where the big bang took place."

The woman looked at the girl. "So, you're the famous Rachel."

Rachel lowered her head but lifted her eyes to keep them on the woman, who introduced herself.

"I'm Pam. I'm the one who sent the email about the DNA match, not realizing at the time you would be seeing it. Sorry about that, but nice to meet you after I've learned so much about you. What do you think? Is he going to be an okay dad?"

Rachel blushed and looked at Rent. "I guess so."

"Only if I figure out how to get Taylor Swift to sing in my old truck."

Pam chuckled. "We're just wrapping things up and about to take off. "Once we're gone, feel free to look around. But be careful near the mine shaft. It's unstable. We don't want any more rescues out here."

"We'll be careful," Rent said. "Find anything of interest?"

"Oh, yeah," Pam replied. "You'll have to get it officially from Alvarez, but we found quite a cache of weapons in the container, in addition to what remained of those in the mine. Pistols, semis with bump stocks. How any of you got out of there alive is a mystery to me."

"Yeah, we got lucky."

"The way I heard it, you shouted the alarm and got everyone moving," she said and looked at Rachel. "Did you know your dad is a hero?"

Rachel looked up at him and grinned. "He already was a hero to me."

"Well, I guess you two will get along just fine," she said. "I have to finish up and get this stuff to the lab. Talk to you later."

Rent and Rachel explored the site, and Rent pointed out what was left of the mine shaft where he had been held hostage.

"Wow, that's totes amazing. Can we go over there?"

"You heard what Pam said. We have to be careful. But first I have something I want to show you.""

Rachel's shoulders sagged, and she gave him a look of disgust over the delay.

"It's a surprise. A very cool surprise."

He opened the door of the truck, reached behind the seat, and withdrew a Trader Joe's shopping bag, He held the bag open so she could peer inside.

"Go ahead. Take it out."

She rolled her eyes but did as instructed, reaching into the bag and extracting a dull metal box. She examined it, then looked up at him, questioning. "Mail Pouch?"

"That tin is more than one hundred years old. And . . ." He reached into the bag and pulled out an acid-free sheet protector that contained a faded piece of paper. ". . . this is the original document that staked the claim to this mine. Maybe we can find the claim monument, if it wasn't destroyed in the blast."

Rachel's eyes widened in awe as she glanced at the document. "That was in this box?"

"Yes. It's a piece of history. I found it the other day when I came here the first time. Before the big bang."

"That's double totes amazing."

"The tin originally contained chewing tobacco."

Her face crinkled. "Ew."

"Let's put these back in the truck while we—"

"Look!" Rachel shouted and pointed toward the western edge of the canyon, where Chariot Creek, still flowing freely with storm runoff, cascaded over boulders on the steep hillside. "A rainbow. That's good luck." She began singing softly, "Somewhere over the rainbow . . ."

The mist from the waterfall had refracted the light and formed a small arc of a vivid spectrum hovering in mid-air.

"I've seen that phenomenon before, in the Grand Canyon of the Yellowstone, only on a grander scale. Maybe we can go there some day."

"Do you think there's a pot of gold underneath it? We could go look."

"If there ever was a pot of gold there, it would have been discovered long ago."

He put the Mail Pouch tin back in the truck, and they strolled closer to the crumbled mine shaft, where bits of wooden timbers and rubble lay scattered in the mouth of the yawning hole in the hillside. They came to a small depression in the ground, where a puddle of rainwater had formed during the storm, but had nearly dried out, leaving only moist sand.

"Look," Rachel exclaimed again. In the dark sand, particles glittered in the afternoon sun. "It's gold. I told you."

Rent knelt down, picked up a handful of the sand, and held it in a shadow cast by his body. The golden glitter had faded.

"Fool's gold," he said and began to explain.

"I know what fool's gold is," she said. "It's in my report. I've just never actually seen it before."

They drew closer to the exposed pit and looked it over. Rent pointed at a particular spot, where a cart rail lay, contorted in ironic agony.

"That's where I spent the night, sleeping on cases of gun-powder."

"That was dumb."

He looked at her, hands held out, palms up. "Hey, it was the only dry spot I could find. I crawled under the tarp, and that kept me dry and from freezing to death."

As he turned back toward the ruins, a flash of light caught his eye, then vanished. He slowly reversed his movement until he saw the flash again. He rotated his head back and forth until he could pinpoint the spot where the flash originated. He kept his eyes focused on that spot and, step by step, moved closer, careful not to stumble.

"What do you see?" Rachel asked.

"A shiny object. Probably just a tool, or a piece of metal reflecting sunlight. But let's check out it. Tread lightly. You don't want to break your other arm."

They stepped over and around and on bits of rubble as they drew closer to their target, at times arms waving wildly to maintain their balance.

Rent stopped and leaned over. "Holy sh—"

"Schist," Rachel corrected. "Holy schist." She, too, leaned over and peered at the rubble. "I don't see anything."

"Look at the white rocks, the quartz."

He struggled to work free a piece projecting from the debris, finally kicking it with his boot to break it loose. He picked it up, examined it, then handed it to Rachel.

She held it close to her face, her mouth agape. "Oh, my gosh." She looked up at Rent, a broad smile creating a chasm on her face. "It's just like the pictures in the book. It's real gold. Gold nuggets! *Holy schist!*"

Rachel began jumping up and down. "Eureka!" she shouted. "I learned that in a book about the gold rush."

A shadow passed over them and they looked skyward. "A golden eagle, like the name of the mine," she said.

Rent stared the bird for a moment. "I think it's a turkey vulture."

"No, it's bigger. And look at the wings. They're straight out and steady. A turkey vulture's wings are V-shaped, and they wobble back and forth. That's definitely a golden eagle. We see them at our house in Boulder Creek—"

In an instant, Rachel's face transformed from one of genuine joy to utter anguish and she sank to the ground, sobbing. Rent knelt beside her and wrapped his arms around her small frame.

"I know it's tough," he said. "You miss your mom."

Rachel nodded and sniffed. Rent found a tissue in a coat pocket and handed it to her. She still clutched the gold-bearing ore in one hand, and she took the tissue in the other. She dabbed her eyes and wiped her nose, then she leaned her head against Rent's.

"I have a friend," he said. "She's a therapist and works with people who have lost a loved one to violent death. I think she could help you deal with your grief. Will you think about that?"

"She's here," Rachel said. "I can feel her spirit. It's in the eagle, looking over us. She led us to this gold."

"You know, I think you're right."

They watched in reverent silence until the eagle disappeared behind the silhouette of Volcan Mountain.

"I take back what I said to you," she whispered, her eyes still aimed skyward.

"You what?"

"You're not a dirty bastard."

"Oh? Does that mean I'm a clean bastard? I do bathe regularly, you know."

She straightened up, looked into his eyes, and gave him an affectionate slap on the arm. "No, silly. It means you're a nice man. I only called you that because that's what Mom called you. Any time I asked her who my father was, she'd say, 'He's a dirty bastard. Forget about him.'"

"I see . . ."

"Remember? At the bookstore she called you that? And I looked in your eyes? Your blue eyes? That's when I knew. That's when I knew you were my dad. That's why I drew that picture of you, so I would have a picture in case I never saw you again."

Rent drew her to him. "And here we are."

Rachel examined the fist-sized piece of quartz, marbled with capillaries of gold and an occasional jagged, pea-sized lump of gold projecting from the ore.

"I think this is blue quartz," she said.

"Is that good?"

Rachel nodded, grinning. "It's the best. It has the most gold." She pocketed the piece of ore and began searching for more. "We need a miner's pick."

Rent stood up. "I have a hammer in the truck. Will that do?"

"For now."

"You keep looking while I go get it."

When he returned, she held up more small pieces of gold-bearing ore.

"It's ironic," he said. "Gabe the fool, in his attempt to blow me to bits, unwittingly opened up a new vein in a gold mine he believed was worthless, only useful as a place to hide things. When he hears about this, he's going to sh—"

"Schist," Rachel said. "That's what he's going to do. He's going to *schist.*" She punctuated her pun with a girlish giggle.

Using the hammer, they managed to break off more chunks of the gold-bearing quartz. They kept hammering as the sun edged closer to the western ridge looming over them, lengthening the creeping shadow.

"We're gonna need a jackhammer to much go farther," Rent said.

"Or gunpowder," Rachel replied.

"Let's not go there."

"Can we keep this gold? Finders keepers."

"I don't know. I'll talk to the folks at the BLM office. Maybe we can take over the claim. But for now, this is our secret. Okay?"

"Cross my heart," she said, then pouted.

"What is it, Sweetie?"

"I want to tell Grandma and Grandpa that we struck gold. They're coming for dinner tonight."

"Don't tell them tonight. After we know for sure we can take over the claim, then and only then. If word gets out that we discovered a vein, there will be bad people, people like Gabe Turner, showing up in hordes, trying to get their hands on it. You can count on that."

"You mean like claim jumpers?"

"Exactly. So, mum's the word. Got it?"

"Got it."

"Pinky swear?"

She nodded and held out her right hand, extending her little finger. Rent did the same and they locked their fingers together. "I swear," they said in unison.

"One more thing . . ."

A look of apprehension gripped Rachel's face.

"I know you like to say 'holy schist' but no one other than us gold miners and geologists get the joke, so it's okay for you to say it around me, but do you think you could tone it down around the other grownups, especially your grandma? It can be our secret."

Rachel's shoulders sagged and she clenched her jaw. Then sighed. "Oh-kay . . . Dad."

"Come on, it's getting late."

"Are you staying for dinner?"

"Do I have a choice?"

"No."

AT THE KITCHEN TABLE, Rachel gave Rent a conspiratorial look and he winked.

Agnes Powell glowered at Rent, then at Rachel. "What are you up to?"

"Nothing, Grandma. "Me and my dad just had—"

"You say 'my dad and I.' I don't want you sounding like a darn hillbilly. And DNA or not, I don't like you calling him your dad."

Rachel sighed. "I do. I've always known he's my dad since I saw him at the bookstore. And as I was saying, *my dad and I* had a fun time at the gold mine. He showed me where he almost got blown to kingdom come, and . . ."

She hesitated as a look of alarm crossed Rent's face.

"And we saw a rainbow over the creek, and a golden eagle flew over us. It was magic. I know it meant that Mom was with me, her spirit was watching over me."

"Stop talking nonsense and eat your dinner."

Rachel glanced at Rent and winked in return, then resumed eating.

After they finished and moved toward the living room, Agnes stepped in front of Rent. She glared at him, her features hard.

"We need to talk."

"I'm all ears," he said.

"Don't get smart with me. We've talked to our lawyer . . ."

Not Tucker, I hope."

"No, he's an ass, if you'll pardon my French."

"At least there's one thing we can agree on."

"We found someone else, a woman, who specializes in family matters and custodial disputes."

"I didn't know there was a dispute."

She eyed him warily. "Don't play games with me."

"Agnes, I am not playing games. I only want to do what's best for Rachel. End of story. I'm sure we can come to an amenable solution."

"We'll see about that. You don't just come like a ghost from the past and take our granddaughter away from us."

"I have no intention of taking her away from you. Just tell me when and where. But let's try to keep the lawyering to a minimum. Ultimately, their priority is billable hours so they can drive a pricey car to the yacht club and lounge on the poop deck, drinking margaritas, martinis, and bloody marys."

They seated themselves and an uncomfortable silence hung over the room. Rachel began fidgeting and asked about Abby. Rent described his visit to the hospital and her departure for Idaho.

"I hope she comes back," the girl said.

"She's planning on it," Agnes replied. "She called me before she left and said we could stay at her house while we look for something more permanent. She didn't want to leave it sitting empty. And someone has to feed the deer."

"So, you're staying here?" Martha inquired.

"At least until school's out," Agnes answered and looked down at Rachel, who sat on the couch between her grandparents.

Rachel had a look of disbelief on her face.

"Yes, young lady, you are going to a real school. No more of this homeschooling nonsense."

"But all my friends—"

"They belong in a real school too. You can still do your other activities with them."

Rachel crossed her arms and feigned a pout. "Can I still do 4-H? And get a pony?"

"We'll have to see about that."

"I might be able to help you in that regard," Martha said.

Rachel perked up. "Yes, please."

Rent checked the time and said he had to be going.

"It's about time," Agnes muttered.

"Do you have to? What about—" Rachel slapped a hand over her mouth.

"I'm playing for a dance tomorrow night. I will be debuting two new tunes, *Skulking* and *Chariot Canyon*. I need my beauty sleep."

Rachel looked at her grandmother. "Can we go? Please, please. I've never heard him play his fiddle in person. Only on YouTube . . . He plays a tune named *Rachel*, just like me, and I like that song *Squirrel Heads and Gravy*."

Agnes puckered her face. "Ew. . . . Let's just see what tomorrow brings. Now, isn't it about your bedtime?"

36

Rent entered the newsroom and all those present stood and clapped. He bowed, then winced as a jolt of pain from a playful elbow in the ribs reminded him that he had yet to fully recover from his injuries.

"The prodigal returns," said Naomi Clark, who then leaned toward him and added, "You know Meriwether Lewis got shot in the ass, right?"

"Oh, yes. We play a fiddle tune related to that, *Old French*, but some call it the 'shot in the butt' tune. Your point being?"

She flicked her eyebrows. "Just sayin', *Lewis* . . . but seriously, well done."

"Thanks, and, seriously, thank you for stepping in."

"No problem. Any news from the DA's office?"

"That's my first call, but I suspect there's going to be a bit of plea bargaining in the offing."

"Rats on a sinking ship. I suppose you have a fiddle tune for that as well," she said and turned away.

"Off she goes," he said to Clark's back as O'Connor approached.

"You two still bickering like an old married couple?" the editor asked.

"Something like that. The growling old man and grumbling old woman."

The editor smiled and shook her head, then continued. "We may have to do that Pulitzer submission yet. You've created quite a tsunami."

Rent shrugged. "Your call."

"What's next?" she asked. "Got any more windmills lined up?"

"First, I have to wrap up the fraud story as much as I can while we wait for the prosecution," he replied. "But there's never a shortage of scandal or malfeasance the citizenry ought to know about."

Stabbing his fingers, he ticked off several topics: "The troubling number of inmates dying at the county jail; the ironic gaslighting by the gas and electric company trying to pull a fast one on unsuspecting ratepayers; SANDAG and the toll scandal on the 125 freeway; the school board debating the merits of resurrecting the teaching of phonics; San Diego has a new distinction: It's gone from America's Finest City to America's Filthiest Beaches; illegal dumping of toxic waste; the insidious aspects of AI; or my latest pet peeve, idiots on those damned e-bikes roaring through public parks. Did you know there's no law against operating electric bikes in public parks, even though their gas-powered equivalents—mopeds, dirt bikes, et cetera—are not allowed?"

She waved a hand for him to stop. "Okay, okay, Don Quixote, I get it. Just let me know what to expect," she said and began to walk away.

"I'll start making some calls and see which rats come crawling off the ship."

O'Connor turned back. "By the way, although I'm sure you've heard the rumors, some pink slips are about to come floating down from on high. And before you ask, I haven't a clue who's getting axed. I could be first in line for all I know."

He scoffed. "We've gone from 'all the news that's fit to print' to 'only the news that fits between the ads' and humans replaced by bots and AI. Maybe we can get jobs at CalMatters or go back to the journal —at half the salary and fewer benefits."

Rent sat at his desk and stared at the mess of paper strewn across its surface.

"Screw that," he muttered and called the Bureau of Land Management field office in El Centro. "Hi, I'm inquiring as to how one goes about taking over a mining claim . . ."

He learned that Gabe Turner had not made the annual payment to the BLM to retain his claim on the Golden Eagle mine, which meant his claim was forfeit. If he had continued occupying the claim, that made him a squatter, a claim jumper, with no legal hold on it. Therefore, the mine had no current claimant.

He must have figured he no longer needed it once he had taken up residence at the surf camp south of the border.

Rent downloaded the application form from the bureau's website. The person he contacted at the BLM office said it would take a few weeks to process the application. The fee total would be $274.

With gold in excess of $2300 an ounce, thanks to the Chinese, it may well be worth it. Golden Chariot Mining might even be interested in getting involved or buying the rights to the claim. That could provide money for Rachel—her proverbial pot of gold at the end of the rainbow.

He started to fill in the form, then stopped.

Rachel's name needs to go on this claim too. We'll fill it out together, as joint claimants. This may not make us millionaires, but with any luck it will be more than enough to get her a pony, maybe pay for college. And maybe even buy me a vehicle with modern electronics and Bluetooth so she can listen to Taylor Swift. Lord, help me.

Rent's phone dinged. Text message. Irritated by the interruption, he muttered, "Now what? A rat come crawling?" He tapped the Messages icon.

PI Alicia Velasquez:
Meet for coffee? Or drink?

His reply: 👍

Skulking

Rent Beacham, 2024

Downoad the sheet music and audio files at
https://www.larryedwards.com/music/

Chariot Canyon

Rent Beacham, 2024

Downoad the sheet music and audio files at
https://www.larryedwards.com/music/

Watch for the next Rent Beacham Mystery

Construction workers in the San Juan Islands of Washington State discover the body of a man who had disappeared thirty years earlier. Death threats again haunt investigative journalist Rent Beacham as he turns to the news archives to investigate the man's disappearance following a toxic-waste scandal during the 1995 America's Cup sailing regatta in San Diego, California. Rent confronts the former owner of the San Diego boatyard, whose son-in-law has thrown his hat in the ring to become the next congressman to represent California's 25th Congressional District, which encompasses the Imperial Valley.

Rent discovers that father and son-in-law have close financial ties to an entity operating a geothermal plant and solar arrays near the border with Mexico that will power an artificial intelligence data center being built in Mexico. Rent's life—and the lives of his loved ones—come under threat as his investigation leads him into the closeted worlds of toxic waste disposal, alternative energy production, and the emergence of generative AI.

Acknowledgements

I could not have completed this book without the inspiration, assistance, and encouragement of many, many others along the way, some living, some long gone although their legacy lives on.

Among the living . . .

Influential authors: Fredrik Backman, Harlen Coben, Michael Connelly, Mary Karr, Jonathan Kellerman, Elmore Leonard, Cormac McCarthy, Walter Mosley, T. Jefferson Parker, Annie Proulx, David Rosenfelt, and Tobias Wolff, to name a few.

The Ocean Beach Writers Networking Group for their support and encouragement over the years: Terrie Leigh Relf, Martin Hill, G.M. "Jerry" Ford (RIP), Corey Lynn Fayman, Pendelton Wallace, Chris Enni, Sarah Galarza, and Linton Robinson.

The La Jolla Writers Group, from whom I gained indispensable critiques and feedback on my writing: Kathy Foley, Lynn Gahman, Mike Irbi, Penelope James, Walter Karshat, Melody Kincade, Cathy Lubenski, Laurie Richards, and Jenny Russell.

The San Diego Writers & Editors Guild, in particular Sally Gary, Margaret Harmon, Arthur Raybold, Mardie Schroeder, and Ruth Wallace.

Private eye Edna Trigo for providing insight into the operations, training, and licensing of a private investigator, not to mention the important roles played by a dog, a bird book, and sunflower seeds.

Kate Miyamoto, a public information officer with the Bureau of Land Management, for helping me gain a better understanding of the responsibilities and the inner workings of this federal agency.

Tom Blackman for telling me about the Mail Pouch tobacco tins.

Carolyn Goben for informing me about Lions Tigers and Bears.

Martin Hill for introducing me to the survival bracelet.

Kirby Nellis for demystifying the term FNG.

Mountain man re-enactors Chuck "Strummer" Preble, Mike "Hatman" Robinson, and Ken "Flyrod" Wright, among others, who taught me how to use a muzzle-loading rifle, and and together we played the folk music of the early 19th century.

Among those long gone (and not so long gone) . . .

Connie Saindon, a dear friend who left us mid-stride, yet her kind words and encouragement continue to keep me going on dark days.

William Shakespeare, the Brontë sisters—Charlotte, Emily and Anne—Jane Austin, Edgar Alan Poe, Fyodor Dostoyevsky, Anton Chekhov, Mark Twain, F. Scott Fitzgerald, Ernest Hemingway, Maxwell Perkins, Jack London, John Steinbeck, Robert Service, Robert Frost, Louis L'Amour, John Kennedy Toole, Lawrence Sanders, and G.M. "Jerry" Ford, to name a few.

I give a special shoutout to a few (still among the living) closely involved in the process of completing this work:

Timothy W. Brittain for another excellent cover design and layout.

Donald E. McInnis, lawyer and author of the A.J. Hawke legal thriller series, who (often unwittingly) provides knowledge of and insight into the practice of law, as well as the criminal justice system.

Linda Caruso, Rich Hazelton, Ian Law, and Naomi Lewis for giving the book a critical read and pointing out plotholes in the story and errors in the text.

M.L. Meurs, fellow author and musician—and my sister-in-life —for her encouragement, feedback, and contributions to this book, offering a view through the lens of a girl, a woman, a wife, a mother, and a grandmother, and her vast, if not bizarre, knowledge of topics ranging from Chekhov, Dostoyevsky, and Jesus to chimpanzees, bonobos, and orangutans—and let's not forget her true loves: horses and wolfhounds.

Janis Cadwallader, my beloved wife, with whom I am celebrating 37 years of marriage, and who has supported and encouraged my creative—if not always financially rewarding—meanderings over these past decades, and for her critique of and perceptive feedback on this book, as well as her patience and understanding, and putting up (mostly) with my outbursts of cursing (primarily directed at Microsoft products), and who makes sure I eat plenty of leafy green veggies, bathe regularly, and get the occasional haircut.

What's that? Oh, yes . . . last but not least, Bob T. Parrot, self-anointed executive editor, who squawks raunchy and distracting non sequiturs at the most inappropriate moments, yet sharpens my tongue when the need arises.

About the Author

A scribbler by preference and profession, Larry M. Edwards is an award-winning investigative journalist, author, editor, and publishing consultant. He has written five books and has edited more than 500 fiction and nonfiction books.

As journalist he has won numerous awards from the Society of Professional Journalists and the San Diego Press Club, including four Best of Show honors. As business editor for *San Diego Magazine*, his reporting fueled the resignation of a corrupt CEO and an ineffective San Diego mayor.

As a nonfiction author, he wrote *Dare I Call It Murder?—A Memoir of Violent Loss* (2013), which took top honors in the San Diego Book Awards and was nominated for a Pulitzer Prize.

As a book editor/publisher, one of his proudest moments came when *Murder Survivors Handbook: Real-Life Stories, Tips & Resources* by Connie Saindon (2014) received the prestigious Benjamin Franklin Gold Award from the Independent Book Publishers Association.

As a musician, he plays fiddle and bass, and has composed nearly two dozen melodies. While "stuck at home with the Pandemic blues," he produced *The Pandemic Sessions: New Tunes in the Old-time Style (mostly)*, a book and CD featuring the sheet music and recordings of his own compositions, including the "Billboard worthy" *Got the Pandemic Blues.*

He also prides himself as being a birder S.O.B. (spouse of birder).

Larry lives in San Diego, California, with his loving wife, Janis Cadwallader, a serious birder, fellow fiddler, and world traveler.

Website: https://www.larryedwards.com/
Facebook: https://www.facebook.com/FiddlinFriar
LinkedIn: https://www.linkedin.com/in/larrymedwards/
X: https://x.com/LarryEdwards
YouTube: https://www.youtube.com/@FiddlinFriar

Other books by Larry M. Edwards
- *Dare I Call It Murder?: A Memoir of Violent Loss*, Winner, Best Published Memoir, San Diego Book Awards, and Pulitzer Prize nominee
- *Food & Provisions of the Mountain Men: A Guide to Authentic Provisions of Fur Trappers, Traders & Explorers in the Early American West*
- *The Pandemic Sessions: New Tunes in the Old-time Style (mostly)*
- *Official Netscape Internet Business Starter Kit*

A selection of books edited by Larry M. Edwards that you may enjoy reading or find useful:
Fiction
- The A.J. Hawke Legal Thriller series by Donald E. McInnis, including *Return of the Sphynx*, BookLife Editor's Pick
- *The Fourth Rising*, Martin Roy Hill, Winner, Best Mystery, Best Indie Book Awards
- *Camp Salvador*, M.L. Meurs
Nonfiction
- *Murder Survivor's Handbook: Real-Life Stories, Tips & Resources*, Connie Saindon, Winner, Gold Award, IBPA Benjamin Franklin Book Awards
- *The Journey: Learning to Live with Violent Death*, Connie Saindon
- *She's So Cold: The Stephanie Crowe Murder Case—A Defense Attorney's Inside Story*, Donald E. McInnis
- *What the Private Saw: The Civil War Letters & Diaries of Oney Foster Sweet*, annotated by Larry M. Edwards
- *They Must Be Monsters*, the untold story of the McMartin Preschool scandal, Matthew LeRoy and Deric Haddad
- *Outlasting the Nazis and Communists: My Life in Vienna & Prague*, Paul Vantoch

www.ingramcontent.com/pod-product-compliance
Lightning Source LLC
Chambersburg PA
CBHW071148020726
47502CB00002B/326